TOWNS
WITHOUT
RIVERS

TOWNS
WITHOUT
RIVERS

Michael Parker

wm

WILLIAM MORROW
75 YEARS OF PUBLISHING
An Imprint of HarperCollins*Publishers*

HarperCollins books may be purchased for educational, business,
or sales promotional use. For information please write:
Special Markets Department, HarperCollins Publishers Inc.,
10 East 53rd Street, New York, NY 10022.

FIRST EDITION

Designed by Oksana Kushnir

Printed on acid-free paper

Library of Congress Cataloging-in-Publication Data

Parker, Michael, 1959–
Towns without rivers / by Michael Parker.
p. cm.
ISBN 0-380-97860-1
1. Brothers and sisters—Fiction.   2. False imprisonment—Fiction.   3. North Carolina—Fiction.
4. Ex-convicts—Fiction.   I. Title.
PS3566.A683 T6 2001
813'.54—dc21
00-052089

01 02 03 04 05 QW 10 9 8 7 6 5 4 3 2 1

For Maryann Peterson

ACKNOWLEDGMENTS

I would like to thank the University of North Carolina at Greensboro for providing a research leave during which this book was written. Thanks also to the following for countless acts of encouragement and kindness: Chip Greer; Lee Zacharias; the inspirational Emma, from whom I've learned so much; and another teacher, Daphne Athas, for decades of priceless lunches and letters.

PART ONE

One

Listening to the coeds brag about how much money they planned to save in a summer of selling books out west, Reka Speight considered the phrase "freedom of speech." A right of all Americans, guaranteed by the Constitution according to the correspondence course in Civics she'd taken while serving time for injecting her lover with a lethal dose of morphine, yet who was ever free to speak as they wished? Sitting in the back of the classroom on a muggy morning in April 1959, pretending to be a college student, Reka felt doubly inhibited: Not only could she not say the things she thought, but she had to slave over the way her words sounded lest some niggling rhythm or swampy pronunciation reveal who she really was.

She'd had to teach herself to talk again. She spoke slowly since her release, and said little. The man she'd served five years in prison for killing had taught her a lot, but the most powerful idea that lingered from her brief time with him was the irrevocable power of words. With him it had been the words themselves, what damage they might do if allowed to convey what he really felt. In the years since his death, she had learned to disguise not only what she thought, but the pitch and timbre of those thoughts. Reka spoke with the halting precision of a traveler trying to pass as native in a foreign land. Some people thought her dim-witted, or at least speech impeded.

If she was to get this job—and she longed for it with a passion she'd not felt since Edwin's death—she would have to appear glib. Words were the only currency; if you could not talk your way past a threshold, you would end up stranded and penniless in some windswept Nebraska town, said the man leading the information session. A representative for the McMillan Book Company, he had come to Greenville to recruit summer crews from among the coeds at the state university. Reka happened to be walking across campus—she spent her Saturdays in Greenville, reading in the university library—when she'd seen a flyer posted on a telephone pole. NEED MONEY FOR SCHOOL? EARN YOUR TUITION IN WEEKS WHILE TRAVELING IN THE WESTERN U.S. Because it combined two of her dreams—to go to college and to travel westward—Eureka found the classroom where the recruiting session was being held, and tried to pass herself off as a coed.

She was fortunate enough to look much younger than her twenty-five years, despite a life that should have wrinkled and toughened her skin, turned her hair limp and gray. Her hair was so inky black that strands of gray had already appeared in a vibrant afternoon light, but even if visible her face was so open and unblemished that graying hair seemed an anomaly. She'd been told by her co-workers at the laundry that she looked seventeen still, which made sense to her, as she was seventeen and a half when Edwin died, and her own life had hesitated for the five years she spent in prison and the two more sluggish ones since she'd returned to Trent.

The recruiter intimidated her, as did the perky girls clumped in groups around the classroom. After explaining how his company worked, and promising vast sums of money for a few hours of work each day, the recruiter asked each girl to take a stab at selling him a set of encyclopedias. He swore this was not a tryout—whoever wanted to could sign up, no one willing to work hard and see the scenery would be turned away—but Reka was skeptical. If everyone was welcome, why put the girls through such trouble? The others seemed to think it was a joke. They took it lightly, without the slightest show of nerves, but Reka felt on the verge of hyperventilating even when there were a dozen girls in front of her.

It wasn't what to say—she felt confident that she could talk her way into any stranger's house, for despite her silence she was adept at putting people at ease if need be. Reka did not want to reveal who she was—a high school dropout, a convicted felon, the daughter of a drugstore janitor and sometime farmer, a resident of that part of Trent bordering Johnsontown, where no respectable college-bound girl would set foot. She wanted to believe that she was as smart as anyone in the room, tried to convince herself that she was as smart as the recruiter, a sharply dressed man about her age named, incredibly, Bob Smart—but she'd learned all she knew from books, in silence, in the gloomy privacy of a prison cell. History, evolution, literature: ideas needed to be consummated, like passion, but she felt too much the unrequited lover, as she'd had no one to talk to about what she read save for Memory Wright, a wealthy lady who volunteered at the prison, and Edith Keane, the mother of the man she killed, who'd come to visit her faithfully during her entire sentence. Memory was so kindhearted that she didn't really count—she would talk to her purse, and accepted so guilelessly the abiding good in everyone that she would never pass judgment on someone because of how she talked. As for Edith Keane, Reka suspected she had never heard a word Reka had said in all their hours of tortured conversation. She wasn't there to listen, and she appeared so self-conscious about what she doubtlessly considered the charity of her visits that what passed between them could hardly be called conversation.

ˎ "How about you, in the back?" said Bob Smart. Reka looked up to see the room staring back at her corner, the girls twisted in their seats to see whom he'd chosen, since he'd been letting the girls go in order, left to right, front to back.

Reka swallowed, but it did no good; her throat was rusted shut. Her hands shook and she felt through her thin cotton dress—a gift from Edith Keane, who not only paid the rent on her one-bedroom apartment but provided her with clothes she would have otherwise donated to Goodwill—the terrified flutter of her heart. All eyes on her, her own eyes on the desk, covered with initials and juvenile graffiti she was shocked to find in a college classroom. *DR. LONG IS A MEANIE*, someone had carved into the wood, and Reka decided that Dr. Long was not a meanie at all, that whoever had written this imbecilic slur was lazy and spoiled, miffed at a grade given fairly for shoddy work or excessive tardiness.

Because she was reading the desk instead of talking her way into the house of the midwestern stranger Bob Smart was pretending to be—because she had no right to be there, because she had success-fully avoided for years any situation that might call attention to her struggle with words—Reka stood up and walked out of the room. In the hallway she began to run, the slap of her flats echoing like gun-shots on the waxed tile. She was halfway across campus when she slowed to a walk again. For the first time in years—since those mid-summer nights in prison when the heat swamped her cell and the noises of her fellow inmates kept her wide awake even though she was exhausted from a fourteen-hour day in the work camp fields—Reka found herself crying.

If at first she blamed the coeds for their easy confidence, the far-ther away she strayed from the classroom, the more it seemed her fault alone. If she was to leave—if she was to be able to put all this behind her—it would have to be as Reka Speight. Too much dam-age had been caused by acting. She had suffered enough from pass-ing herself off as someone she was not.

For the rest of the day she tried to lose herself in the routine she'd established in her ritual Saturday trips to Greenville. She went to the library and wandered the stacks, choosing books whose titles or covers appealed to her, often standing between the tight shelves for an hour, turning pages, trying to lose herself in the rhythms of someone else's desire. But the fear she'd felt in that classroom, and the blame she placed—unfairly—on the coeds, kept her from getting lost this time. The day was ruined. Reka skipped lunch and walked downtown to wait for the early-afternoon bus back to Trent.

She was sitting in the grass by the post office when she heard someone call her name. Or attempt to.

"Miss Spite?" Bob Smart said. Reka wondered how he knew what to call her, until she remembered the sheet she'd signed when she'd first entered the classroom.

"It's pronounced Spate," she said.

"You're just saying that to spite me," Bob Smart said.

Reka could not look at him. Thank goodness the three o' clock sun was brutal and low, burning a hole in her vision, blocking all but the shape of a man in a sharp suit. She shaded her brow with a sweaty hand and stared at a place just above his belt.

"Sorry," he said when she did not respond. "A harmless joke."

"It's okay," she said, too shyly. She felt as if she were being sized up still, though surely she'd already blown what chances she ever had for passing herself off as a coed.

"What happened back there?"

Again Reka was silent. She searched for an excuse, but every line she could think up to explain her sudden and embarrasing flight reminded her of the line scrawled across the dirty desk—*DR. LONG IS A MEANIE*. Like the author of this line, Reka was about to make excuses for her behavior, place blame where there was none. She was so disgusted by the impulse that she spoke, finally, without self-consciousness, with an honesty and ease that shocked her.

"I lied to you."

Bob Smart shrugged. He squatted next to her so that he might see her eyes.

"Lies aren't all bad. In fact, in my line of work, they ain't that big a deal. Sometimes they're necessary to make the sale."

"I'm not a student here."

He smiled and sat next to her in the grass.

"So?"

"So you want students, right? This job is just for college students?"

"I want someone who can sell some books, Miss Speight."

"Reka," she said.

"Reka," he repeated. "Pretty name. What's it short for?"

"Nothing," she lied. Her name had been Eureka until she emerged from prison, at which point she did everything she could to distance herself from the girl whose name had appeared in the *Trent Clarion* every day for months. She'd never liked her name anyway—her mother had named her, and her mother had died when Reka was small, taking with her the mystery of such an odd and cumbersome name. Forever after, the name had reminded Reka of what she could never know about her mother, and about other things as well. In school she'd been teased because of it. Boys called her "vacuum cleaner." They made sucking noises when she passed them in the hall.

"Family name, I take it?"

"So you *aren't* looking for college girls?"

Bob Smart smoothed his seersucker suit jacket and laughed. His laugh was canned and untrustworthy, different from the laugh she remembered from when he'd stood in front of the classroom holding forth for a roomful of callow coeds. Eureka was used to seeing through people, and was never surprised to find out that someone was not who he pretended to be. Still, Bob Smart's real laugh unnerved her.

"I like the way you carry on a conversation."

"What's that supposed to mean?" She acted more suspicious of this comment than she actually was—if he was going to put on an act, she had no problem pretending in return. She'd begun to think a job was possible after all, and she regretted for the first time bolting from that room. She thought of her little brother Randall, who loved to talk. He would have been the first to volunteer for Bob Smart's simulated sale, and he would have talked his way into any house and even the tightest wallet in the vast West. Randall should be the one talking to this smarmy salesman. He should be the one venturing out west, instead of living up in Norfolk with their sorry brother Hal. Randall should be seeing the world instead of standing atop a scaffolding in the naval shipyards.

"Wait, now. Don't take it wrong. I like it, Reka. You won't let a sucker get away with you. You hold the fort. That's what it takes to move books."

"I don't guess I'm right for the job."

"I don't guess you know as much about it as I do. You've got drive and you've got hunger. The rest of the girls—I'm going to tell you this, but I don't want it repeated, though, hell, I did tell them all, not that they ever believe me—the rest of those gals will last about three days. I'd say sixty percent of the girls who sign on with us end up stranded and broke within the first week. They have to call their daddies and beg them for train fare home. It's hard work, selling books—especially out west, worst market for knowledge there is in this country. You'd think it'd be down here, but people down south want a book on the mantel even if they never crack the spine. They like the idea of books, read 'em or no. Ain't that way out in the prairie. Those people—Swedes and Germans, most of 'em—they're some cheap people, I'm telling you. They ain't going to spend a dime on anything they can't eat."

"So why should I go there? I don't have a daddy who'll send me train money."

"I highly doubt you'll need it. I'm not saying it can't be done. Just that it takes a special kind of salesperson. How old are you, if you don't mind me asking?"

Reka said her age. She ignored his whistle, his bumbling flatteries, his professed disbelief. She saw what was coming and did not care enough to discourage it, for since she'd come back to Trent and taken work in the laundry she'd taken a vow not to consider herself above anything if it would get her somewhere. This included sleeping with boys she didn't much care for. Trips to places she wasn't interested in—dance halls and juke joints and even churches—were not out of the question if there was the slightest payoff at the end of the evening.

"Had lunch?"

"I'm waiting for the bus back to Trent. It's where I live—a town about twenty miles from here."

"Still?"

Reka winced. Was he asking why she still lived there? After all that had happened, all she'd gone through in order to escape from that place, which, out of penance, out of punishment for her impatience to leave, she'd returned to without question? In prison she'd decided to rot there, like her four older sisters, who never even considered anyplace else. Trent to them was the big time—they'd lived the first part of their lives on a muddy piece of bottomland her father pretended was a farm—and her sisters thought they'd died and gone to Raleigh when they'd arrived in the snide, dusty town she'd accepted as her next and final prison.

"What do you mean still?"

"You don't need a bus back anywhere. You need a train out west."

"You're offering me the job?"

"Let's go somewhere private and discuss it. I've got a little something to drink back at the hotel. I can drive you home later on in the evening."

Eureka took Bob Smart's hand when he offered it to her. She took a drink of his whiskey and she took her clothes off in the airless hotel room and she took what she could from him only because she'd reached that point where she could no longer punish herself by staying in a place she'd hated so much she'd killed a man to leave it.

When he offered to drive her home, she took him up on it, though she asked him to let her off in the country, at Speed's store.

"I thought you lived in town," he said.

"I got to see someone. Tell them I'm leaving."

"Don't let them talk you into not."

"You don't know me very well," she said through the window as his car idled in the parking lot of Speed's store.

"Enjoyed getting to know some of you," he said.

"I guess you did, didn't you."

"You're going to show tomorrow morning, now."

"I said I was." She feigned indignation even though she was tired of pretending. It had occurred to her in the middle of their arrhythmic lovemaking that she did not really need to sleep with him, that she already had the job if she wanted it, and—like he said—she could talk her way into anything if she just put her mind to it. But there was still too much of the old Reka left, the one who would let herself be led into almost anything, who could not rouse herself for a fight, who would just as soon go along with it, fake it, than stand up for herself. She had the feeling—and this was the only feeling she had, for Bob Smart was a talentless and grunty lover, like all of them since Edwin—that this would be the last time she'd allow herself to be so led. That it was her last opportunity lay made it go faster, though the hair-triggered Bob Smart would not have prolonged it under any circumstances.

He left her in the parking lot with plans to meet her the next morning in front of the courthouse. He'd wanted to come to her apartment, but she'd lied and said she lived with her sisters and did not want them to know she was leaving. She did not care to tell them she was leaving—she had nothing in common with them, not even blood it seemed, as she and Randall were the only two of the eight siblings who shared the same swarthiness. They had long since decided that their mother was some stranger, made believe she was a mysterious maiden who stalked the swamps around the farm where they'd been born, who'd seduced their father twice, enticing him into the purple pockets of the woods bordering the fields he failed to turn into money.

It was dusk, and she was dirty and exhausted, a numbing fatigue that seemed more emotional than physical, a depletion that came when her way out presented itself without warning. Or perhaps she knew she was going to leave, and just could not bring herself to admit it; she hesitated to give credit to Bob Smart, who could probably care less if she did not show up in the morning. The ache in her body came from her very marrow, and was too total and relentless to attribute to any outside party. Exercising will took more energy than a week of twelve-hour days at the steamy laundry. It was a good tired, though, and she did not mind it at all, even though she had two more country miles to her father's house.

Speed himself was working the counter. Reka fished a cola from the icebox and placed it on the counter, ignoring the invasive gaze of this man she'd known and disliked all her life. Before they moved to Trent they had lived a half-mile from this store, and her father was forced to trade here even though Speed gouged his customers with high prices and cheap merchandise. Though he billed his store as an unofficial community center for the poor whites and blacks who sharecropped the tobacco and produce farms around the crossroads, he took advantage of everyone who could not afford the trip into town to the A&P or Colonial stores. He sold whiskey, too— white liquor he made himself in a shed behind the store. On Saturday afternoons a line snaked out to the gas pumps sometimes, half the men in the community come to blow their wages.

"You Speight's girl, ain't you."

You know who I am, Eureka thought to say, but she did not have the energy for Speed tonight. He wore a t-shirt stained with some kind of animal blood, and smelled of cigar smoke and whiskey and the manure he bagged and sold out front as fertilizer.

"Yep," said Reka, awaiting her change.

"He was by here earlier."

This meant only one thing: that he was drinking again. She'd heard him swear he'd rather starve than trade with Speed again, and she could imagine him wasting to cartilage and bone rather than line the pockets of the greasy merchant. Though Reka visited him rarely, she kept abreast of him through her oldest sister, Ellen, whose husband drove her out once a week to check on Speight. As far as Reka knew, he'd been sober for six months this time, a record, though since he lived alone in the middle of the middle of nowhere, who but the squirrels knew what he did with his nights?

"Why'd you sell it to him?" she asked, tapping the dime change he gave her on the counter. Speight had even started attending those meetings held nightly in town—a neighbor drove him in a couple of times a week. This time she'd thought he'd licked it, or at least had it under control.

" 'Cause he paid me to. You best be glad I did. He'd of gone up the road to Joyner's if I'd of denied him. He might of got run over walking back from that joint, plus my liquor's pure as mother's milk compared to what Joyner and them sell. Those crazy niggers will strain their mash through any damn thing. Car radiators, filthy t-shirts. It'll blind you sure as hell."

Speed paused, as if he wanted to be thanked for his humanitarian effort. As if he was ever motivated by anything besides money.

"Why you acting so goody-goody? I know what you done."

"Thanks anyway," she said sullenly, too tired to talk back to him. She was accustomed to this—the residue of *what she done* affecting every simple transaction, every conversation, even a stroll down the street. Porchsitters falling silent as she appeared, their susurrous gossip rising faintly like wind through pine needles as she passed into what they considered out of earshot. But she was never out of earshot, never unaware of their scrutiny. Reka desired it at first— she'd returned home to suffer it—but she'd had enough of it now.

Tomorrow she was leaving. She tried to imagine her escape as she took the left fork at the crossroads, trudged down the dirt road that led to her father's farm. Alongside the road ran Serenitowinity Swamp, peaceful and dark, though she knew its blackness to be alive with threats: bobcat and bear, the bloated roots of cypress threaded with moccasins, coral snakes, timber rattlers. It seemed as if even the wildlife hushed and froze to watch her walk by, as if they too knew her past. Such scrutiny encouraged her fantasy of way out west, land of two point three people per square mile, two point three trees. She craved a landscape as unlike home as possible. It must be arid, for there was too much water everywhere here, underfoot and in the heavy air itself, swamp and pocosin, river and creek, the ocean a scant fifty miles east.

If she were someplace dry and well above sea level, a valley ringed by mountains still snowcapped in July, where she would have to wear sweaters year-round and would never again suffer from the stultifying heat of eastern North Carolina, she would not have to think of what really killed the man she killed. Here everything reminded her of him, of them; even this last trip to see her father was sure to be tainted by the needle she had plunged into Edwin's vein to hear him tell her he would take her away from Trent. Her father had not looked her in the eye for more than a shifty second or two since she was released from prison. He had not been able to bring himself to touch her, not even a tentative brush on the shoulder, not once.

A dusty pickup bumped up the road from behind.

"Want a ride?" a boy's creaky voice called.

She turned to look. The bed was crammed with more boys, filthy from a long day's work, their skin glazed with a paste of sweat and woodchip. Sawmillers, pulpwooders maybe. She kept walking, as if she did not hear, as if they did not exist. The pickup coasted along-side her for what seemed to her a quarter mile, the boys asking their fool questions, trying to cajole a response. Finally they spun off in thick red dust, coating her with another layer of this dirt she would wash off behind her father's house, for she could not tolerate the filth for another minute. It confined her like a baggy second skin, and she vowed not to take any of it with her when she left, even if it meant washing every garment she owned by hand, packing a suit-case of still-wet clothes.

She came to the overgrown two-track that led through the wood to her father's shack. It was nothing more than a shack—a single room and a lean-to porch converted into a listing kitchen, bare bulb light but no heat besides a smoky trashburner with a rusty length of stovepipe, no furniture to speak of save the things Speight had sal-vaged from the roadsides where his neighbors dumped their castoffs into the ditches. He'd lived here since her trial, trying to convince himself that the worthless soil might suddenly turn fertile. He made less than enough to live on—she sent him money from her wages at the laundry through Ellen, though she made her sister promise never to tell her father where the money came from. Ellen was con-tent to act as if she were the only one of the Speight children who saw to it that their father did not starve. Reka suspected she skimmed a healthy commission for her "trouble," though she never bothered to confront her about it.

She made a point to stamp her feet on the buckled porch floor-boards to warn him of her arrival. He was not used to visitors. Ellen came at the same time every week—Sunday afternoons—and even then, according to Ellen, he appeared annoyed by her presence. Just as Reka had returned to Trent as penance, determined to rot there, so had her father come back to the country as punishment for tak-ing his family into town. He'd asked Randall to write her letters while she was in prison—her father could not read or write—and he'd said in one of these letters that she would be a free woman, married, fat, and happy, had he not given up on his first farm and carted them into town. Reading this letter she'd allowed herself to cry, for it crushed her, his innocent suffering, the way he blamed himself for things he could not understand. She knew she'd disappointed him, she and Randall both, and she knew as all her siblings did that she and Randall were his favorites. His preference had always showed, because he took such pains to hide it, punishing them more severely for the slightest thing, expecting more of them than the rest. She loved him deeply even though she had not had a real conversation with him ever. He distrusted words even more than she did. She remembered Randall telling her once that the soda jerks at the drugstore where he had made deliveries and his father had swept the floors had referred to him as the cigar store Indian. See-Gar for short, Randall claimed.

Her noisy warning did no good, as she pushed open the door and found him passed out on the floor, an old army blanket of Hal's tangled around his feet, cigarette butts stubbed out on the floorboards around him. Rather than wake him, she decided to sit and wait for him to come to, for sooner or later the sugar in his bloodstream would plummet and he would wake up wanting more booze. She searched the room for his bottle but found nothing, not even an empty. He was a bottle-hider—when they were little they used to discover his stashed whiskey in the woodpile, dare each other to take swigs—and even when dead drunk he took care to hide the bottle before he passed out.

Reka listened to his ragged drunk breath for a half-hour. She hated it, this waiting for a comatose man to come to, for she had been through it enough times with Edwin Keane, and knew well that she was no match for whiskey or morphine. Sitting vigil beside him depressed her so much that she considered leaving without telling him or writing him a note, but he would have to get Ellen to read it for him and she did not want Ellen to be the first to know. She knew, but hated to admit, that she was here more for Randall than her father, for he would tell Randall about her plans, would pass along a message to him, and she was not about to trust her sisters with such an important task. She could not tell him herself because they had talked for years of leaving together. Yet now that the time had come, now that she had found a way out that promised so much of what she desired—the wide blue sky of the far west, good money to put away for college—she had come to the conclusion, while riding down the highway with the insufferable Bob Smart, that she would be better off alone. Randall would disagree, which was why she did not try to tell him in person. It would be easier this way, easier for both of them.

Reka rose and searched the cupboards for food. She was certain he had not eaten—he didn't eat much when sober, never when drinking. She wondered what had set him off this time, though she did not pursue this thought, since what, finally, did it matter? He was drunk, and needed to get sober again. If she allowed herself to ponder for very long the reason for his fall, she was sure to blame herself in the end, for every bad thing that happened seemed the result of her past.

Nothing in the larder but a few desiccated turnips, three new potatoes, a can of condensed milk. She washed a pot and peeled the potatoes and turnips, heated a soup with thin milky broth. She would not eat it herself, though she was starving—she'd not eaten since lunch with Bob Smart, and she was so excited about leaving that she'd only picked at her ham sandwich. Bob Smart had even finished what she couldn't, which told her a lot about him, though she couldn't care less what kind of cheapskate he was so long as he made good on his promise.

"You'll need some money," he had said to her in the car. "For train fare, to get out there. You got some saved?"

"I can get some," she'd said, and she knew she could—Edith Keane would gladly bankroll her escape from Trent. Edith had spent weeks trying to talk her into leaving, had offered her a year's wages at the laundry if only she would settle in Norfolk or Raleigh, anywhere but Trent, where the sight of her on the street would remind everyone of what Edith called "the incident." With Reka around, Edith's friends would feel forever sorry for her, treat her like a victim, which seemed to bother Edith as much as, maybe even more than, Edwin's death.

Her husband had been responsible for Reka's trial—Edith was against charging anyone in what she argued would have happened eventually anyway, and she never believed that Reka had done anything wrong, never believed that it was her hand that had delivered the final dose of morphine.

"You're just grieving," she'd said when she came that first night to visit Reka in the Trent jail. "It wasn't your fault any more than it was mine or his father's or that pharmacist at the drugstore, though if anyone should spend time in jail, that Mr. Green should." She'd even tried to get the sheriff to charge the pharmacist with illegal dispensation of a controlled substance, though the pharmacist was innocent, had just been following the orders of Lehmann, owner of the drugstore, who rented his building from Edwin's father.

Thomas Keane had never laid eyes on Reka until his son was dead and buried. He'd known about her—the whole town knew about her and Edwin—but he'd thought their fling a phase. Surely his son could not be serious about this girl who had dropped out of school to work in the German woman's laundry, whose best friend was a black girl, and who lived with her many siblings in a creaky clapboard eyesore in Johnsontown. Edwin was only stringing along with this white trash because of the dope. He'd get bored with her, he'd get bored with the dope, he'd come out of it and get himself healthy again and return to Chapel Hill to finish his degree and go straight through law school and come back to Trent to join the practice. Thomas Keane believed all this with the single-minded obsession that had made him one of the wealthiest men in the coastal plain. He did not take Reka seriously until Edwin was dead, at which point he took nothing else seriously, certainly not his wife's pleas to leave the girl alone.

When the soup was ready, Reka knelt by her father and shook him awake. He cussed and sat up to spit, squinted at her, called her Ellen, told her to go the hell on home, it wasn't her time to visit. He said he wasn't feeling good. He claimed to have a touch of the crud, and he said this with such a drunken pantomime of a straight face that Reka felt like laughing, even though it was far from funny.

"It's me, Pa. Reka."

He blinked. Raised up on an elbow with much effort and less success. Appeared wobbly and still drunk even on the floor.

"Reka? Damn sure is you."

"I fixed you some soup."

"You eat it. You look tired. You walk out here?"

"I was over in Greenville. Caught a ride to Speed's. He told me he saw you."

"Fat bastard."

She reached for his arm to help him up, but he appeared overcome by a dizzy spell, put his head on his knees as if he was about to be sick.

"You want a pot?"

"I'm okay," he mumbled.

"You were doing so good, Pa."

"Don't even start. Sound like Ellen."

"She's just worried about you."

"Ain't nothing wrong with a drink every now and again."

Reka let this go. He made this claim every time he drank, and he said it with so little conviction that it seemed pointless to argue.

"Let's get cleaned up. I really think you should eat."

"What kind of soup?"

"Cupboard special." She'd grown up on it, a clean-out-the-shelves concoction, also known as neighbor soup—what they could borrow from whoever had the misfortune to live alongside them, or what Hal and Ellen could steal from a nearby garden.

"I'd a known you were coming I'd a got something real to eat."

He'd have shot and dressed a squirrel or rabbit, his standard offering to guests. She had not had a bite of either since she'd come back to Trent, determined to eat only store-bought meat. Even in prison they did not feed her gamey yard animals. He meant well—to him it was a fatted calf killed for the prodigal—but she was glad she'd shown up unannounced.

"I didn't really know I was coming 'til I passed by Speed's." As soon as she said this, she realized how wrong it would sound when she told him she was leaving. As if stopping in for goodbye was a spontaneous decision, as if Speed's store, perhaps the sight of his bustling lean-to business, reminded her of her old drunk daddy, wasting away in the country.

"I mean, I didn't decide to come until today, when I was in Greenville."

"Over there reading books?"

"At the library."

"They let anybody up in there?"

She bristled at this; she was not exactly anybody, she could read, after all. She'd learned enough in prison, from correspondence courses and the patchy and tendentious tutelage of Memory Wright, to earn her visits to the library.

But her father did not know this. He thought, as she had once, that universities and their offerings were closed to people like them.

"I don't check books out like I do at the Trent Public. I just sit in there and read them."

"Long way to travel just to sit and read."

"I don't have nothing else to do on my day off."

He looked her full in the face then. His eyes were watery and bloody-veined, his face pale and whiskery. Randall had once told her that he'd seen a house that looked just like their daddy's face, and ever since, when her father went a week without shaving, she saw that shabby bungalow of Randall's, its shingles stained with mildew, its windows black as her father's sunken sockets.

"I'm going to have a drink now, Reka."

She nodded. What else could she do? She knew from experience with Edwin that she would never talk him out of it, and her resistance would only encourage belligerence.

"I'll get it for you," she said. "If and only if you promise you'll eat a little something."

"In the woodstove."

She opened the stove door and retrieved the bottle from a bed of ashes.

"I'm leaving, Pa."

"Stay a bit. You just got here."

"No, I mean I'm leaving Trent."

"Up to Nawfolk?" He favored the Tidewaterese she'd tried to shed while in prison. She spent nights trying to teach herself to talk, but around family, especially her father, she often found herself slipping back into the mother tongue.

"No. Out west."

He stared at her as if he had not heard.

"I got a job selling books. I'm going to save some money so I can go to college."

"You ain't finished high school yet," he said with what she felt was satisfaction.

"In prison I did. Got my degree through the mail."

"Don't tell me what you done there. I don't want to hear it, Eureka."

She winced at his use of her former name. She'd told him she'd preferred to be called Reka now, but Speight hated change with the recalcitrance of a grade-schooler. He tried sometimes to call her Reka, but as soon as he grew upset or anxious he reverted to that horrid word she'd borne for her first twenty-three years.

"Well, I'm leaving tomorrow. Taking a train. I got a job with a company called McMillan. Met a man at the college who hired me. I'm going to leave you the name and number of this man, he'll know where I am. I want you to make sure Randall gets it."

"You thinking of taking him away from here, too?"

Reka remembered another time the two of them had sat awkward and alone, discussing this same subject: her leaving, his begging her not to take Randall along. But that was seven years ago now, before Edwin's death, and she had gone away, but not to a place where she could take her little brother. Had Edwin not died, she would have taken him away from Trent, and Speight knew this. After her trial, he'd taken Randall with him to the country, leaving the rest of her sisters in town—Hal had found work in the Norfolk shipyards by then—and he did his best to keep the boy there, though there was no work for him and what Speight called his farm could hardly support two mouths. Randall had been in Norfolk for a year now, too long to Reka's mind—she'd always imagined him in some foreign country by now, or at least in college. She'd always had more plans for Randall than for herself, for he had not yet succumbed to the entanglement of Trent. He had chances, options. She'd lived through them for years, and now it was she who was leaving, Randall who was staying behind.

"You've got to promise me you'll tell him."

Speight sipped his whiskey, grimaced at the taste of it, as if it truly was poison to him, though that did not stop him from taking another slug when she tried to stare a promise out of him.

"You promise me you won't take him away and we'll see."

"I promised you that already. Years ago. And I didn't take him away. But now he's grown, Pa. He can go anywhere he wants, it ain't for us to say where or when."

Speight considered this. Or at least he appeared to consider it; she could not tell if the whiskey had come over him, carried him off someplace else. He fell silent, stared at the floor. She got up and went to the kitchen, returned with the steaming soup.

"Turnips?"

"Make-do soup, I warned you."

"Don't go too good with whiskey."

"What does?"

"I can name some things," he said. "Peanuts. Beefsteak."

"Fresh out," she said, smiling, trying to lift him from his funk.

"A man taking you west?"

"I told you I got a job."

"You tell him about . . ."

"No," she said, "and I'm not going to, either. They didn't ask me to list my last five places of employment from last to first like usual. They just hired me on the spot, I guess because I seemed like I was willing to work."

"I don't know," he said. "How you going to get out there? They paying your way?"

"I can get some money to tide me over."

Speight put down his soup, which so far he'd done nothing but blow on.

"You still taking money from that woman?"

"She's still fool enough to give it to me."

"That don't mean you got to take it."

"It's not like I'm living off her, Pa. I got my job at the laundry."

"I reckon she'd pay a fortune to get you away from here."

I reckon she would, Reka thought but did not say.

"It's the last time I'll need her money. I don't plan on ever laying eyes on her again."

"So you don't plan on coming back here ever?"

She had not anticipated such resistance, especially when she had found him passed out on the floor. It flattered as much as annoyed her, and she was both impatient to get going before he finished his bottle and ready to sit and talk all night, for this conversation was the lengthiest and least self-conscious they'd shared in years, since that day he'd shown up at Edwin's bungalow to encourage her to leave Trent and to beg her for the first time not to take Randall away from him.

She reminded him of that day then. "You told me I should leave. Remember? Told me to find someplace better, a long way from Trent."

"And I meant it, too. But even while I was telling you to leave, I was hoping you'd stay. I never wanted you to leave. I never asked neither one of y'all to leave here. After all that's happened, I don't see why you won't stay around here like your sisters."

Reka turned away from him. She rose suddenly and walked to the stove to turn off the soup, where she lingered, wiping away tears with a chili-stained dish towel. It shocked her, his admission—she was convinced at the time that he did want her to leave, that she had failed him by taking up with Edwin, that the trouble she'd brought to them all was too much for him to bear. As touched as she was to learn that he felt differently, it was too much to think about, especially now that escape was only hours away.

When she returned he was propped up on his cot. He studied her through his bleary, red-veined eyes. She reached for his hand and held it, and it felt bony and raw-skinned and unaccustomed to holding anything besides a hoe or a bottle.

"I've been back here two years now, Pa. Nothing's changed, either. Nobody forgot about it like I prayed they would. I'm still the girl that killed Edwin Keane."

"I reckon you always will be," he said. "To them. But you don't need to see yourself like they do."

Maybe it was the whiskey that made him so open, so honest. Believing so made it easier for her to lean over and kiss him on the forehead.

"I'm going to go now," she said.

"I can't stop you. But hell, Eureka, I'm an old man now. I might not be here when you get back. If you get back."

"I'll get back, and you'll be here. You'll be sober, too."

"Oh yeah," he said, unconvincingly. "As a judge."

"Give Randall the note. Don't you dare forget."

"I ain't seen Randall in two months if it's a day."

"You'll see him soon enough. He'll be down here to see you."

"Promise me you won't forget your old man, now."

"I told you I'll be back, Pa. You got to believe me."

"I believe in both of y'all. Always did. Got us all into some trouble, too, but even that ain't made me give up on nobody."

She stood in the parking lot of Speed's store until she spotted someone she felt comfortable enough asking for a ride into town: a teenaged couple bound for a night of slow and repetitive cruising up and down Main. On the ride into town, Reka tried to make conversation, but the girl, who looked to be about fourteen, suctioned herself like a barnacle to her boyfriend and said not a word. The boyfriend answered her questions shyly; twice he called her ma'am. Reka felt ancient in their company, even older during the thick silences that fell between her stabs at talk. She felt for the two of them—in a year the girl would be pregnant and would walk the aisle of some cinderblock Holiness church to the unanimous disdain of the audience, shunned by her parents, whose own marriage like as not was just as forced and hurried. She wanted to tell the girl she had other choices, she wanted to grab her by the collar of her too-tight sweater and wrench her from the car before the evening ended on some desolate back road with what the girl would claim was an immaculate conception. Yet another part of her grew queasy dispensing such judgment, for she had seen the damage done by thinking you're right, always right.

The couple let her off at the Little Pep Drive In, where she used the pay phone in the parking lot to call Edith Keane.

"I'm sorry to bother you so late," Reka said when she answered on the first ring.

"No bother." Edith always sounded surprised when Reka called, though she encouraged her to get in touch if she needed any little thing, and she discouraged her from showing up at the house, for she did not want her husband to know the extent of her involvement with the girl. Thomas Keane knew that his wife had "done some things" to make Reka's transition easier. He knew of and reluctantly accepted the magnanimous charity that allowed her to befriend the enemy. He did not know the half of it—rent paid and loans written out on the sky-blue checks drawn from the account she kept separate from her husband's fortune—but then again, perhaps he knew everything and chose to ignore it, as he had chosen to ignore his son's morphine habit.

Edith Keane was a lonely, stubborn, handsome woman whose shame would never lessen. Reka had learned things from her—the ravaging effects of an apparently half-pleasurable guilt, for one—but the things she'd learned had not been the things Edith meant to impart.

"I'm leaving town tomorrow."

A crackly silence. The noise of teenagers pulling in and out of the parking lot, their radios tuned unanimously to Buddy Holly's "Not Fade Away," their shouts and gravel-spinning scratch-offs patching the silence with an incongruent frivolity.

"For a vacation?"

Reka laughed. She didn't mean to, and felt immediately sorry, for she tried never to reveal her true feelings to Edith. But the sarcastic chuckle was out before she could stop it, and she could not take it back.

"I can't afford a vacation. I'm leaving for good."

"Wherever to?"

Edith's voice was small but incredulous. Obviously she did not think Reka capable of ever severing their arrangement. She wanted her to leave, she did not think her capable of leaving. Maybe she *doesn't* want me to leave, Reka thought; maybe my staying is key to the guilt she seems to need to wallow in to survive. Reka thought of

what Edith's life would be like without her "project" around to remind her of the life she had once. She felt sorry for another person
for the second time in an hour. Again the pity struck her as dangerous, this time because she needed the money to leave and did not
want to pity the lender.

This time it would really be a loan; all the other payments were
called such, but she'd yet to pay back a dime and when Edith never
mentioned it, she assumed it was understood that *loan* was only a
euphemism for *handout*. Reka would feel differently about not re-
paying this getaway money, though. She'd send Edith her money
first thing, before she even started saving for college.

"Out west. I got a job out there, selling books."

"What kind of books?"

"Books to help schoolkids study. Reference books, abridged encyclopedias, stuff like that."

"And who . . . I mean, how did you . . ."

"I met a man in Greenville. I was over there using the college library, he was recruiting for his company."

"It sounds awfully difficult. Will you be going door-to-door?"

No, thought Reka, I'll be contacting potential buyers through
the U.S. Mail. She had thought this would all be over in a few minutes, like most of her transactions with Edith, but it seemed a full-
fledged conversation was in order.

"I guess." Reka suspected Edith thought she was lying. Thought
she needed the money for something else, an abortion, or to bail
out some ne'er-do-well lover in the tank on a drunk driving charge.

"I can give you the guy's name who hired me. He's staying in a
hotel in Greenville, you can call him."

Reka knew this would get to her. They had long since learned to
manipulate each other; though they saw each other rarely now and
talked even less, they knew ways to rankle each other. In her more
lucid moments Reka attributed this pettiness to the sickness of their
arrangement, which could not help but breed resentment. Edith's

need to redeem herself, Reka's desire to punish her—what good could come from such a warped situation?

Blaming the nature of things was something Reka had been trying to avoid lately, as she was not convinced that any given thing came with its own set nature. Not even nature itself, which was not fixed but capricious. The trick was to learn how to adapt to extremes. For too long she had thrown up her hands and sighed at the things she thought unchangeable.

Edith Keane always made her contemplate such things, which might well make their arrangement worth it in the long run. If Reka had learned things from Edwin, the most lasting lesson of her time with him was the way he refused to learn from things. He theorized—he loved his theories, his elaborate and overdeveloped ideas—but his theories seemed rooted more in fear and defensiveness than a desire for clarity or survival. That Reka did not realize this at the time was understandable, since Edwin was the first man—the first person—she'd ever met who lived more from his head than his gut. Randall was the exception, but at the time she met Edwin, Randall was only eleven, his mind as wild and deep as a river that threatened always to swamp the shore with torrents but that flowed backward and forward and sideways at once, and led to no sea.

"I don't need to check up on you," said Edith. "I'm just curious about what you'll be doing. As long as you're sure it's legitimate."

Did she think Reka had sold herself blindly into a white slavery ring? Signed up unwillingly to be auctioned off on the streets of Laramie, Wyoming? Reka was torn as always between indignation at Edith's assumptions about her intelligence and gratitude for what seemed, at least at times, genuine concern.

"It's a national company," said Reka, aware of how naive this sounded. "They go all over, recruiting college girls for summer work."

"College girls?"

"I want to go to college, Mrs. Keane."

"Good for you, Reka. Certainly I'll do anything I can to help."

"I just need train fare to get out there. Maybe enough money to tide me over for a week or two, until I start making money."

"And what if you don't make any money?"

Will you come back to Trent? That was the rest of her sentence. Not *How will you survive*, not *Will you pay me back?* but: *Will you come back here and make me responsible for you again?*

Reka watched a group of teenage girls pile out of a family Dodge and strut in a giggly clump through the gauntlet of leering boys leaning on the beds of their pickups.

"I'll find some other kind of work out there," she said, and she knew she would take any kind of work to avoid coming back here.

"Edwin always wanted to go west. He had some silly notion that things were less complicated there than here. Did he ever mention this to you?"

Edith's words ushed in a memory so vivid it transformed the parking lot of the Little Pep into the cluttered kitchen of the bungalow where she'd lived with Edwin Keane. They had talked so often and so grandly of escape, had spread atlases and maps across the kitchen counters and called out the names of places in far western states, reciting them as if they were love poems. Had she never met Edwin she doubtless would have thought of the Blue Ridge as west, might have traveled no farther west than Raleigh in her life.

"No," Reka lied. She did not want Edith thinking she was merely aping Edwin's plans, though she suspected that it was fruitless to deny it, that Edith assumed every idea, every ambition Reka entertained was provoked by her time with Edwin. It was hard to dislike Edith for this, as Reka often felt this way herself. Even while serving time for Edwin's death, Reka continued to love him as fiercely as before, to see him as her savior. What she felt was hard to call grief, for it was not really until her release, and her return to Trent, that she was able to think of him as dead. Even the living were lost

to her during those five long years; because no one but Edith Keane
came to visit her, Reka quickly convinced herself that everyone she
knew was simply walled off from her. Besides Edith, only Randall
attempted to cross the wall, and because she could not bear to see
him in the stifling Quonset hut where visitors were brought for
thirty-minute reunions on splintery picnic tables, she refused him
every time he came. Tell him to write, she'd instruct the guard
who announced his arrival, and she ordered Randall not to come
in every letter she wrote to him, and after a year of monthly visits,
he gave up.

She needed to feel as if everything she'd left behind was there
waiting for her exactly as she'd left it. It puzzled her now to think
that she had craved such stasis, for the desire for change, for movement and travel and growth, was what had led her to pick up the sy-
ringe and empty the morphine into her lover's veins. And surely she
had changed in prison—under Memory Wright's tutelage she
learned more than she would have in college, and she learned things
from her fellow inmates that she surely would never have picked up
in late-night pillow talks in some college dormitory. But time itself
felt frozen there, suspended; because her days were so uniform and
her routine so colorless, it was easier to think of them as the same
day, and of the world outside as weathering the same interminable
blandness. Randall remained eleven, brilliant and curious and will-
ful; he spent his days as always, exploring the back alleys and side
lots of Trent, cataloging subtle mysteries and collecting things no
ordinary eleven-year-old would even notice: strange sayings from
the mouths of speakers who did not know the meaning of their
words, blue bottles, funny names, rusty parts of cars and washing
machines that he kept in the basement for a sculpture he claimed
would one day make him famous. As for Edwin, he lay in the cot
where she'd last seen him, though he was alive still, frittering away
his days according to his custom, long naps alternated with a stab at
one of the dozen books lying open-spined on the kitchen floor

around the cot, his jerky jazz revolving constantly, lopsidedly, on the warped turntable.

Of course the world she entered when she walked out of prison resembled this image only faintly. Randall was sixteen years old, a man almost, living in the country with her father, who soon after her imprisonment had returned to the shack on the edge of the swamp and lapsed into a meager and bibulous subsistence. And Edwin was dead.

He had remained dead during the two years she'd spent here in self-inflicted punishment. He was still dead, and she was on her own now, and even if the idea to travel west had originated in his passion for someplace unfettered and sparse, someplace free from the gnarled greenery that overtook this landscape in March and clung to it, suffocated it, until November, Reka was the one moving now. Edwin will always be here. He'll disintegrate in the loamy soil he claimed to hate. He already had disintegrated, she realized, and it seemed to her suddenly, linked to his mother by wires, that he never would have left this place any more than Edith Keane herself would pick up and flee.

"You seem to have made up your mind. And of course I can help out."

"I want to pay you back," said Reka.

"Oh, don't worry about that, now, just . . ."

"No, really. I know I haven't paid you back a dime in all this time. But this time I mean it. I want to pay it all back."

After a silence, Edith said, "Of course. You mail me what you can, when you can. I'll send Tillet over with a check first thing in the morning."

"I want to thank you for all you done." *You've* done. She reddened under the brash lights of the parking lot, embarrassed at her slip. Of course she knew better, but when she was nervous or angry she often fell back into the lazy speech of Johnsontown. Her relapse made her all the more anxious to leave.

"Thank *you*, Reka. It's helped me, helping you."

A project, an arrangement. If taking care of Reka was the only way she could get through her days, Reka was even more committed to escaping. Staying would be as bad for Edith Keane as it was for her, but as they said their awkward goodbyes, Reka knew that she cared for this woman. Despite the ways they'd used each other, Edith had stuck by her, which was more than she could say for her own sisters.

Bob Smart was waiting for her in front of the courthouse, as threatened. He was shaved and seersuckered and he looked at her dress—the same one she'd worn the day before, which she had slept in—as if he could see through it.

"Where's your luggage?"

She had only a small suitcase filled with underwear and a single dress, for she could not imagine taking along on her new life the clothes that hung in her closet—Edith Keane's castoffs. She'd been so tired when she returned home the night before that she'd sprawled fully clothed and shod across the bed. She did not even bother to turn on the fan, and her dress was still heavy and damp with sweat. She had not bathed, had barely eaten: There was too much to think about to prepare for her departure in the conventional ways, and she had thought so long about leaving that the usual preparations—change-of-address forms, goodbyes, boxing and sweeping—made no sense to her. There was nothing she'd wanted to bring along save a stack of Randall's letters and two or three crumbling letters from Edwin. It was all she had to remember him by, all she needed, for his words were what remained. Now that she'd had more experience, the sex had faded; he was her first, and he was a dope addict, more willing than able, not always willing. She might have forgotten what he looked like had she not kept up with his mother, whose rooms were filled with photographs of Edwin and even an oil portrait of him at age eight hanging above the landing of the stairs.

"This is it," she said to Bob Smart. She climbed in the front seat of his roadster.

"You're kidding. You're going to need a wardrobe, sweetheart. You got to dress the part."

"I'll buy more when I get there. Couldn't find anything around here my style. Let's go if we're going."

He sighed and climbed in. In three minutes they were out of Trent, traveling west on 64, which they would take to Raleigh. In Raleigh she'd be rid of him—he would put her on the train, and though he might try to get her to stop off for a repeat of yesterday's "interview," she would not oblige this time, as she had what she wanted already.

Nevertheless he tried. "I know a place in Raleigh, not far from the train station. Sir Walter Hotel. Nice place, at least for around here. We could put up there for the night, get a steak dinner some-where, go dancing. You could leave in the morning."

"You're just being smart with me, aren't you?" When he did not respond, Reka said, "Sorry. A harmless joke."

"I've gotten that one before."

"So have I. Been called spiteful all my life."

He took his eyes off the road to study her. "You seem different."

She flushed at the thought of it coming on so suddenly, apparent even to someone as single-minded and unimaginative as Bob Smart.

"Listen, Bob," she said. "Did I get this job because I slept with you?"

Bob Smart returned his gaze to the road. He gripped the steer-ing wheel with both hands, as if he were being tailed by the police and wanted to at least appear as if he was obeying the law.

"Well, according to company policy, we hire girls with some col-lege under their belt."

"And you hired me because of what I have under my belt?"

"You do look younger than you are."

"Which is why you hired me?" She watched him light a cigarette, toss the match out the window, blow his smoke contemplatively out the side vent. She watched him begin to sweat.

"You thought you'd give me the slip, right? After we put up in the Sir Walter Raleigh Hotel. After you got your steak and after we—what did you call it?—go dancing?"

"I'm not supposed to hire anyone who hasn't had a little bit of college." He would not look at her now. She looked at nothing but him.

"There's a Mrs. Bob Smart, right?"

He looked down at the steering wheel, at his hands tightening around the grip.

"Least I didn't try to hide it. You saw the ring. Didn't seem to bother you yesterday any."

"Doesn't bother me today any either, if you want to know the truth. Mrs. Bob Smart has her own troubles, I'm sure. I'll let her take care of them."

"What the hell does that mean?"

"It means I'm not about to let you make me feel bad for sleeping with you because you're married. Nor am I the type to run back to your wife and tell her what you've been doing on your recruiting trips. I doubt I'm the first without any college under my belt to get hired by Mr. Bob Smart."

"I wish you'd quit calling me that."

Reka laughed. She felt a little sorry for him then, for she too had suffered a name she did not care for, and the thought of asking not to be called by your name struck her as sadly comic. Bob Smart was a liar, a snake, but she was far more angry at herself for almost being duped than she was at his pathetic scheming.

"What should I call you?"

"Just Bob," he said petulantly.

"Bob, okay, Bob. Look, Bob: You're going to take me to the train station and tell me where to go. I might not have any college, Bob, but I know as much as most of those girls in that room, and you know it."

"Yeah, you're right. I do know it. But a rule's a rule. Someone was to find out, it'd be my job on the line. They like 'em in college for a reason: People trust a college girl. They'll ask her into their homes and they'll even buy a book they won't ever crack open just to help some girl get her nurse's degree."

"So I'll act like I'm in college. I plan on going anyway."

Bob would not look at her at all.

"Think I'm too old?"

"Oh no. It's just, well, I don't know the first thing about you. For all I know, you could have just gotten out of jail."

"I'd be offended if you didn't have such a smart mouth, Bob." But she was more shocked than offended; she thought of Randall then, of how she'd tell him this story later, how Bob Smart's innocent guess would amaze him.

"Oh, no offense. It's just, we usually check up more."

"I'd say you performed a pretty thorough checkup."

"You're making it sound like I do that all the time."

"I don't care how often you do it. I don't think your bosses will care, either. Once is enough, right? But you don't want them to know about it."

Bob let his foot off the gas. The engine roared, the car slowed. "You wouldn't do that."

"The hell I would not."

"Can't we work this out some other way?"

"Take me to the train station. Tell me where to go, what to do, who I'll be working with and all. And one more thing: I gave my father your phone number to give to my brother. He's the only one in the world who really cares where I am. I want him to know, and I want you to promise me—all hard feelings aside now, I promise you that—I want you to swear you'll tell him the truth when he gets in touch with you."

Bob Smart sighed. He said, "Why would I lie?"

"Revenge?"

"Look, no hard feelings is right. You got the job. I promise you I'll tell your brother where you are if he calls, and I'll take you to the train station. But can't it wait one day?"

Reka allowed herself laughter then. "You're a little smarter than I thought, Bob."

Two

_____

From the beginning it was to be temporary: living with Hal, working at the naval shipyards, Norfolk itself. Since that day in March 1958 when Randall had left Simpson County for the first time in his eighteen years, everything he'd seen had felt tentative, ephemeral. On the bus up to Norfolk, he'd tried making eye contact with other passengers, but the others, mostly big-boned people trembling in hot shallow sleep and a couple of hungover soldiers staring out at the black wet fields of the Tidewater, never moved their eyes. They seemed to Randall unfazed by their passage from one place to another, as if this bus ride was only another link in a lifelong series of moves. When the bus jerked to a stop in one of those lone gas pump towns, Randall watched the sleepers lift their heads, blink, and return to their naps, the weave of the seat cushion imprinted on red and sweaty cheeks. He envied that imprint, a tattoo of transience he would soon wear on his own skin.

But that day he could never have slept. He kept his nose to the window, trying to see what there was to see. He did not see much: a man moving slowly through a big flat field, his head down, hands in his pockets. The man's dejected lope made the field seem end-less, like a dead-end job in which he'd never get ahead, never break even. On the rickety porch of a roadside shack, Randall saw a woman cutting a girl's yellow hair, scissors flashing in the sunlight. He saw too many towns like Trent, their particulars—drugstores and churches, redbrick schools, a row of has-been Victorians lining Main—so similar that Randall felt he wasn't moving, wasn't getting anywhere.

He wore loose flannel pants that younger boys made fun of in the bus station at Norfolk. Sunday shoes handed down from Hal, and a white cotton shirt buttoned to the neck with no tie. He did not need a tie to work in the shipyards, though his sister Ellen had ordered him to dress nice for travel. She had given him a piece of paper with Hal's address on it, instructed him to "inquire as to the where-abouts" of this house; the advice she gave was bossy, though she had never traveled as far as Norfolk herself. His father, talking over Ellen in the way that the furnace used to come on over the teacher at school, said just stop somebody on the street who looked crazy enough to know Hal, ask where he's at.

But Norfolk was huge. People he stopped to ask said, Hell, I don't know, who? Randall trudged the wide sidewalks, holding his cardboard suitcase with both hands. The suitcase was secured with a belt, and the belt was trailing flakes of leather as he lugged.

He went to the shipyard and waited all afternoon until he saw men streaming out of the gate. When he saw Hal pass by he got up and followed. He knew if he spoke to Hal in front of his friends his brother would tell him to get lost. Randall followed him to a bar and waited for an hour, then two. Dusty men came out singing. They looked past him, stained the sidewalk with spit. He took his suitcase across the street to avoid their indifference. It got dark, then cold. His pockets were warm and he dug his hands deeper into them, fingering lint.

Finally Hal came out with an ugly older man. This man's hair was bent back like a field of windblown weeds. The sun had gotten to him bad; his skin looked singed, like a piece of iron you might find rusting in a junkyard, tawny skin flaking in crusty sheets, revealing the bright and tender layers beneath. As for Hal, he looked the same, only skinnier and drunker.

Randall tailed the two of them a half block behind. He wondered if the ugly man worked alongside Hal building ships. He imagined himself among men in a line, handing, lifting, hammering, talking idle trash. Randall liked music, and he wondered if he'd get to talk about music, and who he'd get to talk to. He wondered if it was expected of you to talk to the man next to you in the work line, to find something in common and dig away at it while you worked, getting sweaty and tired, exhausting one subject, then moving on to a barely related one.

Hal's buddy split off finally, and a couple of blocks later Hal left the street to climb the steps of a huge white house. The house had so many staircases climbing its sides that it resembled a beach palace with landings and porches for ocean views, only what it overlooked was a sea of more of the same creaky houses. Randall stood for a moment on the landing, looking out over the shipyards and the blue bay beyond, before he knocked.

A woman came to the door. Very curly yellow hair and a tight gray dress and a way of looking over him on the landing that made him wonder if he was even there. She said, "What?" and Randall said, "Hal," and she disappeared into the darkness of the apartment, the screen door slapping the jamb.

Hal took her place behind the screen. Dirty in his work clothes and bleary-eyed. For a few seconds he stared at his little brother.

"I knew it," he said. "I damn well knew it."

"Knew what?"

"He give you the address?"

"Martha and Ellen and them did."

"They told you you could stay here?"

"They just told me to come by here," said Randall, ashamed. "They didn't tell me where to stay. Said for me to get a job."

"And send them back the cash?"

"Yes. Well, some of it."

"Well, come on in, then," said Hal. "I'll say this: We'll see about getting you a job, but as soon as you got some money saved you got to move. We got a sofa, but we have company over a lot."

"Unannounced," said the woman. She was sitting at the table in the kitchen, smoking a cigarette with a red filter.

"So you need to find your own place, little brother. Understood?"

Randall was staring at the woman. He asked her if she worked in a store.

"What?" said Hal. He turned to the woman himself. "See what I told you about them?"

The woman studied Randall. For a second she seemed like she wanted to laugh, but the impulse passed quickly without her giving in to it. Randall could not look at her. He watched the smoke curl lazily from her cigarette, up to the low ceiling where it hung in a cloud.

"My name's Delores. I work in a restaurant."

Hal got some beers out of the icebox. He handed one to Delores and sat down across from her at the table. After a few slugs of beer he turned to Randall, got up and got him a bottle also, handed it to him along with a rusty church key.

"Drink this," he said.

"I'll drink it," said Randall. He opened it and the cap landed by his suitcase on the linoleum, and when he bent to retrieve it he saw pieces of cheese and crumbs dotting the washed-out floral pattern of the floor. He stared at his feet.

"Why are you standing like that?" Hal said.

"I'm not standing funny," said Randall. He had one hand in his pocket, fingering the lint he'd discovered while waiting for his brother outside the bar. He was leaning on the edge of a cabinet, his feet crossed at the ankle.

"See?" Hal said to Delores.

She said, very slowly, "I do see."

This woman Delores scrambled eggs. Bacon popping in a greasy skillet. Hal singing a song called "Breakfast for Supper, That's the Way It's Done," and washing down breakfast/supper with beer. He only offered Randall the one beer, which Randall made last, as if food and drink were going to be hard to come by in Norfolk.

After supper Hal went out and Delores disappeared into the bedroom. She closed the door. Randall sat on the couch. He had nothing to read, nothing to do. He thought of going for a walk, but he'd been walking all day and he was a little scared he'd get lost and have to stop and ask someone how to get back to this place he never would have found had he not trailed Hal home. He sat outside on the steps for a while, and later he took everything out of his suitcase, spread a towel over the couch, refolded all his clothes. *Here I am and look at me. Free at last and folding clothes.*

From the bedroom he heard soft singing. Then rustling noises, as if she were folding clothes also. He was scared to knock but wanted to very much anyway, if only to see what he would force himself to say to her when she answered.

Randall went to bed without seeing Delores again that night. She did not even come out to go to the bathroom. Much later Hal came in drunk.

"Goddamn it to frozen hell," he said as he passed by the couch. Randall could smell the sweetly sour beer on his breath. Finally he fell asleep on the couch. The bristly weave of the fabric and nervous dreams in which he was fired for dropping a hammer on a bald man's head from atop a sixty-story ship needled him awake from time to time during the night.

Early in the morning before the others got up, Randall changed into overalls and one of his father's dirty work shirts. Hal came out of the bedroom with his eyes half closed. He stood at the kitchen sink with the water running into a kettle. When he could see again he turned to Randall, rolled his sleepy red eyes and started whistling "I've Been Working on the Railroad."

"Shut the hell up out there," Delores called.

"She's a princess, that girl."

"Doesn't she have to get up now?" said Randall.

"What are you worried about it for?" said Hal. "Anyhow, she's sort of her own boss."

"She has her own restaurant?"

"Hell, no. She just does what she wants in this world. Gets there whenever she gets there. She's twenty-six."

On the way to the shipyard Hal said, "Nothing easy to do in a shipyard. It's all hard and since there's always going to be some fucking war it's gotta be done in a hurry."

"What's it like?"

"Hard. I weld. This guy we're meeting up the street taught me how. This guy, if he wouldn't of taught me how to weld I'd still be a rope boy like you're gonna be, hauling tools and scraps all day, at the beck and call of every sonofabitch in the whole yard."

"Why'd he teach you how to weld, this guy?" asked Randall.

"Hell if I know. Did me a favor I guess."

Randall wanted to ask his brother a lot more questions before they met up with this welder, but he had time for only one.

"You're not married to her, are you?"

Hal looked at him. "Don't you tell nobody at home about her. Not even Reka, though she can't say a damn thing, can she? Don't you tell them nothing about me."

"What am I supposed to say when they ask how you are?"

Hal considered this. "Just say, 'Oh, you know Hal.' That ought to shut their faces."

The older man from the night before, the one with the sun-ravaged skin, joined them at a corner.

"This is my little brother," Hal said. "He's looking work."

The man studied Randall and said, "How old are you?"

"Nineteen," Randall lied.

"You don't look it," he said, and then he seemed to forget all about Randall. Hal called him Cheap Blade. They talked fast to each other in a tongue so crammed with cusswords that the cusswords lost all meaning. Words so watered down and common they didn't sound bad or wrong, just empty. Randall could tell that Hal loved these words because they made him sound tough and worldly. But the one called Cheap Blade did not seem to know any other words; Randall could tell by the way he spoke.

Randall dropped back, following as he'd done the night before, and it was as if they did not know he was there anymore. He watched Cheap Blade from behind, trying to figure him. He thought of writing Reka about him; she would dearly love his name. They had always delighted in oddly comic names. In Trent there lived a Ponce de Leon Sutton, a Pocahontas Britt. A woman in the Trent phone book named Minnie Monk got so many crank calls from kids she had her number changed.

Cheap Blade knew people on the streets as they passed by the warehouses on the way to the shipyards. The wide wood doors were wheeled back, and men stood before them in the cool dark, smoking and calling, "Cheap Blade, hey, whattayasay, Cheap."

Randall didn't know where the name came from, but he thought it could either be from a knife he carried or from the splotchy scars on his neck.

All the men on the way to work spoke to Hal and Cheap Blade by name. Walking into the shipyard with a hundred other men, everything gray beyond—the skeletons of boats being built and farther the grayish glint of wave, the sun on the water, the flashing scraps of metal that everyone stepped on, not bothering to look down—Randall felt as lonely as he had since Reka was taken away from the courtroom by the heavy female bailiff.

Hal told him where to go and headed off to another part of the yard with Cheap Blade. Randall stood in a line and talked to a man in charge who asked only if he was a U.S. citizen. He looked Randall over and said, "You'll do for something around here," and took him and two others out by the ships where men moved about on scaffolds, yelling and throwing ropes down. The man said: "Y'all gonna be rope boys. Get back out of the way good and when the ropes hit look up at who's holding them and whoever that is will tell you what he needs and you boys tie in tight and yank the rope twice and get back out of the way. If there ain't no ropes coming down, y'all pick up some of these scraps, tote 'em over to that trash bin across the way there.'"

He was gone. Randall and the others stood gazing up at the slippery steel sides, searching the air for unfurling ropes, only Randall was looking beyond the boat to the sky, the clouds, when the rope snapped at his capless head.

Back at the apartment that night, sitting in the cramped kitchen eating food Delores brought home from the restaurant, Randall was nervous and sore from work. He said very little, ate his meat loaf sandwich and coleslaw. He was conscious of every noise he made, eating noises, the noise he made in the bathroom. Hal, as always, made enough noise for a half-dozen of them, but Delores made noise only when talking, which wasn't much. Mostly she sipped gin and stared at Hal as if her stare could keep him home.

Randall decided the less noise he made the more she would take to him. He loved to talk but he knew that Hal, despite his bluster, would let him stay as long as he wanted. It was Delores he had to please.

Delores said to Hal, "Want me to talk a little about the earliest stages of our love affair?"

"Not really," said Hal, reaching for more coleslaw. They ate from paper carryout tubs. Randall had yet to see a dish.

"In the early stages of our love affair," she started, "we went at it so hard we did not eat for days. I lost six pounds, he lost ten."

"It was mostly water weight," said Hal.

"We went at it hard, I'm telling you. I had bruises. We weren't living here. We were living in my place over by the water and we got kicked out—well, I got kicked out. Hal didn't since he wasn't really living there. I shared with this bitch Roxanne who we locked out for the duration of our hunger strike and lovefest. Finally she came in through a window and Hal here threw a piece of toast at her that had sat in the oven for a week and was more deadly than a brickbat. To top it off, he threatened her pitiful life. After that the landlord came with Norfolk's finest and kicked me out and we moved to this palace."

"Is this all true?" asked Hal. The whole time she was talking he had been shoveling coleslaw down his throat and pretending to read the newspaper.

Delores ignored him. "We lost all this weight."

"Mostly water weight," said Hal.

"No it wasn't, Hal. The hell you say. It was a sacrifice, an offering of substance."

"Water," Hal whispered to Randall. "Tell her, boy genius. The human body is two-thirds water, right? Old mother earth is three-fifths water. Randall's head is one hundred percent H_2O."

Delores got up, pushed the table into Hal's stomach and went into the bedroom, slamming the door. Randall heard that rustle he'd heard before.

"She gets mad, she tries on dresses," said Hal. "There's nothing anyone can do about this type behavior. We got sisters, but she ain't like any girl either of us have ever known."

"Where does she come from?"

Hal pushed the table away from his stomach and lit a cigarette.

"Be glad you didn't ask her that. She'd of knocked your big bobbly waterhead off."

"How come?"

"She don't like to talk about anything pre-Norfolk. But I done some snooping. She's from some chicken-bone town south of here. You know Cheap Blade from work? She claims he's from her same town. But Cheap says he's from all over. She says he grew up out in the country not far from her, says his real name is Ronnie Anderson and he used to sing in a church choir."

"Cheap Blade in a church choir?"

"Free Will Baptist, too. Down in that place where she's come from. What a hole, I bet. Cheap denies hell out of it, of course."

"Doesn't she ask you where you're from?"

"Naw. She don't care, Randall. She could care less about stuff like that. She just likes to have a good time, go out dancing, smoke those long cigarettes she favors. When she gets mad at me or when I leave the house with Cheap Blade for a little R and R, she likes to try on damn dresses. I guess if you wouldn't have showed up I could have told her I was from all over, like Cheap Blade."

"I don't see where my showing up has anything to do with where you come from. I could be from all over, too."

Hal reached over and yanked a shoulder strap of Randall's overalls. "You from all over, all right. Go look in the mirror, hayseed. Got Pa's old overalls on, clomping around in my old shoes. Whose underwear? Your jailbird sister's?"

"Don't you talk that way about her. She's your sister, too."

"She ain't none of mine. Not after what she did. I would of left that town anyway, matter of time, but after she killed that rich bastard boyfriend of hers, I had to leave."

"She didn't kill him."

"What did they send her to jail for then, Judge? Littering? Jaywalking?"

"He killed himself. She just happened to be there when he did it."

"Goddammit, Randall, how stupid are you? The girl confessed. She's your sister, you love her and all, but she's a murderer. What would she turn herself in for if she didn't actually do it?"

"You know why. She felt bad about not doing anything to stop it."

"You always were a fool when it came to her. Believe anything she tells you, take up for her when the whole state knows what she done wrong."

Randall pushed the table away this time. He got up and went into the bathroom, the only place in the tiny apartment to hide, the only other room with a door.

"What you going to do, try on some overalls?" Hal called after him.

At work Randall tilted his head so far skyward, watching for ropes slinging down from the sides of the ships, that his neck hurt always and a ring of sun burned itself in his vision, upsetting his balance when he looked to the ground. He carried this ring home with him nights, a searing hole in the center of everything that Randall, to amuse himself, filled with incongruent images. A seahorse in the middle of a barbershop door. Where a woman passing him by on the street might have had breasts, a ghastly purple cabbage bloomed.

The other rope boys kept up a steady chatter. Randall talked some, but he did not have any talks of the sort he'd envisioned before he'd arrived in Norfolk, the sort that deliver part of you away to some distant land where things changed and anything was possible. Most of the rope crew was young like him; they talked of cars and girls, detailing the innards of both in the same crude ways. Randall found himself working alongside the one older man in the crew, a soft-eyed man named Granger who told Randall he was twenty-six.

"What's that like?" Randall asked him.

Granger looked sheepish and said, "It ain't nothing to write home about," which made Randall laugh. But after this exchange Granger returned his gaze to the sky and said little. Everything he did say Randall asked him to repeat, because he chewed his words too long before he let go of them.

In the apartment one night three months after he'd arrived in Norfolk, Randall heard Hal and Delores yelling in the bedroom. He thought he'd better leave because most of the arguments that his sisters got into with Hal had ended up sweeping through rooms, through whole houses, down both sides of a street. Randall had never known a fight with Hal in it to stay sealed up in one place for very long. But he had finally found his way to the Norfolk Public Library and gotten himself a card and some books, and since he had something to do now besides stare out the screen door at the slice of faraway water, he did not want to leave the apartment.

The yelling swelled. Delores hit this high creamy note, calling Hal a "goddamn so and so." Hal said, "Bitch, I'll pull your hair out." Delores begging him to try. The two of them yelling right into Randall's ear. He could tell her words were seeping out from between clenched teeth, could see the blotches of red soaking her face and neck.

It scared Randall much more than all those family fights he'd witnessed between Hal and every combination of sister. This had the potential to go so much further.

When the door opened, Randall hid behind his book and did not breathe. Hal passed by without looking at him and left. Delores stayed in the room with the door open still, and after a long silence during which Randall read one paragraph seventeen times, he heard the rustling again. All night long she kept it up, the rustle of fabric, a steady high-heeled stomp across the warped floor. After a few hours of this someone below broomhandled their ceiling and yelled something unintelligible but obvious up at her. After a spray of "To hell with you, too," the room went quiet except for soft crying, muted it seemed by something—a pillow maybe, maybe a dress.

The next morning, walking to work, Randall passed the place where he and Hal usually met up with Cheap Blade. He wasn't there. Randall waited a while on the corner, then took off slowly, glancing back occasionally, thinking Hal must have told Cheap Blade he'd meet him at work. But all day he saw neither Hal nor Cheap Blade.

"What did Hal say today?" Delores asked Randall that night when she came in after her shift.

"He wasn't there."

"Wasn't at work?"

"I didn't see him."

"That doesn't mean he wasn't there," she said, passing by him to go to the bedroom.

An hour later she came out and sat across the kitchen table from him. She heated up some okra and tomatoes and picked at it, pushing her hair out of her eyes.

"What's that book?" she asked.

"A novel."

"Yeah, a novel, okay. About what?"

"These farmers that get driven from their land by dust storms. They leave the plains and head out to California and . . ."

"That's enough of that," she said. "I lived that mess, I don't want to read about it or hear you talk about it."

Randall was about to ask if she was from Oklahoma when Hal and Cheap Blade burst through the door, carrying two bulging grocery bags from which they pulled bottles of beer. Hal slid bottles across the table to the two of them, but neither Randall nor Delores made a move to pick one up.

"Where'd you go to college last night, Cheap Blade?" Hal asked his buddy. Cheap Blade was unshaven and wore a greasy hat crushed up along his crown.

"Old Do-minion, Willum N'Mairy, Warshington and Lee."

Delores looked at Randall. She watched him so closely he was scared to avert his eyes from her. Finally he got up and poured the morning's leftover coffee in a pot to heat up for them.

"Damn, Delores," said Hal. "Cheap Blade's smart. He's got three degrees."

"He's a genius," said Delores.

"You're just jealous," Cheap Blade said to her. "I got all them degrees in one night."

"You never even graduated high school, Ronnie," said Delores.

"You don't know me," said Cheap Blade.

"You don't know me," Hal said to Delores. He turned to Randall and said, "You don't know me, either."

Hal got up and went into the bedroom. They could hear him pulling drawers out of the dresser until they fell to the floor. He came back carrying Randall's suitcase, tightened with Randall's flaky belt.

"We're going to continue on our drunk," he said. Cheap Blade chuckled and tipped his hat. He got up with the bag of beer and went out the door. Hal stood above them at the table, staring at his brother. Randall knew better than to mention their father, but the sight of Speight struggling across the yard, home from another one of his three-day blows, was all he could think about. It would take another month or two of rope boy wages for him to save enough to get his own room somewhere, what with all he had to send home to Ellen and them.

But Hal was his brother, just as much as Eureka was his sister. He would never allow himself to abandon Hal the way Hal had shed Eureka. In each of them there was some thriving chord of curiosity and intelligence that set them apart from the rest of the world. Randall thought this even about his sisters, who were uniformly complacent in their Trent lives. They worked out at the blender factory and married linemen and heavy equipment operators and they talked bad about the niggers and they stayed all day long at church every Sunday, but they were not hopeless. A day would come when they would allow themselves the liberating expense of all the right questions. Randall thought the family cursed and blessed at once. Eureka used to make up stories for him about how their lives would turn out, and after she was sent away he continued to add to these stories. His endings weren't exactly happy—even at age twelve he'd known better than that—but they were messy in ways he thought balanced. Small triumphs of will and luck mixed in with the tragedy and injustice.

Randall said to Hal, "But what about your job, Hal? You got a good job. They taught you how to weld and all."

"That's the difference between you and me," said Hal. He left. Delores had still not looked at him. The entire time she stared at Randall.

In the middle of the night, asleep with one cheek ground into the rough ridges of the couch, Randall awoke to find Delores leaning over him. She grabbed his wrists and held them tight with her thin fingers. Her knees dug into his sides, her kneecaps wedged sharply into his rib cage. His first thought was, Boy she's skinny. She's a stick girl.

"You're going to stay here a while," she said. "Until I deal with you."

Where else would I go? Randall almost said. But instead he thought of work, of the shipyard at dusk, of moving in rhythm to the day's rising heat, building his muscles and raising his arms high in answer to the questions asked of him by the unfurling rope. Moving and working until dead bone tired, then returning nights to Delores, to be Dealt With.

"Yes," he said.

"Everything bad he done to me, I'll do the same to you."

Hal had been gone close to a month, and this was the first time she'd mentioned him by name, yet everything she said—pass the salt, close that window, will you—seemed to carry some trace of her desire for him.

"Why?"

"You come along and ruined it. You're the one who drove him away from me."

"He's no good. He was supposed to send money back to us when my daddy was out of work and he never sent a red penny."

"I don't give a damn about any of that," she said. "I don't want to hear about it ever. I can't be worrying about what happened to people before I met 'em. The last bad thing I know about him now that I don't want to is you."

"He would of left anyway," said Randall. He thought this might infuriate her, but he was mad enough now to stick up for himself, for she was crazy, deluded. But she didn't seem to hear him.

"This is Norfolk. You don't just up and move in with somebody just because he's your brother."

"Fine," said Randall. "I was going to move all along. I'll leave tomorrow."

"You'll stay. Tomorrow you'll bring me money."

She got up then, opened the door and stood in front of the screen, looking out over the shipyards. It was almost sunup and folks were waking on the floors below, shuffling around at the sluggish pace of dawn. After a long silence she said to Randall—as if they had been talking all the while—"You'll stay. You'll bring me money."

For the rest of that summer and into fall, two or three nights a week, when Delores was working the dinner shift at the restaurant, Randall went home with Granger. They stopped at the market and bought fresh produce and sometimes a half-chicken or a cheap cut of beef. Granger had a sweet red-haired wife named Melissa and two buck-toothed sons. On Saturdays when the sun was out but not

too formidable, Randall picked up the boys for an outing, so that
Granger and Melissa could work on another baby. Randall knew
that Granger was too strapped to hire a babysitter and he enjoyed
the boys, who took to calling him Uncle Randall even after he asked
them not to. They took a bus out to Virginia Beach.

While it was still warm enough to swim, Randall took the boys
one at a time out into the ocean, lifting them squealing and kicking above the waves. He bought them hot dogs from the boardwalk and read to them from books he brought along from the
children's section of the Norfolk Public, for Granger had admitted one day at work that neither he nor Melissa could read. On the
long bus ride back to town, the boys, wasted from the sun and
swimming, fell asleep against him like bookends. Their skin
burned with heat from the sun's rays and they smelled of sea salt
and ketchup. Randall thought of how much he would like to have
children someday.

He could not get enough of the ocean. Sometimes when the boys
were unavailable he went alone for the day with his sheet and a
book. He swam away from the crowds and sometimes took his suit
off and tied it around his waist with the drawstring and swam naked.
One Saturday in September he asked Delores to go with him, and
was surprised when she accepted, for they had lived as strangers in
the weeks since Hal had gone. Randall paid the brunt of the rent,
which came due weekly and left him nothing to send home, only
pennies for himself. There had been no word from Hal in weeks
now. Randall assumed he was locked up somewhere; it had happened before, minor alcohol-related confinements in small-town
jails. Or maybe he really had left the area, which he had always
threatened to do. Randall never believed him—Hal was all talk, all
the wrong kind of talk—but perhaps he didn't really know his
brother at all, as Hal had claimed that night he disappeared. He was
nine years older, and was never around much when they lived in
Trent. Randall had always assumed he knew everything about his

siblings, and was a little pleased to find out that Hal was capable of mystery.

But he did not say as much to Delores, who would have taken no comfort in Randall's pleasure. They hardly spoke to each other at all, and after she agreed to join him at the beach, when they were seated next to each other on the bus, Randall staring at the passing neighborhoods, Delores paging through a movie magazine, Randall wondered why he'd even asked her along. Her presence unnerved him in a new and loathsome way. She seemed too much *there*; in this new and awkward silence she was impossible to ignore, and Randall was even more aware of his gestures, his breathing, the things that came or did not come out of his mouth.

At the beach she stretched out on a sheet she'd stuffed in a straw basket and sunned herself in the noon heat. Randall sat beside her in the sand, trying to read a novel he'd brought along, but he found it impossible to concentrate and soon gave up to watch the people parade by. She fell asleep. He could hear her breathing quicken, as if she were having a nightmare. He stared at her back, naked to the waist, as she had untied the straps of her suit to avoid lines. In sleep her shoulder blades raged, small and delicate wings. He thought of the story she'd told about her first days with Hal, of the weight she'd shed that Hal had claimed was only water. Randall understood: the expendable weight of infatuation, lost in the first flush of passion but sure to return as the heat cooled and routine set in. She could do so much better than Hal. She could find someone who would at least allow her to believe that the weight she'd shed was forever lost. Or maybe Hal was right to be truthful about such things. Maybe, thought Randall, it is wrong to pretend that things last, that the temporary is anything but.

A tide pool had appeared in front of them. Sunlight shimmered on its surface, and mothers led their toddlers down to splash safely in the shallow water. Randall went down to investigate. The pool was warmer than the ocean, warm as a freshly drawn bath. He lay down in it, only his face above water. The sun touched him, yet the water made it seem as if he was protected from its rays. He closed his eyes and sculled, floating in the knee-deep water, trapped until high tide.

He opened his eyes to splashing. A pair of legs appeared alongside.

"Feels good," said Delores.

"It's a bathtub," said Randall. "Lie down in it."

She gave him an incredulous look. He had to shield his eyes to see her face.

"I have my pride," she said.

She stood there for a while, then returned to her sheet. Randall walked into the sea. He swam parallel to shore, floated on his back, dove to the bottom to run his hands across the sand. When he was younger—ten or eleven—he'd thought often of the ocean. Only fifty miles from Trent, but he'd never seen it until he'd come to Norfolk. Reka had promised to take him in Edwin Keane's car—they had a driver to take them anywhere they wanted, though Edwin rarely went out of the house—but they never got the chance. He'd had a teacher who passed a conch shell around the room for those students who had never been to the ocean—well over half the class—to put to their ears. Randall was not impressed. He'd dreamed often of the sea, and in his dreams it sounded different, wilder. Beneath the hiss and slap of waves upon the sand were voices. Waterlogged words of those who'd lost their lives to storms or had been marooned by a sudden doldrum and had gone crazy and jumped overboard. Pirates and explorers. Convicts sent from England to populate the colonies. He heard the neigh of horses brought over from Spain, the cackling of drowned hens. Slaves from Africa moaning low spirituals. He used to think fish made noise. On the afternoons when business was slow at the drugstore, when there were no deliveries for him to make, he'd ride his bike down to the river and wade into the current and put his ear toward the muddy stream, craning to hear fishtalk.

Now here he was, faced with the truth, the ocean itself, and he could not convince himself that those voices he'd heard in his dreams were not real. He still believed that fish made noise. You must be accustomed to the water to hear it, to understand it. He practiced diving, held his breath as long as he could under water, listening, waiting.

He surfaced to see, a few feet out from the shore, Delores standing in the surf. He swam toward her.

"Come on out," he said.

"Nothing doing."

"It's not rough."

"I can't swim."

Without thinking he waded up behind her, circled her thin waist with his arms, lifted her out of the water as he had Granger's boys. She was almost as light.

"Watch it, mister." But she was smiling. He could not see her face but he could feel it in her rib cage, her sudden excitement, a childlike delight in the whimsical waves.

Later, on the bus ride home, he told her about Granger's boys, how much they loved the ocean.

"They're cute kids," he said when she didn't respond.

"Kids? Cute?"

"You don't like kids?"

Her face soured.

"You don't want any?"

"Not in this life."

She was the first woman he'd met who openly admitted to not wanting a family. It was shocking to him, like someone getting up in church and blaspheming the scriptures.

"Why don't you want any?"

"I have my pride," she said.

Randall couldn't tell if she was serious. He said, "Oh, you mean you don't want to go around all big and fat for nine months?"

She sneered at this. "I imagine I'd be excused for my fat belly if I had one in the oven. No, I can't do it. Not cut out for it. What would I teach a child? I know all the wrong things. And don't care to learn the right ones."

Randall wondered what things she was talking about, but he did not pursue it because something told him he would rather not know. They had talked more that day than in the previous weeks since Hal's departure. He had to take care not to interrogate her. She went sullen and quiet if asked too many questions.

A couple of weeks later, during a blast of heat at the end of September, a foreman pulled Randall and Granger out of the rope line, told them they were to weld. Two of his welders had quit on him. He explained the danger and the importance of the job, looking at Randall as he talked. Randall looked at his feet. He thought: He'll think I can't do it. Here I am looking away when it's dangerous blinding fire he wants me to wield.

"Ain't you his kid brother?" the man said suddenly. Randall raised his eyes to him to protest, but the thought that he might not get the job because of shiftless Hal angered him. Hal might claim that no one knew him, but Randall knew him well enough to know he wasn't like him. It was Reka he was like. He thought of what he'd write her about welding. He knew nothing at all about it, but like the ocean in his dreams before he ever laid eyes on it, he thought he knew how it would feel. The torch in his hands spewing flames. The muted rosy world through the safety shield.

"If you mean Hal Speight, yes, I'm his brother."

"Not like him, I hope."

Randall said nothing. He wanted to, but could not bring himself to spell out how he was different. Granger looked at him expectantly. Randall always knew what Granger was thinking. For a man of twenty-six he said very little, yet like a small child he transmitted a great deal. Randall knew that Granger wanted him to defend himself, to tell how different he was, but still he said nothing. He knew there was a difference, but suddenly he did not know exactly what the difference was.

"Well, you're here, and you look sober enough. That's two strikes for you right there."

To learn they stood on scaffolds high above the ground. The cluttered shipyards and all of Norfolk spread behind them. When Randall looked down, he could see the order of the town, unnoticeable from the ground: lining the blocks of buildings downtown, those neighborhoods bushy with ancient trees, the tall white widow-peaked houses crowding the wide view of the bay; closer to the yards the apartment houses settling for wisps of salty ocean air.

Looking toward his house, Randall thought of Delores sleeping tangled in the yellow sheets, her hair streaming across pillows as it had this morning when he'd peeked in at her. Now that Randall was welding, she would want more money. He would not tell her, even though he wanted to.

He put on the clunky visor, the big armored helmet that the sun beat iron-hot, and he pushed the sharp blue finger of flame across the steel as they'd shown him, watching the panels fester and bubble in the wake of the fire, fester and fit seamlessly with another piece of burnt-rimmed steel, thinking as he worked, I am a welder. This ship is mine.

Randall welded ships through that winter of 1959. He climbed the scaffold in the frigid air, shed his overcoat to sweat again under an April sun. One night in May he came home late after eating supper at Granger's. The only light came from the bedroom where Delores, flat-voweling his name in a Tidewater drawl he'd never heard from her before, called for him to come to her. The night was humid and loud. All the men seemed to have brought noise home from the shipyard. All through the neighborhood in the houses he passed on his way home Randall heard voices raised with whiskey. Jimmie

Rodgers on the radio. The sounds of payday. Knockings from one house, a bed frame beating against a wall, and outside on the porch a silhouetted audience drinking in the dark, laughing at the thumping, amused, maybe aroused by its rhythm.

He stepped into the shadowy kitchen and froze.

"I said come in here," she said.

He walked softly to the bedroom, as if he'd shed his workboots. In the harsh circle of lamplight she lay on her belly in bed, wearing one of Hal's long-sleeved shirts, which came to her knees. Nothing else below so far as he could see. Sweating and drinking something clear from a cup. On the floor a half-empty bottle of gin.

"Bring me some ice, will you?"

He went to the icebox and returned with the tray. The metal lever cracking the ice echoed in the room. He dropped ice in her cup and refilled it with gin. Her legs moved in a lazy swing from her knees, into the air then down again so that her feet hung limply from the edge of the bed.

"Come here," she said.

Randall stood still by the bed. Hal's shirt was unbuttoned, and a patch of coarse white bra soaked up sweat that streamed from her neck.

"I quit my job today," she said.

He said, swallowing, "Why?"

"Get in," she said. "Maybe you're bigger than your big brother."

Nervous, tight-limbed, he climbed in beside her on the bed, his dirt-caked boots hanging off the edge. He did not feel like he could touch her without his nervousness shooting right through her like a current, shaking her and the bed and the floor and the house, the neighborhood and all of Norfolk. A tidal wave in the Atlantic. Houses flooded, streets swamped.

She was so loose, so limp, such a part of the damp sheets. He held his breath and touched her back, but she did not seem to notice his fingertips feathering her shoulder blades.

"Once I had a man who thought so highly of me that he paid my rent throughout the entire winter."

"Where is he now?"

"Where is he now?" Her repetition unnerved him, as if he was chewing his words like Granger, though he felt he was speaking clearly enough.

"Long gone, like your brother, Mr. King of Can't Believe a Word He Says."

She reached for the bottle and dragged it across the floor in a slow sweep. She turned to him, glassy-eyed, and seemed about to cry. Suddenly she slammed the bottle against the floor and grabbed his wrist.

"Where is he?" she said. "You know, you're just not telling me. No reason to try and spare me any pain. I don't need your pity. Where? Gone back to that hick town of yours?"

"I can't imagine he'd ever go back there."

"You can't imagine? I didn't ask you to imagine. What good is your imagination to me?"

Randall stared at her helplessly. He had no answer to her question, though he felt he should be able to explain it, the good his imagination could do for the both of them.

"Never mind," she said, drawing him closer. She put her cup down and draped her arm around his neck, tightening slowly.

"Let's roll," she said.

Sharply the night noises of the neighborhood floated in through the half-open window on a breeze that kept the rust-smudged curtains rippling slowly an inch from the sill. Besides those noises—a car idling high on the street, men calling to each other, cross children raging against bedtime—there were noises from inside the building that Randall wanted to ignore but could not: another radio in a nearby apartment broadcasting a show filled with vibrant applause and a phony laugh track, an older woman moaning her way through a sweaty, fitful sleep, busy pipes, an infant screaming, more steady knockings against the pocked plaster walls. How was it possible he could hear so much? Like fish noise; like the sound of the sea he heard before he ever laid eyes on the sea. But what good did it do for him to have heard it before he really knew it? He thought she might be right: What good could his imagination do either of them?

The noises dimmed as they rolled. Rolled? He kissed her and she pushed him back until he was still and then brushed her face against his clumsily, her eyes closed, her lips finding his, grazing them. Randall's lips were cracked and dry at first until she painted lightly with her tongue the gin-sweet saliva that softened them. She slid her hands to rest below his ribs.

He thought he'd best not breathe. That his heavy breath would interrupt them. That, hearing him huff, she would know the truth about him, a truth he did not understand himself.

But Delores, breathing as loudly as a woman he'd once seen climb out of a wrecked car, peeled off her shirt and lay in her underwear while he struggled with her, holding on tightly. She smiled at his embrace and pulled his shirt out from his jeans, her hands working slightly without effort, with no noise now except the light rustle of clothes he'd heard coming from behind the closed door so many times before. She climbed atop him and moved slowly at first, and he stared at the dim light above them, its crooked bug-dusty globe dangling, rocking slowly as the bed bumped the wall and the wall shook the fixture, the trembling light shrinking and swelling the shadows of their bodies together as they rolled, another noise now in the Norfolk boarding house night.

Afterward they lay awake late in the night, into the morning, as Randall would later learn that lovers do. The hours seemed charged with wonder and meaning, though he could not remember what they talked about until, somehow, against his wishes, they got on the subject of Hal again.

"You're like me, you know. You're not like Hal at all."

"What do you mean?"

She put her chin on his chest and stroked his cheek. "Poor baby. You don't know, do you?"

"What are you talking about?"

"I'm talking about love. You ain't got it to give away. Can't dish it or take it, either one."

"And Hal can?"

"Oh yeah. He wouldn't care to admit it, he'd like to think he's above that kind of thing, but inside he's eaten up with it. There's a difference between him and you. You act right almost all the time, but if it was to come to it, you'd do anything. And it wouldn't bother you in the least."

"I don't know what you're talking about."

"I know, baby. That's why I like you. That's how come you're lying where your big brother ought to be."

"Did Hal talk about me before I came up here?"

"He told me about you, yeah. You and that sister of yours. The murderer."

Randall held his tongue. He hated to hear her called that, but he wanted to know what Hal had told her, and didn't want to say anything that might cut her off.

"She's his sister, too."

"See, he doesn't really think she is. He said to me once, I've got five sisters and no brothers. Reka and Randall, they never did seem like they were kin to me. They're different from the rest of us."

"Different how?"

"He didn't say. But now I know."

"Know what?"

"I told you. Y'all'll do anything. You don't care about other people so much as you care about yourselves. I take it back, I'm not like you. I want to be sometimes, I've wanted to be since Hal left, but now that I think about it, I'm just like him."

Randall didn't argue with her. He wasn't interested in what she was like, or what she thought she was like.

"What makes you think I don't care about other people?"

She swept her hand across his hairless chest, rippled her fingers up to his throat, chin, stopped when her palm was flat against his lips.

"Sssh," she said. "Listen. You hear anything?"

He heard only the usual din of the boarding house, the music of weary people trying, mostly failing, to find some late-night peace.

"No."

"I do. I hear things you don't, I see things you don't. I been some places, see. Whole hell of a lot more places than Hal has. I don't give a damn where he's off to, he could be in goddamn England now and I would still win the been-all-over award. And I haven't even left the state of Virginia."

"What are you talking about?"

"Sssh," she said, palming his mouth again. "Shut up and listen. I'm talking about the things I see that most people don't. I'm talking about people, baby, men mostly. Hell, men only. I don't care too much for women. But men I know, and I can tell things about them just from watching. I can see right through the things they want everybody to believe about them."

Randall reached up to pull her hand away. "And what is it I want everybody to believe about me?"

Delores laughed. "You got me, baby. I can't figure you the way I can figure most of them, the way I got your brother figured. Beats the hell out of me what you go around thinking, much less what you want somebody to think about you. Only thing I know is this: You don't have it in you to love anybody but yourself. You might get with a woman, might even stay with her for a while, but she won't ever have you, not the part of you that counts."

She moved her long-nailed hand to his chest and scratched.

"That part."

Randall did not consider her charge so much as subsume it. Perhaps it was the shock of being told he was incapable of something so obligatory and necessary that made him trust her. Whatever the reason, it did not occur to him at that moment that she might be wrong.

He got up and pulled on his clothes.

"Where you going? It's not time for you to go to work yet."

He sat on the edge of the bed and double-knotted his boots for the journey.

"No use taking it out on me. I'm not telling you anything you don't already know. You might not want to say it about yourself, but you'll find out soon enough how right I am."

On the stairs he heard her call out to him a final time, but he could not hear what she said, only the desperation beneath her words, the mood that would fill the hot boxy apartment. She would bake in it, broil slowly in her own misery.

First light found him on the Suffolk highway, thumb in the moist morning air. A black man hauling pulpwood took him all the way down to 158, which ran between Virginia and North Carolina for miles, a border visualized so men could feel themselves passing physically into some other territory. Outside of Roanoke Rapids he got stuck. Car after car, but no ride. He stood by a cabbage field, which smelled to high hell as the sun rose and noon approached. Finally an older couple on their way to Duke Hospital stopped for him. They took turns detailing their various and debilitating ailments. Randall felt fortunate to have snagged a ride with them, as he did not feel like talking and they did not expect him to talk.

He arrived in Trent at a little past five. A muggy morning in mid-May. Walking the streets, he felt like a stranger. As he passed the drugstore, Ruby McClaurin waved to him from her perch in the show window, but Randall pretended not to see her.

Reka was not home. Her apartment was unlocked, which wasn't unusual—no one locked their doors in Trent, unlike in Norfolk, where thieves were known to scoop shoes off the floor of a closet, steal butter out of the icebox. There were dishes in the sink, crusted with food, as if they'd been there for a while. The two small rooms were lousy with flies. Randall found a screenless window wide open in the bathroom. He stared through it to the overgrown back yard, aware that something was wrong.

At the laundry where Reka worked, he found Mrs. Ilgenfritz working alone behind the counter.

"Where is your sister?" she asked before he was even across the threshold.

"What do you mean, where is she?"

"Where is she gone is what I mean. Disappeared. No word, no note, nothing. Vanished. I call up your other sisters who say they know nothing, either."

"How long?"

Mrs. Ilgenfritz lifted her heavy round shoulders. She let them sag. "A week now? Long enough for me to get behind on everything."

Randall thanked her and left. He was halfway out on the River Road before he let himself wonder why she'd left him again. It happened before once, when he was eleven. She'd gone to Kentucky in the middle of the night, had stayed away for a month almost. No word then, either. He made her promise she'd always let him know where she was. She'd asked for the same from him. He thought they'd understood each other, thought that this was the one absolute in his life, the one thing he could count on always knowing.

As he passed out of town and into the country he wondered what, exactly, he wanted to tell her. That he was incapable of love according to a woman he'd slept with? Reka would probably laugh; she would probably explain to him Delores's motivation, make it sound petty but excusable, nothing to take seriously. Yet because she was not there, because she had fled without telling him, Randall was even more convinced Delores was right. It wasn't because of what had happened between them. True, he did not feel bad for sleeping with his brother's girlfriend, as his brother had left her, and even when he was around he took her for granted, treated her so poorly that he had no right to expect fidelity from her. Even if Hal found out—which he never would, she would never tell him, she would be too scared he'd leave again—Randall would not feel bad at all.

Speight was sitting on the porch when Randall came down the road. He was fiddling with some ancient piece of machinery, oiling its rust-choked innards. He did not notice Randall's presence for so long that Randall thought he might have gone deaf. It had only been a few months since he'd last seen his father, but his aging seemed accelerated by Randall's absence.

"You come home for good?" he said when Randall took a chair beside him. Randall did not take offense, as he knew Speight was not doubting his independence. He expected such a greeting, as his father was incapable of a simple hello, good to see you, anything that might show emotion. There was emotion to spare in his question if you knew him well enough.

"I came to see Reka."

"What for?"

"I need to talk to her."

Speight looked across the field to the line of pines. "Ain't it a Wednesday?"

"Yep. I took the day off, though."

Speight grunted. He said, "I never did get to take off a day in the middle of the week. Well, when I was working steady anyway."

Randall knew he did not count the days he could not remember. He had a strict system of accounting that excused binges the way an asthmatic might not count those work days missed when the wind was thick with pollen. His drunks hit him like the flu, took him down for a week sometimes, then lifted, leaving him weary and depressed and sheepish. He used to spend money on his children when he was recuperating from a drunk, but never during the drunks themselves or his periodic, short-lived stabs at sobriety.

"I got promoted. I'm welding now."

"A welder? That's a good trade, son. You can carry that with you anywhere. You could get on out at McCullen's Ironworks. I hear he's always looking a welder."

Randall would not tell him what he already knew: that he had no intention of spending his life joining pieces of metal and iron together. That it was only temporary. Hal might be able to admit as much, but for Hal, welding was as good a skill as any. Randall wanted to learn other elements besides fire. He wanted to travel, to live somewhere besides the flat and sun-baked Tidewater.

"Pay's good up there. They got the union coming in."

"I were you I'd stay clear of a union. You end up paying them dues every month just so some fatass can ride around in a Buick giving speeches about what he's going to do for you directly. Only from what I've heard there ain't no directly."

"You seen Reka, Pa?" Randall hated to change the subject, as his father seemed more talkative than he had in months. He seemed lonely—Randall knew he often went a week without seeing anyone but whoever he ran into down at Speed's store—but Randall did not have time for a properly indulgent visit.

"No. I ain't seen her."

"In how long?"

Speight thought about it awhile. He had the slip of paper she'd given him, the one with the man's name and number on it, stuck up under the cutlery in the silverware drawer where he kept all his paperwork. But he had already decided not to pass it along. It would kill Reka—she had made him promise—but it was for her own good. Randall's, too. They'd always been too close, and now that they were grown, it didn't seem healthy. Especially considering what had happened with Reka and Edwin Keane. He'd never let himself forget the role he played in that sorry affair, but it was Randall and Eureka's love for each other, their clingy devotion, the way they acted like they were more kin than the others—and Speight's special love for the both of them, together—that was partly to blame for the trouble. He would not let it happen again. He would rather Reka hate him forever than give away her where-abouts to Randall. The boy had a good job, making good money, a future ahead of him, even if he did get mixed up with a damn union.

"Long time. Maybe a month. Why?"

"She's gone. More than a week, according to Mrs. Ilgenfritz."

"Maybe she finally got tired of that German woman's mess. She might of took Reka back after she got out, but to hear Reka tell it, she treated her like she owed her something. Worked her to death, didn't pay her hardly nothing. Reka was scared to leave, told me she couldn't find no other job around here. I told her time and again she didn't know 'til she tried."

"She left all her things in that apartment. Looks like she went out for a walk. I couldn't find a thing missing."

Speight feigned a look of concern. "That right?"

"Neighbors haven't seen her in seven or eight days."

"You go see Martha and them?"

"You think she'd tell them her business?"

"No," he said. "Come to think of it, she wouldn't tell nobody her business. Not even me. If she didn't tell you where she was going, she didn't tell nobody."

Randall got up and paced the short saggy porch. "What are we going to do?"

"Ain't nothing we can do. She'll get in touch when she's ready."

"You're saying just wait around for her to write us a letter?"

"I don't know what else to do. You know she'd never go too long without getting in touch. She loves you, Randall. Maybe you're the reason she come back here. I know it won't me."

"You don't know that. You keep on blaming yourself for what

happened, you're going to worry yourself into the grave. I hope you don't still take responsibility for everything."

Speight took a pouch of tobacco out of his overalls, rolled a thin cigarette. "What was it you wanted to talk to her about?"

"Nothing," said Randall, staring at his feet.

"Got to be something for you to lose a day's wages. Something important."

"I guess it will wait."

"I guess it will have to."

They fell silent. There seemed nothing more to say; both were resigned to her disappearance, though Speight of course was faking it. Watching his woebegone son pace back and forth in front of him, he began to wonder if he was doing the right thing, lying to the boy. Clearly something was bothering Randall. He thought of offering to listen, but it had been years since he'd talked seriously with the boy—eight or nine at least—and it wasn't like he could just up and start in on something like that after all this time.

"I guess I better get," Randall said, standing up. "Now that I'm welding I'll be able to send some more money. I'll send you something soon."

"You needn't worry about me," said Speight. "I'm getting along all right out here. Not much I need I can't go without if it comes to that."

"You'll let me know if that changes?"

"Ain't nothing gone change," said Speight.

Randall reached over to clasp his father's bony, raw-skinned grip.

"Watch the oil," Speight said, and he laughed as Randall pulled his hand away to find it blackened and greasy.

Randall stared at his stained hand and said nothing. It was an accident, an innocent mistake on his father's part, but Randall could not hide his annoyance. He felt tainted, marked. As soon as he passed out of sight he stopped to wipe his hand on his jeans.

* * *

Back at the shipyards the next day, Randall found that Granger had covered for him. He caught obligatory hell from his supervisor for not calling in, but they put him right back on the job. He climbed the scaffolding, busied himself with fire. Granger left him alone all day, aware that he did not want to talk. Randall took his lunch break on the scaffolding. He stood to better see the world stretching away from him. The sea was white-capped, wind-whipped. She could be out there somewhere, on a boat, her stomach churning to the chop of the waves. Or she could be smack below him in the swamp of boarding houses, sucked like half of the able-bodied Tidewater up to Norfolk to make money from some looming war. She could be around the corner, across the river in Hampton Roads. He turned to the west. Saw the highway snaking away from downtown, toward Richmond. Heat blurred the horizon; squinting, Randall transformed wavy clouds into mountains. The worn and ancient Blue Ridge, rain- and wind-softened to a gentle, dignified hump. Eureka in some cool mountain hollow, a deep and shadowy valley that saw no sun before ten in the morning. He looked farther west toward the white-tipped Rockies, jagged and angry in comparison to the sleepy Appalachians. He'd heard it was hard to breathe there. Imagined Reka in Denver, learning to breathe all over again, the altitude making her act half drunk.

She could be anywhere. All afternoon he worked alone and silently, the flame moving on its own, his hands someplace else, searching for his sister. Thumb in the air, begging a ride. He would not rest until he found her. Now Norfolk was all the more temporary.

Granger seemed to know already that he needed a place to stay. On the way home he and Randall stopped by a junk shop and bought a pee-stained mattress. They lugged it down the sidewalk, displacing kids on bikes, sending drunks out into the street. The boys were thrilled to find Uncle Randall stretched out in the corner of the parlor where they slept when they woke in the middle of the night. He took them to the bathroom, soothed their fear after nightmares and the rude noises of the neighborhood. On Saturdays he took them for the entire day, part of his payment to Granger and Melissa for putting him up. They would accept only a nominal dollar or two for rent. It was worth it to be able to spend time with his sweetheart, Granger said.

Randall went to work and came home and read to the boys. After Melissa put them to bed the three of them sat out in the yard watching the sun fall behind the shabby houses across the street. Granger and Melissa were respectful of Randall's worry. They never asked; he never volunteered. He was grateful to them, so grateful that sometimes he wanted to be them, either of them, both of them. He wished to be the entire family, the four of them, poor and destined for years of poverty but happy in their meager lives. In their house there was more love than Randall thought capable in such scant square footage. At night when the boys were sleeping he whispered things to them from across the room: You boys are lucky. You boys are blessed.

There was no sign of Hal, no word from the men around the yard who knew him well, but his brother's disappearance was rarely on Randall's mind. He would come back soon enough. Bruised and sullen, wanting his job back. When he found out that he had been replaced by his own brother, he would be furious.

One night in July, a month or so after he returned from Trent, Randall was walking home from work with Granger. A Friday evening; they had worked a full ten hours that day. Empty bottles clattered in the gutters. Everywhere along the avenues people laughing, eating hot dogs and bags of boiled peanuts. Leaning against parked cars, smoking, showing teeth.

They passed a bar. The plate-glass windows were painted a streaky purple. Tinny music drifted out past a man smiling drunkenly into the street, a run of tobacco juice staining his chin.

"Let's have us a short one," said Granger.

He went in and Randall followed, peeking over the partition

blocking passersby from seeing inside. He saw rising smoke and the hats of men who sat at the bar, their moony smiles reflected in a grease-stained mirror. A radio played on a shelf behind the bar. They elbowed their way through the three-deep crowd, which was moving off somewhere, it seemed to Randall. The feel of the room was of a slap-happy effortless indulgence, the first of the weekend. Unshaven men, smelling of sweat and machinery. A peaceful lull before the sun set and the drinks spilled, words slurred, someone in the crowd got sucker-punched or stabbed.

Turning sideways in the line of men clogging the bar, Randall spotted Delores. He saw first her red-filtered cigarette, high in the air above a table in the back of the room. She was sitting with a woman whose laugh rose high and flirtatious as birdsong above the crowd. Men hovered around the table. Delores watched him for a moment through the smoke, peering around her audience before pretending to laugh at something her friend said.

Randall pushed his way back to her. A ceiling fan chopped overhead, making a slow, bothersome sucking noise. A man only inches away from his face told Randall to get lost, they won't giving out numbers. Randall ignored him and made his way to the table. Granger had followed him from the bar, and grasped him lightly by the elbow, as you might a child standing at a crosswalk.

From across the table, Delores dipped her cigarette toward Granger and said: "Is he your Cheap Blade?"

Granger introduced himself. He said his full name—Lawrence Granger—which Randall had never heard before.

"This ain't church, Lawrence," Delores said. The men crowded around the table laughed. Someone elbowed Randall in the ribs.

"He's back?" Randall said to her.

"He's coming," she said. "I heard from him. He was delayed in Richmond, Virginia. Took a trip to Washington, D.C. I suppose he found work up there."

"Vice president, no doubt," said Randall.

Delores's female friend laughed shrilly. She was very drunk, but did not seem to realize it. Delores, on the other hand, seemed stone sober.

"He's coming back."

"I don't care," Randall said to her.

"I know you don't. I told you already: You don't care about anybody but yourself. And maybe that slut sister of yours."

Randall put his beer down on the table. He felt Granger's fingers tightening around his elbow, heard Granger's gentle urging. Let's go now. Just forget about it. Let's go home.

"What drove you away is the same thing that will bring you back. I told the truth, only you were too scared to hear it. But you know I'm right about you, and that's why you'll come crawling back. Only you needn't. I'll be occupied. You know who with, too."

"Can't you two take this outside or something?" said the drunk woman. "Y'all working my nerves, talking so serious. It's Friday night, dammit."

"He's coming back," said Delores. "And you better care."

Out on the street Granger said, "I ain't going to pry."

"My brother's girlfriend."

"She smelled like trouble to me."

"Oh, she's harmless," said Randall. "She's in love with a sorryass is all. It's not easy for her."

"Y'all act like y'all pretty tight."

Randall said, "I thought you weren't going to pry."

A few weeks later, in the highest heat of August, Randall was at work on the side of a ship, his torch spitting flames in the mid-morning breeze, when an office boy appeared atop the scaffolding to tell him he had a visitor.

"Who?" he said.

"Some old fucker," said the boy, nodding toward the ground.

Randall flipped his visor up and peered down. His father stood with his eyes shielded from the sun, staring up at the men teeming on the sides of the ship.

"That's my father," he said to the boy, who put his hand over his mouth and disappeared down the scaffold, grinning stupidly.

Randall tried never to look down when he was on the scaffolding. He loved the view of the warehouses and drydocks of the shipyard, the shiny bay beyond, Virginia Beach stretching out to the flat Atlantic. Often he volunteered for the highest jobs, the ones most of his co-workers were wary of. Looking down did not make him dizzy or scared, only uninterested in returning to earth, where things seemed so much messier. The sight of his father in his standard uniform of overalls, tractor cap, and long-sleeved work shirt even in the heat of summer made him all the more reluctant to leave his perch.

But something was wrong for his father to have traveled this far. So far as Randall knew, this was the farthest he'd ever been from home. Something must have happened to Reka, or maybe he had word of her, and had come to pass along her whereabouts.

Randall crossed the yard to where his father stood.

"I come up here to see how you were getting on," said Speight by way of a greeting. He was sweat-drenched, his face blanched. He wheezed when he spoke and breathed big afterward, and Randall suddenly felt guilty for thinking he'd brought news of Reka when it was himself, obviously, who needed help.

"Is anything wrong? You don't look too good."

"Left out of the house before sunup. Longest I ever traveled in my life. It'll take it out of you, even if all you're doing is riding in a car."

"You're not sick?"

"Tired's what I am."

"I'm gonna tell my bossman you're sick. You look sick."

"Don't go lying if it's going to get you in trouble. Wouldn't want you to lose your job."

"I'll take you back to my room. It's only a mattress on a floor. I stay with a family, guy I work with. But you can rest there."

"I'm wanting to see the ocean."

"Do what?"

"I said I want to see the goddamn ocean. I come up here to see it. I never seen it and I want you to take me over there."

"Now?"

"I waited sixty-two years already."

Randall was both surprised and puzzled by the request. He'd rather take his father to the ocean than haul him off to some doctor's, spend the day in a waiting room reading old magazines and listening to people describe their illnesses to each other. But his father was not one for fun, and he could not imagine him waking up one day and deciding to indulge himself in things he'd never found time for. Maybe he was sick in the head. He didn't smell like he was on a drunk, but he could have just come off one, a bad one.

Randall went off to square things with his bossman, who seemed suspicious of his excuse—after all, he was Hal's little brother—until Randall led him across the yard to get a look at his father, whose soaked shirt and sagging posture made good his lie.

"He don't look too spry, I'll grant you that, Speight. You best take care of your business, but I want you back here in the morning."

"I thought you were staying with Hal," Speight said as they sat on a bench waiting for a bus. He seemed to be having a harder time trying to catch his breath, and he was obviously trying to hide his wheezing and gasping. He smelled worse than Randall remembered. Randall was well aware of his own stink, but his father's odor was outrageous. A sickly sour smell from his overalls and workshirt or from his hair, wet and hanging in matted gray strings beneath the brim of his hat.

"I was staying with Hal," said Randall. "But Hal had a girlfriend."

"Living in the same place with him?"

"For a while. Then he left. I didn't feel right living there with Hal's old girlfriend."

"I imagine not. I imagine you got better sense than to live with some woman you ain't married to."

Would that I cared about such a thing, thought Randall. But he thought this only for the benefit of his father, to whom he felt suddenly close enough to pretend to have scruples. His father seemed so frail and winded, and he saw no reason why he should burden him with the story of what had happened with Hal.

"I reckon I ought to try and see him while I'm up here."

"Let's go to the beach while there's sun still. You can worry about Hal tomorrow."

"I ain't been swiming since I was a boy," said Speight on the bus. All of a sudden his spirits lightened, and he found enough oxygen to support a tepid laugh.

"What?" said Randall.

"I was thinking about something I did when I was a boy. Me and Dexter Howell stole us a little skiff, took off with some blankets and a bag of apples down the Tar. We were going to follow it to the sea."

Randall laughed. "Get very far?"

"Lost is all we got. My daddy beat the stuffing out of me."

"What was your daddy like?" asked Randall. He could not remember ever hearing about his grandfather, who was long dead before Randall was born. Speight wasn't much on talking out his past. Randall knew only that he'd been born in the country, that he'd gone to school through seventh grade, that he had some sisters and one older brother who stole a train in east Tennessee and drove it to Texas before he was caught. The uncle-stole-a-train tale was the only family lore from his father's side. Though Randall could barely remember his mother, he knew more about her relatives.

Speight told his son a little about his own father: how he got work logging cypress and juniper in the Great Dismal; how he befriended the band of hermits who lived in the swamp around Lake

Drummond, and when the logging was done he stayed on with them, fishing and trapping and hiding out from the world in the miles and miles of government-forsaken tangle. He told Randall that his mother was the daughter of one of those men his father met in the swamp; he claimed she had Indian blood in her, or Melungeon, which seemed to have passed on to Reka and Randall but not the others, who favored their mother's side, straw-haired and pink-skinned Taylors with finicky stomachs and swollen lazy bones.

He talked until they reached the boardwalk stop at 24th Street in Virginia Beach. Randall had to lean in close to hear him over the noise of the bus—his father's voice was a near whisper, and grew fainter as he spoke, as if he was losing his voice along with his breath. Sweat poured from his forehead, and his face had turned a veiny red, then a splotchy white, but Randall thought it was only the exertion of a day's travel, which his father was not used to. He'd hardly been out of Simpson County. Sixty-two years in the same place. Randall was thrilled to show him the sea, and he even made him close his eyes as they crossed the street and the boardwalk to the sandy strand.

"Take off your shoes, Pa," said Randall. But his father did not seem to hear him. He was staring out to sea, a look of confusion on his face, as if it wasn't what he expected. Or perhaps he was figuring it like he often did things, trying to make some sense of it, put it into some box in his mind. Randall knew this look from helping his father fix things. He was a studier, and yet the bewildered scowl did not leave his face, as he could find no point of reference for this melding of water and sky.

"Let's sit," said Randall. "I swear, you don't look like you're feeling good."

"I feel fine, goddammit, Randall," said Speight. "I told you I'm just tired. How do you go about getting in there?"

"What?"

"Who do you pay and all?"

"It's free, Pa. They can't charge you. They got people coming all the way from Ohio and Missouri to swim. It wouldn't be right to charge money for something that belongs to everybody in the country."

"What about them houses?" said Speight, nodding toward the line of cottages that began where the boardwalk ended.

"Yeah, that doesn't seem fair to me, either. You ought not to be able to buy a piece of the beach. Or else they ought to divide up the whole coast so that every citizen's got a foot or two to call their own."

"Sounds like something you heard in that union of yours. That's the swimming area right there?" he said, pointing to a group of teenagers playing in the surf.

"You can swim anywhere," said Randall. "But you need a suit."

"A suit?"

"Bathing trunks."

"I never owned a pair."

"I never seen you go swimming."

"That don't mean I can't swim. I lived for a long time on this earth before you showed up. And I didn't need no bathing suit, either. Still don't."

"You can't swim in those overalls."

"Either that or my shorts. 'Course I never was one to wear any clothes at all."

"They'll arrest you if you go in there buck naked."

"Who will?"

"The police will."

"What do the police care?"

"It's called indecent exposure. You can't go flashing your private parts at innocent women and children."

"Innocent women," Speight repeated. "What woman over the age of fifteen ain't seen a naked man before?"

His father's immodesty amused Randall. He had always been this way about these matters, except where Reka was concerned. Once, making a routine delivery for the drugstore, his father had walked in on Reka and Edwin, and because Randall had introduced his sister to Edwin, Speight took Randall down in the basement and broke his cheekbone with a belt buckle. He beat him until he could not cry and left him there in the dirt-floored basement with the shards of canning jars from previous tenants and the rustling of cave crickets.

They walked down the beach, away from the crowds to a point where the cottages stopped and dunes sprinkled with sea oats took over.

"This is good," said Randall. He shed all but his shorts, waited for his father to extricate himself from his overall straps and double-tied brogans. Speight's boxers were worn to a threadbare transparence; Randall was glad there was no one around to witness the sorry state of his father's shorts, but his shame disappeared as he watched his father's face when his toes touched the water. They waded out knee-deep, Speight stepping gingerly as if he feared what lurked on the bottom of the ocean. He hesitated with each new wave, and Randall thought at first he might turn back and run from the surf, as Granger's boys loved to do.

"It's thick-feeling," said Speight. A skeptical frown on his face.

"That's the salt."

"Don't feel like any river."

"Let's go farther out."

"I ain't lost nothing in China," said Speight.

Speight's chest—sunken beneath a patch of white hair—disappeared under water. When the sea rose to his shoulders he relaxed a bit, let the current carry his legs out in front of him. He floated on his back, and once again it seemed to Randall that his weariness, his struggle to breathe, lessened. Randall thought he should have asked him to come up here before now. It never had occurred to him to ask his father to do anything outside his normal and unvary-

ing routine. He knew a few things well, had repeated them endlessly. Mostly work. The countryside where he was raised and
would die. Farming, though he never made a decent wage from it.
Whiskey, which he'd treated as just reward for hard work and a wid-
ower's loneliness.

Randall knew from Reka that when he was an infant, his father
had barely been able to bring himself to touch him. Because he was
the youngest and had been showered with the brunt of his mother's
emotions in the last weeks of her life, his father had, according to
Reka, ignored him for the first few months of his life. He'd wanted
to hold his wife Rosa, to curl alongside her and whisper things to
her, but she was holding Randall, there was already a body con-
forming to the curve of hers. Maybe in his father's eyes, Randall
wasn't even a child then, wasn't even human: he was a threat, a
grudge, an excuse.

His father had turned his raising over to Reka. Reka and her sisters, though Reka had insisted on most of the work, the diaper
changing and the lugging around, the feeding and the singing to
sleep. Only when he was drinking did his father call for Reka, ask to
hold his son. Of course Randall could not remember this, but he
often imagined it: his father out on the porch nights with his bottle
nearby, rocking his youngest with a rhythm new to him, foreign,
like jungle drums disrupting a marching band cadence.

Only when Randall began to talk did his father come to see him
as something other than a rival for affection that finally had nothing to do with him. Randall wondered if his father had ever really
understood his error, confusing a mother's love for her child with
what she withheld from her husband during those last days when
her body was all ache and shiver. His father had made the mistake
of thinking of love as gasoline, cordwood, money—an allotment to
dole out, spread thin.

Out in the water, Randall taught his father to duck when the
waves came. Speight waited until the wall of water was almost upon

him, then put his head beneath it and held his breath. When the water once again grew shallow and he could stand, he searched the horizon as if anxious for the next wave to lift him from earth, above the troubles that come when your feet touch ground.

"So what do you think?" Randall asked him.

"What do I think about what?"

"The ocean," said Randall.

Speight smiled despite his irritation. Randall knew how much his father despised questions like these, but he could not refrain from asking them. He always wanted to know what his father was thinking, how he felt about things.

"I wouldn't mind one of these in my back yard. If I had it to bathe in every day, I believe I'd be young as you."

"I'd like to see that," said Randall.

"It makes you want to chase women, don't it?"

Randall said, "It makes me hungry for peanuts. But yeah, it does something to you down there." He thought of holding Delores above the waves, his hands around her tiny waist, lifting her and pulling her close so that their bodies touched. Her skin felt different, softer and alive in the salt water. He desired her suddenly, furiously. You'll come crawling back, she'd told him, but I'll be occupied.

"It makes me think, too," said Randall.

"Everything makes you think," said Speight.

Randall was surprised at his father's response. He'd never thought his father took note of such things. Where do you think we come from, Reka once asked Randall on one of their walks, and when he said he didn't understand the question she told him she used to think that she and Randall were not really Speights, that they were someone else's children, misdelivered by the stork. But I don't think that anymore, she'd said; now I think that whatever makes us different from the others comes from Pa. There's so much you can't know about him, so many secrets. We're like a part of him he never got to use. That's why he lets us get away with murder sometimes: because it ain't us, it's him.

"I mean it makes me think about different things than usual."

"Yes," said Speight, and it seemed he understood this, that he too was thinking different things.

"I lied to you," he said. Randall watched him, waiting for the rest of it, but Speight fell silent, studying a ship on the muggy horizon.

"I lied to both of you. Reka and you. She come by before she left town. I was drunk, and it took me a few days to even remember she was by there. But when I sobered up I remembered she give me a piece of paper with some man's name on it. He's supposed to know where she's at always. She asked me to give it to you. Hell, she made me promise."

As anxious as he had been for news of Reka, Randall found himself a little disappointed that his father had not come all this way to see the ocean. It meant Randall had to go back to thinking of him the way he always had, that his father could not just up and surprise him one day, appear on the ground below him desiring something unpredictable that only Randall could show him.

"Why didn't you tell me when I came down there, Pa?"

"I thought it best for you two to go your own separate ways. I thought if I give you that paper, it might lead to more trouble. You're both grown now, and it seemed like to me you were better off apart from each other. Needing to settle down and all, which it felt like y'all weren't capable of that as long as you had each other."

"I'm glad you changed your mind," he said.

"It's not for me to fix up your future," said Speight. "Whatever happens to y'all is going to happen. It's none of mine, finally."

"Well," said Randall. "I guess I can kind of see where you would think it better for us to not be together."

"I'm glad you understand it," said Speight. He took his eyes from the ship, turned to his son. He seemed calmer, almost content. Randall imagined him rising in the middle of the night in need of air.

He pictured the shack—the windows propped open with lengths of two-by-four, the low-ceilinged room where his father ate and slept and cooked unbearably still and warm. He saw his father pull himself up off the mattress and sit for a long time on the edge of the cot, his head between his knees, fighting dizziness and nausea. Shaky and uncertain, the slightest movement bringing back every drink he'd had in his life. The shack seemed unfamiliar to him, as if he'd gone to sleep elsewhere and been lugged home by a ghostly samaritan.

Randall watched his father make his way out on the porch. Roll a smoke out of habit, though it was the last thing he needed this morning. Even outside there seemed no air available to him. If I can't breathe in the country, he imagined his father thinking, well then hell, I just can't breathe. He wondered what his father thought about when he thought of death, if he would be happy to die out in his shack, the place he'd fled to after all that had happened in town. He knew his father regretted ever moving to Trent in the first place, that he blamed everything that happened with Edwin and Reka on this move. Randall had heard him say many times that what he should have done was stick it out. The country always comes around, his father was fond of saying. There comes a drought, the corn burns up in the field; locusts descend from black clouds and devour everything in sight. Blight and boll weevil'll rob every penny of profit, and then the next year the sky up and treats you right, sending sun when you need it, enough rain to get by.

Randall knew what his father thought about town. In town, he'd once said, you could wait three lifetimes waiting on things to turn. Some might have a run of luck, but most get further and further behind, end up owing and broke, buried in a muddy cemetery, red clay holes in the earth as black-bloody as open wounds. Once Randall and his father had cut through the graveyard on their way to the drugstore and his father had pointed out how the rich people get all the shade, choice spots on the only hill for miles. What good's a view to a dead man, his father had asked.

"You call that man, he'll tell you where she's at," his father said suddenly. "She's out west somewhere. She got on with a company sells books. She's wanting the money to go to college."

Selling books out west: Randall found it hard to believe. He was happy for her—it seemed like a dream job—but furious at the same time for not telling him everything.

"Where's the note?"

"Top pocket of my overalls. Go read it, tell me what it says."

"What are you going to do?"

"Float," said Speight. "I told you I been waiting sixty-two years for this. I ain't ready to get out just yet."

Randall nodded and waded ashore. He retrieved the note and flopped down in the sand beside his clothes. Held it in his hands for a minute, watching his father's head bob between waves. It had taken a lot for him to admit his lie. Maybe his lie was what had robbed him of breath this morning, forced him out of the shack and into the yard and onto the highway where he caught a ride with a bread man for the longest trip in his life. Maybe his chest tightened with the intolerable weight of his lie, and maybe it would have killed him dead, this lie, felled him like a windblown branch out in the yard one morning had he allowed things to stay put, kept to himself the letter Randall held in his hand. Maybe he realized that his children's destinies were beyond him, and that even if he kept this note to himself, took it with him to that muddy hole in the ground where he'd one day end up, they would find each other anyway. Maybe he'd learned something after all from trying to keep Reka away from Edwin Keane, drafting Randall to deliver the drugs Edwin would use to kill himself. Last time he'd tried to stop fated things, his favorite daughter had been put in prison for it.

Dear Randall. Randall read the note once and then again, and already his mind was long gone from Norfolk, hitching a ride on old 64 toward Kentucky, riding a train toward whatever western hamlet she'd landed in. It did not say here—she'd only given him the name of a man to call to find out where she was—but she'd made it clear that she wanted him to join her when he could. And he could now, for his father had finally made things right for all of them.

He was reading the note for the third time when he heard the shouts. At first he did not even realize who the people gathering at the water's edge were pointing to, did not recognize whose body the two sailors were tugging swiftly ashore. He was too caught up in Reka's letter to do much but stare until he recognized his father's wilting gray hair, his head cut off from his shoulders by some stranger's elbowed clutch. When he reached him, Randall pushed away one of the sailors and cradled his father's heavy dripping head in his hands and spoke to him like always, as if his words were the only thing that could wake him. And then he put his lips to his father's mouth and blew in air stolen from him by the lie he'd made right, until someone in the crowd took him by the shoulders and pulled him gently away and told him it was too late for that.

Randall let the arms that held him lower him to the sand. He stared out over the ocean and tried to see and feel what his father had experienced in his last minute. He closed his eyes to the glare of sun on water. Let the waves take the rigid pain from his limbs. So long as he could float, he would feel alive; the moment his feet searched for the sandy bottom he felt a crushing pressure in his chest. Better to close his eyes and drift. Better to allow himself this final pleasure, for he was certain now that he'd done what he could do. If he did not tell the truth always, well, so damn what. The simple deed he'd just done would rectify the largest lingering sins. Randall opened his eyes. People were gathered around him, asking him questions, offering him water, but he looked beyond them to the water. A wave approached, towering and furious, taking him and his father by surprise. Together they somersaulted backward, making final contact with the earth before the undercurrent emerged, its glorious surge ripping them wildly away from the land they'd come to the end of now, away from the responsibility of shore.

Randall had to wait a week for the body. An autopsy was ordered by the coroner, and his father's corpse had to travel to Richmond to be sliced open and examined. Speight would have hated this, a final and fruitless violation. Dead's dead, Randall could hear his father say. What damn difference does it make?

It made no difference to Randall when the doctor in Richmond told him his father had died of a heart attack. At least he didn't drown, said Granger, who had traveled up to Richmond to keep him company while he waited. Randall nodded, but it was no consolation, for either way he might have lived had not Randall left him alone in the ocean. He'd been sitting in the sand, reading over and over the name and number of the man who knew Reka's whereabouts, trying to figure out from her handwriting where out west she might be. He'd looked up occasionally at first—he was so accustomed to his Saturday trips with the boys that checking on them periodically was reflexive—but at some point he let his mind take him away. Waking dreams of Reka in some far western town, surrounded by the desert she once claimed to desire. He saw her wearing a cowboy's hat in a dance hall, her black hair spilling out from the stiff brim, her face shadowed but beaming, happy. He saw her walking along a high mountain road alongside stark buttes, rocks rising like tables from the desert floor. He did not even notice the commotion when his father's body was spotted floating face down in the surf, so entranced was he in his sister's new life.

He should have known his father was sicker than he claimed, should have known better than to let him go swimming in the ocean when he could barely breathe on land. When he got the body back to Trent, his sisters were so angry they would not look at him. Martha told him he ought to just go on back to Norfolk. They took over the arrangements, treated him as though he had no right to voice an opinion on the matter when he tried to talk them out of a church funeral. His father had no use for preachers. He'd put a church in the same category as a union.

There was only the briefest mention of Reka. Already Randall had decided not to contact her about their father's death—she had finally managed to escape, and he worried that if she returned she would get stuck here again. He would have that on his conscience as well as his father's drowning. Delores was wrong, she was dead wrong about him. He cared, he worried, he spared other people's feelings.

"She's the one left without telling anybody where she was going," said Ellen. They looked to him as if he was going to protest, and when he said nothing, his sisters' looks turned from expectant to pitiable, contemptuous. He was too sorry now to even care about Reka. They blamed it on Hal, his influence, and on sinful Norfolk, Gomorrah of the Tidewater according to the preachers they put all their blind trust in these days.

"Where's Hal at?" said Martha. "How come he didn't come down with you?"

"I haven't seen him in months."

"You mean you didn't even bother to let him know his own daddy died?"

"He doesn't work at the shipyards anymore. I sent word to his girlfriend, or the girl who used to be his friend."

"Hal's girlfriend? I can't imagine she'd be anybody you could count on," said Ellen.

"He knows," Randall lied. He had asked Granger to pay Delores a visit, tell her to pass on the news, but in the weeks since he'd seen her in the bar there had been no word or sight of Hal, and Randall had decided that she had been lying about Hal's return.

But midway through the funeral, which was attended only by Randall's sisters and their husbands and in-laws, a few neighbors from down Devone Street and Ruby McClaurin from the drugstore, the sanctuary door blew open and Randall turned to see Hal and Delores making their way up the aisle. Hal looked heavier—jail food, obviously—but Delores was as bone-thin as ever.

Randall drifted during the inappropriately lengthy service, making up his own stories about the crude figures in the stain-glassed windows while the preacher read verses that had nothing to do with his father. Didn't have much to do with anything, Randall thought as the preacher touched on the evils of drink. His sisters heaved and cried, though only Ellen had taken the time to visit Speight in the seven years since he'd moved back out to the country, and then only because she made a little money off of it. Randall wished Reka were there with him, if only to witness this travesty, but only for a moment. He was certain he had done the right thing by not letting her know.

After the service, Hal strutted up to him in the churchyard. Delores hung back beneath the pecan trees, watching and smoking from a safe distance, as if she knew already what was going to happen.

"You ain't got the goddamn sense you were born with," said Hal. "Letting his sick ass go swimming in the ocean."

"I don't guess I knew how sick he was, Hal. He wasn't one to complain. You might remember that, though it's been so long since you laid eyes on him I can't imagine you remember much."

"He's my goddamn daddy, too. Far as I'm concerned, you sat there and watched him die. Had your nose in a book I bet."

"No," said Randall, thinking of the slip of paper he carried in the breast pocket of his borrowed suit, of the mountain ranges he made out of Reka's schoolgirly curlicues.

"Delores told me everything, little brother. After all I done for you. Putting you up, getting you a job. I leave town for a little R and R, you snake my job, fuck my girl and kill my father."

"He's my father, too."

"No, hell, he ain't. He ain't ever been. Yours nor Reka's neither. Y'all act so damn goody-goody, but you're the worst there is. Delores told me what she said about you. She claimed you didn't believe her. Acted like you possessed what in a court of law I've heard called a fine moral character. You'll do anything. Just like her. Where is she, by the way? Too good a moral character to show up for her daddy's funeral?"

"She's gone. Moved out west."

"You best join her. Nothing left for you here, little brother."

Three

It was true what Edwin had told her about the train: The sink in her skinny sleeping berth folded into the wall, water and all. There were things he'd told her that she'd come to doubt in the years since his death. He'd said so many things, used so many words; the longer she outlived him, the more she suspected that his stories were only stories, tales designed to take her away from her father's house, bed her in that sallow-sheeted cot where he spent his days. He'd written her long and tortured letters, every word of which she'd believed at the time. But after he was gone she began to wonder if those letters weren't just another form of seduction. It had worked, but wasn't it finally no different from the clumsy trash talked by men in the street? What was the difference between Edwin's stories and the boozy comments tossed from the windows of cars passing in the night? From Edwin's driver Deem's blunt come-ons, the transparent compliments of Bob Smart?

The sink folded into the wall, water and all. He'd told the truth, at least about this detail that to most would be niggling, yet to Reka it was as profound as prophecy. To Reka it was not a feat of modern engineering but a confirmation of his love for her. He could have told her anything, as ignorant and gullible as she was then. Yet he cared enough to hold himself to the truth.

As the train lurched away from the station that morning in June 1959 and she settled into her berth, Reka felt as if she'd made this trip hundreds of times already. She'd dreamed of escape by rail so many nights that the slow and bumpy acceleration seemed like sleep itself. Raleigh fell away reluctantly, tall government buildings and side street warehouses giving way within miles to a straggling outskirt of mill house and country stores, finally to field and forest. She was to change trains in Chicago for Duluth, Minnesota, where she would meet a representative of the company and be assigned her territory. From the porter Reka borrowed scrap paper and a pencil stub, made a list of names for Bob Smart's co-worker. Richard Dense. Les Intelligent. Tommy Sharp. She crossed out words and drew sights spied outside her window: the first mound of clay separating coastal plain from Piedmont; an only slightly higher hill signaling the modest rise of the Blue Ridge.

Once, on her way to Lexington, Kentucky, with Edwin, Reka had spent the night in a roadside tourist court west of Asheville. She'd had trouble sleeping there, hemmed in by dark, looming ridges. The mountains seemed filled with water, about to explode. So different from the flatness down east, which seemed suddenly safer, more conducive to escape. She liked being able to see past the next curve. She was used to the sight of the sun in the sky from dawn until dusk, merciless as it rose and hovered but visible, trustworthy. She was a little surprised to feel nostalgia for a landscape she associated with heartache and penury. She vowed to rid herself of such sentiment, for she'd waited for this moment for years.

She'd sprung for a private berth, an inexcusable extravagance. She'd squandered one third of the sum Edith Keane had lent her and she still had to pay for clothes and support herself until she started selling books, yet she could not imagine sharing this berth with a stranger. Only Edwin, for he was the one who had first told that such a thing existed. Still, she worried. What if she had to pay for the samples she carried from house to house? What if there were hidden charges, what if this was really a scam, some form of indentured servitude, as Edith Keane seemed to suspect? She knew too little about the job. Bob Smart had promised to "go over the ropes with her," as he'd put it, but as soon as they'd reached the Sir Walter his promises went the way of his seersucker suit, which spent the night crumpled on the floor by the bed alongside Reka's dress and her common sense. She worried now that sleeping with him again would hurt rather than help her, that he would not keep his word when Randall called because he would, like most cheating husbands, feel so guilty at the mention of her name that he would turn vindictive. *No, I have no idea where she is. Nope, never heard of her.*

But she had to trust someone, and Bob Smart was all she had for now. She'd be damned if she'd wait around for the next chance, the next ticket. She had the feeling she'd narrowly avoided the fate of Edwin: dying in a town you lived to leave.

In Chicago she had a six-hour layover for the Duluth train, and she forced herself to leave the station even though she worried about getting lost and getting stuck in Chicago. She took to the streets, blown about by a wind so furious she feared she'd end up smashed against one of the huge buildings lining the avenue. The buildings were made of granite and were decorated with ornate scrollwork and gargoyles. They looked like they would hurt if you were to rub against them.

The street she took by instinct happened to be State Street, home of the gigantic department stores. She passed by Montgomery Ward, then Marshall Field's, which took up an entire city block. She loitered in front of each one of the show windows, which lined the street one after another. When she came to Sears Roebuck she felt a little breathless, for it seemed unreal to her to be standing in front of this place she had never imagined existing except in the catalog that her father had stashed in the outhouse when they'd lived in the country. Her sisters used to read the Sears catalog nightly, planning their wardrobes, picking out house fixtures and bedspreads, toys and dollhouses for their future broods. It was the only book she ever saw them read, which was reason enough for her to shun it in their presence, as if she had her mind on loftier things. But when they were gone she used to sneak into Ellen's room and pull the fat catalog from under the bed and take it to the sleeping porch where she and Randall would pore through its pages all afternoon. You could buy a house from Sears. It would arrive in your town on a truck, in pre-assembled sections. A bungalow of the type Edwin's father had bought for him. It made sense to her now that Mr. Keane had chosen mail-order lodging for Edwin, as if he knew it would be only temporary and he need not invest much in it.

In front of a Sears show window she encountered a crowd blocking the sidewalk. She pushed her way into the back of the crowd to find a television blinking in the window. The Chicagoans stared dully at the box, as if they did not want to appear too impressed, they had several of these at home, just killing time. She passed on, let herself be sucked inside the revolving doors. The glass wedge spun her onto a sales floor as vast as the entire two blocks of downtown Trent. She rode an escalator up to the women's section and shopped hurriedly, an eye on the clock. It pained her to rush, for she knew she could stay here all afternoon and into the night deliberating over styles and colors, but she had a train to catch.

After she paid she asked if she might go back in the dressing room to change into her new dress. The salesclerk said, "Anxious, aren't you?"

"I have a train to catch," said Reka. She liked the way it sounded, and despite the clerk's impertinence was happy to have a chance to say it aloud.

"You'll have to leave your purchases with me."

"Why?"

"Store policy. You could stuff that bag with clothes on your way to the dressing room for all I know."

You don't know nothing, Reka thought. She'd never stolen a thing in her life, and wasn't about to start now. She could imagine what might happen if she was caught. She'd be back in jail by nightfall, and there was no one now to come to her aid.

Outside on the street, Reka stuffed the dress she'd worn for the past two days into a trash bin. The last of the Edith Keane hand-me-downs.

She tried to sleep on the Chicago-to-Duluth leg, and even though she was tired from the day's travel and the lack of sleep the night before—for Bob Smart had wanted to make sure that his breach of company policy was worth the risk—she felt a little guilty sleeping on the train. Even in the dark there were things to see, things to pay attention to. Not much was visible from her window—there were few towns once they got north of Milwaukee, only unbroken forest. Occasionally a light would blink in the distance and Reka would try to imagine what it would be like to live so far from others in a country so frigid, so prone to snow, wind and ice. She wished she was here in winter, though Bob Smart had said in the classroom that the girls would have to hustle, as winter came early where they were going and was no time to be out in the elements. The girls had fake-shivered and moaned about the cold, but Reka felt she could endure anything after so many years in the broiling coastal plain. She felt she'd been born in the wrong place, to the wrong people; that she and Randall were supposed to have grown up ice skating on some quaint village pond, trudging to school through snowdrifts.

"How will I know who to meet when I get there?" Reka had asked Bob Smart, and he'd told her that a company representative would be holding a sign with her name on it. She saw it first thing as she lugged her Sears Roebuck bag into the station, a chubby man as old as her father holding a piece of cardboard. Her name, spelled out in large blocky letters, seemed not to belong to her.

At least he's too old to pull a Bob Smart, thought Reka as the man introduced himself—Torkelson was his name, Olaf Torkelson—took her bag and hurried off into the surprisingly chilly morning. Duluth was a smoky, ragged, mill-ridden town, and Reka was rather glad that there was not much to look at, for suddenly she was nervous, terrified that her secret would be found out. Olaf Torkelson's silence in the car only encouraged her fear, and after trying and failing to engage him in a conversation about Duluth, Reka thought she might prefer him to be a lech like his colleague if only he'd talk.

They stopped at a downtown hotel, where Torkelson explained that she was to get a room and rest until that evening, when the other girls would arrive.

"What other girls?"

"The ones you'll be working with. We send you out in groups, Miss. You didn't think we'd send you out alone, did you?"

"No," Reka said. She didn't need company, especially if the company was anything like the girls who'd attended the orientation back in Greenville. What if she had to live with them? She'd rather sleep in the woods than room with those girls whose chirpy innocence depressed her. But she couldn't very well sell books after sleeping in the woods. She wasn't thinking straight, and there was no law that said she had to socialize with her co-workers.

Of course she would have to pose as one of them, which meant that her outfits were all wrong, but she'd be damned if she'd spend more money on clothes. She'd just have to fake it, to act as if she had more class, but that night, when the group of them met in a room of the hotel and the girls mingled nervously and one of them asked—first thing—where she went to school, Reka came close to blowing her cover.

"School?" she said.

"Yeah, what school? I'm at Indiana University, studying music."

"Oh, I'm at Carolina. Chapel Hill." This was where Edwin had gone, where he planned to go back someday and finish his degree.

They'd made plans for her to come along, working for a while, then attending herself.

"Studying what?"

Reka smiled to stall her. What would she study? What could she study, what could she do in the world to survive? She only really wanted to read books and to hear what other people had to say about these books, for even though she read as much as she could, she had not had anyone to talk to about books since Memory Wright used to visit her in jail.

"Books," said Reka.

The girl screwed her face up for a minute, as if she was trying to figure Reka out, then laughed.

"Good one," she said, and drifted quickly away, looking back over her shoulder as if she expected Reka to slink away.

Mr. Torkelson made them each stand and tell where they were from, what school they attended, and what their major was. Reka had no idea what he meant by a "major"—she thought at first that the girls had something to do with the military—but she soon figured it out from the girls who went before her. She was not used to talking in public, not really used to talking to people period, and she was shaky when she rose to speak, but she knew she must get over her shyness if she was to make any money at all. Making money was the point. She couldn't care less whether the girls liked her, what kind of house she found to live in. She did not plan to spend any time at all away from the job; she'd sell books from dawn until eleven o'clock at night if she could get her foot in a door that late.

"Says here you're from East Carolina," said Torkelson when she told them she attended Chapel Hill.

Reka colored. Her first words were already exposed as a lie.

"No," she said. "Just plain old Carolina."

"And what are you studying there?" asked Torkelson.

"She told me she's studying books," the girl from earlier said from the front of the room, and Reka shot her a look but was glad for the distraction, for everyone in the room laughed at what seemed a pretty good joke, though it wasn't Reka who got credit for it.

Olaf Torkelson explained the job to them. He offered sales tips and wardrobe suggestions. He quoted someone named Dale Carnegie, whom everyone in the room except Reka seemed to know. He told them that they would rent their sample books from the company and their money would be refunded in full if the books were returned in good condition. He held aloft a briefcase provided free of charge by the company and distributed company ID cards printed with each girl's name, which the girls should always wear clipped to their blouse so that people knew they were on the up-and-up. He emphasized the importance of living a clean and upstanding life while in these towns, as they were there representing the McMillan Book Company, and any scandal would reflect badly on the company and would not be tolerated.

"When will we have time to mess up?" one of the girls asked. Olaf Torkelson answered her question as if it was meant to be answered, which amused Reka and made her like him.

"A good point. You ladies stand to make a pile of money," he said. "But it's hard work. You can't sell books if you're sitting in a booth at the drugstore."

He handed out samples. There were encylopedias and one-volume histories of the world—ridiculously thin, thought Reka, to cover the world since the time of dinosaurs. There were cookbooks and tales of moral instruction for teens. There was even a facts-of-life book that Olaf Torkelson referred to as *Birds and Bees*, a euphemism that drew titters from his audience. This one sells like hotcakes, but only to women, he said. No use even pitching it to the man of the house.

After three days of sales tips and training, Mr. Torkelson read out the names of girls and the towns where they would be based for the summer. The girls were divided into groups of two; when their names were called, they were asked to stand. Reka sighed when she found herself paired with the music major from Indiana in a town called Red Fork, Montana.

But that night, trying to sleep, she decided it would be good for her to have someone she knew in the town. She'd not counted on getting lonely, yet the thought of Red Fork, Montana, on her own intimidated her for some reason. She tried to imagine it, tried to envision the fork of a reddish brown river for which the town was named. A stretch of weather-beaten buildings clinging to the banks. Dirt ravaged by a season's worth of snow, scratched and patchy after the thaw, as if the entire town had been one big chicken yard.

The next morning, after a quick breakfast and last pep talk from Olaf Torkelson, Reka and her new mate boarded a bus for Red Fork. The music major's name was Cecelia Bannister. Cecelia talked all the way through North Dakota and well into Montana. She announced that she was to be married in a year and a half; the exact date was soon to be set. She had to have money, as her husband was going to be a famous cellist but that would take some time, for artistic genius could not be rushed. In the meantime she was sacrificing her summer, which she usually spent with her parents at a family cottage on Lake Erie, to earn money to support them in their earliest years of marriage.

"They're crucial, you know," she said to Reka.

"Who, your parents?"

"The first years, silly. They say most marriages break up within the first eighteen months. Don and I are crazy about each other but still, I don't want to take us for granted. Don't you know anyone who has made a dreadful mistake?"

Reka knew plenty of people who had made dreadful mistakes, but none of the type Cecelia described. Where she came from, people stayed married to their mistakes, and simply took up with other mistakes when the spirit moved them.

"Sure," she said, because she wanted to sound worldly.

"What about you? Why are you here?"

"I need money," said Reka.

"I know *that*. What do you need it for?"

"School," said Reka.

"You mean to finish? Don't your parents help out?"

"My parents are dead." She had no idea why she said this, and the ease with which it came out terrified her a little. Of course her mother was dead, long dead. But her father, she thought, would live forever. Despite all their troubles, she could not imagine this world without him. He was all she'd known in the way of a parent, and as awkward and ineffectual as he'd been, she had come to respect his way with them all, the sacrifices he made to keep them all fed and together.

"I'm sorry," said Cecelia.

"What kind of instrument do you play?" Reka said quickly, to change the subject.

Cecelia described her voice training for the next forty miles. She sang her way through a desolate patch of North Dakota, offering the highlights of her leading role in the spring production of *The Pirates of Penzance*. Reka decided to admire Cecelia's lack of self-consciousness, even though sleep-disrupted passengers gave them the evil eye and one whiskey-breathed man rose in his seat to ask her to pipe down, which caused Cecelia to erupt into giggles, Reka joining in, happy for laughter to ease her anxiety.

They arrived in Red Fork after eight hours in the cramped and stuffy bus.

"My legs don't work anymore," said Cecelia as they stood in the parking lot of the bus station, surveying the town that would be their home for the next few months. Reka wanted to walk the streets, to explore the place; this was what Randall would do if he were here, she thought, take off down the streets first thing, trying to see what he could see. He'd make up stories as he went along, piece together some crazy history of the town's founders, speculate on who had the most money based on the size and grandeur of the faded Victorians lining the main drag.

"Let's get some dinner, I'm famished," said Cecelia. Reka let herself be led to a diner, where everyone stared as she and Cecelia deposited their suitcases and book samples in the aisle beside their booth.

"Hi, I'm Cecelia Bannister, and this is Reka Speight," Cecelia said to the waitress, a high school girl who looked at them as if they were from another planet. "We're here to sell books."

"What kind of books?" a man sitting at the counter leaned across the aisle to ask. Reka did not realize that the entire restaurant was watching, listening. She was a little embarrassed, and intimidated too by Cecelia's bluntness. She felt a surge of competitiveness, vowed to learn how to be as assertive as her partner. I will outsell her two to one, Reka thought. I need the money more than she does.

"All kinds," said Cecelia to the crowd. "Enclyclopedias, dictionaries, books on health and hygiene. We're with the McMillan company. Working our way through college. I'm a music major and she is studying to be a teacher."

Reka stared, amazed.

"Everybody loves teachers," Cecelia whispered to her. "You'll sell more that way, I bet you a dollar you will."

Reka nodded and smiled at the crowd. After they ordered and their food arrived, Cecelia kept jumping up to talk to people about her wares. Reka watched her work the crowd, unable to do much but pick at her blue plate special. Maybe I'm not cut out for this, she thought. She could certainly learn from this girl whom she'd dismissed too early and for all the wrong reasons.

"I got four addresses!" Cecelia said when she finally returned to the table. "Why'd you just sit here, they're dying to meet some interesting people." She lowered her voice. "I don't think they get too many strangers in Blue Spoon, Montana," she said, and she laughed loudly, her mouth filled with succotash.

They shared a room that night in the town's only hotel. Reka rose early the next day, bathed and dressed before the sun rose, determined to outsell Cecelia, who made no sign that she would rise before noon. Reka slipped out of the room quietly, leaving Cecelia a note detailing which side of Main Street she'd take.

For an hour she walked the streets, trying to work up the nerve to knock on a door. She told herself it was too early yet, that people needed time to wake up and eat breakfast, get ready for the day. Red Fork, it turned out, did not have a river after all, a discovery that depressed Reka. Towns without rivers should not be, she thought. In a landlocked town there was only one way out. . .

Beyond the town rose a range of barren hills, sparsely treed and sun-withered. They appeared covered with threadbare throw rugs, and the lack of greenery bothered Reka even though this was what she'd craved back in Trent: the absence of undergrowth. A higher line of peaks framed the distance, craggy and brilliant in the wide sky. The sky was huge here, curving away to the end of the earth. She felt tiny walking the streets with her sample case, a sweater tightened across her neck to protect her from the unseasonable chill.

Finally she ran out of excuses to put off her first attempt at bookselling. She chose a large and prosperous-looking house next to a church. An older woman answered the door wearing a smile as loose and tentative as the housecoat wrapped casually over her nightgown.

Reka made her pitch. She stumbled over words and was aware even as she spoke of the note of apology in her tone. Sorry to bother you, I know it's early, would you like me to come back?

"This is the manse," the woman said. "My husband's the minister."

"Oh," said Reka. She did not know what this had to do with anything. Did preachers not read books?

"We'd have to take it up with the congregation, you understand," said the preacher's wife. "We're really not at liberty to make purchases without their consent."

Reka thanked her and hurried away. Only when she reached the sidewalk did she begin to wonder if she had been told a fib.

All morning she knocked on doors and was rebuffed in ways that revealed themselves only after she was on to the next house. A woman whose yard was littered with toys and tricycles claimed to be childless, and therefore had no need of an encyclopedia. Reka was plagued with delayed I-should-have-said thoughts, which she filed away for the next encounter, but no two excuses were the same. It seemed the citizens of Red Fork had caught wind of her coming, and had gotten together to make sure they did not repeat themselves in their refusals.

The only times she was asked inside, she did not want to go: leering men in undershirts and morning stubble who offered her breakfast and—twice before nine o'clock—a little eye-opener. Men were rare, though; mostly she was met by women, and the women who came to the door and looked her over seemed hard, suspicious, distant: there were no Edith Keanes in this neighborhood, and this seemed the only neighborhood where one might turn up. These women run the houses, she decided; the men go off to work and the women stay home like elsewhere, but the task of running a house seems to require more stamina here. There was little time left to be polite to strangers.

She worked until three o'clock in the afternoon without once completing her pitch. She skipped lunch, and though she was starving by midafternoon she would not allow herself to quit until she'd crossed at least one threshhold. She finished Main Street and worked her way into the neighborhoods beneath the hills, choosing a street that reminded her of Devone Street, her former home in Trent. Shabby-shingled houses, small bungalows, the occasional characterless brick Cape Cod. In one of these a woman came to the door on the first knock. When Reka explained her purpose, the woman invited her in for a cup of tea.

Olaf Torkelson had said that if you could get in the front parlor, your chances rose to at least fifty-fifty. If you could manage the kitchen, you were looking at a ninety percent chance that you'd make the sale. She'd thought his prediction silly at the time, but when the woman asked her back to the kitchen, where, she said, things weren't so damned formal, Reka found herself growing excited.

While she put a kettle on to boil, the woman told Reka an abbreviated version of her life story. Her name was Maggie, and she lived in this house with her husband, who worked for a logging company and was often gone overnight. Maggie did not work. She looked to be in her early thirties, and she looked to Reka like a high school beauty who had let herself go as soon as she was married, for she carried in her thighs and stomach a heaviness that seemed recent, yet did not mask totally the shapely beauty she had once been. She was warm and open, but her eyes brimmed with some need, some undefined and no doubt undefinable wanting that made her impossible to turn away from. Reka looked at her in the way that she'd looked before at people who were too beautiful, unblemished—the kind of people Edwin once described in one of his letters as possessing a cleanliness that went beneath the skin. A black bear could have come down from the hills and waddled into the kitchen and Reka would not have been able to take her eyes off Maggie's. So long as Maggie looked at her, Reka had no choice but to return her gaze.

But what did she want? The rest of her—her clothes, her figure, her posture, her lank and unwashed hair—suggested some insufferable sadness, but her conversation was vibrant and witty and included occasional questions for Reka. She did not make fun of Reka's accent like everyone else had that day, but instead she claimed to like it. She's lonely, thought Reka. Her eyes burned with the please-talk-to-me desperation of the lonesome. Yet the desperation was not off-putting, as it usually was among people who crave other people. It was somehow more touching to Reka, and she decided to go slow with her pitch, as she was worried about reminding Maggie that she was here on business, worried about hurting her feelings.

Halfway through her spiel, Maggie said, "Why are you doing this? I can't imagine it would be very much fun, especially in a place like Red Fork."

Reka put down her one-volume history of the world. She was inclined to make a joke about it every time she fetched it from her sample case, but resisted only because it would be harder to sell a book you'd made fun of.

"Oh, I like it here. It's pretty."

"You don't have to live here," said Maggie. "I grew up over in Bozeman, which at least has the university. My husband's older than I am—he came back from the war and went to school on the G.I. Bill and that's where I met him, when he was at State getting his degree in forestry. I was still in high school, can you believe it? I waited tables at this place down by campus where he washed dishes. We moved here because of his job. He could go anywhere, really—there are trees all over the country and they need people to tell them which ones to cut, I guess. But he won't ever leave this place."

Reka was beginning to worry. She'd been here an hour or longer and had yet to even mention prices. Olaf's kitchen theory seemed to her nonsense cooked up by managers who had never actually tried to sell a book.

"I think you might find this informational, really," said Reka, trying to return to the book she held in her hand. But what need did Maggie have of a history of the world? She seemed to have lost control of her own tiny corner of it. Reka hadn't counted on feeling guilty about selling her wares. She had not anticipated how hard this was going to be.

"I don't know," said Maggie, flipping through the history of the world. "One of those cookbooks you mentioned, maybe? Let's see what else you got."

Reka went through her entire sample case. Maggie looked as if she was listening, interested—her eyes as intensely needy as before—but Reka began to worry that she was only prolonging the visit so that she would not have to face the rest of the afternoon alone. Torkelson had said you develop a hunch right off the bat if you're going to make a sale. With time, he said, you'll figure out which people are worth lingering over, which ones are only being polite. Reka was sure that Maggie was not worth two hours of her time, yet she was unable to tear herself away.

"Well, why don't you think about it," said Reka. "I'll come back if you want."

"Could you?"

"Sure. I'll be in the area tomorrow."

Maggie said she'd talk to her husband, and made Reka promise to return. At the front door, Reka said, "This is a nice neighborhood. You wouldn't happen to know of any rooms to let around here, would you? I'm looking for a place to stay."

Maggie looked past her, out into the street, as if she were considering who might rent a room to a stranger. When after a few seconds she met Reka's eyes, Reka knew what she was going to say next.

"You could stay here. Why don't you stay here? Jake won't mind, I'm sure he won't. He's gone so much of the time, he'd love for me to have the company."

"Oh, I won't be around much at all," said Reka. "Just to sleep here, really. I'll be up and out of your hair in the morning, and won't be back until dark."

"Well, you could come back for supper," she said. "You don't want to eat out all the time. We've got an extra room upstairs, and there's even a private bath up there."

"Why don't you check with your husband?" Reka wished she'd never mentioned it, for Maggie seemed too eager. She saw no way out of it now, however, and it was true that she would be gone most of the day.

"Jake won't mind. You bring your things over whenever you like."

"I guess we need to talk about what you'd charge."

"I won't charge a dime. I wouldn't feel right, charging you. You need your money for college."

"I'd have to pay you something." Reka knew better than to accept her offer for free, which would make it even more difficult to come and go on her own time, beholden to Maggie's neediness.

"How about we work out a deal with one of those books?"

"Okay," said Reka. She didn't much care for this idea—it meant she would have to buy her own merchandise, that her first sale would be out of pocket—but in the end, it would all even out, wouldn't it?

She made plans to return after supper, and headed back to the hotel. It was past five, and she was starving; she planned to collect her things, leave a note for Cecelia telling her she'd found a place, but Cecelia was sitting in the lobby flirting with the young desk clerk, and followed her up to the room.

She closed the door and lowered her voice as soon as they were alone and said, "How'd you do? I sold thirty-two dollars' worth. On my first day! Wasn't that Main Street a gold mine? It took me all morning just to work through one block."

Reka must have picked the wrong side of the street. She hated admitting the truth: that she'd sold only one measly book, and to herself.

"I did okay. Not great, but I guess it takes time."

"Let's go to dinner. My treat, okay?"

Reka allowed herself to be taken to dinner only because she hated spending the money. Why shouldn't Cecelia pay if she made so much money? After her first good day she'd return the favor.

"I found a place to stay," Reka said while they waited for their food.

"Already? Hey, why don't you just stay at the hotel with me? It's only six bucks a night. I figured I can stay there easy, what with all the money I'll be making. And plus I'm not crazy about living with strangers, are you?"

"Six bucks is six bucks," said Reka. She spoke as if Cecelia were a spoiled girl used to her summer vacations on Lake Erie, who had no inkling of the value of money. Cecelia understood, and looked a little hurt.

"Who'd you find a room with?"

"Some couple," said Reka. Their food had arrived. She took a bite of roll so she would not have to talk, but Cecelia would not settle for silence.

"How much are they charging you?"

"Nothing," said Reka, and immediately she regretted it. "I mean, no money. The woman asked if I could do some things around the house for her."

"You're kidding! She just wants a maid. You better watch out. She'll have you up all night long polishing her silver or something."

"I don't mind helping out if I don't have to pay."

"You better be careful."

Reka put down her fork. Who was Cecelia Bannister to tell her to be careful? She'd survived more already than Cecelia would read about in one of those true crime magazines she flipped through on the bus ride from Duluth.

"I guess I can take care of myself," said Reka, in a tone that made it clear the conversation was over.

"Your part comes to two sixty-five," said Cecelia when the check came. Reka smiled and counted out the amount slowly, along with twice the tip Cecelia left.

Maggie's husband, Jake, answered the door. He was tall and bony-faced, and his brown hair was sandy with gray that shone in the late evening light. She had a good look at him, as the sun was in his eyes and it took him a few seconds to adjust, and during this time she stared. His skin was tanned and wrinkled, as if he spent much time out of doors, and his hand was sandpaper-rough. Shaking it reminded Reka of her father, whose own grip was almost dangerous from his years of manual labor.

"You must be Reka. Maggie's upstairs getting your room ready."

"I hope it's no problem, my staying with y'all."

"No problem at all. In fact, it will be good for Maggie."

Reka hesitated, then said, "Well, I won't be around hardly any. I mean, I'll be out all day, working."

"Just having another body in the house will be good for her," said Jake. Since they were still standing in the foyer, and he was half-blinded by the sun behind her, she could continue her scrutiny. His eyes were green, and his hair seemed to her the exact color of the grasses covering the hillocks beyond town. He appeared very much of this place, as if his features were camouflage almost, an adaptation of the landscape. She stood close enough to smell his body, which also reminded her of her father, of hard work in the elements, of men more comfortable outdoors.

He took her upstairs to her room, where Maggie was making her bed.

"Here you are," said Maggie, opening her arms wide. "I hope it's okay."

"It's fine," said Reka. She thought of emphasizing again how little time she'd be spending there, but it seemed rude to keep repeating herself. The room was small but neat, with tall windows recessed in dormers and a walk-in closet. It seemed to be a child's room, a boy's; there were model airplanes and board games on a shelf, a collection of metal cars and marbles in a box by a desk, rows of Hardy Boys mysteries she recognized by their spines, as she used to check these out of the Trent Public Library for Randall.

There had been no mention of a son. Perhaps he was away somewhere, at camp? But surely Maggie would have said something about him earlier, when she talked on the subject of her life.

"Oh, don't mind those things," Maggie said. "My nephews come to stay a lot. We like to keep the room set up for their visits."

Reka smiled and looked—accidentally—at Jake. She noticed the look he gave his wife, a glance both caustic and filled with the same kind of wanting Reka had detected earlier in Maggie's gaze.

Well, it was none of her business, what went on between them. She was here only to sleep, and because she wanted to be alone, she excused herself to do just that. Jake had to lead Maggie out of the room; Reka thought she would have flopped down and tried to have a slumber party had Jake not been there to take her away, leaving Reka free to collapse onto the small rickety bed with the wagon wheel footboard and a Conestoga wagon carved into the headboard, where she slept like a little cowgirl.

For the rest of the week, Reka taught herself to sell books. If at first it seemed true what Bob Smart had told her that afternoon in Greenville—that these people had no need of knowledge, that they were unlikely to spend money on anything they could not eat—in time Reka discovered a way to succeed. Rather than sell books, Reka sold herself. She talked more about her desire to teach school than she did the scrumptious, easy-to-follow recipes of the *Everywoman's Time-saving Cookbook*, and she made sure to emphasize how crucial this job was to the completion of her degree. She pretended to be Randall's age, though she feared the customer who noticed in the afternoon sunlight the strands of gray flaking her hair—but it took only a day or two for Reka to convince herself that it was the truth, that she would soon enter college and feel eighteen again. Reclaim those years lost to hoeing weeds in a prison garden, start all over from Edwin's last night on earth.

She had Cecelia to thank for the teacher line, which soon became less a pretense than a sincere desire. She could see herself in front of a room of children, crouching by a tiny desk to help a child sound out a difficult word. It would probably be her only chance to be around kids; she loved them, wanted them, but doubted she would have children, since sooner or later she would have to tell them about her past. Finding a man willing to marry a woman who had served time for manslaughter was a tall enough order; she had all but resigned herself to the occasional coupling, like as not with a now-you-see-him-now-you-don't lover like Bob Smart.

She made money. These people in Red Fork knew and respected hard work. They bought books from *her*, not *for* themselves, and even though it saddened Reka to think that the *History of the World* might gather dust on a shelf alongside bric-a-brac and gloomy portraits of Old Country ancestors, she was flattered to find complete strangers capable of believing in her future.

Maggie insisted she take supper with them—it was part of the package, she said—and by the end of the week, Reka was doing well enough to linger after the meal for a cup of coffee. Mostly it was the two of them. Jake worked long hours, and this far north it stayed light well into the night, but Reka preferred it when he was around. Maggie doted on her. There was still, in the back of her eyes, some deep and ineffable longing, but Maggie tried so hard to make Reka feel at home. Reka could not dislike her for her kindness, even though it made her nervous. She knew there was something huge lurking behind Maggie's elaborate meals and the flowers she placed on Reka's nightstand that might explain the mood of this house, yet she was determined not to get involved.

When Jake was around, the evenings were less intense and more enjoyable. Reka could never decide whether Jake was relaxed or exhausted. He seemed so easygoing, so gentle. Reka had never known a man whose manner was so quietly effective. She thought Jake might be a good teacher; she could imagine a classroom full of smart-alecky fourteen-year-olds settling down to work as he entered the room, listening closely to his soft-spoken western drawl. Learning things from him.

Often, from a distance, Reka observed the way they spoke to and

touched each other, the way they did not speak or touch. She stood
sometimes on the staircase in the morning and eavesdropped on
their truncated conversations, and she often lingered in the dining
room when they retired to the kitchen to wash dishes together. She
had never seen a man do the dishes, or even help with the housework, and she thought how wonderful that would be, to share a
meal with a man and then have him in the kitchen to talk to afterward. The few times she had cooked for men, she felt like a waitress. She couldn't imagine Edwin drying silverware; she could not
even see Randall helping out with the housework, even though she
thought her little brother might grow into a considerate man. He
was still a boy, though; she couldn't imagine him with a woman at
all, much less in a scene of domestic stability.

Maggie and Jake might share the housework, but that did not
make them happy. Even in those moments of sharing they did not
talk much, and though Maggie was chipper and smiley when both
Reka and Jake were around, when she was alone with her husband
her tone changed. The words Reka overheard passing between
them sounded angry on her part, tentative and wreathed in a thin
patience on his. It seemed that she was trying to hurt him by how
she said things and by what she did not say, and it seemed he was
aware of it, used to it even, and had decided out of frustration to try
his best to humor her. Reka knew they had another life, the behind-
closed-doors life that meant so much more than anything she could
observe, even those moments when she spied on them. But she
knew also—unfairly, mysteriously, but resolutely—that very little
passed between them that she did not witness.

Reka had been there a month when a freak storm swooped down
from the Canadian plains. She was working her way down a dirt
road alongside a railroad track when the wind began to pick up.
What at first she mistook for a higher, darker range of peaks in the
distance turned out to be thunderheads, gathering and shifting in
the intimidating sky. She stood under a tree in a vacant lot, watch-

ing the sky flash and blacken and wishing she'd brought along her sweater, for the temperature plummeted in a matter of minutes, until the wind felt laced with slivered ice. There was something horrifying about such extreme shifts in temperature, something malevolent and apocalyptic to Reka.

Shivering in the driving, leaf-flecked wind, she decided that the world existed only in moments of extremes—in ecstatic bliss or severe sadness—and that what you saw in between was like the silence on a phonograph, when the needle has yet to slide inevitably into the groove of the next tune. Maybe some people aspired to live their lives in these empty moments of what they called existence, but she never could. She would not be satisfied waiting around for the next bout of happiness, or sadness if that was all that was available.

A small Indian boy appeared beneath her.

"My mama says come inside," he said, and he led her into the house next door where a woman not much older than her and buried beneath babies—lap baby and knee baby, child at her breast and one clinging wildly to her skirt—told her she could wait out the storm there.

Reka thanked her and tried to make conversation, but the woman had her hands filled with children and only smiled, as if she did not quite understand why Reka was there. At one point she said, "Snow's coming," and Reka, incredulous, said, "But it's July," and the woman said, "It's coming." After a while Reka rose and crossed the room to the small greasy window, where sure enough the bushes were already catching great fat snowflakes.

It had been snowing for an hour when it occurred to Reka that it would not stop anytime soon. She thanked the woman and left, shielding her head from the snow with her sample case, hobbled through town in her heels, her dress soaked from the wet flakes, her teeth beginning to chatter.

"Back here," a voice called when she reached the house. She made her way back to the kitchen, where Jake was banking the woodstove.

"Welcome to Montana in the summertime," he said, glancing at her and smiling. She collapsed into a chair by the stove, stuck out her hands to let them dry.

"This happen a lot?" she said.

"Enough to remind you that it can happen," said Jake.

"That's too much," said Reka.

"You don't like snow?"

"Not all that much in July, I guess. Not that I've ever seen snow in summertime."

"You'd get used to it if you lived here."

He brought her a towel from the bathroom. She rubbed her hair dry, excused herself to change.

"You have any winter clothes?"

Of course she didn't. Bob Smart had not warned her about summer blizzards.

"Why don't you borrow something of Maggie's. She's got sweaters and warm pants in the bureau. Be a little big on you, but you'll be more comfortable."

"Oh, no thanks. I've got a sweater."

"I'm afraid it will be a bit on the nippy side tonight. I don't turn on the heat for a freak storm like this. Tomorrow the sun will come out and it could be mid-fifties by afternoon. It's likely to be freezing upstairs in your room. You're welcome to fix a pallet up down here by the stove, or sleep in the parlor by the fireplace. Oh, I forgot to tell you, Maggie's gone to visit her sister in Bozeman. She's having a baby. Maggie wanted to be there, to help. She'll be gone for four or five days, until her sister gets settled, and she asked me to tell you to help yourself to anything we've got in the way of food. She didn't want you to have to eat out while she was gone."

Jake straightened up from the woodstove and seemed stunned by how much he'd said. It seemed to Reka that he wasn't used to speeches.

"I don't mind," said Reka. "Y'all've been so nice, feeding me and putting me up for free."

"My pleasure," said Jake. "But I thought we were getting a book out of the deal."

"Of course," she said. "I'm sorry, I didn't mean . . ."

"I know you didn't," he said. "Why don't you get changed and help me figure out something for dinner, and then I'd like to take a look at those books of yours. I've been working so much I've hardly had the chance to see what you've got to offer."

It felt funny at first, wearing this man's wife's clothes, working alongside him chopping carrots, potatoes and beef for a stew, but Reka soon forgot all about Maggie.

They ate dinner at the kitchen table, Jake regaling Reka with tales of snowstorms past. Drifts higher than cars, chimneys clogged and roofs caving in. Reka told him about Hurricane Hazel, which had passed through Trent two years earlier one early autumn after-noon, trapping her at work with the fraulein and her friend Rose until morning, a night of airborne trash cans and breaking windows, of two-hundred-year-old oaks uprooted, trunks flying past the plate-glass windows of the laundry. They seemed to need to talk of disaster to keep themselves from falling into shyness, but only at first. By the time they finished eating, Reka was no longer unnerved by silences, and Jake appeared even more relaxed than usual, which made her think that his easygoing demeanor around his wife might well have been exhaustion. Reka insisted on helping with the dishes, and though he protested, he clearly welcomed her company, for they talked and joked as they worked, and Jake seemed happier than he ever had helping Maggie out in the kitchen.

Jake made coffee. They took mugs into the parlor, where Jake lit the fire he'd laid earlier. Reka stretched out on the floor to watch the flames.

"Let's see these books you're making a killing off of," he said.

"I wish."

"I can't see how anyone could say no to you, no matter what you're selling."

"Happens more often than not." She took the compliment with only the slightest unease. She knew he was sincere, but she cared suddenly and too much about the things he said. She did not want from him the glib, hollow praise of a Bob Smart. And when she considered this, she wished he'd said something crass and obvious, if only to disabuse herself of her idealized view of him: the most interesting man she'd met besides her brother.

Jake seemed interested only in her *History of the World*, the same volume she'd felt guilty trying to press on his wife. He flipped through it, began to read. Reka watched the flames, content to be sitting quietly with a man absorbed in a book. It was, she realized, a long-standing fantasy of hers: to sit quietly with a man while reading before a fire.

Yet soon she wanted him to talk again.

"How's the world turning out?"

He closed the book and leaned back, propping himself up on an elbow. He watched the fire, spoke to her.

"I was reading about the war. D day, the Allied invasion and all. It's strange to have lived through something, been right there, then read about it years later in a book."

"So did they get it right, or am I peddling a pack of lies?"

He laughed, shrugged. "Both, I guess. They got it as right as they could, but it doesn't sound anything at all like what I saw over there. 'Course I only saw a little part of it. Guess you got to take the wide view if you're going to write it up in a history book."

"What was your little part like?"

Jake told her how he'd enlisted without telling his mother. His older brother was already overseas, and even though his mother made him swear he would not leave her alone in Red Fork, he laid out of work one day and hitchhiked to the recruiting station in Billings.

"I don't regret going, because I learned more in those three years than I ever would have staying here. And even though it seems like a high price to pay for an education, I never would have been able to go to college if it weren't for the G.I. Bill. But I hate how I lied to my mother, left her alone here. Three weeks after I left—I was out in Tacoma doing basic training—she got a telegram about my brother Richard. I don't think she ever got over that month."

He told her how excited he was when his unit was deployed to England.

"I was so stupid. I treated it like the senior trip or something. My mother never told me about Richard, see—she told me later she thought I'd go AWOL if I knew he'd been killed, would have come straight home, gotten in trouble with the army. But it would have only made me more determined.

"To me it was a vacation. See the world. I spent my twenty-seventh birthday in Plymouth, England, drinking too much of that English ale with two boys from down your way—Alabama and Texas. Had us a good old time. The next day we shipped out for Normandy. I was so seasick crossing the channel that I almost didn't care what was waiting for us on shore, so long as I could get off that boat. We landed two days after the first troops hit the beach. The area was secured, but there were still body parts lying around in the dunes. Bloody patches of sand. Is this too much?"

"No," she said. She wanted more. Hearing him talk of hardship and tragedy made him more real to her. She was used to seeing him humoring his wife, playing along with her transparent gaiety. She wanted to hear all about the horrors he'd seen, wanted to know most of all how he'd managed to put it behind him.

"Maggie can't stand to hear it. We've never talked about it, really. Once when we were dating I started to tell her, but she cut me off when it got the least bit gruesome. She doesn't care to talk about unpleasant things. I guess I see her point."

I don't, Reka almost said, but she stopped herself when she remembered she was draped in Maggie's sweater, wearing a pair of her old corduroy pants.

"Two weeks after we arrived in France I took a bullet in my shoulder. We were crossing a field at dusk when the Germans opened fire from the woods. Fifteen men in my company dead inside of three minutes. I managed to crawl into a stump hole where they couldn't see me. I was bleeding bad, in and out of it, but I could hear someone moaning nearby and when it got dark I dragged myself through the grass to where my sergeant lay clawing the ground. He'd been blinded by a grenade. I got him back to the hole and we lay there, huddled up, hugging each other all night to keep warm. I was as cold as I've ever been and that's saying something for somebody who grew up in central Montana.

"When the sun rose I figured the Germans would drift out of the woods and check to see that no one was living, but we waited and waited and they never arrived. So we headed back toward the line and met up with a medic who wrapped my shoulder and gave me a shot of morphine. That fixed me up, I'm telling you. If God made anything better, he kept it for himself."

"He made a lot of things better," she said. She felt the capillaries in her face burning with blood, heard the vengeance in her voice. She could not meet his stare. She bent toward the fire so that the color in her cheeks would seem the fault of the heat, but she knew he heard it, knew he realized he had said something wrong.

"It's just a saying." He spoke gently enough that the defensiveness of his words softened her mood. After all, he was merely repeating something he'd heard others say. He had no idea what this meant to her.

"I've heard it before," she said, "but it's not true. What happened after that? They send you home?"

He was silent for a minute, watching her watch the fire, before he started up again.

"They sent me back to England. I spent six weeks in a London hospital recuperating. One morning I was told to get my things ready. I said goodbye to all my buddies, some of them I was sure wouldn't make it home alive. I thought I was going home, but they shipped me right back to the front."

"I guess the worst was over, though."

"No. Things got a whole lot worse before they got better."

She waited for him to elaborate, but he seemed to have run out of words. He stoked the fire, asked if she wanted a drink; she accepted a small glass of Canadian whiskey and ginger ale, and he had his whiskey over ice.

"I know what you mean," she said after a while. "About how you think the worst is over and then it keeps on going downhill."

"You do?"

Maybe it was the hint of surprise in his voice that made her talk; maybe she wanted him to know her fully, as fully as she felt she wanted to know him. Either way, it was a risk, and it was the first time she'd told anyone about Edwin since prison, though back in Trent it wasn't as if there was anyone within miles who did not know her story.

She told him about their earliest days together, about getting caught in the act by her father, running away to Kentucky. Describing what happened next—how the druggist and her own father had cooked up a scheme to get Edwin back on morphine, ostensibly to save her from this spoiled, drug-crazed rich boy—she noted how absurd it sounded, how implausible it was that these things had happened to anyone, much less her. She told him about the day Edwin died, how he had taken more than she knew about and promised to take her away that very afternoon, if only she would give him one more shot.

"I would have done it again, I guess," she said. "I mean, I wanted out of that town so bad I would have done almost anything. I didn't mean to kill him, of course, but in a weird way it's good I did. Who knows what would have happened to us. I can't see us married, or even staying together much past a few more months."

"Why did you hate that place?"

She hesitated, scrambling for a way to be both honest and cautious. Because he liked it here in Red Fork, and she saw little difference between the two towns, she worried that he'd be offended if she admitted as much, that he'd gulp his drink and pad off to bed in another part of the house and their night would be over.

"You like it here, right?"

"Red Fork? Yes, I do like it. I know it, anyway, and I like knowing it. I guess if you were to put a gun to my head and ask me which I liked best, the people or the place itself, the land, I'd choose the latter. The people, well . . . they're like the rest of the world. No difference far as I'm concerned. I've heard others say how nice people here are, how hardworking and respectful of your privacy. That's not the Red Fork I know. But here I am going on about my town, when I asked you to tell me about yours."

"I went to prison to get away from it."

"You mean you didn't have to go to prison?"

"I could have claimed he did it himself. No one would have doubted me, everybody knew Edwin was a morphine addict. He didn't try to hide it, I'll say that for him. He didn't give a damn about that town, at least to hear him talk. But when it came down to leaving it, he chose to stay. Forever."

"How long were you in prison?"

His voice was soft, tender, respectful; it was easier to talk about it than she thought, at least to Jake. She could not imagine telling Maggie, who would worry her for details and throw her arms around her and cry at the thought of Reka in a hot, moldy cell, curled up in a wool blanket to ward off the roaches and mice, even though it was hot as hell in there year-round.

"Five years. His mother, she used to come see me, but his father was convinced I killed his boy. He didn't know a thing about what Edwin's life was like while he was living—he kept his distance and paid the bills—but all of a sudden after Edwin's gone, his daddy's some kind of expert witness. He said I was after money. Said it in court, his hand on the Bible and all. If I'd been after money, seems like I would have married him instead of killing him."

"And after all that happened, you went back there again?"

"To punish myself some more, I guess. And my little brother was there still, I wanted to keep my eye on him. He ended up leaving before I did, though. He's eighteen."

"How old are you?"

Reka realized, too late, that she might be caught in a lie. She saw no way out of another at first, but when she turned to Jake he had fixed her with those generous green eyes of his and she understood that she'd found someone she could never lie to.

"Twenty-five. I'm wanting to go to college, but I haven't had the money. I was told by the guy who hired me that I look younger than I am. He let me have a go at it, so long as I promised not to tell anybody I'm not really a student. So much for that."

"Hey, it doesn't bother me. I won't tell anyone. I imagine you make a lot more when you say you're training to be a teacher."

"I plan to be one someday."

"You'd make a good one.'"

They sipped their drinks. Jake finished his and went to the kitchen to pour another. When he returned she said, "Why doesn't Maggie like it here?"

Jake stared at the fire, took a healthy gulp of whiskey.

"We don't have any nephews," he said.

She hates it because of that? Eureka decided she was even more spoiled than she seemed, but she said nothing, only nodded.

"The room you're staying in," said Jake, "belonged to our son, Heath."

"Oh," said Reka. She felt bad then, though she wasn't yet convinced that Maggie wasn't spoiled, or at least fragile, easily bruised. "She wants to live closer to him?"

Jake attempted a laugh that ran out of steam and ended up a botched sigh.

"That's what drove him away in the first place, her wanting to be close to him. She could not let the boy alone. Not from the time he was born until the day he left, when he was sixteen."

"He ran away?"

"Three years ago last August."

"Because of her?"

Jake got up to stir the fire. He busied himself with poker and shovel, and she could see that he, like the men she'd grown up with, like her father and whoever she would have married had she stayed in Trent, found solace in work, only in work. Needed something to do with his hands that would leaven the weight of words. Houses painted, fields cleared, fences mended by men made busy by the intolerably unsaid.

"She worried over everything he did. She picked his friends for him. Disapproved of his girlfriend. Fought with his teachers, the ones she wasn't satisfied with, which there weren't many she thought a thing of, and those she liked she annoyed so bad they ended up taking it out on Heath. The boy got to where he hated her. He would tell me that, tell me he hated his mother. But I would not let him hate her. He could get mad at her, God knows I would have done the same thing—I did get mad at her, still do—but he could not go around thinking those kinds of thoughts about his own mother. I wouldn't allow it."

Jake replaced the fireplace tools and looked around the room for his drink. When he found it he drank and sighed, rested his forehead on the mantle and said with his back to her, "Have you ever heard of such a thing? A man telling his son what he could and could not think?"

"It happens," she said. "A lot, I guess."

"Your parents might tell you what to believe, but not what to think."

Reka tried to imagine her own father telling her or Randall what to think. That part of them he left alone, as if he had a tall enough order filling their stomachs, the most important feature of the anatomy to him. Perhaps in his own way he tried to offer something for the heart. She would allow him that now, for in his terse and raw way he was a tender, exacting man. And a drunk, she forced herself to remember, and not above beating his youngest son purple with a belt buckle. She thought of the last time she'd seen him, coming upon him curled up drunk on the floor of his shack. He'd seemed so harmless and shrunken that afternoon, such a sliver of what he had been to her when she was younger, even up until the day she left for prison. Easier to talk to. She wondered if, had she stayed, he would have finally opened up to her, if age and infirmity would allow her access to those places he kept so vigilantly to himself.

"Heath used to beg me to take him along when I went out on the job. She didn't like to let him go anywhere, and it got to the point where I spent all my hours trying to talk her into letting him be. Just be: be a boy, be idle, be bad, be in trouble if that's what it took for him to learn something. But she wouldn't listen to me. To hear her talk, I was the one messing him up. She said I was remote and selfish, a coldhearted bastard. I got to where I believed her, and finally I just gave up. Started staying later at work. Sometimes after the crews went home I would drive around the mountains for a couple hours just to avoid going home."

"So he just left? Without a word?"

He didn't seem to hear her. With his head still resting on the mantel, he said, "I thought I was doing the right thing not crossing her. I thought it would make things worse, the two of us at odds, one letting him fight his own battles, the other making those battles her own. Seemed like to me we ought to at least pretend to be of one mind. It's the way I was raised, and I did not really even question it, until he was long gone of course."

He turned to face her, and she saw the accumulated weight of worry in his eyes.

"To answer your question, yes, there were words. His mother came home one day—she must have been running late or something, because she always made it a point to pick the boy up from school—he'd come on home on his own, and was upstairs in his room with his girl. Melanie. She's older by a couple of years, a nice girl if you ask me, a little lazy maybe. She didn't do much besides paint her face and it seemed like the other kids thought it was kind of strange, a girl going steady with a boy two years younger. That's the one thing Maggie claimed she had against her, her being older, but of course if she would have been Heath's same age, it wouldn't have made a difference. Maggie would have rejected anyone Heath brought home.

"Maggie walked in on them up there. They were messing around, like kids do. Hell, like adults do, like Maggie and I did when she was in high school, for that matter. But Maggie lost her head, called the girl things she ought not to of, especially in front of the boy. I wasn't there, I only have what Maggie told me to go on, never did get to hear Heath's side of it.

"Maggie threatened to have Melanie arrested for corrupting a minor or some such silliness. As if the boy was a victim. She ordered her the hell out of the house, and Heath tried to leave with her, walk her home, I guess. But Maggie grabbed him and wouldn't let him go and Heath, though he was, is, a gentle boy, burned up inside but not at all violent. . . . Heath beat the living hell out of his mother."

Jake spoke without inflection, matter-of-factly, as if he had gone over this so many times that all the emotion had been leached out, yet Reka noticed a vein bulging in his neck, blood pumping at the memory of this day.

"I chose that night to come home later than usual, scared of walking in on what I should have stopped a couple years earlier. Found her on the kitchen floor, door wide open. He beat her bad enough, bare-handed—but she'd gone and taken a paring knife to her wrists and hacked away at them, not enough to do much but scratches, but still. What a sight. She probably could have gotten up and called the office, told them to come find me, but instead she stayed there on the floor all afternoon, holding her breath, waiting for him to come back to her. He didn't and I did. First thing when I walked in the door, before I could even help her up, she was on me to go after him."

Jake stared at a spot on the carpet, as if envisioning the scene he came home to find that day three years earlier.

"I didn't go. Then or later. Won't ever. Can't see what good it would do, bringing him back if he doesn't want to be here. It was too late for me to do anything, I'd let it go on too long. See, she really did love the boy, and I never believed anything bad could come from a mother's love for her only child. I saw plenty of badness, and I did try to say something to her now and again, but it didn't seem like the kind of thing that would end like it did. And what could I have done short of keeping the two of them apart?"

Jake was silent for an intolerable amount of time, during which Reka tried to imagine being loved so much it hurt. She had nothing in her experience to compare Jake's story to—she'd never known a soul who suffered from too much attention, except for Edwin Keane maybe, and Edith Keane's love for her son seemed so conditional and selfish that it hardly applied. She tried to imagine being smothered by a parent's love. Or anyone—a lover choosing her friends, her clothes, sharing every part of her life, even that most private part where she spent most of her hours, waking and dreaming. It couldn't happen—she could not imagine anyone wanting that much from her—and given what she'd known in this world, it did not seem such a tragedy to her.

"She never said a word to me about him," she said, because she felt she had to say something. "Of course I don't know her, really. I mean, I just met her and all. But she does talk to me about stuff sometimes."

"That's one reason I'm glad you're here—it makes it easier on Maggie, having someone around. She's better since you came to town."

Reka held her tongue, did not say what she thought, tried not to even think it: She did not want to take the place of the banished son. She liked it better when the nephews came to stay in that room, which now seemed haunted by a ghost forever visible, present in every toy and book, the kid-sized desk built lovingly into the gable, the skinny, eave-slanted closet where her dresses hung. She wanted Jake to name another reason he was glad she was here, one that had nothing to do with ghosts, the past, his wife.

She wished she hadn't brought up Maggie at all, yet she liked knowing that he would choose to stay in this place even if it made his wife miserable. His refusal to drift off somewhere else to appease his unappeasable wife struck her as noble and right. She thought of herself back home in Trent, and told herself there were things she could learn from this man.

"Maggie never came right out and blamed me for it, but I know she thinks it's my fault that he's gone, like I could have stopped him. Sometimes I wish she would have blamed me, I wish she still would. Instead she talks all the time about how much she hates Red Fork, as if the mountains are to blame, the clouds that settle over town sometimes, the trees I make my living off of."

For a moment Reka wanted to feel sorry for him. She could think of good reason to—all it took was to imagine being estranged from her little brother—but she could not bring herself to pity him. Jake might have taken on more than his share of guilt over what had happened, he might blame himself for things he ought to leave alone, but he seemed the least self-pitying person she'd ever met.

Of course, he remained with Maggie even though it was obviously torturing him. She could have dismissed him for that alone, and it did make her question just how respectable he was, but she saw that this was the only way he knew how to deal with his losses. Not until years after he died did Reka understand how much Edwin Keane relished his martyrdom. With his unlaced work boots, his work-roughened hands and woodsy odor, his childlike attachment to his native terrain, Jake seemed as far from Edwin as it was possible to be.

Reka had never considered what she wanted in a man since Edwin, as she hadn't really been looking for one. Sitting across the room from Jake, sneaking looks when he rose to poke the fire, she reminded herself she wasn't looking now. But being alone with Jake made her consider things she hadn't thought of, like whether he was the complete opposite of the only man she'd ever loved, and if it was too easy, too predictable to fall for him because he wasn't likely to quote some German philospher in the middle of dinner or end up lying in bed for a couple of years listening to jazz in a continuous and debilitating morphine dream. He would never do any of the things Edwin had done, but might he not leave her all the same?

Reka got up and put her drink down. She grabbed a pillow off the couch and lay down in front of the fire so she could watch the flames without having to make eye contact with Jake. He seemed to understand that she did not want to talk, though he sat down on the rug close behind her.

She was confused, and wanted only to stop time long enough to think. Finding a lover was the last thing she'd come west for, and even if she'd been looking, she'd know enough to stay away from the husband of a woman who'd befriended her, let her into her house and made her dinner. True, Maggie wasn't who she pretended to be, but neither was Reka, and just because Maggie drove her son away and neglected her husband was no reason for Reka to let herself go where she felt herself wanting to go.

Was he real? How could he fill up a room with nothing but his acceptance of her, with patience and ease? She felt those things in the air, *heard* them humming above the crackling and whistling of the fire, his steadiest qualities allowing her to ponder all sorts of things she had not thought of in years.

"I had a lot of men after I got out of jail," she said after a while. "Lot of men get suddenly interested in you if you do time. I don't think women find that sort of thing attractive, so don't go getting yourself arrested to find out."

"I promise."

"You'd go crazy locked up," she said. "It's harder if you love to be outdoors. Most people who end up in prison spend their lives in tiny apartments or bars or the backseats of cars. Not much of an adjustment to a cell. Anyway, these guys I went out with, all of them asked me the same thing. They wanted to know if I slept with the guards."

While she waited for his response, she thought of what Edwin would have said to this, decided he would have pointed out that this was an understandable curiosity if not a terribly original one. He would have said something not-so-slightly autobiographical about the way men needed to dirty up sex, and she would have accepted his opinion as fact. But Jake said nothing at all—he only waited and breathed—and she knew without looking back that he knew what she was up to, knew she was testing him.

His silence both pleased her and prodded her to keep going.

"Most of these men were married. The single ones asked me about the guards, too, but they didn't pursue it, they accepted it when I told them no, I did not sleep with any prison guards. Oh, okay, they said, and they left it alone and never brought it up again. But the married ones didn't believe me. They kept asking, as if they could wear me down, and no matter how many times I told them no, they always thought I was lying. They didn't always say so, but I could always tell. What is it about married men that makes them think everyone's lying to them?"

"You want to know if you can trust me," he said.

"No," she said. "That's not what this story is about."

"Okay," he said. "But you can't scare me away from you."

"I don't have to. I can scare myself easily enough."

"Oh, I'm not saying I wouldn't be scared."

Reka smiled, but at the fire. She wanted to turn to him, to see the expression on his face, but instead she let the heat blush her cheeks, and she was still smiling and couldn't stop smiling, as his answer pleased her and made her want him all the more.

"What would you be scared of?"

"That's not what this conversation is about."

She turned to face him then.

"No?"

"Not anymore. I'm talking now, and I don't see the point in listing all the things that might scare me. We're both smart enough to figure them out, and listing them might make them even scarier. I'd rather talk about how I'd do it anyway, despite the scary parts, and how the scary parts might turn out to be the most exciting parts, not that I'm up for doing something scary just to make my life more exciting."

"Good," she said, but she didn't say why. She assumed he knew, after all she'd told him about Edwin and prison, that she was not in the market for mere excitement.

"Any more stories?" he asked.

"Not unless you have one you want to tell me."

"I told you all the stories I have."

"That's bad," she said, wagging a finger in mock reprimand.

"I know. Fortunately, it's not true. There are more, but can't they wait?"

She rolled across the floor to him in answer, rested her head on his shoulder. She didn't want to *think* any further, didn't want to talk around it, either. Didn't she deserve him, even her idea of him? He bent to kiss her and she let him, but after a quarter hour of kisses and caresses, when it came time to shed her clothes, she would not let him help, for they weren't her clothes, and she did not want him to touch them.

They slept that night by the fire, on a pallet of blankets, and they slept little, in between bouts of lovemaking made tense by the awkwardness of their first time together, the anxious need to get it right on the first try. They did not get it right on the second try, nor the third, and finally they slept. It was chilly in the house she woke to, the fire having died out in the night; she lay beside him as he slept, reliving last night's passions. She wouldn't have trusted it if it were the most satisfying love she'd ever made, but despite its being only competent, there was enough discovery and surprise to make her want to memorize it, an indelible landmark she could forever and easily recall.

While Jake slept, she listened to the snow-muted world outside. When she was younger, before she went to prison, she might easily have convinced herself that the quiet was summoned by their intimacy, as was the bluish glow of the sun upon the snow-covered lawns. Or even the snow itself, an act of nature that caught the rest of the world by surprise and isolated them in their shared forbearance, brought them together in a room lit and warmed only by fire. But she knew it was only a freak storm in a place where such storms were common enough not to be thought of as freakish. She had just stumbled into this weather, and wasn't fool enough to claim it as her own doing.

"You can't work today, you know that," said Jake when he was awake and scrambling around in the kitchen, fixing her breakfast she was reluctant to tell him she wasn't hungry for.

"I thought you said the snow would be gone by noon."

"It will, but it'll still be messy out. You don't want to be trudging around in the slush all day. I can't work, either. We'll take the day off. I want to show you some of the country. All you've seen since you've been here is Red Fork proper. My uncle owns a cabin outside of town. You wouldn't believe the view from up there."

She accepted his offer even though it made her feel guilty; as eager as she was to spend more time with him, she did not want anything to get in the way of her plans. She was here to make money for college. This wasn't a vacation. And she wasn't used to being coddled—the men she'd been with since Edwin had been as eager to part with her in the morning as she had with them. She wasn't sure what she'd done to deserve such adoration. She wondered if he was merely responding to her patience with him earlier, if all he really wanted was an audience. She'd been happy to oblige, as his story turned out to be as interesting as it was sad, but the reward for her attention—his gentle but obvious doting—made her uneasy.

Yet she agreed to take the day off, and when they got out of town, reached the curly roads rising wildly toward the line of craggy, snow-frosted peaks, she was glad she'd agreed. They packed a picnic, and Reka once again wrapped herself in Maggie's clothes. The day warmed quickly, and soon she was uncomfortable in the bristly wool, that much more eager to shed layers.

High above town, Jake turned off the highway onto a dirt logging trail. His Willy's jeep traveled easily through the snow. On a hillside overlooking a valley so wide and deep it seemed painted to Reka, he parked the car but made no move to get out.

In silence they watched clouds curtain the sunny valley. Reka found a river snaking through the valley, frothy with runoff from melting snow. If only that river could run through Red Fork it would be livable, a place where she could stay. She imagined this stream diverted so that it ran through town, rerouted there for her own comfort and security, and Jake's, too—she wasn't the only one in need of another way out—but way too soon she realized what was happening here.

Another Trent. More beautiful perhaps, higher and more picturesque, the landscape free from the malevolent undergrowth that wrapped itself around everything in sight, wrestling old barns and abandoned cars and even people to the ground, tethering even ideas and dreams to the earth, but Trent nonetheless. She could not hesitate here, could not allow herself to linger. Yet even as she realized this, she acknowledged that this place had changed overnight, that it was no longer some riverless town where she'd come to make money, but home to the man who, as she sat there plotting her escape, took her hand away from her lap and planted it in his own.

Breaking the silence felt to her as disruptive as dumping a load of trash down the pristine hillside, but she had questions.

"What are these mountains called?"

"Those are the Crazy Mountains."

"You're kidding."

"I'd go crazy if I couldn't see them out my window every morning."

"You don't think you'll ever leave here?" Again she felt as if she were violating the moment by talking, bringing up Maggie, leaving, but here was a person who did not care to leave a place that had obviously imprisoned him. This was a curiosity too great for her to ignore.

"I left," he said. "Went farther than most ever get. Across the ocean. But when the war was over I came back because I chose to. My mother died before I could get home, see. There was no reason why I had to come back here. It wasn't as if I had business to take care of or anything. Hell, I could have moved anywhere in the country, could have stayed in England if I'd wanted to. But here I am."

"And here you'll stay?"

He looked at her. "You think leaving would do me some good?"

"I guess I see Maggie's point."

Trying to see Red Fork through Maggie's eyes, Reka thought of how, after Edwin died, she could not walk through town without remembering things he'd said, hearing his voice. She'd first seen him

in the courtyard of the Episcopal church, where she'd been gathering leaves for a botany project. Randall had come along to help,
though he was no help at all. He spent the whole afternoon climbing trees and yelling things at her from above. *Hello down there*, he
said, over and over, and when she was released from prison and
came back home, every time she passed by the church she heard his
crazy call and spotted Edwin lurking in the shadows of a giant magnolia, watching her, linked to her by Randall's call.

It must be like this for Maggie. Every tree in her yard rustling
under Heath's weight as he climbed or swung from a tire. She tried
to sympathize with her, but instead ended up resenting Maggie's
presence in this time which would last about as long as the snow on
the ground beneath them.

Reka reached for Jake's other hand, retrieved it from the steering
wheel; clasping both in her hands, she brought them back to her
lap.

"It wasn't your fault, what happened between them."

"Everything is your fault if you let it be. And I'm guilty of letting
it be. Almost like I want it to be. Like I accept the blame for what
happened just so I can stay here and suffer."

Maybe he is a martyr. She did not want to see him as one, and she
found herself searching for reasons not to.

"And Maggie thinks leaving will make it all go away? She's just as
guilty, seems like to me."

"What do you mean?"

"She thinks if she leaves, things will get better, right? That if she
doesn't have to look out her window every morning and see these
crazy mountains, she'll be able to get over it. That's no more the
truth than you thinking you need to stay here to punish yourself for
what happened."

Searching out the river, following its bends far below, measuring
the distance to town, Reka wondered if this really was another
Trent. Maybe Trent was something she'd brought along with her,

someplace that would color everywhere she went until she learned to leave it behind.

"Let's don't talk about her anymore," he said.

But Reka wasn't through. "You won't ever leave her, will you?"

Jake retrieved his hand from her lap and gripped the steering wheel as if he was entering heavy traffic. "Of course I've thought about it, I think about it all the time, but I can't see how any decent person could do something like that. You lose one person, so you give up the only other family you've got? I wasn't raised to be that selfish."

"You haven't lost your son forever. He'll come back."

"No, he won't. And I can't even say I want him to, really. See, she'd do it again. It's the way she is: she tried to do it to me and I would not let her. The truth is, I let her take him so she'd leave me alone. Sacrificed the boy for what I used to think was freedom. That's something I've got to live with, and if he came back here and it happened all over again, good God. I don't know what I'd do then."

Reka said nothing. She thought of the ways he'd contradicted himself, and started to point it out to him—how he claimed it would be selfish to give up Maggie for Heath and in the next breath admitted that he'd sacrificed Heath out of his own selfish need to be unencumbered—but she suspected he knew already the various ways in which his past proved paradoxical. He'd designed it that way, she thought, just as we all do out of instinct and need.

"I know where he is," said Jake. "Melanie, his old girlfriend, told me. I even know where he works. In Seattle. Slinging fish to tourists at the public market downtown. They all want to go to the cities now. He and Melanie took a bus that very afternoon, only she came back here as soon as she got hungry. She might have been older, but she didn't turn out to be more mature. Then again, she had no reason to run. Her father's dead, her mother let her run wild, bought her clothes and gave her a place to sleep for free. Why should she want to live hand to mouth in some gray city where she doesn't know a soul?"

"You've never tried to contact him?"

"I like knowing where he is," said Jake. "He and Melanie keep in touch, and if he moved she'd tell me. I'd like to always know where he is in case something happens to one of us. But I'm not going after him, and I can't imagine he'll ever come back on his own.'

"Let's eat," she said, to change the subject. His mood was shifting, his sadness looming like the peaks outside the window, and she did not want to risk losing any of him during the few hours they had together.

He led her to the cabin, where they built a fire in the stove and spent the afternoon on the floor. This time it was better. Not perfect—not without false starts and dead ends—but building gradually to a merging of friction and rhythm. She thought of how essential these two elements were to both body and spirit, how seldom it is that they come together in even an approximate coherence. As they lay together afterward, she realized how common these two elements were to almost everything she knew—friendships, family, work, love—and lots of things she did not know.

She thought of mentioning this to Jake, but she did not want to ruin the mood by analyzing their lovemaking in a way he might find pretentious. She'd save it for Randall, this idea. Jake was quiet and still, and she could tell from his touch how long it had been for him; his fingers, his breathing, the feel of him lingering and shrinking inside her as if he did not ever want to separate his body from hers, all told her that he and Maggie were no longer lovers. She knew better than to launch into a breakdown of the essential components of sex to a man who has not had any in a good long while. She knew better than to bring Maggie up again, yet she could not help wondering how she'd face her now.

This time he broke his silence. What was it was like, he wanted to know, her time in prison.

She told him about the women who had shared her cell. Iona, who cleaved her husband with a hoe one night when he came home from a card game with two of his drunk buddies he had promised a piece of his fine-looking wife. Lucinda, who had left her small town in the coastal plain for Baltimore, where she'd developed a serious codeine habit that had finally landed her in an abandoned car on the outskirts of the town she thought she'd left forever. She was convicted of trying to rob a drugstore with the spray nozzle of a garden hose.

"It wasn't as bad for me as for most of them in there," she said. "A rich old lady from the town nearby came out to visit. She kind of adopted me as her project. She brought me books and fixed it so I could take courses through the mail to finish high school, paid for it and cleared it with the warden, and if it weren't for her I don't know that I'd be able to come out of that place and stay out of it."

"Come on," he said. "You're not a criminal."

"I know that. But a couple years in a place like that will make you so bitter that you come out thinking you're owed the world. I can see why somebody'd come out of jail, walk into a store, point a gun at the clerk and take whatever they pleased. Doesn't surprise me in the least, the things people do when they get out of jail."

"It seems to me like you've done a good job of putting all that behind you," he said.

She felt her whole body stiffen at this statement, felt affronted by the innocence and presumptuousness of it. He meant well, she knew that; he meant only to reassure her, to make her feel as if it was no big thing to him, her past. But how could she put it behind her? She wasn't sure she ever wanted to fully; it was too much a part of her now, and as close as she felt to him, as attracted as she was to his gentleness and his quiet resolve, she wondered if she wasn't fooling herself to think that a man who said things like this could ever make her happy.

"I guess I do a pretty good job of acting like it," she said.

He was quiet for a few minutes, then said, "Did I make you mad?"

"Not at all," she said, but she was certain her tone gave her away. Look, she wanted to say, I would much prefer you to respond to my war stories with one of your own, grisly particulars of the carnage and the futility. She wasn't used to being treated like a survivor, someone who had managed to "put things behind her." It was obvious to her that he was as vulnerable and confused about the dissolution of his family as she was about her own past, and she saw no good in pretending wisdom.

"I didn't mean to," he said, "and I'm sorry if I did." He pulled her over to him then, rolled her on top of him, and this time she orchestrated the mix of rhythmic friction, and the blend she pitched was urgent and forceful, more a slamming away toward resolution than a meandering, complacent search for it. It made her feel better to come so violently, and to feel in his simultaneous release a helpless surrender that leavened the naive hopes of his lingering compliment. Look, she said with her body, there are some things you can't get over, and if perspective is possible at all, you have to pound away at it, sweat and ache and strain for it. You can't expect it to magically arrive, or to assume, just because you've kept your lungs full of air during some unendurable tragedy, that you've come out on top.

She felt better, as if she'd taught him a lesson that would make it easier to be with him.

And it was easy to be with him during the next three days, which they spent stealing love when they could. Jake went to work late and reluctantly—Reka had to lead him to the door with both hands, claiming she had her own work to do. During the day Reka walked the streets, knocked on doors, but she was too distracted to sell anything, and even when she was inside some lonely woman's parlor making her pitch she took care to find a seat with a view of the street, where she could watch for Jake's jeep. Twice a day she spotted it, trolling the neighborhoods in search of her; twice a day she tossed her sample case in the backseat and climbed in and sat on her hands until they reached the house, where as soon as they crossed the threshold she began to undress him, and herself. At night they slept on the floor of the living room even though the sun had returned and snow seemed a distant and unfathomable secret. It was July again, early summer. Hard even to imagine the Crazies frosted with snow.

There was no more talk of ruptured families, wars or prison. She was glad to have had those conversations—she needed them to make sure he was real—but she was just as glad to lapse into the idle chatter of infatuation. They claimed words and phrases as their own, repeating them until they were frayed and silly. This was something she'd done with Edwin also, and with no one else since, and though Jake was not nearly so verbal as Edwin or Randall (and this was one thing that attracted her to him), he played the game well. He told her once, in a moment of postcoital rapture, that she reminded him of rain. Thereafter every conversation was studded with meteorological references, self-conscious and extravagant. She came like a thunderstorm, his lips and loins were parched by drought. He hummed-sang an Indian rant chant. He played along, but she knew he was only playing to please her, that unlike Edwin, who had appropriated words and phrases only ironically, Jake was not-so-secretly sincere. He really did think of her as rain, elemental and vital and replenishing. Despite her skepticism, her tendency to lace the references with sarcasm, she fell for it, and felt herself falling for him.

On the day of Maggie's return, a week after the snowstorm, Reka worked well past supper. Forced herself inside houses with a pushiness that seemed more Cecelia Bannister's style than her own. It did not pay, for the women she visited seemed to sense her underlying anxiety, seemed to understand her desperate need to keep herself busy, distracted. She sat with her back to any window facing the street. Still, the whoosh of every passing car filled her with desire, and also with fear, for she did not want to believe that it was over.

Maggie appeared different from the lonely housewife who had hovered over Reka at mealtimes, making sure she had enough to eat. Her trip seemed to have changed her, perhaps because she no longer had to lie about the existence of this nephew who might soon come to stay in the shrine to boyhood where Reka slept. It was dusk when Reka returned—she had hoped they would have retired to their room, or that Maggie, tired from her trip, would have gone to bed already—but she found them sitting up in the living room, chatting. They appeared to be the kind of comfortably married couple who had learned to talk about the mundane occurrences of their days with sincere interest, as if even the description of meals and discussion of debts outstanding were profound declarations of the two of them against the rest of the world.

Reka felt like the rest of the world. She sat with them only long enough to be sociable, staring sadly into the fireplace, at the remnant ashes from that night of freakish and ephemeral snow.

But she and Jake weren't over yet. Maggie was so distracted by her nephew's birth that she paid Reka little attention now; obviously she wanted her to leave, and often looked at her as though she wasn't sure who she was and why she was sitting across the table from her. Reka knew she *should* leave—not only this house, but this town, for even though there was territory yet to cover and she had agreed to stay for the summer, she'd sold only enough to cover her expenses since Maggie's return. She would have sold more had she not climbed into the jeep each afternoon for the two-hour trip out to the cabin.

"I was wrong," he said to her one afternoon a month after Maggie's return.

"About?"

"When I told you I'd never leave her. I would, now. She's different. This nephew thing, it's helped her. She's latched onto him now, as if he's her grandson or something. She's going to be okay without me, I can see that now."

Again, he'd said something that pleased and worried her at once. Did she want him to leave Maggie? She tried to tell herself that she, too, had been wrong. About Jake, his lack of self-pity, his inherent and unshakeable decency. Maybe he was as selfish as she was. But would leaving Maggie be indecent? She liked to think there were circumstances in which anything you did was permissible, where impunity was available to you if your highest aim was the solace of love. And as soon as she settled into this thought, suspicion arrived. I like to think a lot of things, she thought, stretched out naked and suddenly modest on the floor next to naked and immodest Jake.

"Let's go," she said, reaching for her dress. "I have to sell some books."

"You're not listening," he said.

"Sorry," she lied. "Can't we talk about it later? You need to get back to work yourself. What if they call home looking for you?"

"What if they do? I don't care anymore. I'll tell her the truth. I'd rather tell her the truth than sit with her every night and pretend to be her husband."

"So now that she's feeling better, you can dump her?"

She regretted saying it as soon as she saw how he tried to ignore it. His face was slack, his eyes blank, but she could see the hurt she'd caused.

"Maybe we *should* go," he said. "You're right, I have to get back to work. And yes, we'll talk later. But I won't give you up even if you say things like that. You can't drive me away with words."

On the ride back to town she considered this. It thrilled her, his defiance of words, his allegiance to her no matter what came out of her mouth. Twice she came close to telling him to keep going, straight out of town, out of Montana even, on into Idaho, Washington, to the edge of the continent. She sighed twice instead.

"Wonder who that is," Jake said as they pulled up in the drive.

They'd agreed to pretend he came upon her on the street, offered her a ride home, not that they really needed this lie, for Maggie was too absorbed in her new life to be suspicious. Reka searched the street to see whom he was talking about, but saw no one.

"Who?"

Jake nodded at the strange car ahead of them in the drive. It took Reka a few seconds to place Bob Smart's coupe.

"Oh God," she said.

"Someone you don't want to see, I take it."

"The man who hired me."

"The married guy? The one you told me you . . ."

"Yes, him. What's he doing here?"

"I can go in alone, get rid of him. No one's seen us yet."

Reka looked over at him. He was willing to do what he could for her, but it just wasn't enough. She remembered wishing earlier for a river, only a river. Too late she understood how a river contradicts itself, how it never stays and never leaves.

"No," she said. "You wouldn't be able to get rid of him, and besides, he might have some news for me."

"He could have called."

"Maybe it was news he couldn't give over the phone."

"Are you expecting such?"

Jake took her hand, turned it over, ran his fingertips over her palm. She feared this might be the last time she would feel his touch; she resisted the urge to kiss him right there in the driveway.

"Thank you," she said.

"For what?"

She pushed open the door, swung her legs out onto the pavement. "We need to get out now. They might have seen us."

Bob Smart and Maggie sat stiffly in the living room. The way they turned to look as she came through the door suggested they'd been waiting longer than either of them could stand. Reka stepped into a silence intolerable as a blaze. It was hard for her to breathe in the heavy quiet of the room. She looked past them at the hearth, which had been swept clean, yet still smelled crisply of ashes and soot.

"Hello, Miss Speight," said Bob Smart. He pronounced it *spite*; she smiled at this, but bitterly, as she knew already what he was there to tell her. She tried not to look at Maggie, but her gaze was as magnetic as it had been when she'd first knocked on her door, though scornful now instead of eager, needy, hopeful.

Jake had come in the back door and entered the living room with an innocent what-a-surprise-we-have-company smile on the face that minutes before had been tense with worry and longing. He was a good actor, Reka realized; he could let this go on as long as she would let him, despite what he had said earlier in the cabin about hating himself for pretending. She found herself more disturbed by his sudden presence in the room than she had been by the sight of Bob Smart's car, which she took as proof of how much she had fallen for him. She watched him suffer through introductions and a few seconds of awkward small talk, and when the thick silence returned, she noticed Bob Smart watching her watch him.

"Can I speak to you for a moment?" he said to her.

"We'll leave you two alone," said Maggie, but before she could rise from her chair Reka said, "No, don't get up. We'll go outside."

On the porch, Bob Smart said, "That was nice of you. I can see you don't want to put her out any more than you have already."

"You didn't tell her, did you?"

"I sure did."

"Why? What difference does it make, her knowing that?"

"I believe she has a right to know what she's got sleeping under her roof. I'd want to know if I was playing host to a convicted murderer."

"You really trusted me, didn't you?"

"Matter of fact, I did. I don't know why I did, since you weren't exactly the kind of girl I'd want to bring home to Sunday dinner. But I did trust you, until I got a call from that little brother of yours. He's quite a talker."

"You can't expect me to believe that."

"I don't care what you believe. We don't hire ex-convicts to go around impersonating college students. You might have fooled that woman, but she would have found out about you and the hubby sooner than you think. See, there's a reason why we don't hire people like you. I had a little talk with Cecelia Bannister this afternoon. She's the one who told me where to find you. She also told me about you and the husband."

"She doesn't know anything about me."

"You're denying it?"

"My brother would never have told you that."

Bob Smart laughed. "Then you're not denying it."

Reka looked beyond at a flash of movement behind a window. Maggie, certainly; Jake would not care to watch, would not allow himself to watch. She hoped he would leave before she went back in to get her things. She prayed that he would have enough sense to leave.

"I never told you because you never asked. If you remember—and I imagine you've found a way to forget—nobody asked me to fill out an application, and the interview was kind of informal."

"I remember it pretty well, thanks," he said. "For instance, I remember saying to you that I had no idea who you were, that for all I knew you could have just gotten out of prison."

"That was a statement, not a direct question."

"See why I can't have you selling books? First of all, you're going around acting like a college girl, but you don't think like some college girl. You think like you've spent some time in a court of law."

"So I'll say I'm studying to be a lawyer."

"I'll give you a ride to the train station," he said.

"Fine," she said, and she went in to collect her things. Back in the kitchen she heard them arguing, Maggie's voice loud and desperate, Jake's tamped low with a calm desperation only she could recognize. Upstairs Reka found her clothes already packed, her suitcase by the door. She tried and failed to summon anger at the thought of Maggie going through her clothes; after all, she'd worn Maggie's clothes, let her husband take them off her body. Looking around the room at the cowboy bed, the shelves of Hardy Boys mysteries and the model planes, she wondered if Jake would find the courage to leave Maggie now that she was gone. She wondered if he would look around the cabin where they'd spent their afternoons and see, instead of dingy furniture, cobwebs and dust, instead of deer and elk heads and some relative's ancient bowling trophies, Reka as palpably present as his son in the room where she stood.

She found herself rummaging through drawers she'd never bothered to open before, searching idly for something to remember Jake by. In a desk drawer she found photos of Heath, who looked so much like his father that Reka at first thought it was a teenage Jake standing on the shoulder of a mountain road, the Crazies looming beyond. It was only when she noticed the date on the photograph that she realized it was Heath, whose hair was slicked and trained in the style of a few years ago. After staring at it for a full minute, Reka slipped the photo in the pocket of her dress.

Downstairs, she went to the kitchen to say goodbye, to thank them for their hospitality, which seemed proper even considering the circumstances—they might treat her like trash, but she would never act that way—but they were not there. She heard voices from behind the door of their bedroom, and twice she held her hand aloft to knock, but both times she chickened out. I can write them, she thought, returning to the parlor, retrieving her bag. I can write him and say goodbye, at least. What right do I have to write to her? Anything I could say to her—Dear Maggie, Sincerely, Thank You, I'm indebted—even the most tiresome and familiar espistolary conventions would be hypocritical, spiteful, wrong.

"Take me to the bus station," she told Bob Smart as he backed out of the drive. "I don't have enough money for the train after I pay you what I owe you."

"We might be able to work out a little deal," he said.

"I believe I've had enough of your charity."

"Seems to me like you did have enough. More than enough, I'd say."

"About my brother," she said.

"Quite the talker, I'm telling you. Smart boy, too. He doesn't sound like a welder to me."

"What did he say? Where is he?"

"We didn't get personal. He shared with me some choice details about your past and I told him you had gone to Minnesota and were to be assigned a territory by Olaf Torkelson of our Duluth office. I gave him Olaf's number, then I called Olaf immediately to find out where you were. Came out here as quick as I could get away, before you got both of us in a whole lot of trouble. I hope for your sake you didn't tell anybody."

"Why would I? I doubt those choice details of my past would have fit in real well with what I'm trying to do out here, which is raise money for college. But back to my brother . . ."

"Don't go thinking you need to bump him off, too," said Bob. "It was an accident. He didn't mean to get you in trouble. He just thanked me for giving you a chance. Said not many would have taken the risk."

"That's all?"

"That's all, I swear. But it was enough for me to get interested, do some checking up. So if you're thinking of blaming him, well, you needn't. It was an innocent enough mistake: He assumed you told me the truth about yourself. Y'all must not know each other so well."

Reka considered this as they pulled into the parking lot of the bus station. We used to know each other better than we knew anyone else, she thought. She would rather believe they still did, which meant doubting Bob Smart's claim that it was an innocent, trusting remark. Maybe Randall wanted her back. Pa told him she was gone and he knew he couldn't talk her into coming back, so he did what he could to force her return.

"Anyway, if you're looking to blame someone, you might look in a mirror."

"I guess if I need advice on morals, I'll find someone else to tell me how to act."

He got out first, opened the trunk, handed her suitcase over. When she gave him her sample case and paid him what she owed him, he counted the bills, handed a part of it back.

"Don't bother. Your advice was worth so much to me, I'd hate to take your money."

Bob Smart laughed. "I did trust you, girl. I sure did. But, hell, it wasn't enough to lie to those nice people. You had to go and try to split them apart."

She turned away from him then, for the thought of reminding him again of his hypocrisy made her tired. She did not turn back until he called out to her, but even then she did not really see him when he told her, oh yeah, there was one more thing her brother wanted him to pass along. Her father? He died.

Four

And then he was free to leave the place his sister had grown to hate for its slow midnight torpor, its invisible, relentless weight, its bugs, heat, dust, syllables of words stretched out into ignorant song, neckless old triple-jowled preachers, earth-colored serpents coiled and nervous in the woodpile. Walking out of town he thought of all the things she said she hated about it, the list she'd made on crinkly prison-issued paper, and he added some things and subtracted others and said them all aloud, a chant to bring fortune to his search for her.

He kept his thumb to himself, stood immobilized on the shoulder by the September humidity. Until he got out of Trent no one would stop for him and he didn't mind the walking, kept his pace slow, even, taking a last look around for the sake of some night in the next millennium when he finally got back around to remembering the place. He saw a tire-kneaded carcass staining the sun-dyed macadam. He kicked a chunk of this macadam and remembered putting a similar-sized piece in his mouth when they first paved the country road that led away from Speed's store to his father's farm.

You could chew on it like bubble gum and it left your mouth gritty and black. Randall kept his eyes out for things to remember. Driving a tractor with his head turned right around behind him as if it had been put on that way in the first place was a man named Lacey Houseman, rumored to be a hermaphrodite. Randall waved goodbye at Lacey Houseman's head and wondered if hermaphrodites existed elsewhere in this world, or were they local and was Lacey Houseman one or not and was he the only one and what did his wife think about it if he even had a wife. Lacey Houseman and hermaphrodites in general kept his mind occupied for a good quarter mile until he came up on the river, crossing it on a bridge where back in the horse-and-buggy days a horse had been spooked by a thigh-thick moccasin and a baby got dumped into the Tar. They claimed you could hear it cry nights when the moon was right, and sometimes boys brought girls out here on dates and the sheriff had to come along every fifteen minutes to clear the cars off the road.

Away from Trent he walked, looking around for things to remember, but after a mile of straggling outskirt nothing much announced itself, and the sky grew gray, then furious with thunderclouds. When the rain came Randall soldiered on until it came down so hard he could not see, at which point he took shelter beneath a railroad trestle and for want of more distraction imagined that day, years away, dim in the future, when he would return to Trent.

As the rain poured through the overhead track, Randall saw everyone he knew, and lots of people he did not know, seated inside a church. Some sort of services were under way. An unlikely site for his prodigal return, since he'd been inside a church only a few times in his life, only once for worship. He and Reka used to sometimes sneak into the Episcopal sanctuary when they had exhausted the corners of its gloomy courtyard. It was a beautiful room, high-pitched and dark, its moods various but all tinged with a sanctified loneliness, for its shadows and smells and secrets were of a room used only once a week.

He stood in the vestibule, home from years of wandering. His hair was as long as those disciples he'd seen in doctors' office picture books, and his clothes were not Sunday ones; he wore jeans and brogans and a workshirt sprinkled with the dust of the road. Seemed he'd been dropped in from another time, according to the faces of those gathered there—an absurd and implausible lot, a dream lot of kith and ex-schoolteachers, estranged second cousins and the victims of junior high crushes. He spotted his father who looked as he had ten years earlier, before he left the country the first time and took his family into Trent. He sat stiffly in a back pew, his eyes on the stained glass behind the altar, staring at the window expectantly as if it owed him something—a vision, a miracle even—for being so ostentatiously pictorial. Randall tried to replace this younger, harder Speight with the man who'd come to see him in Norfolk bearing news of Reka. That Speight had sacrificed his life to let Randall know of Reka's whereabouts made Randall curse the thunderstorm that confined him there. Every minute lost seemed a stain on his father's memory. Wouldn't he have lived longer had he chosen to keep that note to himself? Wouldn't he be alive still, and wouldn't his first instinct—to keep his two favorite children apart from each other, to force them to live their own lives—have worked out in the long run?

But there he was wasting time with daydreams about his triumphant return among bloodred carpets and heavenly organ chords. Maybe Pa would not mind his taking his time to find Reka, maybe he would approve. Give Reka time to get set up, make some money. Maybe she didn't want to see him just yet and that was why she had not come up to Norfolk herself to say goodbye. Maybe Pa would say to him if he was here still, You go on up there and see that she's doing all right but hell, boy, take your time. Look around some. See what there is out there.

After all, it was his escape, too. He had a reason to leave and a quarry to track, but hadn't he always known he would leave when the time came? He found himself torn between the need to find his sister and honor his father's sacrifice and the desire to see what was out there, as his father would have wanted him to do.

A train passed overhead, rocking the trestle and sending torrents to soak the parts of him that had managed to remain dry. She took a train west; he'd learned this from his phone call to the man whose name was printed on the paper his father had brought with him to Norfolk. Bob Smart. He remembered how uneasy the man had seemed when Randall expressed his gratitude to him for giving Reka a chance. He'd acted as if he did not want to be reminded of it; the long pause on the other end of the line made Randall think he was talking to someone in Poland. But he felt uncomfortable on the telephone himself, distrustful of disembodied talk. He talked with his eyes, with his entire body sometimes, never with his lips alone.

The phone call had left him feeling more frustrated, yet it was important to Randall's mind as the resolution of the last act his father had performed in this world. It had seemed a destiny to pursue; his father had made things right by bringing Randall that number. And then he'd let the ocean take him away.

But despite the guilt he'd felt since that day at the ocean, Randall was glad now that his father had died in the sea. He remembered his face, boyish and wondrous when the first waves hit. His toes wiggling beneath a thin sheath of sand when they stood ashore surveying the sea. He thought of his father's voice rising in an underwater cacophony only Randall could hear. Joining the slurry whisperings of Blackbeard, the sharp, harsh cries of deckhands from downed Spanish galleons. Citizens of lost Atlantis, his father among them now, at home with the Lost Colony Randall had studied in school, whom Sir Walter Raleigh had sent to colonize America. Randall had long ago decided this colony disappeared into the sea instead of the forest. The continent was not yet ready for pale, strangely dressed intruders, and it blew up a storm so wild it sent them flying into the surf, sinking the ship they rode in on. He thought his father lucky to have been claimed by the waves, so much luckier than if he'd died in the saggy cot back in his shack. Randall did not think it spiritually profitable to choose the place where you would breathe your last. He saw nothing but sorrow in the way people came home to die in a spot of earth they loved. He'd heard of people demanding their bodies burned instead of buried, their ashes scattered over someplace special to them in life. Did they think they would stay there? That the earth itself, particle and molecule, mote and seed and spore, would remain in one place?

When the storm settled into a steady gray pelting he left his spot beneath the trestle and made his way down the muddy shoulder. It seemed easier to get a ride in the rain anyway. He was lucky with truck drivers, and in a day and a half he made it as far as eastern Kentucky. He found himself in a small town not unlike Trent, the same faces staring at him from shaded porches, the same teenagers cruising the streets in their treasured '55 Fords and Chevys.

Out on the highway he walked for ten minutes before he found a spot beneath a shade tree where he could wait out of the heat for a ride. He stuck his thumb in the air and soon a dented Ford station wagon bobbed over to the shoulder and he braved a small dust storm and climbed in the back. He found himself in a car with two colored men, which surprised him—where he came from, most black men would have let a white man walk and vice versa. His surprise must have been apparent to his saviors.

"We ain't gone to lynch you," said the driver. "Where you headed?" He was freckled and reddish, and talked in a high, sour, rapid way that Randall liked. The other one was overweight and sleepy. He seemed to have been poured into the passenger's seat, and his voice, when he bothered to speak, was a low sardonic croak.

"Minnesota," Randall said.

"Minnesodacracker?" said the sleepy passenger.

"Ain't no Negroes going to Minnesota," said the driver. "We'll take you up to Chicago, but that's all. We ain't studying no Minnesota."

"What you lost up there?" asked the passenger.

Randall was put off by the question; the black people around Trent would not ask a white man his business so boldly.

"I'm going to see my sister. Where y'all from?"

"Raised up in Mississippi, but we ain't down there no more. Now we stay in Chicago."

The driver explained that the two of them were on their way back from visiting family in Itta Bena, Mississippi. They'd found work in factories in Chicago and wouldn't think of returning south.

"How come you like Chicago so much?"

"How come I like it? I can go about my business, that's how come. Won't nobody bother me for being darker than them so long as I keep to myself and stay out of the way of them Irish."

"So would you say you're a different person in Chicago than you were in Itty Bitty, Mississippi, or whatever y'all called it?"

"He ask me if I'm a different person in Chicago," the driver said to his pal.

"Damn sure did. I believe we accidentally picked up a preacher."

"I ain't no preacher," said Randall. "I don't even know no preachers." He'd slipped easily into his mother tongue, which down in the county south of Trent was shared by white and black alike. Since arriving in Norfolk he'd tried to speak good English, which was one of the reasons he made no friends in the shipyard save for Granger. He talked funny, which is to say correctly, and only Granger gave him the benefit of the doubt and hung in there with him long enough to hear him break down into the sloppy English he was raised to speak.

"You must never spent time in no hospital, then. They stuck Cyrus here in the VA hospital for his phlebitis. I went down to see him, but I couldn't get in for all the preachers. It was standing-room-only preachers over there, all lined up in the halls trying to save some sick somebody."

"I saved them some breath is all that got saved," said Cyrus. "I told them they needn't start quoting no Bible to me. I told 'em, said, 'I done been saved three times, and two of them times it was in a pond so nasty took me a month to wash that smell off.' "

"You might have stank, but you were right with the hereafter," said the driver.

"I might have been right with the hereafter, but I damn sure won't getting any loving in the here-and-now."

The two men launched into a vibrant and swaggering aside concerning matters of the flesh. Randall enjoyed it so much that he interrupted them to tell a joke he'd heard that ended in a punch line about a mixup between a Chicago ho and a Navajo.

The two men twisted around in their seats to study him, then traded looks of weary familiarity.

"I swear he's a preacher," said the driver, whose name was Benny.

Randall stretched out in the backseat in reply. Soon he was asleep. When he woke, in Crawfordsville, Indiana, it was getting on toward dusk. They were at a gas station, and Benny was shaking him awake.

"What?" said Randall.

"Gas money, preacher. Got to tithe for the fuel tank."

Randall hesitated. He realized he should have admitted earlier that he had no money.

But they took his news well enough.

"Well, I guess we ain't no worse off than before we picked you up," said Benny.

"Long as you don't tell no more jokes or start witnessing, I reckon you can ride for free," said Cyrus.

Randall went into the station to get the key to the bathroom. The station was filled with idle men in oil-stained work clothes, just like every gas station and country store he'd been in back home. He realized that there wasn't much difference, really, between Trent, North Carolina, and Crawfordsville, Indiana. It smelled different, there were a few modest hills, but as far as the inhabitants, these loiterers seemed cut from the same greasy cloth as those who stood in line for white liquor around back of Speed's store.

"You riding with those niggers?" asked one of the men. He was rail skinny with a flattop the color of a freshly picked, dirt-flecked carrot. Before Randall could reply, the man reddened at the very idea of a white boy traveling with black men.

"Oh, that's Benny and Cyrus," said Randall, pushing himself right up against the man and spreading his face into a smile so wide it hurt. "They're cultural emissaries from Chicago, on their way back from a goodwill trip to their home town in Mississippi."

"I ain't impressed," said the man. He grunted to underscore his indifference. Randall could tell he had no idea what a cultural emissary was; he wasn't so sure himself, but it sounded like something dignified, and his fellow travelers behaved themselves like dignitaries, though of a decidedly informal ilk.

"You want white or nigger bathroom?" asked the boy behind the counter. His audience found this funny, but their laughter was eerily inaudible, a snort, a gust of Camel smoke, a hiccup, beltcreaks from quivering bellies.

"Nigger will do fine," said Randall.

"You don't need a key, then. Ain't no sense in locking up the nigger bathroom. Nothing in there to steal."

There was no light in the bathroom save what duskiness leaked through the grimy window. Randall was about to flush when the four men entered.

"Let me guess," he said. "Cultural emissaries from Crawfordsville on a goodwill trip of their own."

"You chose wrong," said the orange-haired man. "You ought to of chose white."

"I guess I ought to be glad I have a choice in the matter," said Randall.

"What's your business with two old niggers, boy? You got to be up to something, stringing around with them two."

"I guess my business is getting to Chicago," said Randall. "I stuck my thumb out and they were big enough to stop. Unlike a whole long line of white people."

"You guess too much," said the carrot-top. "We ain't asked you to guess."

Randall thought of how many times he'd walked down the street with black boys in Trent without any incident but a turned head or two. Hanging out with black boys had earned him a reputation at school, but this mattered little finally because there was not much a reputation for nigger-loving could do to harm his truck with his classmates in the first place. He wanted badly to laugh at the absurdity that what he'd gotten away with down South got him beaten in the enlightened North. He thought of his father, who had never said one word in favor of blacks nor a word against them. He had never preached tolerance to his children, nor had he ever disparaged the race or blamed them for his problems, as most of his neighbors in Johnsontown were wont to do.

"What are you grinning at?" said the carrot-top. Randall wasn't sure what was making him grin. Certainly it wasn't an appropriate response to the situation, though he did not feel as if his responses had been appropriate for some time. While his father died he read, over and over, a note from Reka. While his father was eulogized and buried he thought not of his father but of his sister, who seemed farther away to him, more dead and buried, than his father who had opened himself up to Randall in the last minutes of his life and drifted off in what seemed to Randall a bit like bliss. His response to his father's death was inappropriately nonchalant, according to his sisters and brother. He seemed doomed to inappropriate responses. Perhaps this was connected to what Delores, in her lovelorn cups, was trying to tell him.

Of course, it could also be that the stimuli he responded to were themselves questionable. That might explain why he said things like the next thing he said.

"I guess I'm grinning at you."

The carrot-top blanched before turning purplish. He seemed to suffer violent aches each time Randall ventured a guess, as if Randall's tentative responses led to heart blockage or muscle spasm.

"You forgot to flush," he told Randall, and as Randall looked down he realized what was about to happen and he did not fight it, allowed the men to force his head into the bowl and breathed deeply through his nose just before his forehead dipped beneath the bubbled surface. It was not the worst, the flushing; the worst was afterward when they let him up and held his hands behind his back and urine, his own and others' before him, streamed down his face and chest and sides, soaking his shirt and humiliating him and drawing grins and more silent amusement from these goodwill emissaries. The leader told Randall he was welcome to go back to his buddies now before he and the others slinked out into the parking lot, where their laughter for the first time became audible.

One of the men remained behind to guard the white man's lavatory when Randall finally emerged from the Colored to look for a sink that actually dispensed water and was not clogged with beer cans and spent towels.

"Whites only," said the guard.

The station wagon was gone, which neither surprised nor particularly bothered Randall. Surely they were looking out for themselves as well. He'd covered a good deal of midwestern space and he'd stiffed them in a way and had they stuck around for him they would surely have ended up stinking of piss themselves if not bloodied or broken.

He stripped off his shirt and strolled barechested down the sidewalk, too preoccupied to notice the people staring from the windows of cars. Two blocks down the street he spotted the station wagon in the empty parking lot of a shut-tight hardware store. He kept right on going out of courtesy; they did not need any more trouble of the type he was sure to provide for them, nor did he want to stick his head in a foul toilet again. Seemed to Randall an appropriate response, though Cy and Benny, when they pulled the car alongside him a half block down the street and coaxed him inside, seemed from their respectful silences to feel that he was blaming them for what happened.

"We would of stayed but . . ."

"No, we wouldn't of, Preach," said Cyrus, giving Benny a sidelong look infinitely patient and exasperated, as if he understood the impulse to lie but found it finally futile.

"Naw, we wouldn't of. Cy's right," said Benny. "See, whatever they done to you wouldn't of been half of what they would of done to us."

"Don't worry about it," said Randall. He wanted to somehow let them know that he had been acting not out of social protest but had instead been unable to respond in any way that might save himself from being dunked. Had he been able to talk himself out of it, he surely would have done so. He wanted to say, in language they would listen to, Look here, boys, I would have sold your asses south if it got to looking like I was going to get seriously hurt. He wanted to explain to them how he did not make moral judgments so much as react in the ways that came to him, which he was beginning to realize were not, as they should be, negotiable or alterable.

"Shoo," said Cyrus, cranking open the window to let in the rank air of departing Crawfordsville.

"Just let me out at the next gas station," said Randall. "I'll get cleaned up so I can catch another ride, and ya'll can go on ahead."

"We ain't about to leave you in this town," said Benny. "You with us for the haul, Preacher."

"He ain't no preacher," said Cy. "Wouldn't no white preacher use the colored men's unless there was some newspaper boys around to take his picture going in."

"Y'all ought to have believed me up front," said Randall.

"All due respect, ex-preacherman, but we don't believe no white men up front," said Benny.

"Down behind, either," said Cyrus. He twisted his slow head to take in Randall, shivering shirtless in the backseat.

"Pull over, Benny. Let him get cleaned up."

Benny parked on the street a block from the gas station this time. Randall approached alone, on foot, wearing a sweater on loan from Cyrus. When he climbed back in the car Cyrus said, "What you going to do when you get to Chicago?"

"I don't know. I told you I'm broke. I guess I'll find a tree to sleep under."

Cyrus croaked out his sardonic laugh. "Naw you won't. Ain't no trees in Chicago. Unless you planning on staying in the park. Get yourself locked up sure as hell if you lay your head out in the open where some tourists can see you."

"I guess I'm a tourist myself," said Randall.

"Naw, hell," said Cy. "A tourist has got money."

"We got you covered for a few nights, Preach," said Benny. "You stood up for us back there, least we can do is pay you back."

Randall started again to explain why he did what he did, but opted instead to return to his nap, which lasted all the way to Chicago. The city made Norfolk seem in memory a sad-sack, slightly stretched-out Trent. On his first day there Randall read in a castoff *Tribune* that several thousand transplants arrived in the city each day. More than Trent had gained in a quarter century. His daddy told him once that Trent had shrunk some since he was a boy. The incredible shrinking city, Randall called it. He drew a picture: townspeople wrestled to the ground by snaky vines protruding from Serenitowinity Swamp, undergrowth creeping out of ditches,

snatching cows, pianos, ovens, chickens. The courthouse repossessed by beautiful, red-flowered foliage. He showed it to Reka,
who said only that she wished it was something she'd seen in the
newspaper, something real instead of right out of Randall's big
head.

Cyrus and Benny lived together in a one-room apartment in a
wheezy wooden building they called a tinmint. The tinmint was
four stories, six apartments to the floor, though it was obviously
built for only two. Each apartment had a sliver of a kitchen, and
there were two baths at the end of the hall. Their building was
wedged in a sooty row of other tinmints, identical and bursting with
people, mostly blacks but also Italians, Germans, Poles, Lithuani-
ans, quite a few Mexicans. Randall knew how to act around colored
people, but he was at a loss around these immigrants. The men
went to work early and came home late coal-blackened or caked in
flour, and those wives who did not work crowded the streets during
the day, children clinging to their skirts, draped in strange black
shawls and horn-toed shoes that made them look like buzzards.
Randall was fascinated and terrified by the chattering of foreign
tongues, especially from the children, whose switch from some gut-
tural overly consonanted throat-clearing to a slangy Chicago drone
seemed as incongruous as Thelonius Monk transforming the
rhythms of a staid old standard.

"I stay away from Germans," Cyrus said when he and Benny got
home from work that first night. Randall had been asking about the
various nationalities, querying his new friends as to how they got
along with their neighbors.

"Cyrus here's a bigot," said Benny.

"Naw, hell," said Cyrus. "My daddy died in the big war's what it
is. I ain't got nothing against a Pole, because a Pole ain't killed my
daddy."

"Them Germans downstairs didn't kill your daddy, either. You
blaming the bunch for what one did. Just like white people do us."

"One thing about Germans, though," Cy said to Randall, ignoring his friend's charges. "German women like a colored man. Guy at work, he got up with a fraulein, moved back to Germany with her. He sent a letter to his old buddies at the shop saying how nice everybody over there treat him."

"I know Hitler didn't love no colored people," said Benny. "And if it's so fine over there, how come your black ass is still hogging a chair in Chicago, U.S.A.?"

"I don't love cabbage," said Cy. "Cabbage and some link sausage, that's about all I ever seen a German eat."

Randall asked if he might stay for a few more days. He planned to pick up some day work, save enough for a bus ticket to Duluth. He liked what he'd seen of Chicago, liked the way its tallest buildings hugged the great wavy lake, liked its many foreigners and even the wind that blasted either fire or ice with the force of the industrial blowers that hung from the rafters of the warehouses back at the shipyard. He liked that you could walk everywhere or take the train above the streets; he watched the windows of el-level apartments and offices as if they were words he needed to form a single and meaningful sentence. The meaning of Chicago grew more mysterious the longer he stayed there, and it occurred to him that should he stay long enough the meaning would either become irrelevant or be subsumed in the simplest acts of his living there: waiting in line for a bus, flirting with an Italian waitress in a delicatessen on Halsted, threading the crowds gathered for a sunny day at a Michigan Avenue beach.

Stay as long as you need, said Benny and Cy. He slept on a pallet in the tiny kitchen for the first few nights, until Benny suggested he move to the front room so he would not be disturbed when the men rose at four-thirty to cook their breakfast. Randall had no intention of taking advantage of their kindness, yet he was unable to resist stretching out on one of their saggy cots as soon as they left for work and sleeping until the tinmint came alive with the shrieks of children, and the slice of open air between their building and the next filled with laundry unfurled at the slightest showing of sun.

Soon it was mid-October of 1959. Lying abed listening to the city rouse itself, he thought of his sister. She would be at work now, would have been at work for hours. He should leave her alone for a few more weeks, give her time to adjust to the Wild West, save some money. He would be a distraction to her if he showed up suddenly and unannounced in her new life, yet it never crossed his mind to track her down and let her know he was on his way. Back when all they ever talked about was escape, of life after Trent, phone numbers and forwarding addresses were never mentioned, for it seemed understood that wherever they were, however many miles they managed to put between them, they would always be able to find each other in a matter of hours. Even now, a third of the way into the continent, Randall did not feel that their certainty was naive. He did not feel foolish because he believed still that he would find her when he wanted and that he would stay here in Chicago until she needed him.

For he had begun to doubt his need for her. What spurred him to leave Norfolk was starting to seem laughable, ignorant, naive. Delores was crazy. Water weight—Hal was right, it was only water weight they'd shed and her insistence that it was substance, flesh burned away by something less ephemeral than the first firing of lust, should have been enough to teach Randall not to listen to her proclamations. Why should he pay attention to this woman who was so sick she closed her eyes, climbed atop him and pretended he was his big brother Hal. Everything she said came from some wet and clingy place inside her which had nothing to do with reason or even thought.

Rousing himself from bed hours after he should have hit the streets in search of work, Randall felt as foolish as he had when he'd realized his father and that druggist had used him to try and tear Reka away from Edwin Keane. It was only after Keane was dead and

Reka was charged with his murder that Randall allowed himself to understand why he'd been sent daily to the dark bungalow with a package and instructed to wait in the Johnsontown woods until Reka was gone to make his delivery. All along he knew from the fussiness with which the druggist instructed him that he was involved in something secretive and undoubtedly wrong. But even then it seemed that Reka was lost to him, lost to them all, and even though he told himself he had no choice but to follow orders, he knew also that, though his father and the druggist saw only salvation for Reka in their plan and could find a thousand ways to justify their behavior, he was finally on the side of the enemy. Reka against the world and in this world lived a boy in love with a bicycle and his afternoon freedom and three dollars a week. He sold her out, and he swore to himself the moment she was sentenced to prison he would never again forget or forsake her.

In the mornings he would borrow an egg or a sausage patty from his benefactors and have a slow breakfast before braving the streets. He would stroll to the corner store for a paper and a cup of coffee and would light a butt crushed out in an ashtray. It was then, after reading each line of the *Tribune*, while he struggled to leave the apartment and look for work, that he wondered whether he should even visit Reka at all. He thought again of his father's death and it occurred to him that by honoring his father's first impulse—to keep the two of them apart for their own good, so that they might have a chance to leave behind all the bad that had happened back home—he would be absolving himself of some of the blame he took for sitting on the beach reading a note from Reka while his father's heart gave way. This thought always disturbed him so much that he left the apartment quickly, for it seemed both out of the question— he had come this far, she was all he had in the world, they'd talked for years of making their way across the country together—and an irrepressible idea whose vigilant rejection would supply him with the focus and energy needed to survive the bluster of Chicago.

He walked the streets, aware that the denial of what seems like fate can keep a man from conceding to the inevitability of fate. Like pathological exercise to ward off the eventual rot of muscle and organ and brain tissue. During those brief periods when his father, toward the end of his life, refrained from the call of Speed's shed, staying sober seemed for him less absence than presence. It gave him something to live for, even though the point seemed to Randall to rid your days of something you could live without.

Benny left him train fare every morning. He rode the elevated for hours. People suctioned themselves to his sides, breathed in his face, crowded him against a pole. A slinky woman in a dress as silver as tin foil, black high heels and red red lipstick sat down in front of him once, her knees touching his. She took a compact out of her purse and arranged her face in a mirror, looking up occasionally, hoping to catch him staring. The Chicagoans were oblivious to the stone wonders outside the window. Randall could not imagine burying himself behind a newspaper while such curiosities flashed by within inches. So much to see, outside and within. Uniforms soiled from sweaty factory work right upside a three-piece pin-striped suit, as if the men had been pinned randomly alongside each other on a clothesline. They let anybody on, colored, white, Chinese people reading their chicken-scratch newspapers. The blond skyscrapers down by the Chicago River closed them in, as if they were shooting through a high mountain pass. In the belly of this city, shadows never lifted. A wash of cold shade painting the sidewalk, the gargoyled buildings, the faces of passersby. He wore his windbreaker, the one with the zipper-gnawed track he'd inherited from Hal. Pockets bulging with balled fists. By midmorning the pavement radiated heat unlike any he'd felt in the tobacco and corn fields of eastern North Carolina.

One Saturday he took the train to Grant Park. In a grocery bag he packed a book and some crackers he borrowed from Cyrus.

From a sidewalk fruit stand he snatched a banana and a measly bunch of grapes. He read his novel beneath a tree—*L'Immoraliste*, by a Frenchman. After noon the park began to fill with people out to stroll. Randall took a walk himself, down through the park until he came to the grand museum, which was sucking people in from the street in a steady stream.

Randall joined the flow. Crossing the high marble foyer, he was stopped by a guard. He did not hear the man calling to him at first, and when he did hear him he assumed he was talking to someone else.

"You have to check your package," the guard said to him.

Randall blinked at the guard, at the bag he held in his hand.

"Your package," the man said loudly. Randall understood then— the guard thought he was a foreigner, assumed from his mute confusion he did not speak English—and even though the guard's curt orders unnerved him, he was pleased and amused to be mistaken for an immigrant.

He handed the bag to the guard, who refused it and pointed to a small room off the foyer where a girl sat behind a desk reading a book. Randall slinked off across the lobby, the guard watching him closely.

The girl behind the counter looked right through him when he handed her his belongings. She was an insolent beauty with a bored blank smile.

"It's a book by a Frenchman and some fruit and some crackers," he said. "Oh, I forgot, and a comb."

"What?"

"It's not a bomb," he whispered, lest the guard find out he spoke good English.

"Who said anything about a bomb?"

"Why else would you want to confiscate my personal effects?"

The girl got up and disappeared behind a high bank of pigeon-holes. She returned carrying a ring with a numbered tag attached.

"What a trade," said Randall. "I can't eat this or read it more than once."

"You're joking, right?"

"Am I?" said Randall.

The girl sighed and went back to her book, a thick novel by Henry Fielding, which it happened Randall had read.

"That book cracked me up," said Randall. "I don't ever laugh out loud at things in a book, but with that one I came close. Old Squire Allworthy."

"Can I help you?" the girl said to a woman over Randall's shoulder.

Randall shrugged and wandered into the museum. It seemed to him that the rooms opened into each other oddly, as if in a dream, but he was soon absorbed in the paintings covering the walls. He had never been to a museum before. Once, in fifth grade, Mrs. Tarkington had brought in some paintings by a man named Turner, soft fuzzy scenes of clouds and ships at sea. Randall liked them enough to want to be in them, sailing the blurry waters, but the paintings he saw on the walls in front of him—strange dripping colors swirling like swarms of no see-ums back home, a series of blue boxes arranged on a canvas as high as a house—made him feel different. Instead of wanting to be in them, he felt that these paintings were inside him.

He did not bother with the plaques identifying the painters, their dates, the occasional commentary of some expert. He did not care for the kind of facts you learn in a class to write down on a test. He would rather know one painting well than be able to identify the work of every painter represented here. In time he found one he wanted to know, to subsume—a huge sallow square fading into burnt edges of ochre. The painting made him think of welding, of his work in the shipyards. Rivets and soldered squares of steel put together like words into sentences that held some incontrovertible truth only he would understand. And the rest of the world saw only the lurking hull of an ice cutter, a battleship, an aircraft carrier. The blocks of color, bleeding into each other, struck him as a vision he alone was blessed with, that only he could trust. There are things in this world I will never be able to share with anyone, he thought, things I cannot even explain to Reka. With a shiver of embarrassment, he thought of living his life inside his head, an idea everyone had, nothing new at all, yet for some reason, standing in front of this painting, he understood it fully.

And in that moment it felt like a sentence to him rather than an abstraction, a brain-teaser college boys argued about over beers at the tavern. What was real and what was not: he and Reka had even talked about this, plenty of times, in words that weren't terribly technical or sophisticated. Despite their ignorance, they understood that their world wasn't the one found on the front pages of newspapers or in the textbooks doled out at the beginning of the school year. Without words, they understood that the world they saw was the same one, colored and slanted the same, a world made whole by a single, shared desire: to burn through it, exhaust it, outrun it.

People drifted through the room like dust motes stirred by a wind, invisible to Randall as he stood staring. At some point the guard stationed in the corner of the high-ceilinged room was replaced by another. Once Randall looked up to find the girl from behind the counter watching him from a corner of the room, which he found curious but finally not interesting enough to distract him from this painting he felt on the verge of knowing. As defiantly abstract as it seemed at first, in time it struck him as wonderfully representational, a map, a rendering of an empty but luminous spirit. It had to do with searching for things that had no form except in the mind. A landscape that existed only until it was discovered, at which point it bled into some other, unknown shape.

A guard moved through the rooms announcing the closing of the museum in ten minutes. When the time had passed and he stood there still, the guard reappeared to escort him to the lobby. He had to wait in line at the desk, and the girl was so busy fetching coats and hats and briefcases for dour people in their Sunday best that she did not see him until he was standing before her.

"I want to talk to you," she whispered.

"What?"

"I need your tag," she said, loudly this time.

Randall gave it to her, and she disappeared into a room behind the desk. She returned with the bag and said, "Look in the Gide."

"The who?"

"The novel," she said, smiling. "André Gide."

"I never heard his name said," said Randall. "It's not what I'd have called him."

"Can I help you?" she said to the woman behind him.

Outside he ate his grapes slowly, then his banana, before allowing himself to open the book. A postcard fell from between the pages. On the front was the very painting that caused him to swoon. On the back was one line—Wait for me outside—and a name. Constance.

Randall sat in the grass, saying her name. A name out of a book, it sounded like to him. Who would name a child Constance? A name for middle age. He could not imagine her answering to Connie. Yet Constance intimidated him, as it seemed such a stubborn name. Monied, too.

He read his Gide in the shadow of the Art Institute, though it was impossible to concentrate now. He merely pretended to read, dragging his eyes across the chain of black marks on the page, attempting to glean from their shape some trembling mood like the one cast off by the painting on the postcard until he looked up to find Constance standing before him. Her face was blurry, backlit by smoky Chicago dusk. She wore a sweater over her dress that came almost to her hemline, for she was a small woman, petite she was probably called by salesladies, though she had a disproportional presence.

She flopped next to him in the grass, stretched her sweater over her knees.

"Hey," he said.

She laughed at his greeting, which made him wonder what was funny.

"You are so strange," she said. "Where are you from?"

"North Carolina."

"Aren't you going to introduce yourself?"

He said his name and she said it back to him in a way that made him think she liked it. She would, he thought, as it was formal in its own way, though not as stiff as her own.

"You do realize you almost got yourself arrested in there?"

"For what?"

"You can't walk in a place like that and mention bombs."

"I was joking," he said. "I didn't mean . . ."

"I know," she said, "but there are some things you can't joke about. At least not in some places."

Randall considered this statement. He knew not to take her too literally, though he felt, finally, that the only sacred things, the only subjects free from irony and darkest humor, were personal. Institutions and objects and even philosophies were far from sacrosanct.

"We've had paintings defaced in the past."

"Who would want to do that?"

She shrugged. "Sick people. You'd be surprised at how many times we've had to usher out crazies who claim the paintings on the walls are sending them messages. Lunatics are particularly susceptible to great art."

"And you thought I was a lunatic?"

She smiled her answer, which was ambiguous and made him smile in return.

"I have to report stuff like that to the guards. It's my job. So they had someone watching you the whole time. They even sent me in there for a while when the guards took their break."

"I saw."

"Really?" she said, leaning toward him. "I didn't think you noticed. You seemed transfixed."

Randall looked down at the postcard he still held in his hand. He studied the painting again, unsure of what to say next.

"What are you doing in Chicago?"

"Doing?"

"Yeah. What do you do? Work? Independently wealthy? What?"

"Oh, I'm just passing through. On my way to see my sister, in Montana. I'm staying with some friends."

"What's your sister do in Montana?"

Randall looked down at the postcard again. He wished he was still in front of it, for he did not want to talk at all now, especially about Reka. The whole time she was locked away he did not mention her name to anyone in his family, certainly not to anyone else. Telling her story would not have made her imprisonment any easier to bear. He'd grown used to holding his tongue. Around Reka, he talked nonstop; in those days his father was forever telling him to hush up. But after Reka left, Randall lost faith in words. He was curious still, he wanted desperately to know how things worked, where they came from, why they were there—but he had convinced himself that had he not been so eager to talk, to tell tales to any sucker who asked him an innocent, casual question, she would never have gotten herself mixed up with the man they claimed she killed. It was Randall who met him first. He'd delivered his medicine and answered his questions about Reka: *Who's that girl I've seen you around town with?* The two of them came to trust him with words; back and forth he ran between them, delivering letters, messages, desperate and anxious sentences. In penance it was words he gave up, for words had started all the trouble.

"Okay, sorry," said Constance. "I shouldn't pry." Gently she lifted the postcard from his grasp, held it at a farsighted distance, studied it herself. Randall came close to asking her what she thought of it, what she felt when she looked at it, but he wasn't sure this was the kind of thing you can just up and ask a stranger, and before he could speak she sprang up from the ground, offered him her hand.

"Come on," she said. "We can talk while we walk."

But they didn't talk, not much, and not at all about the painting that had brought them together. After a few dull exchanges they lapsed into a silence. She walked ferociously, like everyone in the city; struggling to keep up with her, Randall remembered his father huffing along behind him on that last afternoon of his life.

They came finally to a slender building fronted on the street by a dark-windowed typewriter repair shop. She led him up three steep flights of stairs. He stood in the dark hallway while she fidgeted with her keys in front of a dim door, its frosted transom made even more opaque by decades of dust and grime. He made a game of imagining what was behind the door—horrors, treasures, sexual adventures—but this interest in options, surprises, quickly soured. This was a bad sign; he had never before been uninterested in possibility.

Suddenly Randall felt ancient. As old and seasoned as the floorboards beneath his feet, the lumpy plaster he leaned against. He missed the painting he'd crawled inside earlier; if he was going to be subsumed in space, it might as well be of his own choosing.

Finally the key fit and engaged, the door swung open, his hostess patted the wall for the light switch. Inside was a studio. Paintings stacked against the walls, an easel and a drafting table set up by the window. The smell of paint, canvas, turpentine. The room was larger than he expected, and the ceilings were high and of peeling pressed tin, and there were windows along both walls taller than Randall's six feet. Late-afternoon light quivered on the floor, bubbled by the thickly blown glass. He moved to the window to see a gray inch of Lake Michigan slivered between two tall buildings.

Constance excused herself and disappeared down the hall to the bathroom. Randall crossed the room slowly, studying the paintings. They felt unfinished to him—or rather abandoned, as if she had gotten so far with an image and had been paralyzed by the severity of her choices. Even after a cursory survey of her work he understood that she, like most people, loved beginnings: the first chapters of novels, the slow disrobing in the dark, the first two glasses of wine. Yet what she had already accomplished was interesting enough, even though he knew nothing really about it; he'd just visited his first art museum minutes ago, he was no expert. But he liked the way her colors seemed at once violent and blissful, as if one mood was impossible without the other.

"They aren't done," she said when she returned to the room. She kept her distance, leaning against a refrigerator on the far wall as if out of bounds, immune from his opinion.

"I know," he said.

"You do?"

Turning to her he noticed a flash of rekindled insolence in her eyes, but when he refused to answer her she laughed and loosened up and shrugged. "I guess you do, then."

She announced that they were going to have some soup and busied herself over a hot plate in the corner of the studio.

"You live here?"

"I work here." She nodded at a daybed half-hidden behind a screen, two panels of which revealed a triptych in progress. The third panel was so painfully blank that studying it, Randall felt a crushing anxiety. It was equally suspenseful and antagonizing, like that feeling of realizing in the middle of the day that you might have left the stove on that morning, spending the rest of the day fretting over whether or not to run home and check on it. What he loved and hated about this scenario was the way time slowed to a stutter as he surveyed the risks. Should he ignore the past and make use of the present, or trust blindly in the future and risk incalculable loss?

It wasn't only appliances that elicited such ambivalence, which was why the third panel unnerved him so.

"Sometimes I spend the night if I'm here late and the trains have stopped running. But I live with my parents in Oak Park."

"Where's that?"

"Half hour on the train."

"And you work at the museum?"

"I go to school there, at the Art Institute. It's part of my fellowship, working at the museum. I've just finished my first year, so I'm lowly enough to have to take an occasional shift at the coat check. But by the time I finish I'll be able to actually help hang shows. I really want my own gallery. I'd like to keep painting, I'll always paint, but I don't really think I'll ever be that great at it. I'd love to help other painters get their work shown. And sold."

She stirred the soup, brought a spoonful to her mouth to blow on. Randall watched the steam undulate like an unstoppered genie and wondered, What's the point of doing it if you don't think you're any good? He thought of Reka peddling her books up and down the streets of some foggy mountain town. She would have given up by now if it turned out she could not pay her way. Maybe she'd figured out some darker, quicker way to put herself through school. He knew he could do nothing to save her from danger except stand by her side again. It occurred to him that he might have already lost her, that if he allowed himself to tarry here, their plans for a future together in that much-coveted elsewhere would slip into wisps and vapor.

But he had questions to ask Constance. He could no more leave her now than he could leave Chicago, to which she bore an unnerving likeness: She was all sharp edges, marvelously built, breezy and cool and brilliant in a modestly midwestern way. It seemed to him that she was an idealist gone bad, her hopeful intelligence having festered and soured after some blunt disappointment. He wanted to know her as he imagined he might get to know the city—

quickly and hungrily, with the unquenchable desire of a visitor whose days in town were limited.

"How do you know if you're not that great at it until you finish all those?"

She turned her breezy smile on him, a spoon in one hand, the other on her hip. She still wore the baggy sweater even though it was warm on the third floor, and he found himself wishing she would take it off so he could see all of her. He thought for the first time in months of his own appearance. Since the funeral he had grown thinner than ever, though his chest and arms were still tightly muscular from his shipyard days. He could not afford a haircut and was constantly wetting his comb in public restrooms to slick his long hair back out of his eyes. As for shaving, he had not worked up the courage to borrow a blade from his housemates, and as a result his face was blue with whisker shadow, which did not quite cover his cheeks but made him look dirtier. He wore the clothes he'd brought on his back and a couple of castoff workshirts Benny had lent him. Every third day he washed his underwear in the communal bath while the men were all at work, provoking conversations in foreign tongues from the women of the tinmint, whose eyes and tone conveyed the scorn he understood fueled their words.

"Don't you think the fact that I can't bring myself to finish them says something about my talent?"

"Not your talent," said Randall. He was perfectly content to keep her on the subject of herself, for he had not yet decided how much truth to tell her, if any at all.

"Well, my drive, then?"

"Maybe it just means the end hasn't come to you yet."

"You're sweet," she said. "I bet you were brought up that way."

"Which way?"

"You didn't have one of those genteel southern mamas who taught you that politeness is the most important virtue in the world?"

Randall knew she'd brought him here for reasons other than to patronize him. He hated to pass up a free meal, even canned soup simmered on a hot plate, yet he felt his former indifference hardening into a prickly impatience.

"I was raised by my older sister. She said please and thank you, but she didn't give a damn if I said them or not. You told me back at the museum you wanted to talk to me?"

She brought the soup then, along with a saucer of soda crackers, to a paint-stained table in the corner. He noticed in the corners of her lips slight ripples he identified as a suppressed smile, and when she asked if they weren't talking already, her tone was amused. He was relieved to find that she was not, in fact, genteel.

"Surely you didn't bring me here to get me to talk about your work."

"Oh, I know what's wrong with my work. I know what it's missing, and I know why it's missing: because of the life I've led. Which really isn't my fault, I mean, I can't really control who I am. Only child of a university professor and a violinist. Pampered daughter of fine old leafy Oak Park. But it feels like I've taken it as far as I can with what I know, and that's why I have all that work yet to do," she said, pointing at the paintings stacked along the walls.

Randall kept quiet, though he knew she wanted him to comment on her confession. What was there to say? She's complaining about being an only child? She ought to try sharing a single bath with six siblings, five of them female. She's whining about her parents being a professor and a musician? He made a short list of the jobs his father had held between stabs at farming, tried to imagine Constance walking with her friends down State Street and coming upon her father careering down the sidewalk on the official delivery boy's bike.

He found sympathy only for her desire to be a different person, as who had not wished the same? Yet Randall suspected that Constance wanted to reinvent herself without suffering any of the obvious consequences.

"What do you want?"

"Part of my job at the Institute is to hire models."

He stared blankly, waiting for more.

"Artist's models. For life drawing classes."

He stayed quiet and still.

"All you have to do is be still for thirty minutes or so. Most people can't do it, it drives them crazy or they twitch without even noticing, so much that the artists go crazy. But you already passed the audition. I've never seen anyone who stayed as still as you did in front of that painting this afternoon."

"All I have to do is stand around?"

"You get a break every half-hour."

"You'll pay me money to stand around in a museum?"

"A classroom. The pay's not bad. They pay more for nudes."

"You want me to take my clothes off?"

"Only if you want more money. But if you choose not to, you still wear only your underwear. No shirt. It's all about anatomy. We're not interested in drawing shirt collars."

"You brought me here to ask me that?"

"You looked hungry."

Randall looked at his soup.

"Well?"

He thought to say, as Delores was fond of saying: I have my pride. But instead he said simply: "I could eat."

He ate, slowly and a lot; she watched him eat in a way that made him nervous, for he worried in the self-conscious silence of supper, broken only by the music of spoon against ceramic and the slurping noises he allowed himself in an effort to establish his lack of gentility, that he had confessed to more than simple hunger. Larger needs hovered at the table: a need for sustenance, for guidance in a place he did not know how to navigate. Needs she expected and was prepared to meet. It was the former that bothered him, as if she had sized him up as he stood frozen in front of this painting that he wondered now if she had ever even looked at twice.

It was not like him to suspect even strangers of duplicity, and he was not given to second guesses once he'd decided he liked and trusted a person. Maybe breaking bread with Constance was not a great idea, but he did not stop spooning soup into his mouth, and when he was done and she started in with her personal questions— where are you staying, how are you living—he felt he had already agreed to the offer (slow in coming but genuine, he assumed from the tone of her voice) of her studio daybed.

"I have to go get my things, then," he said. He was too timid yet to admit that he was wearing his entire wardrobe and that his belongings could fit into the bag he'd tried to smuggle past her coat check.

"Let's go," she said.

He did not see why he should stop her from coming along. Perhaps when she saw where he had been living, saw the line of grimy men lined up for a wash outside the tinmint bathroom or picked her skirt up to cross the line of drinkers on the front stoop who would surely turn and stare without gentility as she floated above them, she would change her mind about him. She only needed a model; she only wanted a body with some slight resemblance to statues Randall had seen in the pictures in encyclopedias. His frame was losing what muscle he'd gained at the shipyards, and in a few weeks' time he would deflate back to his slat-and-rail stringbeaniness and she would trade him in for a new model, some muscle boy she spotted hanging out in front of a boxing gym.

"You live alone?" she said to him on the train.

"With Benny and Cyrus. They've been damn good to me, and you know what? At the moment I have absolutely no means to repay them."

"What would you do for them if you could?"

"If I could do anything? I'd pay for them to bring their families up from Mississippi."

She said, "That's sweet," in a way he did not trust, but when she asked him what he would do for them now, tonight, he understood and decided to play along.

"Take them out for a big meal, then to hear some music. I imagine they know the good places to go."

"I know some pretty good places myself," she said. He smiled, imagining Benny and Cyrus and even himself trailing petite Constance into some candlelit Lincoln Park jazz club with a two-crème-de-menthe limit and lacy tablecloths.

"We ought to let them choose," he said, and when she nodded he told her he would pay her back. She patted his arm as if she were his mother, then hooked her own arm under his and scooted closer on the seat.

Randall thought she would grow quiet or stiffen once they crossed a certain line in the city. He had taken note of that stop where the white people like her got off the train and hurried away from the platform clenching umbrellas and briefcases and even rolled-up newspapers as if they might have to defend themselves against bodily harm. But she seemed relaxed as he led her into the rows of tinmints, though she did not let go of his arm.

Benny and Cy were not down on the stoop. Randall was grateful for that. He did not say a word to her about their blackness because he wanted to watch her face when he introduced them as his roommates. She followed him up the treacherous stairway, which even this early at night was as black as the shaft of a coal mine. She hung in the shadows while he knocked on the door.

"Prodigal sonbitch done draggedass home," said Cy. Randall tugged Constance into the light; he watched her face, wanted to see it drop or blanch or tighten, but there was no reaction from her and only a smile from Cyrus who nodded and said, un-*hunh*, said, I see, said, So that's the situation, can't blame you for staying gone so long, and mumbled in his croaky baritone all sorts of other barely audible responses while opening the door wide and sweeping the two of them into the dingy parlor.

"Let me go wake up Benny," said Cy. "Church tired him out something big. I told him not to pray so hard."

He disappeared into the bedroom and came back with Benny in tow. Randall introduced Constance and Cyrus had a way with her name, dropping the second n without apology or to Randall's ear much damage. Even she seemed charmed by it, especially as he found cause to repeat it over and over in the first five minutes of their visit: sit here, Constuss. Where did you meet this bum, Constuss? Preacher, get your Constuss something out the icebox-cold to drink.

"Preacher?" said Constance.

"You didn't know he was a preacher?" said Benny. "Oh Lord. He *would* fail to tell you about that little detail."

"Tonight I'm holding services at the greasy eatery of your choice," said Randall. "Ya'll get dressed whether you already ate or not. We're going dancing, too, Cy."

"You paying, I'm playing."

They walked through the streets to a place called Bone's, where the jukebox rattled like an off-cycle washing machine, it was cranked so loud. Constance stuffed quarters in the slot and Benny chose the soundtrack: Chubby Checker and the Five Satins, Chuck Berry and Elmore James, Muddy Waters and a host of other bluesmen Randall did not know by name. Cy and Benny claimed to have seen them all: Robert Johnson, too, back home in Mississippi. John Hurt and Howlin' Wolf, Fuzzy Lewis and another cat out of Memphis, Phineas Newborn, who they claimed did things to the piano Monk would only dream about. They hunched over their table talking music and drinking sweaty bottles of beer and gnawing on plates of ribs with heaping sides: candied yams, okra crusted with fried batter, rice afloat in rich pot-likkered gravy. Constance only picked at the corn bread, but she matched the boys bottle for bottle and chain-smoked Tareytons and finally engaged Benny in a passionate chin-wag about working conditions in the steel mill and the pros and cons of the union.

Cy whispered to Randall: "She a communist?"

"Don't have the slightest."

"Nor care neither, do you?" said Cy, grinning. He took a swallow of beer and studied Constance. "She over there talking unions, I bet you she's a communist. Chicago crazy with 'em. They like a Democrat around here, no big thing."

"I never met one," said Randall. "I don't think they grow them where I'm from. Let's go hear some music."

"You buying, I'm flying," said Cy.

Down the street and down a flight of stairs into a room packed and loud and smoky, a wide basement of red-painted brick sloping toward a creaky plywood stage. A woman in a white dress and thigh-high purple stockings sang a raunchy, bossy blues. She needed a man what would take care of her, not any man would do; the man she'd find would have a nice be-hind, big muscles to squeeze away her blues. Cy hoisted himself out of his chair, crooked a finger at his head and shouted out, "Look no farther, Mama." He shook his loose belly as the guitarist's fingers pecked notes off the neck of his instrument like a chicken feeding in a barnyard, and three beers later Cy was suddenly up on stage singing a slurry song he introduced as straight out of his own experience on this earth about some crazyass Russians riding around in the skies where they didn't have no business. In his song, which was as slow and lazy as the eyes of old men Randall spotted half-sleeping their days away on the elevated, the Russians ran out of rocket fuel and fell from the heavens, landing in a cow pasture in Mississippi. All the churches in the delta held special services to try and save the Russian Martians, and the verses detailed various strategies employed by the sincere Mississipians and the song itself went right where it wanted to without regard to scale or tone or cadence, though the crowd loved it and even Constance got up to dance with Benny and Randall, the three of them hoisting their beer bottles in the air and enjoying a slight celebrityhood as friends of the spirited vocalist. It became evident from a chorus introduced late in the game that the song itself was entitled *Russian Martian Mississippi Methodist Y'all Fly Away Home*, and it broke off in the middle of a Cyrusian croak, leaving the crowd in wanton clamor.

"Cyrus Interruptus," Randall said to Constance, who pulled him close on the dance floor and made frothy promises with the dart and flicker of her tongue. I.O.U. more later, upon a daybed behind two thirds of a triptych in a studio filled with half-finished canvases clamoring for life experience of exactly this stripe. It occurred to him in a drunken miracle of prescience that he was Raw Experience.

She said, "How I love your friends."

"Tonight you have missed your train to Maple Glen or Pine Commons or Sycamore Square."

"Oak Park," she said. "Let's go home."

On the train they kissed and laughed at recast and embellished moments of the night's hilarity. He found himself missing Benny and Cy, whom he had promised outside the bar he would see in a day or two, though as the elevated crossed Halsted he acknowledged the unlikelihood of this happening. Once again he had forsaken them. Remembering the first time, he found himself telling Constance the story of the carrot-top vigilante of Crawfordsville, Indiana, and his crew of mute enforcers, though before he could even get to the point, the part where Benny and Cy misinterpreted his cowardice as valor and he failed finally to disabuse them of this notion, Constance clasped his head between her hands and pulled him over to her and would not let him finish.

"I want you to tell me everything about your life," she said. "All of it, even the worst parts."

So she could put it into a painting? Embarrassed almost to sobriety, Randall renewed the warmup for the daybed. Despite the bibulous elasticity of the last few hours, he was certain that he had met her that very afternoon, yet here she was pleading for his life story.

They kissed along the tracks to their stop and bumped to a halt on the landing of her building to explore and unbutton.

She left the lights off and went to the bathroom, but Randall, propped naked on the skinny daybed, was glad to see that the room was lit from the streetlights, the details of the half-finished paintings as clear to him as they had been earlier. He saw no reason to ever make love in the dark. He had all kinds of ideas about love, how to make it and how to make it fresh if it ever became stale, which he was certain it would for him, as it seemed something that could only be done in a finite number of ways, and the idea of holding onto one partner for life, without infinite barriers broken and taboos laid to waste, was about as interesting to him as staying perpetually in school. He had all kinds of ideas despite the fact that besides Delores, he had only slept with one other woman—a girl, actually, seventeen-year-old Shelly Dunne, whom he worked with at the Phillips Ice Cream Shop back home. Shelly Dunne was a predictable and petulant beauty with whom he had nothing in common save the daily operations of the store and the fact that they attended the same school, though they never talked or even acknowledged each other outside of work. Shelly's boyfriend had dumped her and she wanted him back bad, and to get him back she would do anything, including ask Randall out on a date even though he did not have a car and drive him around town so that everyone could see the two of them together and be seen with him again later that night, leaving the car in the parking lot of Japarks Lake and leading Randall into the shadowy woods, where even though Randall had figured out what she was up to and came right out and told her to forget it, she didn't actually have to sleep with him, everyone would think they did it anyway, Shelly Dunne held herself to her skewed sense of honor, which resulted in a consolation lay for Randall, who had successfully fulfilled his role and therefore deserved his reward.

It wasn't that big a deal to him, his first time; he had never been one to attach much significance to initiations, since he lived it all so thoroughly in his imagination. Everything—riding a bike, dragging a razor across his neck for the first time, losing his virginity—took place in vibrant reverie first, and he expected and even encouraged discrepancies between the real and the imagined, for the alternative, that things would turn out exactly as dreamed, seemed intolerable.

When Constance returned, still draped by her sweater and nothing else, he pulled her to him and made love to her and to the city that hummed three floors below. It was not a tender place, but it was open to adventure and fueled by a wind as brutally steady as he could imagine, and when it was over and he lay crumpled alongside her he felt that this was the way he would feel leaving Chicago: comfortably ravaged, broke, having spent more than he'd brought along.

When he awoke she was gone. He lay in bed with his big head throbbing until he felt stable enough to rise and drink several glasses of water and snoop around the studio for clues to the last twenty-four hours. On the table he found a note from Constance telling him to be ready for work by late morning. She would stop by for him. For a second he worried about what to wear until he remembered that with this job it mattered not at all.

In a box beneath the daybed he discovered a stack of notebooks that he flipped through, skimming notes from some class. Dates and names, the opinions of some expert professor. He thought it silly to study painting at school; if it was within her to paint, she'd be better off spending her days in this beautiful room. But he knew nothing about it, really. He'd only finished high school himself and had no plans for college, unlike Reka, who since meeting Edwin Keane had wanted college more than a man, children, a settled life in a place she loved. In her letters from jail she'd repeated this desire endlessly. He wouldn't mind knowing the things found at college, but he'd just as soon spread it out over a lifetime, as it seemed to him that many people give up on their minds after their structured stints at Higher Learning and even in those years did not learn to think for themselves.

He found her full name in the front of the notebook: Constance Rachel Kernstein. Knowing her name embarrassed him in a way that he could not quite fathom; it seemed to have so little to do with the part of her that he was destined to know, nothing at all to do with what she wanted from him. He was glad when she arrived to take him to his job and teased him for his bleary dishevelment and with the bossy insolence of the coat check girl distracted him from his suspicions about what really was going on between them. On the street he told himself that she was in charge of hiring models for the art classes, and he let her buy him breakfast and a cup of coffee and again they went over the events of the night before, filling in the gaps but leaving unsaid those things they did to each other in the first beatific light of day. He was still a little drunk when she led him into the room filled with easels and stools and pale artists and talked with some of the people while he stripped in a closet first to his underwear and finally, why the hell not, he did not know anyone and had been told by Delores that even compared to his big brother Hal he had nothing to be ashamed of in the proportion department, to the bone. He took a seat on a stool in front of the class and let his mind drift for half-hour segments of quiet save for the rasp of charcoal on rough paper and the erasure of wrong strokes and occasionally the sighs and sophisticated curses of the pale and tortured artists.

Of course he worried that his mind, in its dilatory drift, might snag on some image of carnality, sending a bloodsurge southward and embarrassing him, perhaps even leading to his dismissal. This was his only worry, for he was not the least bit modest about exposing himself to a roomful of strangers. In fact, he liked it. Constance disappeared as soon as he took his seat, and as she left the room he sought her gaze but found it averted, as if seeing him in the flesh she might weaken and attack him right there in front of the class.

He found a way to keep his eyes open without meeting the stares of the artists, but even while focused on the tops of trees out the window he detected from both men and women in the room an interest in his body that exceeded form and balance and anatomical accuracy. So long as he did not acknowledge this interest, he felt appreciated in ways that he could treat with indifference, and it seemed to him that he was in control here and that the painters below him were the subjects, created and controlled by his coy denial of their hidden desires.

Randall realized that he had never consciously considered the notion of power, having been bred to believe that meeting the simplest of bodily and emotional needs was all he need know of the subject. It occurred to him as he let his mind drift that power for him would always be contained in moments like these, in which through pure force of imagination he crowned himself emperor of a fable in which the lack of clothes was not at all the proverbial delusion but rather a source of incontrovertible strength. That his audience looked at him and pretended in their uptightness to connect leg bone to thigh bone was a failing of their own courage and had nothing to do with his need to be coddled with lies and hypocrisy.

When it came time to take a break he rose so casually from his throne that you would have thought he was brought to his feet by the stirring chords of a church organ announcing the final hymn of the coronation. He felt the power in the balls of his feet as he padded barefoot to the closet for a scratchy communal robe and out into the hall for a drink of water from the fountain. Even off duty he would not look them straight in the eye, for if he did his power would evaporate and he would turn into a poor fool too lazy to earn a decent day's wage. He would turn into the person his father would think him if his father were here to see how he paid the bills.

But Constance Rachel Kernstein took care of his bills. Not that he did not attempt to pay his way. He came every day to disrobe and take the throne, and the artists so admired his ability to hold a pose that they requested him more and more until by the end of two weeks he was working steady six-hour shifts of idle free-floating thought.

For the next three months, Randall earned his way in the world by taking off his clothes and holding his breath. A rhythm was established: He would walk to work in the mornings and strip and sit and let his mind graze. Sometimes his thoughts were vivid and specific and other times they were so loose and lazy that he thought of them as shades of this or that mood, more color than shape or image, as if the work being done in the room before him entered his consciousness in hue or brush stroke. The artists seemed aware of their ability to color his psyche, and in these moments they worked intensely and with pleasure and he felt that he was not body stripped and exemplary before them, but spirit created by their desire to articulate the slightest shadings of their own inexpressible emotion. They liked him from afar; their admiration came close to worship even, yet at first they kept their distance and he kept his eyes averted and was careful not to acknowledge their desire.

Constance also kept her distance, in public at least. She took classes in another part of the building or put in her hours at the coat check and met him at a prearranged spot after they both were through with their days, for she did not want any of her fellow students to know about them. They would return to the studio after a meal in one of the Italian restaurants she favored and spend the evening making love in various and progressively less conventional sites among the untouched paintings. She never painted. After their lovemaking she opened a bottle of wine, curled up beside him and asked him questions about his past. He welcomed the opportunity to talk after so long a silence, for it seemed ages since he had been allowed to talk freely—since he had introduced Reka to the man she would go to jail for murdering, to be exact.

But the more he told her about his past, the more Constance

seemed to cling to him. What she needed from him was as unacknowledged as it was obvious, and even though Randall felt like a library book renewed for weeks and thumbed through, skimmed, ransacked for pertinent and inspirational passages—even though he knew that one day soon his past due date would arrive and he would be dropped in a dark slot in the side of some cold marble tomb and forgotten—he knew also that he was not without guile. Still, he was motivated mostly by curiosity, which had been his motivation for almost everything else he had done in his eighteen years.

After a few months of modeling some of the artists sought him out on break or sometimes waited outside the building in the frigid Chicago morning and engaged him in supposedly spontaneous chatter. The women tried hard to be both blasé and suggestive, and this strained subtlety Randall found irresistible. One of the boys sidled up alongside him while he was eating his lunch one day. His name was Hans, and he was a rangy pale midwestern peasant whose artistic ability had liberated him from the northern Michigan forest where his father and brothers felled trees for a living, and his interest in Randall was so direct and uncomplicated in comparison to the scripted insinuations of the women that Randall gave in to him on the first suggestion. They met at a movie house one afternoon when Randall was off and Constance was checking coats and watched a tepid war movie while noisily eating popcorn and disparaging the fight scenes, then off to a dirty Mexican restaurant for beers and tortillas and finally to Hans's rented room for an hour of tumbling so brutal that neighbors pounded on the thin walls.

Randall could not say he'd prepared for this, or that he'd planned for it to happen, but once it took place he saw no reason to interrupt it, for it felt so compatible with some untested facet of his desire that it seemed to him inevitable. There were things in this world he'd learned to do solely in dreams—driving a car, swimming, parting a woman's legs with his fingers and aligning his torso atop hers—and when it came time to experience these things for the first time, his body performed with such intimacy and calm that it hardly seemed an initiation. Running his fingers through another man's hair was not one of these things, yet it did not seem unnatural, at least enough to stop.

The strange thing was, he felt no shame. If the world was fifty percent male, he thought, it seemed rather silly to limit himself to women before at least testing the pleasures of his own sex. He remembered the time in sixth grade when he'd shown up for tryouts for the school orchestra, not knowing that only those students who could afford instruments were allowed to join. The bandleader had asked him what instrument he wanted to play, and he told the man he did not know, he guessed he'd try them all until he found one he liked.

He thought fleetingly of Delores, of her prophecy. "No woman will have you, not the part of you that counts," she had said. But he knew that he could love women completely, and he knew he enjoyed their bodies with an abandon he did not feel as Hans bobbed steadily between his legs, bringing him to a different kind of culmination, almost violent in its crass physicality, enjoyable but finally unfulfilling. There was too much missing; the pleasure came too completely from the flesh. Nothing at all took place in his head

Afterward, Hans walked him to the train station, talking all the way on the subject of Old Masters drawings with such absorption that it seemed he had forgotten the way they had spent their afternoon. Randall was not required to contribute to the conversation, and it occurred to him that Hans had chosen him because he did not speak. He was sitting duck, still life, skeleton, Burt Lancaster emerging shirtless and dripping from the heavy melodramatic surf of *From Here to Eternity*. He was not real and could not talk back, and at the el stop they shook hands and nodded goodbye.

There were women. Three in the six weeks that Randall made his living off his body. Lydia, Catherine, Denise. Unlike Hans, each made a noticeable pretense of her pursuit of him, as if it had nothing to do with the fact that he had posed naked in front of them for hours, was not at all connected to their mechanical and painstaking rendering of *his* muscle, *his* bone into some idea of men or man or even universe they seemed so eager to translate from the inchoate images that had appeared to them that morning outside the windows of trains or lingered long and misty from the chaos of their own small-town childhoods into the obsessive achievement of what they called Style. Vision. Form. They were after something inscrutable, some flinty wisdom earned by color and line and perspective alone; they would rather marry a banker and recede into bourgeois domesticity than be accused of sentimentality, unlike Hans, who seemed to Randall eager to paint the world as he saw it without regard to charges of mawkishness or influence. He was a painter and he painted and he lusted and so he had sex with whomever he was attracted to, and though Randall was drawn to his openness he was equally seduced by the inventive pretensions of the women.

Part of their pretense was a fascination with a Randall clothed and verbal. A slab of stone suddenly capable of laconic greetings and merchant marine peacoats purchased from the seedy Army/Navy outlets. They asked him questions, mimicked his accent in a way that was affectionate and without sarcasm. As he talked they watched his mouth so intently that he grew self-conscious and wondered if his lips were not smudged with crumbs. In their presence he ran the back of his hand over his mouth. He looked them dead and unwavering in the eye as he was not permitted to do in the studio, until he realized this was exactly what they wanted from him, to be human, a man, Randall Speight, lean and chiseled and colored like the smudgy chunks of charcoal that stained their hands at the end of the day. Thereafter he avoided their gaze but this did not discourage them, nothing would discourage them, and when he gave in to them they took their sweet slow time stripping him of clothes and seemed to prefer that he make love to them with his shirt on or, in the case of impatient and of-questionable-mental-stability Denise, with everything on, standing up, his pants unbelted and bunched about his knees. They talked as they made love and tried their damnedest to get him to talk back. Asked him to do things and asked how he liked these things; asked what he wanted done to him and if these things felt good.

And every night he came home to the studio where he lived for free, for the few times he had offered to contribute to the rent Constance had waved him off and said without saying that he paid in other ways. Their pattern became as predictable as his clock-punching days at the shipyard: They worked, they ate, they made love, she asked for stories. The tales he told were honest and easy to part with, for what she needed from them was so obvious that Randall in the telling felt disconnected from the events, as if they had happened to someone else entirely, someone he once knew. A boy who did not know his mother and loved his father and hated him a little and was poor but happy all the same for he discovered early and fortunately the redemptive oblivion of his imagination, and learned to see in the thick scrub of the woods behind his house a forest primeval and magical and dense with riches and a thousand personalities to try on when there was nothing to eat at home and his siblings were at each other's throats over who would feed the chickens and his father was busy draining his porchwhiskey and seeking sanctuary in his own thoughts, which Randall in his earliest memories thought responsible for the stubble on his father's cheeks and chin, as if each deep regret—and there was no question that it was regret, for the look on his father's face ruled out any pleasure but the briefest passing cloud provided by the corn in his bottle—produced a single, ungainly whisker.

But he had his sister. His other siblings appeared in these stories as linked dolls cut from coarse paper. When Constance quizzed him about them, he said only what he thought was the truth: that they left him alone because he was Reka's and they did not for some reason, which he had never really bothered to ponder, trust Reka. Constance found this puzzling and would not let it alone, but Randall found ways to steer her away from the subject and in time began to resent her obsession with what seemed to him none of her business, as it wasn't the truth she wanted but some gritty and bleak vision of a life unknown to her.

One day in November he turned nineteen. He did not tell anyone and spent his birthday walking the streets in a funk, missing his sister who had always concocted surprises for him on his birthdays. He missed her so much that day that he bought a bottle of rye and drank it in the broken wasteland of an abandoned freight yard, imitating his father by getting slowly stewed and wallowing in his loneliness. The next day he was overcome with dehydration and hungover remorse, but even in his histrionic self-loathing he did not consider it time yet to join his sister, for there seemed something left to discover first. Something missing, something more than just money and trysts with artists and Constance, who had begun to get on his nerves with her questions that always led toward the tawdriest and bleakest of his memories. As if she could translate his suffering into the last third of a triptych. He knew what she wanted and she knew why he stayed, and even if it seemed an equal trade, still it gnawed at him, the depravity of their arrangement, the way they worked each other and managed to keep up a rhythm that on the surface looked and felt and sounded a lot like a life together. He knew that if he truly cared for her he would have demanded that she introduce him to her parents, but he had no interest in humiliating either of them with a tense trip out to Oak Park where he was certain to be patronized, or put on exhibit, or, worse yet, accepted as Constance's new boy.

The new decade arrived. He watched the world for signs of change, as it seemed possible to him that some change might occur here in Chicago, as opposed to Trent, where the fifties were not noticeably different from the forties and on Saturday afternoons the

farmers and their families bumped into town in mule-drawn wagons left over from the thirties, enraging the town kids in their slick
coupes who sometimes scooped the shit from the streets and heaved
it at the farm kids huddled in the backs of the wagons in their overalls and wide-eyed come-to-town stares. If the world changed with
time, it was imperceptible to his eyes; it was fruitless to expect from
the world some tumultuous action. Something caught his eye, his
ear. Someone left, or showed up unannounced. He thought of Reka
and Edwin, how his death had led to her escape. And Hal, too—had
he not gone away on his drunk, leaving him with Delores, Randall
would at that moment be standing on a scaffold above the Chesa-
peake Bay, spraying the side of a ship with fire. His father would not
have traveled to Norfolk to tell him of his betrayal, there would not
have been a betrayal, his father might still be alive.

So what was he waiting for? Though he knew it was not that
something missing that kept him naked on a stool in a drafty classroom, he imagined he might be ready to move on if Constance
would lift a paintbrush. But the two thirds of a triptych sat unfinished, and it began to irritate him so much that he was tempted to
finish it himself and would have had he not known that he was not
an artist, that his art was contained in his ability to stay still for
hours at a time. He could stay still. The rhythms of the world—the
turning earth, the unending traffic of Chicago, the neediness of
Constance and those he sat for and those he allowed brief offerings
of his body, leaves falling from trees, rain turning to ice turning to
thick drifts of soot-stained snow, a decade exchanged for another—
all this motion continued outside of him as he sat still and waited
for something he was not sure existed. Had someone told him when
he was younger and deluded by the idea of a world through which
he would move with the speed and indifference of a comet that it
would come to this stasis, he would have done anything—lied,
stolen, maimed, killed—to prove them wrong.

One day in late February he sat shivering in front of the class.

The radiators hummed their dyspeptic tune, the steamed windows turned the studio into a space between waking and dream. More than usual his mind drifted, settling uncomfortably on brief and disconnected images from his past. His father in his saggy drawers wading in the sea with a frightened amazement in his eyes. Randall rubbed thumb and forefinger together absently as if the piece of paper his father had left home to bring him was there still as he sat on the sand and read over and over the harried script of his sister's last words. Wet strangers gathering by the surf pointing at the breaking waves, at his father's dead man's float. When he came to he saw the insolent impatience in the eyes of the artists, all of whom were staring at his fidgeting hands. Embarrassed, he sought some other image, something to calm himself, to set him still. Reka in a warehouse he used to take her to on his afternoon walks. Reka in a corner by piles of burlap tatters left over from the tobacco market, her black hair frizzed by the storm from which they'd sought shelter, her thoughts obviously elsewhere, far from Trent, far from him even. He saw in her eyes that afternoon her desire to leave him, leave them forever. It seemed the moment he'd been looking for, isolated and made meaningful, the beginning of the story, a first sentence of a tale he did not know the end of. He watched her from far across the blackly shadowed building, took note now—years later—of how much they looked like each other. They had their father's coloring, everyone said so. But there was something else now besides his father's dominant darkness that occurred to him in the reconstructed gloom of that stormy afternoon. Some other presence, and not his mother's, whom he knew only through photographs and whose lack of resemblance was so profound that Randall had scarcely felt her absence. Reka, too, though she knew her, though she remembered her smell and had sat on her lap and fed at her breast, seemed not to claim her in memory as a child would a mother taken away early and unfairly. Randall remembered the way she would talk about her—as if she was a visitor, a nice lady who came and stayed awhile and then left forever, her memory lingering more like a favorite toy than flesh and blood.

He could not sit still. Some buried secret coursed through vein and crackled through nerve and even bone. Warmth settled in his groin as if the secret so long hidden would emerge only through lust, and he wondered if it had already, if this mounting current had led him to bed women, men, his brother's lover and the friends and fellow students of a woman who said now, nights before sleep, that she loved him. Oh, Delores, maybe you were right after all. Now that it had arrived, turning him restless and disrupting the quiet intensity of the studio, it seemed not at all what she claimed, as it arose not from his own selfishness but from some passed-down part of him he had no control over.

"Do you need a break?" a voice called from somewhere in the room.

"God, look at him, he's freezing," said someone else.

Let them think so. The heat in his groin proved otherwise, and they sneaked quick glances at the blooming between his legs as they put away their pens and brushes and began to file from the room.

When he was alone he could sit no longer and shot up from his stool so abruptly that it tipped over onto the tile, startling him into a shuffle. He hugged himself to calm the shaking but it only grew more intense, sending him out into the sparse forest of easel and stool to examine what had until this moment been hidden from him, for he'd never before been curious about how they saw him and wasn't sure he really wanted to know now. But whatever had taken him over had nothing to do with his desires, at least until he saw—in two, then five, a dozen of the drawings and sketches and paintings—not the earnest rendering of male anatomy he expected, but the face of his sister, shorn of hair and spliced atop a rangy male nude. She is here with me, has been from the start. He moved through the rest of the studio to find more evidence of her presence and it wasn't until he realized what made them different from their siblings and the same, was not until he saw in charcoal and pen and ink the darkly familiar features of his father's secret lover come finally into focus that he felt his nakedness, felt finally the cold of Canada blowing in off the lake and into this room, and in shame or celebration or perhaps something simpler, some desperate desire for hard proof, moved through the room stripping the thick pads of images and rolling them into a thick cylinder of offerings to his sister and—should she still live, should he ever be able to find her—the mother they shared.

Part Two

She came every day to look for him among the bustle of the Public Market, searching the fishmonger stalls where men in bloodied aprons tossed ten-pound salmon through the air to thrilled customers and entertained tourists with marionette moves of limp-legged Alaskan king crabs. To save money she dawdled among the fruit and produce stands, feigning dissatisfaction with the goods so that the keepers might woo her with offerings of Bing cherry and Washington apple. When she tired of wandering she splurged on coffee in a small diner in the back of the market with a view of Puget Sound, where she alternated her gaze between the shoppers and the ferries and tankers and trawlers headed in and out of chalky continents of fog.

The boy's photo remained hidden safely in her purse, behind the only picture she had of her brother, a smudged and curly-edged snapshot taken in a carnival booth. It wasn't a very good likeness—the light in the booth was as crudely blatant as a torch thrust into the blackness of a cave, and the two of them were too amazed at the thought of being captured in time, together forever, to smile. But a solemn blur in a shadow-puddled closet seemed the appropriate image for that time in their lives, and despite the background and their obvious discomfort (for aside from school pictures this was the only time either had sat for a camera), the resemblance between them was tremendous, especially in the eyes, which shone like the beacons on the hats of miners long accustomed to darkness.

It seemed to Reka now that their father was present in that booth. Present but invisible, as they said of God in the universe. He haunted the shadows and sometimes when she pulled the photo out to examine it under glaring fluorescence, she thought she could make out his silhouette standing above and behind them, a holograph that appeared at whim.

Since learning of his death she had seen him everywhere. He'd never traveled west of Rocky Mount in his life, yet on the bus to Seattle she'd seen him walking through a sopping field outside of Spokane, the morning sun in his eyes, his pantlegs muddy to the knees. Here in Seattle homeless Indians slept in wads of blankets in the shallow shelter of storefronts, and several times she'd seen her father among them, his gray-black hair and sharp bones peeking from tattered covers. He walked by her once right there in the market, while she was watching a ferry churn slowly through the water beneath a galaxy of gulls. And when she ignored the water for land, he appeared beneath her on the docks, toting the end of some piece of equipment, disappearing just as she recognized him into the hold of a ship.

Your father? He's dead. As she'd stood there shallow-breathed and broken in the parking lot of the Red Fork bus station, waiting for Bob Smart to continue, he'd thrown the car into gear and left her there. One more thing her brother had wanted to pass along, he'd claimed, as if it were that casual, one of Randall's stray thoughts tacked onto the tail end of a monologue, an "Oh yeah, I forgot," a P.S. scrawled in hasty afterthought at the bottom of a letter. It took her days to undo the hurt this lie had caused, days to remember that

Bob Smart was a liar and a hypocrite and she could not trust anything he said.

Yet she had no choice but to believe that Randall had cost her the job and the solace she'd found in Red Fork, for how else would Bob Smart have learned of her father's death? The more she thought of it the more she forgave her brother, for she could easily imagine Randall in his naive trusting way thanking Smart for taking a chance on her. Still it worried her, his innocent assumption that people are who they say they are. It seemed to her more curse than attribute, a lifelong sentence much worse than her five years in prison. Jail was a sanctuary compared to a world of trustworthy upstanding strangers.

Nursing coffee in the diner, she told herself she'd done all she could to find him. As soon as she reached Seattle she'd sent a letter to him care of the naval shipyards, but of course she had not heard back and did not expect to, given the number of men from Trent alone who made their way to Norfolk to make money off some coming war. She'd tried the telephone listings for Hal in Norfolk, but of course he would not have a phone and even if she could find him she had the feeling that he and Randall had long since parted company, for she could not see Hal putting up with Randall for longer than a night or two. She did not waste the few dollars it would cost to contact her sisters or anyone else in Trent to see if he'd returned there, for to do so would be like imagining him maimed or dead.

If only she could have gotten word to Jake, for she was sure Randall would come west for her eventually and Red Fork was so small that Jake could keep an eye out. But she was on the bus to Seattle before she thought of this and though the idea of losing her brother was far worse than the obvious risks of interfering again in Jake's life, so far she had not been able to allow herself to take that step.

Instead she'd searched for Jake's son. She did so with a purpose articulated only vaguely, in the vigilance of her search, long hours and constant attentiveness to passersby. She did not yet know exactly what she sought him for, though she knew enough to know that it had more to do with others than it did with Heath Whitener.

She took a room in the YWCA and lived as frugally as she could off the savings left over from those few weeks when she'd actually sold books. There was no reason to save for college anymore, and she would have to find work soon, but for two weeks she devoted herself entirely to her search. She had his picture hidden safely in her purse, though she never looked at it. She didn't need to. He was his father. He had his father's build, his father's smile; though in the photograph he stood tall and unnaturally rigid she could tell he had his father's gentle, rangy walk, which she would recognize easily among the throngs of shoppers there in the market. He was as much his father as she and Randall were their father, and this quirk of gene bound her to him even more, for in neither she nor the boy was there the slightest evidence of a mother.

———————

"AND ARE YOU AN ARTIST?" asked the woman seated next to Randall on the train. For a moment he stalled, staring past her out the window at some forlorn Minnesota hamlet, wondering how she came up with that idea. But then he remembered his baggage—a paint-splattered canvas carpenter's bag he'd borrowed from Constance and a roll of newsprint bound tight by shoestrings, wedged between his knees and the seat, too precious to store in the bin overhead.

He said, "Of sorts." Maybe he was an artist of sorts: the sort known as a quick change, whose talent was mysterious disappearance. The view from the train seemed to confirm his art form, for what he passed was the back side of things: sheds, cars, tractors, factories, houses, towns, stores, even animals and people who paid the train no mind as it chugged past them, did not even bother to look over their shoulders. He preferred the vantage point to the pretense afforded by highways; work was done in the back yards of America, buckets held mops and tools lay strewn about in the grass and it seemed to Randall that he'd found the proper escape route—the back door, the unchecked alleyway—by which to mysteriously disappear.

Now that he was gone he realized he'd wanted to disappear for a while. In the last few weeks, Constance had taken to smiling too much. She smiled at everything, pleasure and displeasure, pain and fear expressed in a grin. Like an infant who knows only tears and a wail to alert the world of his needs, she seemed to find only one way to communicate her emotions. Exasperated, Randall smiled back at her, but with guilt and not a shred of conviction.

Now that he was gone she would be well rid of him. He convinced himself that this was so, using as proof her perpetual smile and the unfinished triptych and his serial infidelities that she was surely aware of. He would have liked very much to feel something other than nothing for taking so much from her and leaving her with so little. Five months he'd lingered there, and during those last nights she'd told him she loved him. Had he not gone to bed with his brother's lover and learned from her the secret he longed to share with Reka, he would surely have lingered longer, taken more care with Constance. He would have told her he loved her too, even though he did not and would not. Maybe he had Delores to thank for saving him from a life of telling people what they wanted to hear.

After a time his neighbor fell asleep and he was able to stare freely out at the moonlit desolation of the northern Plains. He thought of the Indians who had once claimed this land, and then of the Lost Colonists, perhaps the first quick-change artists to work the continent. Late in the night he became the train he rode on, blindly following tracks laid out for him, doomed to wander in search of his sister. The thought might have terrified him had he not already accepted it, for he had lost her already, according to the phone call he placed from the train station to the offices of Mr. Olaf Torkelson of the McMillan Book Company.

Mr. Olaf Torkelson was in a meeting when he called. Randall spoke with his secretary, who twice asked him how to spell his last name and after a few agonizing minutes came back on the line to say that her records showed Miss Reka Speight was no longer employed by the McMillan Book Company.

"You mean she quit?"

"Sir, it shows here that she was terminated."

"Does that mean fired?"

"To the best of my knowledge, yes sir, she was let go."

"When?"

"Last September," said the secretary.

Randall did the math, felt the six months he'd wasted in Chicago in every inch of his body, as if he'd aged that much again with this news.

"But why?"

"I'm not authorized to give out that information."

Randall had tried sweet talk and when that failed he had gone for her sympathy: their father was dead and he needed to find his only living relative to tell her and could she please just tell him what happened and where he might find her. Mr. Olaf Torkelson's secretary said in her unyieldingly formal phone voice that she had no record of a forwarding address and was sorry to hear of his tragedy but she was not allowed to disclose information about hiring or firing practices and if he wanted to talk to Mr. Torkelson he could call back later but that she doubted Mr. Torkelson would be able to help him because company policy prohibited and here is where Randall hung up gently on the secretary in Duluth and rested his head on the cold glass of the phone booth and stayed there until a burly sailor rapped on the glass with a bottle of pop.

He had hesitated and now they were both lost. In a way they had gotten what they both wanted, which was to be free forever of Trent and what had happened there, yet in their countless talks of leaving they had made plans and even promises to let each other know always where the other was and even to be together, to leave together.

Now, rocking along on the westward tracks toward Red Fork, Montana, to try and find out what had happened to his sister, Randall felt the roll of paper between his knees and thought that the secret these drawings held changed everything, and made him even more desperate to find her.

TO GET WORK REKA LIED: about her five-year absence from the working world, about her education. So far from home, she took a risk that they would never check up on her and besides, the job wasn't exactly plum, though it did call for a minimum of two years of college. Surely her jailhouse tutorials with the bookish Memory Wright counted for as much.

The tediousness of the job made the pay slightly higher than what she could earn waiting tables or pressing shirts in a laundry, and she liked that she worked mostly alone. She proofread phone books for the Northwestern Bell Telephone Company, which involved either comparing printed proofs to billing information or following along in the proofs while a co-worker read aloud the names and addresses of thousands of Pacific Northwesterners. For the first week or so she found she had to concentrate so intently that reverie or even thought distracted her from the task, but in time she learned the rhythm well enough to take flight without making mistakes.

Just before Thanksgiving she was able to move out of the YWCA and take a tiny room in a building at the foot of Queen Anne Hill. The bed folded into the wall sheets and all, and the stove was a sliver between a few square inches of counter and sink. In the apartment above hers lived two women who seemed to make their living hosting sailors in port for a three-day blow; the walls were thin, the sleep she caught even thinner, but she was happy to be on her own again and she looked upon those walls as only temporary.

The longer she stayed in Seattle the less she saw it as temporary; within weeks she felt she'd found the place she'd been searching for since she was old enough to search. Perhaps because it was the antithesis to muggy, dusty Trent, the rains did not bother her and the fog that even natives complained about seemed oddly comforting, more cozy than oppressive. She liked to see it lift, as it rarely did now that winter had set in, yet there were days when some meteorological grace allowed a midday sun to singe clouds from the city and the surrounding water. From her window she could see the Olympics blue and craggy in the distance above the Sound, and if she went up to her rooftop she could see all of Elliott Bay, West Seattle blinking across the water. Above the skyline of the city the Cascades ranged to the east, crowned by regal Rainier. The mountain reminded her of the lion in the previews for movies, settled in stately repose but capable of a sudden and terrifying roar. The city seemed at its mercy, and she could not look at it without thinking of Randall, of how he too would respect its supremacy and its violence, of how he would turn it into some kind of primitive shrine.

Though Randall was with her always, he was less present in her thoughts now than Jake and the son who favored him. Without giving thought to what she would say to the boy if she found him, she continued her search. At work they allowed her overtime, which she always took, and this left her little of her own time, yet she spent every minute of it—late nights and Saturday afternoons and all day long on Sunday—combing the market and the streets around it for

Heath. At first she was content to wait, and it never occurred to her that she was wasting time, that he had moved on to another town, another state, another country even. The search gave her purpose, structure, rhythm. She knew that she was looking not only for Heath but for other men lost to her as well, and she knew that if she gave up she would be only Reka Speight in a deadly boring job, saving up money for college, living a life as barren as the one she'd led in prison. Oh, she went exploring. She made weekly trips to the library and roamed the aisles of Nordstrom's and the Bon Marché, ogling clothes she could not afford. She took a bus over to the University District and spent afternoons combing the shelves of the used book stores. Once or twice she took the ferry out into the Sound to one of the islands, which rather than explore she studied from the deck of the ferry, more interested as she was in the boat ride, in water than land. But she was still Reka Speight struggling along in the kind of loneliness she'd known since she'd returned to Trent, and she did not want to be that person anymore, had never wanted to be that person though she wasn't at all sure how finding Jake's son and making friends with him would change her life in the ways she so desperately desired.

One afternoon in mid-December she sat sipping coffee in the diner, watching the crowd for Heath. The brusque Greek who ran the place had started refilling her cup without her asking, and though he never said as much it was understood between them that she had won him over with her regular visits and would never have to pay for her coffee again. The diner was empty, the market itself in its last slow hour of trade; idle stallkeepers traded jokes and insults and the place felt easy and warm to her, as if by logging the hours she'd been accepted in the society of people who worked and traded there.

"Who is he?" said the Greek. She looked away from the window to find him staring at her from the counter. He was drinking wine from a coffee cup and smoking a cigar. His bushy mustache was flecked with ash.

"Who?"

"The one you come all the time to look for."

She did not ask him how he knew. She wondered if others knew, if it was clear to the workers and regulars and even the tourists who flocked to see the fishmongers toss salmon to a boy stationed in the aisle with a length of wax paper to catch it.

"Son of a friend."

"Maybe I seen him," said the Greek. "What does he call himself?"

"Heath."

"And what does this Heath look like?"

She retrieved the photo from her purse and handed it over. He popped open the cash register, pulled a pair of smoggy bifocals from beneath the drawer, slid them on his nose and studied the picture.

"Yes, he was around. Selling fish. Not seen him for a while, though. You take it to the fish stalls, they can tell you more."

She thanked him and tried to pay this time for his kindness, but he refused her money on the condition that she come back to see him and not look so blue next time. She made her way up the market to the fish stalls, flashing Heath's picture. All of them knew him and some even called him by name, but it was not the name she knew him by. Flip was his name here. Haven't seen Flip in a couple months, they said. Ask Domino, a man told her, and he pointed up the market to a large stall positioned prominently at the entrance to the market, where the man named Domino took one look at the photo and grinned so openly that Reka felt her own face stretching into a smile.

"Hell yes, I know Flip. He worked for me better part of a year. I'm the one who named him, for the way he could flip a fish to one of the boys out in the crowd and draw us a line all the way up to First Avenue. What about him?"

"Do you know where he is?" she asked.

"I know where he *was*. Alaska. He took off for the season, working a halibut rig runs between here and Ketchikan. He ought to have been back by now, though. You kin to him?"

"Friend of the family," she said.

"He never mentioned family to me. 'Course I don't ask those kinds of questions. You want me to tell him you're looking for him if he shows?"

"I'm around," she said.

"Yeah, I've seen you. You keep checking. He'll be back."

Reka slipped the photograph into a plastic sleeve of her wallet, behind the blurry image of her brother whose absence seemed easier to take now that she had hopes of finding the boy whose father slipped nightly into her dreams and would soon show up right here in the market, years younger and unscarred by war and marriage and heartbreak.

THE TOWN LAY SPLAYED OUT through a narrow valley between mountains as high and hard as Randall had ever seen. He had nothing to compare them to but the sage and humble Appalachians, against which these monoliths seemed arrogant and immature. They had known so much less suffering, were unwizened by the winds of history and fate. This place where she'd come to find her fortune seemed to Randall a place forged by dreamers and escapees, its topography created not by tectonics and seismic shifts but by sacrifice, betrayal, the need of its inhabitants to put heavenly walls and wild young rivers and treacherous deserts between themselves and the lives they cast off like rain-soaked clothes.

But where was the river? Raging through town with his roll of drawings shouldered like a rifle, Randall saw in the patches of earth that showed beneath the sun-warmed snow only pasture and grassland running right up to the base of the mountains. Red fork of what? He saw no water, not even much color save the tawny grasses and the leafless cottonwoods and the dun foothills kneeling at the imminence of the snow-topped heights. The name seemed a joke, or perhaps there was a river once that had dried to a trickle the size of the creek back home he and Reka used to play in, a sudsy little leak they called the Cat Tail. Maybe Reka had not been fired but had left in disgust with this town that could not even support a stream.

Right off the train he started to work, walking the streets just like she did with her books. Have you seen my sister? Once there was a photo he could have shown to passersby and shopkeepers, but he realized only then that he'd left it in Norfolk with Delores. He slowed to mourn it, for it was the only photo he'd ever owned, being too poor to afford his class picture, until he remembered the roll over his shoulder. Proof: she was there in every line, every stroke, every smudge of charcoal. But would they look at him as if he'd strolled into a department store and held up a pair of overalls and said to the salesman, I want a pair just like these except without the straps and no bib and give me summer-weight wool instead of denim, brown instead of blue. Would they think he was crazy show-ing up on the doorstep with drawings of his missing sister hiding in the shadows of portraits of himself? He dismissed the thought on the basis that he was sane for having entertained it and besides, the drawings looked like her, you'd have to be blind not to notice, just as they resembled him and their mother, too.

She could be anywhere, their mother; right here in this town for all they knew. He thought of her running away from his father in the middle of the night because he would not marry her and she was tired of having to meet him in the ephemerally safe places where they rendezvoused. A piney grove just north of the Tar they called Beamon's Woods after a man named Shorty Beamon was shot by a cuckolded husband while sliding the skirt off the cuckold's wife. Some back alley in Trent, the parking lot behind the old Colonial Store. Or maybe she was the daughter of one of those rich people his father had delivered drugs to before they'd hired Randall to make the deliveries; maybe she was some rich man's wife. If so he understood why she fled. But then he thought of her running away for no other reason than it was in her to roam, just as it was in him and Reka, which was why he had to find his sister and soon.

Somewhere in this sleepy town lay her footprints. He would cover every street and knock on every door, all night long until dawn rose like the waters of a flood and the countryside reappeared with fewer secrets. At the first house a grandmother opened the door to him. Toddlers clung with shy wonder to the shawl she'd wrapped herself in against the draft. *I am looking for my sister and she looks like this:* he slipped the shoestrings off the roll and extracted a drawing and held it up without looking at it or explaining that this was not actually his sister, his sister did not have a penis and her face was free of whiskers, but if she were a boy she would look like this, exactly like this, and even though she is a girl, well, woman really, she is here, in this picture, and there is enough of her here for you to be able to tell me if you've seen her.

One woman lingered over the picture. She was pretty and seemed to have been much prettier once, maybe even beautiful in her youth, which was all but drained away now. Her eyes were slow and sad and empty and her mouth hung open slightly as she stared at the picture and in any other woman this slight parting of lips might have been seductive but it did not work on parts of Randall south of his heart. In the few seconds—close to a half-minute perhaps—before she spoke he felt for the first time like setting aside his drawings and leading this poor tired woman inside, turning on a light for her and bringing her a glass of cool water.

And then she spoke. No, she said, I have not seen your sister.

Randall thanked her and pushed on. Three houses down the police car came sidling up to the curb.

———————

WITH WINTER CAME a kind of cold she'd never imagined, thirty-eight degrees and raining, a cloudiness that entered her marrow as if the weather outside when she rose in the morning was only an extension of the fogginess left over from her dreams. Walls wet to the touch, her feet swollen with sock. By mid-January even the natives were complaining. Reka adjusted. She lost two umbrellas in a week to the wind whipping up the steep streets and more often than not she arrived at work soaked to the bone, but she accepted the weather as her own creation and even when it was intolerably raw it seemed exactly what she'd wanted when she'd lain smothered by thick humidity in the Black Lake Correctional Facility for Women Offenders.

She often came straight home rather than pay a trip to the market. She would not allow herself to give up on him, but she learned from Domino that sometimes the hired deckhands without families stayed on to work the crab boats during the winter, especially if the salmon and halibut season was a bust. Don't worry, he told her, Flip will be back. She didn't worry, though as Christmas came and then Easter and the frigid rain turned only a few degrees warmer she wondered how long she would wait. She had nowhere else to go, nowhere else she wanted to go, for she felt settled in this city, as settled as she'd ever felt in her life. Yet so much of her life was on hold, and for what? She did not even know what she would say to this boy whose father she was in love with, and she would not let herself consider what she might gain from befriending him. From time to time she looked at his photograph and allowed herself the most skeletal scenario imaginable: they would become friends, and their friendship would right wrongs. Injustices done to her, to him, to his father, her brother, even his mother, even somehow her own father. Their bond would be miraculous and even though neither of them would feel the need to admit it, the simplest acts of friendship would bring harmony to a small world of people.

This was as far as she'd let herself imagine, and as spring made its belated and barely noticeable arrival, she put it out of her mind. She'd become friends with the Greek. His name was Thanassis and he offered her a job tending the counter in the late afternoons and early evenings, and she took it because she had tired of proofing phone books in her leisure time, not to mention during the day, and it gave her something to do at night and allowed her to look for Heath without looking. She was there in the market for a purpose. She had a job. Thanassis paid her modestly but treated her well. She could eat for free and on Sundays when the market was closed he often invited her out to his house in Wallingford, where he and his six siblings who had relocated to Seattle from Athens got together to sing songs and drink wine and toast the four siblings who had remained in Greece. These slow and festive Sundays made her miss not neccesarily her own family but the idea of family. The men flirted with her and she danced with them and the women treated her coolly at first but when they saw how she ignored the leers of their husbands and fathers they accepted her and allowed her into the kitchen, where they gossiped and joked and smoked cigarettes and chopped olives and fed her things she'd never tasted.

In April Thanassis took his youngest children, those who had been born in Seattle and knew of their father's homeland only through his boisterous stories, back to Greece. He was gone for a month and before he left he begged her to come work for him full-time. He would make it worth her while, he said. She had phone numbers in her head, seven-digit sequences spilling out of her mouth, area codes taking the place of song lyrics. Yes, she said, even though she knew she would not be able to save as much money. She said yes because she had put off her dreams of college and what did money matter to her now anyway when there was so much else she needed?

She worked the counter alone at night, and often she was so busy that she barely had time to speak to the customers as she took their orders and scrambled back and forth from the tiny galley kitchen where the cook cursed over the short-order sizzle of meat and onions frying on the griddle. One night in June she happened to look out the doors of the diner to see him passing by in a crowd of carousing boys. It was as she'd dreamed it, his appearance, and she did just what she'd done in countless dim renderings of this moment: She jumped the counter and gave chase, the strings of Thanassis's floppy apron trailing behind her, a shaker of salt she was refilling still in her hand, a pencil behind her ear.

WHEN YOU ARE LET GO from the jailhouse at dawn by the grumpy turnkey who has been up all night drinking coffee and reading the want ads of the local papers and is eager to get home to his eggs and biscuits, and the streets you meet outside are shiny with rain from a passing storm and the only traffic is a truck with blinking taillights that shoots newspapers from its windows against the plate glass of shut-tight storefronts, each thwack shaking your sleepless bones like a seizure, there are only two ways you can go.

Left. Right.

Not straight. Go straight, Randall said once to his father when he was showing him a shortcut to work, and his father said, Straight hell, boy, you mean forward. Hal said it once too, in Norfolk when he and Cheap Blade had "borrowed" a car and allowed Randall and Delores to accompany them on one of their beery trips to some outskirt roadhouse where they hustled sailors at the pool tables.

They had come to a crossroads and were arguing over left or right when Delores in a voice tinged with such impatience her Tidewater twang seeped through said, "Just go straight," and Hal said, You can't go straight, you can go forward but not straight, and Randall thought, This is what is left of people when they fade away or up and damn die, the phrases they use, the jokes they tell. Words. Randall remembered all this as he stood on the steps of the jailhouse with the bleary-eyed jailer who had lit a cigarette and was mumbling.

"Man come by to see you. Lucky for you it wasn't visiting time."

"Who?"

"Jake Whitener," the jailer said as if Randall would know who that was.

"What did he want with me?"

The jailer yawned. He held his cigarette out in the morning and puzzled over it, as if he did not remember lighting it, then sighed and smoked on it awhile. He said, "I suspect he wanted to kick your ass. I suspect you showed one of your smutty pictures to his wife and he wanted to square it with you. That happens around here a lot. People wanting to square shit with lowlifes like you will come by here and make bail on somebody who's stole from them or knifed their brother in a bar fight just so they can kick their ass. Usually they're waiting right outside here. Looks like you're lucky."

"Lucky," said Randall. He looked down the street ahead of him, then to each side, trying to decide which direction would take him away from Red Fork before this crazy husband returned to take his bail money out of Randall's ass.

———

AFTER SPOTTING HIM in the market, Reka followed him to a tavern on 1st Avenue that he and his buddies took over completely with the nervous thirst of seafarers returning to terra firma. Displaced bums stumbled onto the sidewalk where she stood peering in until it was clear that they had settled there for the duration, at which point she returned to the diner and shed her apron and gave the cook the rest of the night off and shooed away lingering customers with aggressive preparations for closing. Back at the tavern she sat at the bar nursing a beer and watching him through the smoky mirror, his head and shoulders visible above the row of bottles. He was taller than his father and bulkier from his work on the ships, but his resemblance was even stronger than in the photograph, as if their estrangement had enhanced the likeness. Everyone always claimed that she and Randall were the same person save for their sex. She wondered if now that he was lost to her they'd grown to resemble each other even more, if she ever found him would she see herself as clearly as the image before her in the mirror, only younger and male.

She would find him. Hadn't she found Heath and wasn't it a miracle given the size of the city and the odds that he had stayed on in Alaska or departed for parts farther? Or maybe it wasn't a miracle at all but simply the reaping of a stubborn faith in things coming to you if you wait. Prison had taught her to wait. No, she knew waiting well before prison, knew it from the day Trent's secrets had been exhausted and even the places Randall showed her, his sweetly special places, felt predictable and leadened with a history as oppressive as the sticky heat. Now that she'd found Heath the wait would be tolerable. She borrowed a pencil from the barkeep and made a list on a napkin of the things she had in common with Heath, the things she might find to talk to him about when he came to the bar for a refill.

His father. Obvious and inadmissible. She would not dare bring this up first, as for all she knew he had grown to hate his father. It often happens that the farther away you are, in time and space, the larger someone's faults loom until you cannot remember the slightest good. She'd felt this way about her own father once. The time she served in prison seemed also a sentence handed out by a higher court, ordering her to see her father as the source of everything bad that had happened to her, the real cause of her confinement. Had he not conspired with the druggist to get Edwin back on morphine, she would have made her escape and Randall would not be lost to her now.

But she'd forgiven him the moment she walked through the gates to the car Edith Keane had sent to drive her back home to Trent. It wasn't even voluntary, this forgiveness, but she felt so much lighter without the resentment, like a balloon loosed from a child's fist and carried away above the trees.

His mother. A topic even more off limits than his father, guaranteed to send him so far away he might as well be back in Alaska. But the knowledge was there, they shared it; she, too, had known his mother's neediness, and though it was not nearly so smothering or long-lasting or emotionally desperate as what he'd finally fled, it was something they shared, something she could use without using.

What else? She doodled on the napkin until the beer in her bottle was empty and the bartender replaced it with another. Heath's group raised hell behind her and she craned to pick his voice out of the din and suddenly she remembered something so strange it made her smile. It was hardly a pleasant memory, but it was one more item for her napkin: both had been *caught making love by a parent.* For her that was only the beginning of the few months that led to that moment when she kneeled on the floor above the cot where Edwin lay turning blue, but now that she was making a list it made sense to her in a new way, as the beginning of her leaving. He had managed his escape immediately, but not before striking his own mother. Reka pushed away the thought that Maggie deserved it for nearly wrecking her son's life, as she knew that Jake would never say such a thing even if he thought it and his generosity even toward the person who had caused him more pain than a world war made her embarrassed to entertain even briefly such a black idea.

This city. She could tell by the way he held his beer and smiled to his friends and sent smoke rings above their heads toward the open door of the tavern out into the warm night air that he loved it here, that it had become home to him in spite of his frequent excursions away. It was sanctuary from the life he fled, the landlocked and inward life beneath those crazy mountains in that town his father loved, his mother detested. For her too it was a haven, and though she never intended to stay here more than a few weeks—long enough to lay eyes on the boy in the mirror, long enough to maybe share a cryptic conversation with him, to follow him through the streets and gaze from a distance at the Jake in him—she knew now that she did not want to leave here ever.

"Grocery list?"

One of his friends leaned toward her, his hands on the bar, a bill in his hand to flag the bartender. His peacoat smelled of sea.

"Things to do," she said, moving the napkin away so that he could not read it.

"You're not that busy," he said. "Why don't you join my friends and me?"

"Because I don't know you," she said.

"Sure you do," he said. He spun her stool around so that it faced the booth crowded with boys hunched over their drinks watching with tipsy smirks, as if they knew what he wanted and she were only some barfly he had enough booze in him to approach. "That's Robbie and Chief and Gene," he said, pointing at the boys who grinned stupidly at the sound of their names, "and that ugly one is Heath."

"As in Heathcliff?" she said to Heath. He seemed the shyest of all, slightly embarrassed at his friend's antics, his father's gentle humanity lurking beneath the facade of drunken cool.

"Just Heath," he said. He appeared to have heard that one before.

She smiled, thinking of something else they had in common. Eureka vacuum cleaner, Eureka Spite.

"And I'm Terry," said the brazen one. She told him it was a pleasure to meet him and swiveled back around to face the bartender, who pushed the round of bottles across the bar and said, "You let me know if these boys are bothering you."

"No bother yet," she said.

"Aren't you going to say your name?" said Terry, but she had accomplished enough for the night and felt she had more to lose by joining them than by saving more for later, for now that she had laid eyes on him she was certain that she would see him again, and the next time he would be alone and she would make her move.

"No," she said, and got up and walked out into the city she was growing to love.

IN THE BACK BOOTH of a diner next town down the road from Red Fork Randall sat teasing coffee out of a teenage waitress and wondering where in this world was his sister. She could not have gotten far. Maybe she was still here in Montana, which seemed to him a place she'd like. She favored cold and north and used to talk about ice skating on frozen ponds and reading by firelight in a snowed-under farmhouse, drifts rising to the windowsills, soup bubbling on the woodstove, sun on the snow so bright it would blind. He played along—it was his job to entertain her fantasies of elsewhere, her job to entertain his—but now that he was far north and way west and in the middle of a winter straight out of Reka's fantasy, he wondered whether the conduits carrying his blood were not as faulty as the veins of his father, who had been known to bank a stove on a rainy night in mid-June.

Reka used to joke that their father's lone goal in life was to keep his fever from breaking. What he loved to break, what Reka would keep herself sunken in a cool tub all day long to avoid, was a sweat. She did not mind work, but she somehow managed to accomplish her work without perspiring, a feat anywhere, a miracle in sticky Trent. Mrs. Ilgenfritz who ran the laundry where Reka worked off and on from eighth grade until she left to sell books used to marvel at her ability to stay dry in the back of the laundry, which the pressing machines kept as toasty as a boiler room. When she asked Reka how she did it, Reka told her, "I dream north."

The fraulein, who dreamed of money if she dreamed at all, let it be known through one of her Teutonic grunts that she thought this ridiculous. But Randall, remembering, understood completely. She did not dream south, which gave him one less point on the compass to consider. She had come from the east and though there was no real reason to think she had not returned to, say, Chicago or lit out for someplace like Maine or Vermont, he eliminated east

This left west. And north.

From his roll of drawings he extracted a portrait of both of them, made believe it was a map. He studied the lines on their faces, the curve of their jaws and the crook of their hips as if they were highways. The outward line of a left arm became a river, its elbow a westward bend. Of course she would need, want a river: Red Fork had fooled her into thinking there was another way out, which was surely why it had not worked out for her there. She needed water, they both did. The lazy river that skirted the edge of Trent kept them busy well after the town itself, its back streets and warehouses, ravines and back lots, had lost its mystery. It wasn't much of a river—the current was so slow that you could put in a magnolia-leaf boat at the Devone Street bridge after breakfast and have a full day to mess around before you showed up down River Road that evening to watch it swirling indolently into sight. The water was stained with tannic from the cypress knots, and smelled of metal on a good day, sulfur and sewage at its worst. But it came and went, stayed and left, and this was what they loved about it.

The waitress was standing above him.

"You looking for work?" she said.

"Might be. Ya'll need a dishwasher?"

"Not here. You don't want to work at this dump. My daddy needs somebody on his ranch."

"I'm no cowboy."

"You an artist?" she asked, nodding at his drawings.

"Those are my maps," he said.

"Oh," she said, and fell silent as if she did not know what to ask next of a man who traveled with only a paint-splattered bag and a roll of maps.

"There's a dance at the 4-H tonight."

"You've probably got three dates."

"Shoot. Boys around here are a bunch of whorehoppers. They like their horses is about it. You like Elvis?"

"Sure," he said. He'd heard him on the radio, though he did not see what all the fuss was about, preferring the music Edwin Keane had played for him, crazed scale-running saxophones turning tired standards inside out. The old blue-black guitar pickers Cy and Benny claimed to know from back down where they came from. This rock and roll seemed nothing new to him, only a whitewashing of the songs he'd heard busting out of the Johnsontown jukes.

"Want me to call Daddy? He needs someone bad. Last guy stole a saddle and left in the middle of the night. Daddy went after him with his shotgun but my ma called the sheriff and all the deputies went looking for Daddy because they knew he'd kill that man if he found him and they wanted to kill him theirselves I guess."

"He got away, I take it."

"They always get away. Daddy's had bad luck with help; he hires any old thing off the street. But he'll hire you if I say so. You'd get your own place to stay in a trailer house behind the barn."

Her name was Ginger and he called her Ginger Ale, which she seemed to like enough to feed him a full breakfast, and when her father came rattling up in a muddy pickup, a heavy-footed red-faced man in a Stetson, she met him in the parking lot to plead Randall's case with such obvious conviction that Randall felt indebted to her.

"You running from the law?" he asked Randall first thing when he slid into the booth across from him.

"Not anymore."

"Least you're honest. I'll say this: You steal from me, even a length of rope, one single fucking nail, and I'll shoot you no questions asked."

"I'm not a thief."

"I won't ask what you are, then."

An artist of sorts, thought Randall. According to the good people of Red Fork, some sort of pervert.

"Eighty dollars a month room and board. We work when it's light and sometimes when it's dark. Putting up fence mostly. Ginger seems to think you're okay. You touch her and it's same damn thing in my eyes as thieving."

"I'm off of women right now."

"That's your business, stud. Whoever she is, though, whatever she done, only way to get over her is fuck yourself dizzy. When you get some blood back in your pecker, I'll point you to a place here in town's got girls as clean as this table."

Randall stared at the salt- and crumb-flecked Formica, the great lakes of grease staining the finish, and looked up into the rancher's grin.

"Mac McLaughlin," he said, and they shook hands and Randall grabbed his gear and climbed in Mac's pickup while Mac chatted with the regulars at the counter and Ginger ran a rag across the table they'd vacated, staring at him through the plate glass in a way that both scared him and made him want to laugh.

A WEEK AFTER SHE SPOKE to him in the tavern, Heath showed up slinging fish for Domino. She learned from one of the boys he worked with, a regular at the diner, that he was in Seattle only temporarily, until the opening of the salmon season. She did not have much time, according to her source, who said once the pinks started running Heath would be the first to go. He was legend around the market for pulling in big bucks, one of the few hands who managed to make money off the stingy captains who promised boys like them healthy shares in profits but rarely delivered. All the boat captains fought over Heath, though; he worked hard and had learned boats so well he could dismantle an engine and mend a net as if he'd grown up on the water despite having been on the sea only a few years.

From the windows of the diner she watched the boats disappear into the socked-in bay and worried that as soon as she got to know him he would be gone. If at first she desired only the sight of him, his startling resemblance to his father, now that he was here, close by, within sight, she wanted more. To bring them together again, father and son, fractured family—was that too much? And if she was motivated as much by guilt for what she'd done to his parents, if her desire to reconcile his family was fueled by the fissures of her own past, would that make her efforts any less noble?

A departing ferry bleated its horn below her, and she wet a rag with bleach and set to work cleaning the grease Thanassis had let build for years on the supposedly stainless steel fixtures, determined to distract herself, to stave away the second and third guesses that plagued her every thought, every move. She thought of Edwin, of those letters he'd sent her during the first weeks she'd known him. Back then she'd thought them fascinating—he seemed so aware of himself and of his past, as if no dark corner of his psyche was safe from the light of his analysis—but after he was dead and she reread the letters, which she took with her to prison along with the photo of her with Randall at the fair and nothing else, she saw how selfish and vain these letters were, how much of his character was devoured by his narcissistic flaunting of motive and will. He made himself out to be so complicated, so driven by instincts hidden and dubious, yet what had once seemed admirable honesty turned after his death into the kind of self-disgust that should have been convicted of his death instead of her that day in the courtroom, should have been bottled or boxed or clothed and sent to take her place in jail. She decided that she much preferred an enigma to the people who felt they could explain themselves to you, or who even tried. She could not imagine Jake writing a letter like that. He'd write to her about his work, the weather, trees, self-conscious jokes about the deadness of Red Fork. Things other women might find unglamorous or mundane, but to her they would not be descriptions of trees or tepid jokes but whatever she wanted them to be. Jake, unlike Edwin, had a talent for the kind of talk they called small. But there wasn't anything small about it when she remembered or imagined it. In memory the details of his life—trees, streams, storms, food—all suggested one thing: survival. She remembered the rhythms of Edwin's sentences, how his talk was always more about music than lyrics, how he could have said anything at all and she would have listened and been seduced by the electric currents of words. But the sentences were never finished, they were always interrupted by new ones, counter-rhythms, syncopated diversions, and what finally killed him was the fact that they were all sound and no sense.

She cleaned the place top to bottom, closed the grill early to scour. Heath turned up at the counter minutes before the market closed.

"Still open?"

She was on her knees scrubbing the drink cooler. Though she'd heard him speak only once and then only two words above the thrum of late-night drinkers, she knew exactly who it was.

"Of course," she said. She rose slowly and found herself blushing, which embarrassed her so much that she turned away from him again to run her rag over a blender she'd already cleaned.

"Can I get a couple of those good burgers to go?"

"Well, I've just cleaned the grill." She worried that she'd missed her chance—he could be shipping out tomorrow for all she knew—but she remembered how his mother had doted on him and how it had driven him away and it seemed the worst thing she could be to him was another eager-to-please woman.

"But if you hurry up and tell me how you want them I guess I can help you."

At least she'd make it clear that she was making a sacrifice, which she somehow believed he would respect. But he looked away, out the window at the blinking lights of Elliott Bay, and she could not read his thoughts and worried again that she had lost him. Clearly he did not remember her from the tavern. Or maybe he did, and thought of her as some barfly. What other kind of woman would hang out in one of those bars? She imagined he got lonely after so long at sea and braced herself for the words that would ruin everything, for how could she carry out her plan if he came on to her?

"No," he said finally. "I hate to dirty up your griddle after you've cleaned it. I flipped burgers back home for a while, had to clean the grill every night at closing. Sometimes after I was done and I'd scrubbed the grease off my arms and washed the smell of burger away and was ready to go, the manager would decide he was hungry and he'd fry himself up a couple of sausage dogs. Of course it wasn't him who had to clean it. When you get finished with some-thing and it looks just right, like you never used it, and someone comes along and messes it up—-that drives me crazy."

"It's really no problem," she said, smiling, weakening despite her decision not to appear too eager. He'd been talking about burgers, about cleaning a grill, yet there was something so truly Jake in his words—a respect for other people's work, an obvious selflessness—that she found herself a little choked up. This em-barrassed her so much that she took up her rag again and turned away from him.

"I'll go somewhere else," he said. "There's plenty places open up the street."

"Come back earlier next time." She heard herself say this, heard the words, but she was not standing there saying these words, she was not in Seattle but back in Red Fork standing in the parlor watching Jake walk in through the kitchen door and greet his wife and Bob Smart and her as if he'd been at work all day, as if there was nothing between them. Whispering to herself a frantic last-time-I'll-lay-eyes-on-him goodbye.

"I will," he said. But he did not leave. She knew without turning that he was staring out over the water again, and she marveled over the way that water drew his gaze even in darkness.

"I guess you've already eaten yourself," he said.

She had but said she hadn't. He waited for her outside while she finished closing down and locking up.

"What are you hungry for?" he asked her as they left the market and walked along in the misty night.

"Anything but gyros and burgers."

"I know a place down by the piers where the shrimp are big as bananas."

They walked in silence mostly, chattering in fits and starts about the news that the market was soon to be razed, though the preser-vationists were trying to fight it. She spoke as if she'd been in Seattle for ages. Working with Thanassis allowed her to talk with authority, for Thanassis knew everyone and everything about the market and she had grown to feel as if she had been there forever, though as soon as she left work and returned to her apartment memories of other places—Red Fork, Trent, the parched and desolate stretch of field and swamp that was the Bladen Lake Correctional Facility for Women Offenders—kept her awake some nights until dawn.

The shrimp were more like pea pods than bananas, which made him sheepish and gave her something to rib him about. He was surprisingly mature for only nineteen, the result, she decided, of having lived by his wits for the past three years. When they exhausted the market he talked about fishing. She envied him this passion, as it seemed clear that he had found his life's work and would live and die on the water. She thought about Red Fork, of his father's love for the place, his mother's dislike of it. Maybe the lack of water there, the obvious lie of its name, had sent him off in search of real water, and now that he had found it he would never leave. She thought of his father's love of trees, of the mountain pastures and thick forests where he spent his days; Jake would approve of his son's obsession with the sea, for though they were drawn to opposite topographies their passion was similarly intense. She envied the way they found in tree and forest, bay and sound and sea, some way to translate the world into their own articulated desire. As comfortable as she felt in Seattle, as close as it came to the misty place she'd dreamed of when marooned in Trent, it was finally only a place to live, pleasant and fulfilling but not what Heath and Jake had managed to create: a place where landscape and spirit merged like a lunar eclipse.

Heath told her stories about the Inside Passage he traveled to Alaska, the Indians who were native to that coast, Captain Cook and Vancouver and others who had first sailed it. She found herself thinking of Randall, of how much he'd like these stories.

"But enough about me," he said, apologizing for his monologue, as he realized how long he'd been talking. "I've seen you before, you know."

"At the bar," she said.

"Sorry about Terry," he said. "He gets like that when he drinks."

"Friendly? Him and the ninety-five percent of the rest of the men in this world. I didn't really mind."

"You sure took off quick enough."

She found herself flattered that he'd noticed.

"I'm not much for bars. Don't know what made me go in there in the first place," she lied. "Guess I got tired of walking. I'm inside all day, and when I get off work I like to walk around."

"Let's get out of here then," he said. He insisted on paying and she let him, mindful again of his past, the way his mother bought him everything he wanted.

"Ever been to Volunteer Park?"

She hadn't and said so, and he described the view of the city from the steps of the art museum and suggested they take a bus up there and walk around a bit. As they waited at the bus stop he apologized again for talking so much about himself and told her it was her turn but she put him off for the time being, told him there was plenty of time for her story, now she wanted to hear more about Alaska and he obliged, telling stories of the tiny Ketchikan swelling in summer from a few hundred natives and shopkeepers to six or seven thousand of what the Alaskans called outsiders, working the canneries by day and packing the bars by night.

"There," he said when they reached the steps of the art museum and took in the view, which was every bit as stunning as he'd promised. The lights of downtown spread below them, blocks of blinking buildings clinging to the slope that dropped to the bay. "There," he said, "enough about me for a month. Your turn."

She came close to stalling, telling some innocuous story about the market, but the sight of the city below her, perched on the crust of this continent she had come deliberately to the end of, supplied her with the courage she needed to tell the truth.

"I know your father," she said. "And I know your mother, too."

GINGER CAME NIGHTS to his trailer and sat on his bed complaining of the greasy whorehopping boys in her town and gossiping about the kind of high school experience he'd never had himself and could not imagine, though he quickly lost interest and more often than not took up his pen and started another letter to Reka.

In his six months with the McLaughlins he'd written close to twenty. Some ran as long as twelve pages. He filled them with things he'd seen on the road. While he wrote Ginger flipped through movie magazines her mother would not let her read in the house and smoked poorly and interrupted him with queries about what he was writing, who to, how did he think of so much stuff to say, life around here was so damn boring, she couldn't imagine filling a postcard, didn't he hate it here, her daddy worked him too hard, he ought to ask for a raise, let's go into town there's a dance at the 4-H, will you buy me and Cindy some beer?

Dear Reka I am fine. You heard about Pa now let me tell you the truth of it.

It was not bad as deaths go. I have been thinking since it happened of how else he might have gone and every other way I can come up with is worse than how it was. If he hadn't of left home to bring me the number of where you weren't surely he would have died in bed or on the porch of his shack and by the time Ellen or Martha and them got around to paying him a visit the buzzards would have walked right in through the front door and sat down to lunch on him.

One day he showed up at the shipyard where I was working. A boy climbed the ladder to fetch me down from the scaffold and I saw him standing there on the ground and even from up that high he looked pale and broken, I could tell something was not right with him. But he denied hell out of being sick like you know he would and acted like he'd come all that way to see the ocean and he showed up just after lunch that day and said take me down there to see it I came all this way. I asked him couldn't it wait he said wait hell I've been waiting sixty-two years, let's get. You know how he talks.

We rode the bus out there. You ought to of seen his face studying the Atlantic like it was going to wave right away if he took his eyes off of it and he asked me who do you pay if you want to swim and where's the swimming area and when I explained to him how it worked he wanted to swim buck naked. Broad daylight. Probably would of been easier on the eyes than the drawers he was wearing. Rag bag would of turned that pair down. When he was in up to his waist he kind of relaxed and I taught him how to duck under the waves and he said it made him crave women and I said to change the subject that it made me crave peanuts. I never heard him talk about craving women before and for damn sure he would not have said anything like that to you. I can't say I really enjoyed hearing him talk about craving women, to me it was kind of creepy.

We were floating out past the breakers. After a while he told me you'd come by before you left. He told me about the note you left and said go get it out of his overalls but I stayed in the water with him and at first he told me he was drunk when you came by there and he didn't even remember but after a while I think the water worked the truth out of him and he said he lied to me when I came back looking for you because he did not think we ought to be together. Said he'd rather us apart. We were grown and nothing good would come out of us going around together now that we were old enough to settle down. I tried to tell him neither of us is exactly the settling down kind but he wouldn't have any of that. You know how he acts.

He kept telling me to go in, he'd be on directly. He'd been breathing big all day long, I knew he was sick from the moment I laid eyes on him from atop the scaffold at work but in the water it seemed like he got better and could breathe and I thought maybe that's why he doesn't want to get out so I let him stay in there even though the tide was ripping us away from each other. I told him not to fight it just swim parallel to shore like they tell you to you know but he got scared I guess he panicked or maybe he wasn't scared at all maybe he just thought he could outlast the current. I think he thought he could beat it because he was smiling whenever the current took him away it was like he'd been hooked and somebody was reeling him in, God I guess most people would say it was who had hooked him but you know how he felt about all that I guess it wasn't God you know who I think it was? Reka? I think it was our mother, not the one who died not Rosa Speight who is buried in the middle of that muddy cornfield out in the country where we used to live near Speed's store but our real mother.

"Why won't you do it to me?" said Ginger.

"Because you're a virgin and your father would kill me if he found out. That's for starters," said Randall. *He was dying to see the ocean,* he wrote, then crossed it out as he did not want Reka to think he was being disrespectful of their father or the way he died, then he wrote it again as it seemed true and not ironic or smartassed to say that he was dying and that his death seemed hastened by a desire to see the ocean. He got what he wanted and it killed him. But this wasn't be careful what you ask for; it was a fulfillment, death by satisfaction, and Reka would see it this way as surely they saw things in the same way.

"How do you know I'm a virgin? You think you can tell by looking?"

"Yep," said Randall. He looked down at the pad and started to write again but stopped to think again of Reka, how much they thought alike, how it seemed they were the same person. And then he remembered that this letter would end up like the rest of them, rolled up inside his tube of drawings. How did he know she was the same person? Maybe they were never the same person. He remembered Delores and what she had said to him, the very thing that drove him down to see Reka in the first place. So much had happened since then it seemed another life when he had fled from Delores's bed and hitchhiked to Trent to tell his sister what some girl had said about him, some jealous crazy woman who tried on damn dresses all night, went around claiming she wasn't from the Tidewater even though it was as umistakably present in her r's as the sand and pine needles of the coastal plain were in his interminably long i's.

But even if Delores was right about him, he knew Reka was not that way. She thought of him always, had put herself aside to raise him; the only thing she did for herself, the only time she'd ever left him, was when she'd taken up with Edwin and even then she came to live her life for Edwin. And did so until he died. And then they put her in jail, claimed she killed him. If she was like him—if she was like Delores claimed he was—she never would have gone to jail for something she didn't even do.

"You're not that damn stupid," said Ginger. She stood up and stripped off her blouse and bra and stepped out of her skirt and peeled off her panties and said, "Who says I'm a virgin and if you can sit there and write a letter when I'm standing here naked begging you to stick it in me I guess that proves you're a queer."

He looked up at her. "A queer?"

"A fruit. You know. A pansy."

"Calm down now. Put your clothes back on."

"If you don't do it to me I'll tell my daddy you did."

"Did what?"

"It. I'll tell him you came up behind me in the barn and tried to stick it in my other hole."

"Good God almighty." He watched her rub her hands across her naked stomach, awkward pantomime of some supposedly sexy gesture she'd heard about from some boy who'd been to the hootchie-cootchie show at the local fair. He stared and felt more than tempted. He felt inevitable—not that this succumbing was inevitable, but rather that *he* was inevitable. His inevitability was unarticulated and reined supreme; he followed it anywhere without question or resistance. He was following it now; he felt aroused even as he knew he could not do this, he felt the jeans tightening in his crotch, the denim stretching, the zipper creaking. She was small-breasted but beautifully nippled, her nipples hardening in the ancient and perpetual chill of his trailer. She was slight and womanly at once, a girl and not a girl, a woman and yet too young to know what to do with herself, and he felt himself putting aside the letter to his sister as how could he write to her now after understanding for the first time that they were not the same person at all. He was like Delores said he was. Here he was getting ready to prove it. He looked at the letter and brushed it onto the floor as if it was a spider and he knew he would not write to her again, that even though he had nowhere to send those letters he would not write them, that even though they helped him keep her close he would not write them. He had not lost her. She had left him because of how he was. She knew it all along. She could tell it even before he knew it himself. Like looking at a girl and knowing she is a virgin.

Randall looked down at his jeans and smiled. Not at her, not at himself, but at Delores, who told him the truth. Can't dish it or

take it, love. You do what you want and goddamn the consequences.

Here the consequences were several: the loss of a good job.
Death. Maybe that should come first? No, this last should be first:
He knew she would look back on it with hatred and shame, screwing the hired hand; he knew Ginger would move on to other boys
after him and maybe not be able to stop moving through these boys
after fucking him in the hayloft, after she realized her desperation.
Would she end up fucking her way out of insecurity? He knew it
could happen, even if he did not think himself capable of it. He saw
her years later working at the same grill where she'd taken a job to
stay in town with her classmates. He thought of her remembering
the loss of her virginity to a goddamn joke: the hired hand and the
farmer's daughter.

But what did he care that it was a cliché? Wasn't it equally hack-
neyed for him to succumb to the jealous desire of the lover his
brother had abandoned? For a nude model to bed the artists who
drew him? For a fresh-from-the-shipyards naif to be taken in by a
rich artiste who stowed him away in her loft and plundered his body
for raw sex and his tawdry history for raw experience with which to
improve the canvases she never got around to painting? Was this
what it means to have no morals, no center, no regard for anyone
save yourself: that you would turn yourself into something tired and
obvious and lifeless, that you would forgo mystery and discovery
and exploration, all for the sake of a few minutes of friction and the
ultimate and ephemeral blast of pleasure?

"I will," she said. "I'll tell him you held me down and pushed it
in my mouth and told me you'd cut my tits off if I didn't swallow."

"Where in God's name do you come up with this stuff?" said
Randall as he kicked his shoes off and loosened the top button of his
Levi's.

"God ain't got nothing to do with it. I swear I'll tell him. You
know what he'll do to you, too."

Yes, he knew, but he didn't care. Inevitably he rose to lead her to his bed, put her out of her temporary hormonal misery and deliver her to an inevitable, doomed misery not so easily discarded. Rising, he heard a crinkling and looked down to see his bare foot flattening the roll of papers. He thought it was the letter, that dead abandoned letter that he would have easily kicked aside as Reka was not like him and he was a lost cause to her, but it was the drawings that had revealed to him his mother. He stopped where he was. He smiled again and Ginger smiled back tentatively as if she thought this part of the seduction, perhaps the sum and total of their foreplay, but he did not linger on her awkward grinning as he was thinking of Delores, smiling at Delores now. But not with the same cynical glumness as before. There was triumph in this smile. He thought of himself, but not in any way that could be called selfish.

"Okay," he said. "I reckon you seduced me. But I want it to be wild. Go out to the barn. Meet me in the hayloft. I want it to be good and dirty and I want our skin to get all scratched up from the hay and I want us to root around up there like animals and I want to stuff my hand in your mouth so you won't scream when you come."

Her face was splotched and her eyes were wetly despondent. She hugged her arms to her breasts as if she were freezing, but he saw the shame come over her like a shadow.

He said, "You can bite my hand when you come. I don't care if I bleed. You can tell me how big I feel inside of you."

"You bastard," she said.

"Afterward I'll go to town and get some of those whorehopping classmates of yours and we'll have a little party, say three of them and the two of us."

He felt exhilarated. He did not even notice her tears. He did not notice anything but his own redemption and as blessed as he felt, as grateful to his mother, he also felt cheated by time. He'd felt this way before: when he looked up from the scrap of paper bearing the name of the man who could tell him where he would find his sister to see his father dragged dying from the surf; when he had hesitated in Chicago fulfilling his inevitability with Constance and, by the time he made it to Red Fork, missed his sister by months. Even earlier he had felt this rage against time: when the woman they claimed was his mother was taken away before he could even memorize her smell, when Roy Green the druggist sent him on a delivery to Edwin Keane's house down on the edge of Johnsontown and Edwin had paid him money to bring Reka to the courtyard and he had done it, sold his sister out for pennies, the first and heretofore unacknowledged example of what he had let himself believe was his inevitability. Why could he not have come to see this earlier? Why was he being delivered from evil now, after so much wrong had been done?

"You think you're something different with your paintings and writing those letters, but you're just a pig," Ginger said as she struggled into her clothes. "Go away. I hate you. Something's bad wrong with you anyway."

As he gathered his letters and his roll of drawings and prepared to leave he told her she had it wrong, that it was this: there was something good wrong with him. He saw how the goodness and the wrongness were inextricable, and how both were maybe inevitable, and now that he understood it seemed he no longer had to worry about where to go or what to do next.

———

FOR YEARS SHE WOULD REMEMBER the silence that washed over the world after she admitted to Heath that she knew his parents. Her words echoed off the skyscrapers far below, they ricocheted between the ranges of mountains framing the city; they created waves in the waters surrounding the city, silenced car horns and the gray layer of traffic noise from the freeway. The steady thrum of the city stopped as suddenly as if she had flipped a switch.

"She sent you here," he said finally.

Slowly the music returned. She breathed big, too big, gasping at the oxygen as if air was water and she was drowning.

"No."

He did not look at her. He stood up in a bolt of nineteen-year-old agility and sailed away. She knew she should let him go but even though she got up to follow she was not there, with him, in Seattle, Washington, but back in steamy Trent, a long-ago autumn night. She'd told Randall she was leaving him, going to Kentucky with Edwin Keane, and he'd left her sitting on the bench in the courtyard of the Episcopal church. Rustled away through the dead leaves in a jerky trot, and she followed him for her very life, convinced that if she let him out of her sight it would be forever. Now she followed Heath with the same terrified urgency through the park and into a neighborhood of mansions and finally onto a busy street named Broadway where after three blocks of silent single file he ducked into a tavern and sat down at the bar and ordered a drink and said to her as she stood in his shadow, "You might as well have something, too. Obviously I can't shake you."

"I'm fine."

"Well, I'm not." He sipped his beer and fell silent. The frivolous laughter of drinkers made her anxious. Someone called out numbers and letters for their favorite songs on the jukebox and someone else yelled bingo and Reka felt suddenly like getting up and telling him it was a big mistake, she had him mixed up with someone else, goodbye.

"If she didn't send you, I guess he did?"

"No. Not really, no."

He turned to stare. "Not really?"

She looked at the bottles behind the bar, rows and rows and beyond more mirrored rows; she felt she had to choose words from an infinite and unintelligble lexicon. It would take hours, days. Do what Randall would do: just start talking. For God's sake, just tell the truth.

"No, he did not tell me to look for you. Yes, he told me where you were."

"So he knew all this time?"

"Yes."

"Goddamn Melanie. I knew she'd blab. As soon as we pulled into the bus station she wanted to go home and she was the one who talked about leaving always. Red Fork, Red Fork, Red Fork—she's even worse than Dad when it comes to that place. She *is* Red Fork. Can't think of her now without seeing the ceiling of my bedroom where Mom caught us that day I left. Not that this is any of your business. Though you probably know it all anyway. So he knows where I work and everything?"

"Your girlfriend told him you were selling fish at the market. It wasn't hard to find you because I have a photograph."

She reached for her purse but he stopped her. "I don't want to see. Not if she took it, and of course she took it, he would have never been allowed to take a picture of me if she was around. He'd have screwed it up, of course, at least to hear her tell it. How do you come to know them, if you don't mind me asking? You certainly aren't from Red Fork. I'd have seen you and besides, you don't sound like you're from Montana."

She did what Randall would do: just started talking. All of it, every detail, Bob Smart, her arrival in Red Fork, then back to Trent and prison and what led her to it though she did not have to, but staring at his reflection in the mirror, parts of him visible between the bottles, she felt as if she was telling it all to his father and for the first time.

When she came to the part where snow blew suddenly down from the Crazies, burying crocuses and daffodils and the raked infields of ballparks and his mother left for Bozeman and on the floor in front of a fire she rolled around with his father, she stalled, scared of how he might react. Even though his mother had driven him away she was still his mother and even though Jake had allowed it to happen and she was sure the boy blamed his father, still: he was his father. She tried to imagine what she would think if one day she opened her door to a woman who claimed to be her father's lover and wanted to be near for reasons that had nothing to do with her. It wasn't easy imagining her father with a lover other than her mother, *even* her mother whom she barely remembered since she was seven when she died and the years since were the hard kind that erased the good and left the bad.

"And?"

She looked up from her focal point behind the bar into his eyes, which she noticed for the first time were the eyes of his mother, the ones whose sadness had implored her to stay in that house in the first place.

"There's more, right?"

"Listen, maybe this was a mistake." She remembered telling him she was fine when he told her she might as well join him in a drink. She wasn't so fine now, and she wished she had something to sip on, something to do with her hands.

"I thought maybe you would want to know all this and I thought maybe if . . ."

"You and Dad?" he said.

She nodded, but so slightly he did not notice.

"Is that what you're trying to tell me?"

Yes, okay, I should have said it straight out, your father and I.

"And Mom knows?" He was trying to sound indifferent, but she could hear the hurt in his voice and wondered again if all this noble truth-saying was worth anything at all.

"No," she said. Unless Jake told her after she left or she heard it around town from someone who heard it from Cecilia Bannister, but she did not want to think about it, she didn't even care. What difference did it make now? All she wanted was to bring the boy together with his father. She might as well admit what she had not let herself even think: that she would just as soon Maggie go back to Bozeman and instead of Heath returning to his father they could all start over here in Seattle, where already she felt like Before was socked in by a fog as thick as what was gathering now somewhere out above the water as they sat there chipping slowly away at the truth.

"What do you want from me?"

"I have a brother about your age."

He looked at her and laughed, softly but not altogether kindly. "I can't picture you two together. Not the way you talk. Dad's not much of a talker and what he says is what he means, which ain't exactly your way."

"I was changing the subject," she said, though maybe she wasn't at all. She did not know what she wanted from him but she had a vision of that moment when Jake and his son walked across a parking lot to hug each other and silly as it was, silly enough to make her cringe, the hug brought Kennedy and Khrushchev to agree on everything that concerned their countries and made her sisters open up their arms and houses to colored people they'd rather die than call colored and it put food on the tables of the penurious, this hug, it made Edith Keane a happy woman and brought back Memory Wright's sweet old husband she missed so much. Randall showed up to see her graduate from college as father and son hugged and her father lived still and for a long time, long enough for her to get to know him like other people knew their parents. Real people. Like Heath should know his father.

"I won't ever go back there."

She reached for his hand, pulled it away from the mug, warmed it in hers. "Hey, you shouldn't," she said. "Oh, I never would even think of saying you should. Believe me, I understand why you left. I understand maybe better than anyone."

"I got a good life here. Not Seattle, I like Seattle fine but the water I mean. Coming and going suits me better than sitting around in one place saving money for my tombstone. It's hard work and it's dangerous as hell but I'm good at it and now that I found something I'm good at . . ."

"No one's asking you to give that up."

"You think he'd understand? He left Red Fork exactly once since he moved there and that was to take me to the state fair. Mom was all the time taking me somewhere, Bozeman mostly to see my grandparents or on some trip she thought I'd love. I'll say that for her, she got me out of there, which is a good thing though I guess now she regrets it."

He turned to her. "So you want a dime to call him, give him a progress report?"

"He doesn't know I'm here. He has no idea where I am."

She studied his face to see if he believed her, but Heath seemed to find in her eyes something else he was not even looking for and that she had no idea was so apparent.

"God, you love him, don't you?"

She was silent and in her silence he heard her answer and got up without a word and left her there. There were no goodbyes but she knew there was no need, for she was certain from what he did not say that she would see him again.

THEN CAME THOSE MONTHS of slow wandering, neither aimless nor purposeless, though Randall was in no hurry now that he was free from the curse of Delores. As for his purpose, it seemed he had already found the woman whose presence in those drawings had roused him from his complacency and put him back on the trail of his sister. What if he managed to track her down, in the flesh, living in some riverfront manor house on the Tar or in the Seven Lakes Trailer Park out on Highway 403, only to find her incapable of doing for him what a roll of drawings had already done?

Still, he planned to try. If only to see her for a minute. And have something more than faded, smudgy sketches to show his sister.

But for now the sketches were all he had. He took care with them. Every morning, before he ventured out to explore the world, he hid his drawings. Beneath the crawl space of an abandoned house, in a dry culvert, between the bushes of a city park, atop sheds and the flat roofs of warehouses, in wrecked cars and sidetracked boxcars, anywhere that seemed safe, dry, undiscoverable.

In late summer of 1961, after eight months on the road, he found himself in Astoria, Oregon, picking apples. He lived with a family of Mexicans whose kids he grew to love even though he could not speak a word of Spanish and they knew no English. He held them in his lap and made faces and gave them candy and let them know in other ways that transcended language that he was on their side. In time he learned enough Spanish for the Mexican men he worked with to make good fun of his accent, though it was clear from the way that they held things in the air and repeated the words they knew for them that they trusted him more for trying to meet them halfway, unlike many of the orchard owners who communicated with crew bosses or shouted and gesticulated as if his friends were deaf. He grew so deeply tanned from outdoor work that the bosses often assumed he too was a Mexican, which he did not mind even though he grew tired of being yelled and pointed at.

After the season ended he found himself in Portland. Though he had saved enough money for a flop, he slept in a downtown park in front of the art museum and spent most of his days wandering the galleries. The paintings reminded him of Chicago, which bothered him as he would like to be able to stand in front of, say, a Chagall or a Kandinsky and peer into its mysteries without hearing the clack of the elevated or seeing the sliver of Lake Michigan from the window of Constance's studio. Memories tainted by atmosphere and landscape: He sought a way to keep his mind free of such baggage, as it annoyed him that the thrilling discordance of Thelonius Monk's piano chords always ushered in an image of Edwin Keane's cluttered and malodorous kitchen. Just before Thanksgiving, arriving in a northern California town named Eureka, which he combed for hours in search of his sister of the same name, Randall realized without allowing himself to admit as much that he was headed slowly south and east to a place where landscape and memory were one and the same.

A WEEK AFTER HEATH left her in the bar, he showed up at the diner. It was lunch hour, and so packed that Heath had to stand at the counter. Reka had to make herself wait to wait on him. There were customers ahead of him whom she wanted to ignore, but she did not want to appear too eager. While she fetched drinks and took orders, she thought how much like a seduction her situation with Heath was, though that was the last thing on her mind.

"One of those good burgers to go?" she asked when she finally worked her way around to take his order.

"How'd you know I'm going somewhere?"

I always know when men are going somewhere, she almost said, but she knew that anything she said about men he'd likely assume was about his father.

"Off to fish?" She said it as if he were merely strolling down to the pier to idle away the afternoon with a rod and reel and a cooler of beer.

"I'll be gone for a few months."

She nodded and looked down at her order pad instead of at him, for he reminded her so much of his father that she found it hard to hear about him leaving. Even his mother's flat gray eyes brightened into his father's wide green ones if she stared long enough.

"I wanted to let you know I'm leaving. So you wouldn't think I'm, you know, avoiding you. I had a lot to think about after our talk the other night. Brought some stuff back. Some big stuff."

"I know," she said. It did for her, too, but not nearly so much. She wondered if she'd done something horribly wrong, seeking him out—if she'd ripped open wounds of the type that can only be healed by wide-awake headachy nights, months and years of them. But instead of saying more about this big stuff she brought back to him, he asked her if she liked seafood.

"I grew up fifty miles from the ocean, but I only went once. I guess I'm a little scared of it. But that was the Atlantic. I guess yours is different."

"Mine's a lot rougher, from what I hear. Whoever named it got it dead wrong."

"Like Red Fork?"

He laughed openly at this, and his laughter seemed to relax him. For the first time she sensed that she made him nervous, and she understood why. His father's lover, so close to his own age: of course she would make him nervous, and of course she would have to find ways to put him at ease.

"I guess whoever named Red Fork had the same idea. They call it what it ain't to trick you into trusting it."

"Didn't work, did it?"

"Not for me. I heard some piano player being interviewed on the radio once. This lady asked him when he came up to New York from Mississippi and he said, 'Madam, soon's I heard about it.' I've wanted to live by the sea since I learned there was a sea. I've always loved the water. My mom told me I was the only child she ever heard of who didn't bitch about taking a bath at some stage. She could always get me to do anything she wanted by promising to take me to the swimming pool at the VFW hut."

"I guess you outgrew that pool."

"That's about the only water there is in that town. I used to ask my dad why Red Fork was named that, and he claimed there was a river there once, that only the Indians knew where it used to be, and they weren't telling. Who knows if he was making it up, trying to invent some mystery so I'd stay around longer. Of course when it came down to my leaving, it wasn't about any river."

"Might have something to do with going back," she said.

"I'm never going back. He's bound to know that."

This wasn't a question, but she understood he meant it as such.

"He misses you," she said.

Heath looked around the diner. She could see him pulling back emotionally, saw it take root in his body: in the way his shoulders tightened, the way his eyes darted around the room, searching for and finding an excuse to cut her off.

"You got 'em coming out of the woodwork in here. I'm keeping you from your work."

"Burger's on the house if you promise to bring me back some of your catch."

He agreed, then tried to pay anyway, which she somehow knew he would.

While he was away at sea she worked as much as she could stand. Thanassis slid into semiretirement and let her run things, stopping in daily to collect his money and drink wine from a coffee cup and entertain the tourists with tales of Old Seattle, logjams and gold rushes that he recited with the slight irony of an immigrant. She was able to save quite a bit of money, which she put away in what she called her college sock, a red-ribbed knee-length thing stuffed with bills and change that she hid beneath the sink in her apartment.

She was doing so well that she was able to send Edith Keane a letter with a money order for one third of what she'd borrowed. Reka labored over the letter for days, unsatisfied always with the tone—either it was too familiar or stiffly distant, and the failure to find an in-between reminded her of how conflicted and contradictory her alliance with Edith had been from the start. She was determined to pay her off and leave her behind, as this connection seemed—aside from Randall, aside from the guilt she felt over her father dying before he had a chance to see her settled and prospering—her last tie to Trent. In the end she abandoned her attempt to strike the right tone, as she realized her words would always betray her, that words were all she had and they were never enough.

She wrote: Dear Mrs. Keane, Hi. How are you? I'm living in Seattle, Washington. It did not work out, selling books. But I've managed to put away for college anyway and I want to pay you what I owe you and will be sending you some when I can. Thank you for all your help, you have been very generous and I don't know what I would have done without you. I probably would have stayed in Trent forever and though it's a nice place to have grown up I don't think it's the place for me. Sincerely, Reka Speight.

She licked the envelope and taped it shut against her second guesses and nearly ran to the mailbox. She knew she would not be free of Edith Keane until she paid her in full, maybe not even then, but sending her money felt therapeutic to Reka, as if she was finally learning to live on her own.

But she missed the men in her life: Randall as always, and Jake more each day. Since she'd found Heath, she thought of Jake constantly. She thought of writing him, too, sending a letter to him care of the timber office, but she knew she couldn't tell him where she was and who she'd just happened to run into and strike up a friendship with. Not yet. No, it was better to wait and see what happened with Heath. She kept track of how long he had been gone on her kitchen calendar, and although she hardly knew the boy, she found herself missing him as well.

She was pleased when he stopped in at the diner on the very day he returned. He looked both exhausted and healthy, his face wind-whipped, his biceps swelling beneath his t-shirt.

"You're back," she said, feeling foolish for saying something so obvious.

"I am back, you're right," he said, as if he'd taken note of her embarrassment and wanted to make her pay.

She tried to make conversation, asked about his trip, and was surprised to find that Heath had no real talent for small talk. He seemed eager to tell her something, so she let the pleasantries go.

"What time do you get off?" he asked her.

"Never, here lately."

"Where's the Greek?"

"Semiretired. He comes in to collect his money and lecture the tourists about the original Skid Road."

"Bet you need a break."

"I never minded work," she said.

"Neither did I," he said, "but you need a day off every now and again."

It occurred to her that he was about to ask her out. Even though she'd acknowledged the seductive qualities of her search-and-rescue routine, she'd not anticipated that he might want her in that way.

"I've got something to show you. When can you get away?"

How to stop this? She couldn't turn him down for fear that she'd lose him, so she agreed to meet him early the following Sunday in front of her building. She spent the next week worrying. Though she could not look at him without thinking of his father, it had never crossed her mind to know him like she'd known his father. She felt almost maternal toward him, which was preposterous considering she was closer in age to him than to his father, but since he was the same age as the brother she'd raised and had lost to bad timing and what seemed more and more like selfishness, her motherly fondness made sense.

He'd asked her to dress for the outdoors, which she took to mean warmly and dryly, and she made a trip down to Eddie Bauer's outdoor apparel and bought herself a new windbreaker and a pair of jeans especially for the occasion. It had been so long since she'd done anything aside from work and walk around the city by herself. On her days off she was usually so exhausted she stayed home and read newspapers and novels in bed, which she really didn't mind because it meant so much to her to be able to save money for college and pay off her debt to Edith Keane.

"You look prepared," he said when he met her outside her building in fog tinged yellow with streetlight.

"I packed some things from the diner."

"Good. We'll need them. Let's go."

They took the bus over to Ballard and got off at Salmon Bay. He led her into a vast marina hugging Lake Union, rows and rows of small vessels and larger seagoing shrimpers and trollers, until they came to a freshly painted gill-netter. She assumed this was the boat he'd worked on until she spotted the *Red Fork* painted in garish red on the bow.

"Not yours?"

"The bank's mostly. But if I have two or three seasons as good as this one it'll be mine all mine."

She found it odd that he'd named the boat after a place he'd hated, but she knew better than to say anything about it, lest the conversation veer away from his purchase and into the treacherous ground of the past.

"Your father would be so proud," she said, and as soon as she said it she regretted it, for it was both too obvious and too intimate. She saw the way his face tightened at the mention of his father and vowed to get to know him on her own terms, though she knew it was impossible now to rid themselves of Jake's shadow.

He helped her aboard and showed her around with the pride of a boy giving a guided tour of a first fort in the woods. She'd never been on a boat like his before and had to have everything explained to her. She found herself thinking of Randall, of how he'd want to know so much more about the equipment and the terms, and she wished he was here so that she might learn more about things for which she lacked the energy to be curious.

They took the boat out through the locks linking Lake Union with Puget Sound, and he explained everything to her as the iron doors to the chambers clanked shut and the boat began to rise like a child's bath toy to the next level. Again she thought of Randall, of how much he'd enjoy this. In Trent they'd spent much of their Saturdays swimming in the muddy Tar and making boats from magnolia and rhododendron leaves to race in the slow-moving current. They'd like each other, Randall and Heath. She fantasized a meeting between them while half-listening to Heath explain the tricks of navigating Puget Sound.

When they were far enough out into the sound to avoid the ferries and tankers, he let her steer. They fished a little but mostly just buzzed the islands as he described his incredibly lucrative season and told her stories about the Inside Passage and the wild Alaskan towns where he put in occasionally to refuel and carouse.

She waited for a lull in the stories, then said, "Remember that night at Volunteer Park, when I told you I knew your parents? Well, I worried for days that you might not think much of me."

"To be honest, I didn't know what to think. I couldn't say anything then because it was all too new and too damned strange, what you were saying. About you and Dad. And yeah, maybe I was a little ticked that you had been tracking me around, shadowing me in the Market. At least that's the way it felt to me then. And of course I wondered why you bothered to look me up. Still do, in fact. I mean, what did you want me to say? What did you want to see me for?"

Reka thought she'd prepared herself for these questions—she'd spent all week at work rehearsing answers—but she found herself dissatisfied with what she'd planned to say.

"I don't know," she said. "I know that sounds crazy, but I don't really know why I wanted to see you. Because you're Jake's son? I know that's not really a very good answer, but that's all I can tell you, for now at least."

He was quiet for a time, busied himself at the wheel.

"I guess that will have to do, then."

"I can understand if it makes you uncomfortable."

He shook his head at her and scowled. "While I'm out on the water I have a lot of time to think and what I decided finally was that I was glad. About you and Dad. I mean, it's still a shock to have someone come up to you out of the blue and tell you they slept with your dad, especially if you can't really imagine your dad sleeping with your mom, I mean even if they were, you know . . . even if they liked each other."

"I'm sure they did once." She didn't want to think about it any more than he did, but it was the only response she could come up with.

"Maybe. But she would never have done me like she did if she'd been getting what she needed from him. It's not easy to forgive her for what she did to me, but I'm going to have to sometime or else I'll have to forget all about her. I don't think it would be a very good thing if you just trained yourself not to think of your mother ever again."

Reka considered this. She thought of her own mother and the way it never occurred to her to think of her, she'd been gone so long. She said finally and a little shakily that, no, she didn't think it would be a good thing either.

"So maybe you make Dad happy. He deserves it. Mom does too, of course, but I doubt she'll ever get there. I believe she's the type who's always got to be having something bad happen to her so, I don't know, what? She can feel alive?"

Reka knew the type. Edith Keane. And maybe her long-dead son, too. She wondered where she'd be if Edwin were alive, how long it would have lasted, if had he managed to get himself clean and stay that way there would have been some other crippling addiction taking over—booze or gambling or other women or simply staying in that place that he claimed to hate in order to make himself feel— like Maggie—alive, miserably alive.

"We'd better head back. I don't usually waste fuel on a pleasure cruise."

She told him how much of a pleasure it was, and asked if she might fix him dinner sometime.

"Sure," he said. "I'm helping out Domino a couple of days a week while I'm in town. I'll be around the market slinging fish. Which reminds me—I owe you a seafood dinner, don't I?"

She tried to call it even now that he'd wasted fuel taking her on a pleasure cruise, but of course he would not hear of it, and while they settled on a compromise—he'd supply the fish, she'd prepare it—she wished for some way to let Jake know how well his son had turned out.

PEOPLE WOULD PICK HIM UP by the side of the road and ask where he was headed. Forward, not straight. Left. Right. Sometimes he'd just go where they were going. An old couple took him with them to the doctor's office, where he read back issues of *Arizona Highways* and held a sneezy toddler in his lap while the child's mother got help for her diabetes. Some carnies drove him all night to their next gig in a nothing town in New Mexico, where he got some work putting up rides and spent a night drinking with the world's tallest man, who turned out to also be the world's drinkingest man. World's tallest kept up a roll of insults with the fat lady that had the whole carnival spitting laughter, though Randall saw beneath the slurs to a desperation that revealed itself in the way these two put everything into their bodily distinctions, as if height and weight were all they had and as much a talent as Monk plucking his crazy chords. Randall wanted to take them aside, each of them, and tell them he adored the untapped spirit within them. Instead he snuck off when things turned sloppy and the fat lady threw a church key at the world's tallest drinkingest man.

JUST GIVE ME A HOUSE BY THE SIDE OF THE ROAD AND LET ME BE A FRIEND TO MAN. He read these words on a tombstone and they became a song, his song, that he would sing between rides, which as he got deeper into Texas were fewer between. Something about his drawings discouraged the hardworking Texan motorists from picking him up. Carrying a tattered roll of newsprint made him a suspicious character. Was there a gun up in there? A machete? A manifesto, his own Dead Sea scrolls, a map of the end of the world? It got hot and hotter and miles of unbroken road stretched out like a sentence that knew no period. One day he walked for six hours in the world's tryingest heat. He sang his house-by-the-side-of-the-road song dedicated to his mother, who was the object of all his songs and prayers and stray lines of road poetry, who appeared nightly in his dreams and at the wavy edge of desert mirages. Walking down the road talking crazy with a go-to-hell smile on his face. It was not the weather, the heat, the dust and dryness of Texas making him say these things. He had someone to sing to, someone who heard his song.

Later he caught a ride with a couple of boys run off from some snoozy panhandle town, went along with them on their way down to Mexico for a first lay. This involved a hard right turn, but he was in a going-along mood. The boys were named Tommy and Ricky, and when he introduced himself they took right off to calling him Randy as if nicknames were the only names and Thomas and

Richard and Randall belonged to a middle age as impossibly far away as the millennium and if they allowed themselves to be called something so formal and legal they would miss out on the irresponsible idiocy of youth.

They smelled of pimple. Their skin was greasy and so was their hair. The '55 Ford Fairlane seemed powered by their boundless and pent-up horniness.

"What you got inside that paper, Randy?"

"My toothbrush."

Tommy and Ricky laughed. Tommy drove with his smelly feet out the window and Ricky tried to open a beer with his teeth. He pulled it off and Randall clapped and asked for some music to hold off the crazy no-word song that was so loud inside his head he feared it would be audible even to these single-mindedly horny boys. All the boys would listen to was Buddy Holly, who Tommy claimed was his second cousin out of Lubbock. Randall told them where he was when Buddy Holly died and they took turns detailing for him their exact whereabouts when the plane went down and this took them the last thirty miles to Mexico, where the border guard took one look at them and told them to keep their peckers rubbered up or they'd have hell to pay their entire lives.

At the whorehouse Randall sat down at a painted plywood bar and ordered a drink.

"Don't you want none?" said Tommy, pointing toward the lineup of whores.

"I'm not one to pay for it."

"What? I reckon they pay you," Ricky said.

Randall kneed his drawings, which he had insisted on bringing in with him from the car, prompting the two horny panhandlers to rib him about wanting to brush his teeth before he kissed a Mexican whore. He thought of Constance, who had paid him for sex, though he had paid her back with his fair share of tales of hardship and farmwork. Now that he no longer had Delores's curse to worry him he felt less guilty about Chicago, about Constance and the other artists who had used him in their own ways, too, but had given him the roll of paper beneath the bar. The greatest gift he'd known in this life, save for his sister.

The whores came and went, each trying to lead him off into another wing of the labyrinthine bar, but he smiled at them and kissed their hands and whispered to them in his abysmal Spanish and would not think of going off with a whore in the presence of his mother, who sat with him while he drank. After the boys made their choices and disappeared with their rentals, Randall drained his beer and the two bottles the boys had left on the bar and walked outside into the tawdry border town past the blanket hawkers and the boys selling store-bought Chiclets loose from their dirty hands. He had just enough Spanish to converse with an old man on a broken sorrel who gave him a ride back to the border, which did not seem like much of a border to him, given the ones he'd already crossed since he'd left home.

HEATH BEGAN TO DROP BY the diner after he got off work slinging fish, and more often than not, Reka would end up feeding him. She sweet-talked her cook into fixing Heath anything he wanted, on and off the menu, but she did not offer any more free meals, as she did not want to make him think she was buying his friendship. As for what she wanted with him, they did not speak of it again, though it hung about them always, seeped out between sentences. They did not speak of Jake either, and never of Maggie. Reka was determined that the things that brought them together would not turn out to be the only living things between them.

She talked a lot about Randall when Heath was around, and sometimes she made believe she was talking to Randall instead of Heath. This was a stretch given even her imagination and her desire to be close to her brother. Though they were so close in age, Heath and Randall were nothing alike. Heath lived with his hands. What he knew came from his hands, knowledge he won through the tips of his fingers. The bulk of his upper body was not only the result of repetitive manual labor but a repository for the things he'd discovered making his brute way in the world.

Randall, on the other hand, used his hands to illustrate images and scenarios rooted in the deepest shadows of his imagination. She had never even seen Randall shake hands with anyone. He wasn't lazy, and she knew he had found work as a welder, but she saw the torch he wielded as an extension of his fiery and eternally lit inner life.

Despite these differences, Reka found herself seeking from Heath the things she missed about Randall. She realized that this did not exactly fulfill her desire to get to know him on his own terms, but it seemed safer than seeing him solely as the son of the man she loved and did not want to believe she'd lost.

"I rented a house," Heath told her one night when he was waiting for her to close. "Over in Ballard. Not much of a place, but the owner's letting me lease with an option to buy. I hope to make enough off the next run for a down payment. It's pretty small, but all I need is a place to stay while I'm not on the water. I was thinking that I need to have someone staying there while I'm gone. Keep on eye on things for me. It's a shame to let it sit empty for eight or nine months out of the year."

"You thinking of subletting it while you're gone?"

He smiled his most Jake-ish smile. "I'm thinking you could stay there for me. Like I said, it ain't fancy but it's got a back yard and you'd love the neighbors, they're all Finns and Norwegians, mostly women during the season since all the men fish. It's a little like living in a foreign country but only a mile or so from downtown. I love it out there and you will, too."

"Why are you doing this?" she asked.

"Didn't you tell me you were saving up for college? I'll cut you a good deal, and like I said, I need someone in there while I'm gone to take care of things."

She told him she'd think it over, but she knew before he even left the diner that she would accept.

"I'd have to pay rent," she told him the next day. "And of course I could keep house for you when you're in town."

"I need a tenant, not a maid. If you want to pay some on the mortgage, if that will make you feel better, fine. But I'll not have you wasting all your free time scrubbing the floor. We'll share the housework."

This was not a promise he kept. Growing up with a mother who existed only to serve him had made him lazy in some small but nevertheless annoying ways and despite his promise to help out around the house, he spent all his time down at the dock working on his boat, and when he came in he shed his soaking clothes on the furniture and left his soup pot simmering on the stove while he ate out on the porch, talking across the yard to the Norwegian sea captain who lived next door while Reka went around behind him turning off burners and scraping the scalded chowder from the pot and keeping him from burning the house down. He was moody, too, which she at first attributed to his profession, the risks and whims of making your living from the sea. Every night he tried to drag her down to Hattie's Hat, where he and his fellow fishermen drank and played darts. Sometimes she went along and sat silently among the wives while the men speculated about what the season would be like and groused about the Japanese encroaching on U.S. fishing waters and maligned the government regulations and the rights extended to Indians.

She was glad he was not perfect—she expected so much out of their arrangement and it helped that he was human, that she grew annoyed with him for leaving his work boots on the kitchen counter and splicing rope with the only decent knife in the kitchen. Though she was reluctant to take care of him like his mother had done, she felt she had much to offer him in the way of companionship, and it seemed to her that they were both in need of someone to take the place of the families they'd left behind.

She wanted to *be* family, and he seemed to share that need, to want as much as she could give.

But it was awkward at first. For weeks they lived together like refugees, survivors of some atrocity about which they did not speak except in a kind of strained code. They tried to get around it but it was there always and not there, the buried hurts of family and adolescence, and to compensate they talked nervously and loudly when they met in the hallways, as if to ward off intruders or ghosts.

After several short trips, Heath left for a longer run in February, with plans to return in early summer. She was alone in the house, a shingled bungalow built in the twenties. Its rooms were so sparsely and inelegantly furnished that she took it upon herself to haunt the rummage shops up and down 1st Avenue for affordable treasures that did not look as if they'd been donated. She made curtains and painted the kitchen yellow and pretended that this was her home, a starter home, she'd heard it called. She thought of it as a start and she kept busy with home improvements and did not get lonely. With the salmon fleet gone, the streets of her neighborhood emptied of men and the women got together sometimes for huge pots of fish stew. She attended their potlucks regularly enough to be polite, but these Nordic women seemed to her as cold as the climes they'd fled. Reka felt uncomfortable around them. Even though they were immigrants, which Reka felt might make them indifferent to the business of others, they seemed suspicious if not outright disapproving of her living arrangement, a situation she made unwittingly worse by telling one of them she was a good friend of Heath's father. She was torn between a truthfulness she'd vowed would save her and protecting the innocent—Heath and his father—and not for the first time in her life it occurred to her that a lie was the easiest for everyone involved.

When she had the house under control, she decided upon a program of self-improvement. For the next year, as Heath came and went and she saved money from her double shifts at the diner, she read the papers daily, forcing herself through the articles about Cuba and the troubles stirring in Southeast Asia as she realized that she knew nothing at all about the world. From the day she'd been released from prison she had not paid the slightest bit of attention to anything she could not see except for her wispy, mythic future in a landscape so far away and foreign it appeared hazy even in dreams. Maybe her ignorance of the world had begun earlier, as who in Trent aside from Edwin Keane paid any attention to what happened beyond Simpson County?

Of course she knew from books that there were people in the world who had problems like hers, girls in Japan who maybe lived in some Japanese Trent. Maybe the houses were smaller and the doors to the rooms slid to the side instead of opening outright, but the mood of the place was the same and the mood of the girls who lived there and longed for elsewhere was the same as hers had been in Trent.

She realized how much she missed Jake's tales of war, even the worst ones, the ones he told about the concentration camps that his platoon was the first to see after the Germans abandoned them. Sometimes Heath told her about his trips up the Inside Passage and she would squint a little and pretend he was his father and the house in Ballard was the cabin in the Crazies. The mercurial Pacific she would transform into battle-scarred Normandy, the whales he sighted German submarines.

She wanted to know more of the world, and one day she picked up the morning paper to find that the world was coming to her.

RANDALL SMELLED OF BUS. His eyes burned and his limbs trembled from cramped sleep and hunger. The ride from New Orleans to Trent took twenty-two hours and stopped not only in cities and towns but at dismal country stores where stringy women stood in dusty parking lots holding children and paper bags filled with bottles of formula and chicken biscuits.

The bus pulled into the station at four o'clock on a Monday morning. It was January and he was dressed for the flimsy winter of New Orleans, not the upper South. He walked the empty streets carrying only his roll of drawings. That the drawings had survived was more a miracle to him than the shroud of Turin and the seven wonders of the world. Outer drawings had crumbled from the elements, layers lost to wind and dust and rain and grease and less tangible corrosives: despair and loneliness and longing to see the mother and sister whose images the roll contained. But at least a dozen of the drawings survived still. Every few days he would unroll them and stretch them out to make sure they were still there, and what he had first seen in them that afternoon when he walked naked through the empty studio was still present: the mother he had come back here to find.

Not that he knew how to go about finding her. She might not even live anywhere near here now, and there was a strong chance she had passed on from this world like his father. He'd like to think they were together in this fabled afterworld but he was not sure he believed in *this* world, much less another waiting in the wings, and if it was so that we lived on past our last earthly gasp it wasn't, he was sure of it, in a place. In our heads maybe. Freed from our bodies, untethered from all the needless constraints of the corporeal.

In the bus station he sat at the counter eating a Trentonian delicacy called a chuckwagon and listening to a lone janitor sing along to Sam Cooke on the jukebox while he mopped up the detritus of people fleeing this town forever. The janitor looked at him out of the corner of his eye in a way that Randall liked, as his look was filled with distrust of another transient and Randall liked that the road was with him still and would be for however long it took him to find what he was looking for.

Walking down Main, it occurred to him that he'd want to save the sights for later, for daylight. He knew what it would look and feel and smell like at night; even if the town he'd left had burned to the ground and been rebuilt out of Styrofoam he would know the music of a slow, cold Sunday.

He made his way along the River Road, heading vaguely out into the country. There were few cars out and he kept his thumb in his pocket, preferring to walk after a full day on a Greyhound. Lights flipped on in the houses of farmers up early to feed their stock. He passed by Speed's store and did something he'd seen his father do: snuck around back to the crusty oil drum where Speed disposed of outdated stock to see if he might salvage any foodstuff. A roll of hot dog buns and a calendar from Trent John Deere, each month adorned with a busty pinup straddling a late-model tractor. He laughed, thinking of the way the salt water sent forgotten blood down to his father's groin. Heard his father's voice ask, Makes you want to chase women, don't it?

His father's shack was dark-windowed, the small yard grassless and muddy. The two-track leading to it through the woods showed no sign of anything motorized; even in winter the weeds lining the middle furrow came to his thighs. He knew before arriving at the shack that it was his for the taking. Just give me a house by the side of a swamp, let me hide out from man.

What little his father had owned in this world was still there, abandoned, too paltry and worn to bother clearing out. Overalls dripping from nails. A pair of workboots so ancient they put Randall in mind of twin peaks of the Blue Ridge, isolated hills of a range as old as the earth itself. Once everything was under water and the sea stretched across the continent; when it receded things bubbled to the surface, among them Pa's threadbare drawers and the skillet he favored for everything you might fry. Even the few mementos he'd managed to save of his children—a pipe holder Ellen made for him in Vacation Bible School, the curling programs of school assemblies that he was too busy to attend—were covered with a primordial dust, documents from a lost time, lying in wait for an archaeologist.

Randall stuffed what he could find in the woodstove. Lit a crackling fire in honor of his cold-blooded father. He pulled the soiled mattress from the cot where he was certain his father would have passed from this life had he not made it to the sea, dusted it off with a broom, stripped off his clothes and fell straight asleep in this place he'd reclaimed from the past.

THE 1962 WORLD'S FAIR was to be held in Seattle. At the foot of Queen Anne Hill they razed an entire neighborhood and in its place began building pavilions and a spindly mock Eiffel Tower topped with a flying saucer they called the Space Needle. In Ballard the immigrant seafarers and their dour wives made fun of the whole enterprise if they paid it any attention at all, though Reka secretly grew excited as she rode the bus to work every day past the strange buildings and the preparations for an international exhibition highlighting life in the twenty-first century. She read in the papers about how the fair would celebrate faith in American science and its ability to conquer not only the land beneath her feet but also outer space. Outer space interested her about as much as the bottom of the ocean and science had never interested her much either, divorced as she thought it was from the things she cared about, which were people and how they lived, books and learning and travel. Nevertheless the fair made her miss her brother, for he had always been crazy about the sky and had walked around half the time with his head tilted toward the heavens. When Sputnik went up he decided he wanted to be a Russian, never mind the communism. He told her he'd be glad to share a bathroom with half the city if it meant he'd get to circle the sky like the teenagers in Trent who spent their Saturday nights in perpetual orbit from the Little Pep to the courthouse.

Heath's enthusiasm influenced her also. He was as crazy about space as Randall was, which she should have guessed from the model planes and rocket ships lining the shelves of that shrine his mother kept to him in Red Fork. The fair coincided with the height of the salmon season, but Heath was so intent on coming that he'd made plans to have a bush pilot fly him in for a long weekend, which Reka thought extravagant but did not dare say so. She let herself be buoyed along by the excitment and ended up singing the silly theme song that was all over the radio for months before the fair arrived:

> *Meet me in Seattle*
> *That's where I'll be at'll*
> *Meet me in Seattle at the Fair.*

They built a railroad three stories high that ran from downtown to the fairgrounds. The train was mostly glass and shaped like a bullet, and the day it opened the lines stretched for blocks even though it didn't really go anywhere and it was quicker to walk.

Heath arrived one night in mid-August. Although the season was at its peak Heath wanted badly to see the *Friendship* 7, John Glenn's space capsule, which had arrived at the fair in late July. Reka took the bus down to Boeing Field to meet him and they stopped off at Ivar's for dinner. He was happy to see her, though so far the season had not gone so well, and she could tell he felt guilty for flying back home for anything less crucial than death. A lot had gone wrong with the season and he wanted to talk about it, but she found it hard to listen. She could not get her brother out of her mind. She had the feeling—ridiculous, improbable, but unshakeable—that he was here, in Seattle, come to town for the World's Fair. She had a waking dream in which he was hard at work in the shipyards when one of his co-workers mentioned the fair to him and without a word he put down his tools and climbed down from the half-built ship and starting walking westward. She'd known since she'd left word of her whereabouts with her father that he was looking for her. Nights before she fell asleep, in that image-fertile time between waking and sleeping, the vulnerable strip of consciousness where the mind entertains its darkest fears and its most desperate desires, she heard his footsteps slapping pavement, heard his knock on her door.

"You okay?" Heath asked on the bus to the fair the next morning. "You don't seem too excited about the future."

"I've been thinking of Randall," she said.

"What about him?"

"Of how much he'd love the fair. I haven't even seen it yet, I mean it could be real boring or silly or something, but he loves outer space and he likes science and he used to always ask me what life would be like in the year 2000."

"Yeah, well, I think by that point they'll need to do more than get the buses off the ground and build weird monuments in the sky. This town is getting too crowded already. But back to your brother. I just can't believe he's lost. I mean, there's bound to be some way you can find him. Maybe you just haven't tried hard enough."

She gave him a look that he understood immediately, and immediately she regretted her scowl because it was true what he said: She hadn't tried hard enough.

"I guess you don't want to talk about it. Fine. You don't talk to me about my family, I won't talk to you about yours."

She didn't say anything because this was not the deal she wanted: She wouldn't mind talking to him about his father at least, but she had not yet figured out what to say. She'd thought so long and hard about bringing them together, yet so far she'd done nothing about it. She told herself that she needed Heath to trust her first, but if he did not trust her now, when would he?

"I don't mind you talking about him," she said. "It's just that I miss him and I guess I feel guilty for losing touch."

"You did what you had to," he said. "You left. I understand it, believe me. If you want my opinion, you don't have anything to feel bad about."

Still, she entered the fair distressed by this conversation, and all the focus on the future only worried her. Who would she be in the year 2000? She liked to think that she had escaped the kinds of questions that would have haunted her back home, but as she passed through the exhibits featuring robots and futuristic models of cities she felt as if she'd done nothing really to change who she was except save money for college and pay off her debt to Edith Keane.

The fairgrounds were packed, but Reka's desire to see more of the world and its people was dashed when she realized that most of the fairgoers seemed to be retired Canadians and schoolchildren from Tacoma. They stood in a long line to enter the new coliseum, which housed the World of Tomorrow. To take her mind off the past, Reka read from the guidebook Heath bought for them. *"The four entrances to the building lead past industry displays to the center of the building where the present is left behind for a step into the future. In groups of 100, the audience crosses a bridge over a pool and enters the vehicle that transports them into the world of tomorrow. Their conveyance is called the Bubbleator."*

Inside the Bubbleator, they rose from the coliseum floor like a boat in the Ballard locks up to the world that hung suspended from the ceiling of the coliseum. They were allowed twenty-one minutes in the twenty-first century. Otherwordly music, zithery and quivering, wafted in from speakers as they were lifted into the new galaxy. Someone behind her read from the guidebook in a thick southern accent that made her homesick and embarrassed at once. *"Time is relative. In this case 39 years are compressed into 40 seconds as the Bubbleator rises into the honeycomb of cubes that foretell the future. The Bubbleator stops in a pool of golden light."*

Beneath the ceiling they hovered. The light was less golden than the color of bottled blond hair. Behind her the reader droned on. *"This is the prologue—man's already-past futures, linked with the present and stretching beyond into tomorrow and the day after tomorrow and the day after that."* Annoyed by the narration, Reka whispered to Heath, "Seems the future comes from my neck of the woods," but Heath shot her a censorious frown. He appeared transfixed by the view, oblivious to the voice-over that made Reka feel as if the future would be just like that: narrated, dictated by a voice from her past rather than experienced without self-consciousness. She'd had this fear before, and it had terrified her more than her first night in prison: the idea that she was doomed to an awareness so total that it developed into a kind of psychic insomnia in which she remained forever aware of every thought, every move. She worried that she'd not be able to lose herself in a moment, a meal, a bout of lovemaking, even a stray thought without the accompanying awareness that she was living, eating, loving, thinking. She longed for the headlong and blissfully ignorant abandon with which she and her brother used to fling themselves daily, hourly, in words and walks and elaborately scripted fantasies, into escape. Once she'd had a safe place reserved always in her mind, an inviolate chamber filled with dream and image and vision.

Annoyed with the commentary, she tuned it out and squinted at the vision before her, a slide show that the guidebook described as "a panorama that fuses the past with the present," a montage of images so incongruent and foreign to her consciousness (the Acropolis, Christopher Columbus staking his claim on this continent, an atom bomb exploding, Marilyn Monroe standing on the heating grate, her skirt billowing like the mushroom cloud of the bomb) that she immediately replaced it with her own images. She and Randall in one of their secret places, an abandoned tobacco warehouse he had led her to one rainy evening just a few days before she met Edwin Keane. A storm had blown up from the coast, causing them to seek shelter in the warehouse where, isolated in the damp duskiness lit only by lightning strikes and smelling of cured tobacco and the sweet deliverance of rain, they retreated to far corners of building and mind. Randall, eleven then, had taken up a scraggly broom and was from the looks of him engaged in an altercation with an evil foe, singing all the while in the monotonal hum he'd favored since infancy.

Meanwhile, she had dreamed the future. She imagined her siblings in not terribly charitable scenarios: her sisters married to the boys they lusted after then, men for whom high school was the zenith of intellect and emotion. And then Hal, exiled to the forlorn outskirts of some bland southern city, thrice-married, twice-paroled, half-drunk, potbellied and chain-smoking, leaning against the hulk of an abandoned car with a can of beer in his hand, wearing his ex-wife's ex-husband's Hawaiian print shirt.

For herself she allowed a nominal escape in the form of elopement with a boy from the next town over, a stranger to Trent and therefore exotic but—as she would find out as soon as they crossed the bridge over the Tar—different from the men her sisters married only in his address.

In this dream, so clear to her now from the heights of the Bubbleator, Randall was the only one who escaped. When he left he would truly leave. He would not return and (she remembered this now with much more shock than she'd felt at the time) he would forget all about his family. This forgetfulness she'd attributed then not to bitterness or shame but rather a desire to see everything, to talk to everyone, to burn through the world.

She closed her eyes to see Randall standing on the crust of some continent, a compassionate though independent Columbus, friendly to natives but loyal to no power except his own sovereign imagination.

This is what she wished for him, and opening her eyes to the images that flashed across the screen in front of her, she hoped he'd made it. It was worth it to lose him if he'd escaped, even if it meant her giving up that part of herself that she'd shared with him, that part that had kept her alive and hoping during the days of Edwin Keane and later, when locked away.

But what if he hadn't escaped? What if he had for some unfathomable reason hesitated? Or—like she once had—gotten mixed up with someone who delayed his departure? This was the only likely scenario she could imagine, for she had come to believe that nothing could stop either of them from fulfilling their shared desires save another person. Nothing actually happened in this world save for some stranger appearing all of a sudden to stand in your light.

Hard to imagine the woman who could stop Randall from the transcendent escape she'd forecast for him that day in the warehouse. She would be more spirit than animal. Lithe and striking, her beauty off-kilter and creeping, apparent immediately but overwhelming once you grew to know her. Reka tried hard to picture this woman, but her concentration was broken by the singsongy twang of her fellow time traveler, who read, *"Is this truly a projection of the future, or merely an unfounded dream, this city of Tomorrow? The heart of a city is not its architecture, nor its highways and its jetports, as vital as they may be to its character. A city's heart is diffused into the many structures that give its families shelter, where individuals may share their joys or triumphs, their woes and disappointments."*

"I could do without the blow-by-blow," she whispered to Heath even as she found herself paying more attention to the narration than the House of the Future flashing now on the scene. Heath's boyish attentiveness reminded her of the model airplanes lining the shelves of his room. She fell quiet and half-listened to the commentary in hopes that there might be something else that complemented her own visions. *"The furnishings are lightweight foamed plastics, foamed cement and glass. Windows can transform day into night or night into day at the flick of a switch and when it rains the windows close automatically. . . . After dinner there's no need to wash the dishes——they are disposable. The man of the future will be eager to return to his home at the end of the day at the office or factory. Perhaps he will commute to his job in his own gyrocopter, which takes off from his own heliport."*

"What about the woman of the future?" Reka said aloud—too loudly—in the packed Bubbleator. "How's she supposed to get to the space market, on a prehistoric bike?"

"Count your blessings, girl," said the woman with the guidebook. "Least there's no dishes to wash."

Even Heath's obvious embarrassment at her outburst did not assuage her. She longed for the Bubbleator to descend into the primitive present, as the twenty-one minutes were beginning to drag like the centuries they stood for.

"You got something against tomorrow?" asked Heath as they made their way out of the coliseum.

"I guess I'd rather it be a surprise," she said.

"That's funny. I always think of you as someone who's got plans. Seems like you'd want to know what the future holds so you can plan accordingly."

She pondered his words as they stopped for a snack—Tang-flavored ice cream atop rocket-shaped cones. Obviously he was referring to the way she'd come west to find him, which was true—she could hardly take offense at this. But it depressed her to be thought of as someone who had the future tightly mapped out, for it seemed a reminder of another thing she'd shared with Randall—a sense of spontaneity, a passion for the unexpected—which perhaps she'd lost along with him.

"So tell me," she said to Heath as they sat on a bench licking their rocket cones, "what do you want for the future?"

"Not much I don't got already," he said. "My own boat. Good fishing, a dependable crew. A house bought and paid for. Still working on that one."

"What about a family?"

He stopped eating to screw up his face at her. "Hell, Reka, I'm too young for that."

"I'm talking about down the road, Heath. Surely you want children?"

He took his time answering, finished his cone and stood and walked to a nearby trash can to throw away the paper wrapper. When he returned he spent another few seconds wiping his mouth off with a handkerchief before he said, "I imagine it will take a real special woman to want to marry a man like me. I'm already married to a boat. It's funny—you think I'd have learned from my father's example. He spent all his time in the woods, messing with his trees. Neglected my mom. I can understand why he did it, I know it cut both ways, she wasn't easy to put up with and she didn't really give him the time of day either except to complain about Red Fork, go on about how bad she wanted to leave there. But it sure made it a hell of a lot harder on me, him bowing out of the picture."

She didn't know what to say, so she said nothing. It would not be right to defend Jake—she was sure he was guilty as charged, as he'd said so himself. And given the circumstances, she should probably have avoided the subject entirely.

"Maybe I'd be better off staying married to my boat. I don't know that I'd trust myself to raise kids."

"You'd make a wonderful father," she said, by reflex.

"How do you know?"

His tone had changed. She sensed she'd gone too far, but she'd only wanted to comfort him. She wasn't much given to this kind of reassurance, which she had long ago dismissed as superficial, sentimental; she was shocked when she realized what she'd said without thinking.

When she did not answer he said, "You don't know. Sometimes I get the feeling that when you look at me, you see my dad. I'm not him, you know."

"I never said . . ."

"Let's go," he said, bolting up as abruptly as he had that night she'd confessed to knowing his parents. "We're at the World's Fair," he said when she caught up with him. "I paid big money to fly down here and see John Glenn's spacecraft and I'm going to see it or the boys on the boat will throw my ass overboard."

They spent an hour in line to see the *Friendship* 7, by far the most mobbed and, to Reka's mind, least interesting exhibit at the fair. She was losing interest in the whole experience. So far her favorite thing was the Tang-flavored rocket cone. Still, she felt there might be something she could learn here, and she trudged dutifully through the exhibits, tagged along to the places he most wanted to see: the General Motors exhibit featuring cars without steering wheels and exaggerated shark fins in the style of the Batmobile she'd seen in the comic books Thanassis kept behind the counter for his boys to read when they came to work with him. They visited the railroad pavilion to get a look at the Japanese bullet train, the Northwest Airlines exhibit for more propaganda from Boeing. They breezed through the pavilions of China, Brazil, Sweden, Berlin, Japan, all of which she found interesting and would have liked to spend more time in, but Heath had to get back to his boat and they had vowed to do the entire fair in a day.

They skipped the amusement park altogether although she had a wild urge to ride the space wheel and the space whirl. It was close to dusk when they came to the Forest Products Industry Pavilion.

Heath did not even try to hide his disinterest when she asked him to stop.

"I've seen enough of the forestry industry to last three lifetimes. No damn way."

His selfishness irritated her—more lingering damage from his spoiled childhood, she decided. It seemed to her worth fighting for, even though he would see right through her reasons for fighting. It felt almost heretical to pass it by, like avoiding a shrine on a holy day.

"Have I not gone to every single thing you wanted to see? Without complaining, I might add? Did I not sit with you through a twenty-five-minute presentation on the lightbulb of the future?"

Heath's stare was not his but his mother's, identical to that look she'd turned on Reka that afternoon she'd come home to find Maggie sitting in silence across from Bob Smart. She hesitated—do I let him go as his mother surely would, or do I stand my ground—and as she stood in front of the pavilion, waiting for him to come around, it occurred to her that it was not her job to free Heath from his mother's indulgences, or to make him pay his respects to a father he obviously did not respect, for that matter. She thought of what he'd said earlier—how he thought she looked at him but saw his father—and almost said, "You're wrong. It's Randall I see when I look at you."

It was this thought that freed her. She could no more make Heath come to terms with his childhood than she could keep intact that magical connection she'd had with her little brother until she was sent to prison. She had to learn not to live this life for other people, even if they happened to be people she loved as dearly as she loved herself.

"Fine. You go on home. I"ll meet you later, in time for dinner. We'll walk down to Hattie's, my treat since we were planning on eating dinner down here."

He looked stunned. "You sure?"

She leaned into him and sent him off with a kiss, though she noticed as she filed into the pavilion that he stood frozen on the sidewalk still, as if debating whether or not to follow her.

Inside the pavilion she took a seat in the all-wooden theater to watch a film called *A Tale of Two Planets*. The frames alternated between someplace like Mars, where wood was unknown, and a planet as imagined by the Forest Products Industry, where life was dependent upon the more than six-thousand forms of wood products and the cutting-edge research of industry giants, which would allow us to meet the needs of the coming millennium.

When the show ended and the lights came up she sat thinking about the way the fair pitched such a stark contrast between past and future. A common enough approach; she thought of how most people would read her behavior in Red Fork as the epitome of sinfulness and evil—a stranger offered free room and board by a kindly older woman who is repaid for her kindness by lies and adultery. Yet for all her inclination toward guilt, she saw more good than evil in what had happened there. Two people had found a happiness they'd never known, where before three were miserable. Four if she counted Heath, which she certainly should do. Simple mathematics.

The auditorium was empty now, and an usher stared pointedly at her, gesturing toward the door where a few more weary souls sought a break from the chaos outside in the dark cool theater. She filed out slowly, exhausted herself but glad she'd bothered. She would rave about it to Heath if only to make him feel guilty for skipping it, then admit she was teasing and mimic the dull statistics spouted by the stentorian narrator. She felt a little sheepish about her adamant idea that visiting this exhibit might bring her closer to Jake. She'd be better off climbing a tree if she wanted to think of him, but even trees could not bring him back to her.

Through the crowd she glimpsed the back of Heath's head, towering above a group of teenagers. He'd waited, which pleased her, as she took it as a sign that he thought of her as family. She pushed against the crowd to reach him but slowed midway across the sidewalk when she realized that he was wearing a coat and tie and that his brown hair was thin and not even altogether brown but a faded gray. And then she stopped altogether when she realized that she was looking not at Heath, but his father.

WHEN HIS MONEY RAN OUT, Randall found a job welding iron cages used to ferry hogs to market. To get to the job he bought a Dodge Dart on credit from a man named Rooster who made gambling money selling reconstituted wrecks to migrants. The Dart had survived a flood and smelled of the alluvial silt of some primordial delta: the Ganges, the Nile, the Tar when it was not the Tar but part of the wide underwater world of yore. He lived in fear of its throwing a rod on the way to work but somehow it managed to get him there and back, smoking like the truck that roamed town in summers spraying mosquito gas. The bearings were shot and he used a pair of pliers to turn on the heat and the radio, but it served its purpose.

For weeks he went unrecognized. Sometimes people would double-take, sometimes they'd stare. Don't I know you, aren't you . . . ? Something kept them from approaching him, saying his name.

His hair curled past his ears.

One day Martha and Ellen and their two brawny husbands appeared in his front yard. His sisters picked their way across the yard in high heels, staring at the mud in disgust. He was lying abed with a book in his hand.

They called him out on the porch.

"We heard you were back," said Martha. "Thanks a lot for coming to see somedamnbody."

"I've been meaning to do so," he said.

They stared at his hair, his jeans wrenched to his waist and droopy-assed, his soiled workshirt.

"Good land, you know who he looks like?" said Ellen.

"Spitting image," said Martha. "It's like Pa come back to bother hell out of us again."

"I ain't about to take care of him this time," said Ellen.

"It's not Pa, it's Randall."

Randall grinned, pleased to be talked about in the third person. "Aren't you going to invite us in?"

The husbands stared. They rubbed their crew cuts and spit in the yard. "We'll be in the car," one of them said.

"Don't ya'll even think of sneaking up to Speed's," said Ellen. They pushed their way onto the porch, gave him nominal hugs, light and quick and anxious. Just across the threshold they stopped to stare at the drawings tacked on the walls.

"I ain't even gone ask," said Ellen.

"I'll tell you," said Randall. "It's me and Reka and our mother."

They looked at each other. But not at him.

"Where you been, Randall?" Martha asked after a long silence. "With her?"

He knew who she meant. They had never been able to bring themselves to say Reka's name, not since she'd embarrassed the whole family by taking up with that sadsack rich boy and killing him and getting herself in the papers.

"Where is she?" he said.

His sisters traded looks again.

"You don't know?"

"I know where she was. Montana. But she left before I got there and I was hoping you'd heard from her."

"I don't care if I never lay eyes on her again," said Ellen.

Martha shot her sister a go-easy look. "You okay, Randall?"

He smiled and said of course.

"Reason I ask is you don't look like you're taking care of yourself. I don't guess it's any of my business if you want to put disgusting pictures of yourself naked all over the walls. I don't guess you get a whole lot of company. But if there's something you need us to do for you, look, we're still your family."

"I can't think of anything offhand," he said.

"Why'd you come back here?" said Ellen.

"I'm looking for my mother."

Ellen said to Martha: "Come on. Let's go."

Martha said to Randall, "Ma's dead, Randall. She's been dead going on twenty-two years. Are you on dope?"

"Not your mother. My mother. Reka and I have a different mother."

"That explains a whole hell of a lot," said Ellen. "Come on, Marty, I'm going. I don't want no part of this. You know why he's like this, don't you? His own sister did it to him and I guarantee you she ain't any better off than he is. I can't be spending my time taking care of his crazy ass."

They went out on the porch to fight. Ellen stormed off in her high heels, her skirt hiked to her knees and a stream of oaths lingering after her in the buggy air.

Martha came back to say, "Don't worry about her, Randall. We're just right shocked. It's not easy coming in here and seeing them pictures. You better be glad Ronnie and Mike went back to the car to take a drink. No telling what they'd do to you if they saw what you got up on these walls."

"Maybe they'd like them."

She scowled and shook her scowl along with her big blond hair and her entire painted face and said, "You want me to check up on you now and again?"

"I'm fine."

"You ain't even got indoor plumbing. You can't live here."

"It's free," he said. "The old homeplace."

"You don't want my help, I ain't going to offer it."

"You're sweet to offer."

She hugged him again, warmly this time. "She ruined you. I saw it coming. I hate her for it. I just don't have it in me to do this again, Randall. After all she did to us and then Pa out here drinking his guts out and it's hard for me to look at you even now after all this time and not blame you for letting him drown."

"Say hello to your husband."

"His name's Ronnie," she said sadly, and she glanced once more at the drawings before hurrying off to catch up with her sister.

JAKE TURNED SUDDENLY at the sound of his name, and the shock in his eyes brought blood to her face. She did not know how to read it, how to read him; she was looking at him, but seeing his son.

Before either of them had trained their breath into words, Heath appeared.

"Look what the cat drug up," he said. "I went in there to find you, but you must have snuck out the other entrance."

She turned to Heath. He was gesturing toward the theater, which seemed an anachronism to her now, part of a past that she could remember only dimly. Heath seemed unaffected by his father's presence. Obviously he'd had time to adjust, for he was breathing normally and making words from the breath he took.

"What?" she said finally. What else was there to say? How? When? Not *why* and not *who* and certainly not *for how long*.

Heath stepped in to save her, as Jake had still not spoken, seemed incapable of even an interrogatory fragment.

"I was walking out of the fair when I spotted him coming out of the space exhibit."

"You're here," she said, foolishly, although she did not care how foolish she sounded.

"Here I am," he said.

People were pushing past them on all sides, and Heath took both their arms and pulled them away from the sidewalk, as if they were too stunned to avoid getting trampled.

"Let's get out of here, go get something to eat," he said. "This isn't the place to catch up on old times."

She found it odd that he would play the grown-up, though as soon as they left the gates to the fairgrounds, Heath slipped into a sullen adolescent silence. She did not know what to say and Jake made only small talk about the exhibits he'd seen, and the mood between them grew so intolerably freighted that she was relieved to find a diner with a few free booths.

Reka and Heath shared one side of the booth, Jake stranded across from them, constrained in a plaid suitcoat, blue slacks and a badly knotted tie. She'd never seen him in anything other than his work clothes—chinos and boots and a flannel shirt summer and winter—and the Sunday clothes made him seem younger due to the way he squirmed and fidgeted. She had taken a seat first and Heath slid into the booth quickly as if he was trying to protect her from some lecherous stranger. The awkwardness at their table was so palpable that the waitress, arriving finally with menus, picked up on it immediately and treated them with extra deference, as if the three of them were reeling from the shock of some terrible tragedy.

"Well," Reka said, her voice a raspy whisper, "are you going to tell us what you're doing here?"

"It's a fair for the whole world, isn't it? Guess you Seattlites think it's all yours."

His wan smile weakened gradually, as if he was as unconvinced by his joke as Heath, who stared at a picture of Mount Rainier above the booth so intently that she decided he'd rather be there than here.

"No, really. I kept reading about it in the papers for months and had no intentions of coming. But one day I was at work way up in the woods all by myself and I decided I'd had enough of trees to last me my whole life. Me and trees needed a break from each other. I thought about the fair and I remembered I haven't taken a vacation in years and I have something like three months stacked up. Seemed like something I shouldn't miss, fair for the whole world and so close to home."

"Just took off, huh?" said Heath.

"It's not like anybody was going to miss me," said Jake, and as soon his sentence was finished he seemed to regret saying it.

"You would be talking about Mom now," said Heath.

In the silence after his statement, both she and Jake seemed to be waiting for something—a lilt, a follow-up "Is that right?"—to turn it into a question. But the statement remained a statement and all the more ominous because of its certainty. She looked at Jake only briefly, long enough to see the veins in his neck throbbing.

"So what about Mom?" Heath said finally.

"Oh, she didn't want to come." He'd recovered, thankful for a question instead of an accusation. "She doesn't like crowds. Your mother . . ."

He fell silent and looked away, as if trying to remember what to say next.

"My mother, right. What about her?" said Heath.

"She's got her cats. She spends a lot of time with her sister in Bozeman. She's crazy about that nephew of hers. Oh yeah, Heath, you've got another cousin."

"What do you mean, she's got her cats?" said Heath.

"She takes in strays. She's got four or five now she's feeding, I forget exactly. And your aunt Martha and uncle Jimmy had a boy. James Elton Farrow, he's called."

"You leaving her?" asked Heath.

Heath's anger was apparent and apparently growing; Reka could feel it almost, vibrating the Naugahyde cover of the booth, rattling the cutlery of the table. She thought the ice water would spill, the room would tremor, the Bubbleator would burst and the Rainier on the wall and the one above them in the clouds would erupt if she did not intervene but still she said nothing.

"I guess I've said enough for right now, son," said Jake.

"Don't call me that," said Heath.

"You're not my son anymore?" He looked at Heath only briefly, then searched the room for the waitress, as if she was the only one who could help him out of this. Reka felt as if his question was directed at her, as if she was responsible for whatever was taking place between them. She had never seen Jake angry, though she had known him for only a few months and that was a while ago, and she told herself—to protect herself—that she did not know him, that perhaps he was as capable of anger as his son, who'd beat his mother badly enough to run away forever. But she knew she did not need protecting. Or want it.

"Okay, Heath," Jake said when his son did not answer his question. "I've said enough. Time for you two to explain how it is that you're together here."

"We live together," said Heath. It was her turn to look for the saintly waitress. She felt as if Heath was trying to hurt her as well, as if all this time he'd resented what she'd had with his father, resented what she'd done with him, maybe even for his mother's sake. She wondered if this were so, if he'd tolerated her only because he wanted badly to believe that he could, if she was an experiment of his, part of a trial-and-error plan to rise above his past, become a better person.

"Housemates," she said. Her voice came out squeaky and faint, as if she had not spoken in years. She explained as much as she could about the time since she'd arrived in Seattle. Heath kept quiet at first, but as she told Jake about the boat and his father asked him questions about it he opened up and soon he was doing all the talking. Fishing gab, details of the boat, Alaska lore, stuff she'd heard already but the conversation, though strained, was preferable to the previous torture and in time they were calm enough to pick at their burgers and fries.

When they had paid their bill and were out on the sidewalk she asked Jake where he was staying. He mentioned a hotel downtown. The name of the place hung in the air like an insult as she waited for Heath to invite him home with them. It was his house; she paid half the mortgage but she had no right to force them into a truce, though that had been her intention all along. She realized how much was riding on this, how divinely fortunate it was that they had chosen that day to attend the fair. If Heath had not flown home to see the spaceship, she would have gone earlier by herself and she was sure she would not have returned to view the sparkling millennium, as depressingly antiseptic as she found it.

"Will we see you before you leave?" she heard Heath ask. She felt faint, a little sick; he was letting him go again, and she wasn't doing anything about it. She thought of lost Randall, realized she'd made a decision at some point not to interfere, not to cling, maybe even to cut him out of her life. Even though she couldn't remember making this decision, it felt deliberate now as Heath turned his father away. She'd fooled herself into thinking she'd merely misplaced him, crossed wires, missed connections, when all this time she'd meant to sacrifice him for a fresh start, like Heath was about to do to his father.

"I'd love to have a look at that boat of yours," Jake said in answer to Heath's question. He said it without inflection, as if he knew that it was the one right answer, but did not want to reveal any eagerness. Or maybe he wasn't eager; maybe it was all too much for him and he had fallen in love with his wife or was at least trying to make himself love her.

No, not that. She had evidence: *She has her cats. Do you want to hear this?* It would have revealed itself in his words; she would have been able to read it, feel it in his gestures. He had not forgotten her and it was clear that things between him and Maggie were not even things anymore, barely even memories. Just empty white space, colorless and quiet hours, a few necessary words now and again to keep from sliding into the kind of maddening static that afflicts unhappy couples too weary or frightened to part.

"I wish you *could* see it," said Heath, and for a second she wanted to slap him for ruining it until she remembered that the boat was out on the water, that he'd flown in from Ketchikan. As crushed as she was, it seemed to her orchestrated somehow, an accident of timing designed by fate to counteract the miracle of running into Jake. Once before the world had delivered him to her, and what right had she to expect another chance? No, it seemed right that the world should take him back, for she would look next for Randall to show up shopping for socks at the Bon Marché, or her father hawking hot dogs down in Pioneer Square.

"Why don't you come out to the house tomorrow?" she said. She did not look at Heath; she didn't have to look at him to know his reaction.

"I was planning on going back to the fair," he said. He looked to Heath for a sign but Heath had his eyes trained on some far part of Elliott Bay as if he were back on the water already.

"You said you don't have to be back in Red Fork anytime soon. That fair's not going anywhere."

"Well, I'd like to see where you live."

She wrote down the address for him and told him where to get a cab and they agreed on a time, and during all this Heath sailed the high seas with his eyes and she felt like the wife of a sea captain, nervously pacing a widow's walk, scanning the waters for her man to return home safely.

———————

NIGHTS AND WEEKENDS, he searched the county for his mother. He sat for hours in laundromats hoping she'd turn up with a hamper of dirty clothes and maybe a half-sister in tow. He ate at every diner and barbeque joint from Trent down to Wilmington, lingered for hours in the parking lots of grocery stores, awaiting her arrival.

His hair grew longer. His co-workers taunted him. Here comes Miss Speight. Forget your girdle? Come sit on my lap, sweet thang, we'll talk about the first thing that pops up.

After he had been welding hog cages for a few months, his foreman said, "Either you cut that goddamn hair or I got to get rid of you. You're a good welder but the other boys, I'm scared of what they'll do to you. Don't you care how you look?"

He smiled and said it was only the whites who had a problem with it. His black co-workers didn't give a damn how he wore his hair.

"You ain't black, Speight. You got to learn to get along."

Randall smiled and went back to work. A man known around the yard only as Bug slammed him against a wall one day and called him a nigger queer. Randall blew him a kiss. The next day when he came to work the foreman met him in the parking lot with a week's pay and told him to go the hell home.

He didn't mind so much. If he thought about his job at all, he had to accept the fact that he was making cages to carry hogs to their death. He wasn't the type to place animals right up alongside people, and he wouldn't say no to a BLT, but surely there were other things to weld in this world.

Randall came to town every Saturday to search the streets for his mother. Saturday was shopping day for the tenant farmers and factory workers from all over the county. Trent crackled with an energy unknown on the slower weekdays; the back alleys were filled with men and boys sneaking shots or smokes, and the teenagers ringed the courthouse square in their Corvairs and Mustangs. Even the scroungy Johnsontown mongrels put aside chasing birds and rabbits of a Saturday afternoon and bounded out of the woods to parade down the sidewalk in search of dropped ice cream or the boiled peanuts the farmhands tossed their way. Randall hung out in front of Dusselbach's furniture store, searching the faces of passersby for his mother. He would know her if he saw her. He had some drawings at home, her face, her features, her doleful native intelligence shining from smudges of charcoal so old now they looked like liver spots.

On the television at Dusselbach's he watched the news. He saw spaceships and was enamored of the idea of traveling to the moon even as he allowed he had things to do on earth, important things. He watched a war unfold in a place as sunken and swampy and festering and green as Trent, and he saw only snippets of everything, saw things in fragments and was left to piece together the meaning on his own before a sofa salesman came outside and ordered him away from the plate glass, claimed he scared away the customers.

He bought himself a harmonica from the Eagle five-and-dime and stayed home for a while. His mother was not going anywhere, and he needed a break. He sat on the porch for twelve-hour stretches blowing some slobbery harp. When his money ran out he hit upon the idea of ferrying local teenagers the twelve-mile round-trip to the next county to buy beer. Trent had gone dry in the last election and the closest wet town was just across the county line, a place called Warsaw. The kids had all kinds of code words for getting tight: Going Poland, Speak Some Polish Tonight.

Randall set himself up in the reference section of the public library. Customers knew to find him there. High school kids too young to drive, local drunks who'd had their licenses revoked or their cars repossessed. They placed their orders and tried to talk him down from his two-dollar round-trip fee. To keep himself from recognizing the desperate sorriness of this scheme, he pretended that he really was going to Poland. Instead of tobacco and soybeans he passed small farms planted with beets and potatos, larger fields of winter wheat. He'd crack his window slightly for the Baltic breeze, listen for the whistle of the train that ran from Vienna to Leningrad. Beyond the train tracks began the city: palaces and villas, decrepit estates of deposed princes, all of whom were named Stanislaus. He passed the spot where Napoleon once encamped, a copse-dotted meadow now, and pictured it cluttered with tents and campfires and anxious troops. When he arrived in the city it was always winter. Ration lines outside the small markets, Poles queued for quarter miles, exhaling great clouds of fog he took for cartoon bubbles, translating their thoughts according to his mood. The Poles were a sallow-faced but hearty lot and he felt in the Arctic breeze that penetrated each crack of the Dart their age-old struggle with geography, climate, history, and power-hungry neighbors.

As he passed the Church of the Holy Cross where they'd buried Chopin's heart, he leaned on his horn in tribute.

The police got word of his business venture and took to following him. As he pulled into his parking space in front of the library they nosed his bumper with the intimidating lip of their cruisers. He retired from the booze courier business and took to foraging in the Dumpsters behind Speed's store for his one meal of the day. He returned to his search. Where oh where could she be? He looked everywhere, always.

———

AFTER REKA AND HEATH LEFT JAKE in front of the diner, they rode the bus home, talking halfheartedly about the fair. He did not mention his father and she did not feel right bringing it up. Heath went to his room immediately, shut the door behind him. Reka spent the night wavering between defiance—she had every right to push, she'd come to this place to bring them together and she wasn't about to give up now that they were this close—and uncertainty. It was Heath's house, Heath's charity that brought her here to live in daily, if ghostly, contact with her lover; it was Heath's choice finally, whether he wanted his father in his life, just as it was her choice to leave behind her entire family except for Randall.

She slept badly and little. When she got up early the next morning, Heath was gone. He returned in midmorning carrying the largest salmon she'd ever seen. She was sitting at the kitchen table in her bathrobe, sipping coffee. She'd called Thanassis to tell him she wanted a few days off, which he gave her gladly since she'd had off only Sundays for a while.

"Domino special," he said, unwrapping the fish at the kitchen counter. "Let me have it for a song."

"I'll broil it for lunch," she said. "You're not mad at me for inviting him?"

In answer he fetched a knife from the drawer and took the fish outside to clean it. She was too excited about seeing Jake again to follow him outside to talk, and besides, if he was really angry why would he get up at the crack and go all the way downtown and bring home a fish big enough to feed half of Ballard? She decided that he'd hurt so long over this that it would not do for him to suddenly act as if all was healed. Reka had seen enough acting to recognize it, especially in people not given to performances.

Jake arrived an hour later. She'd showered and put on a new dress bought in the bargain basement of Nordstrom's and she showed him around the small bungalow while Heath hung out in the rooms where they weren't, pretending to be looking for something or straightening up magazines and books on the coffee table. Though it was overcast and drizzling, it was warm enough for them to sit on the porch. Heath and his father drank bottles of ale and she sipped lemonade and every time she went to the kitchen to check on lunch she eavesdropped through the window but heard only choked conversation, intermittent and truncated sentences coming from the porch.

After they ate, Heath suggested a walk down to the water. The rain had picked up and Heath distributed the yellow slickers and hats he kept in the mud room to outfit his crew. As he doled out the coats, Reka was struck again by the idea that Heath was in charge here, that she and Jake were the children. They followed him through the neighborhood, where he knew every other person who stopped him on the street or called to him from a front porch. She could see the relief in Jake's eyes, that his son had survived his childhood, that he had turned into a person whom other people obviously liked and—once they got to the shipyard—clearly respected. He stopped to talk to older men about the fishing, as aside from the weekly radio contacts from sons and neighbors his was the only news they'd had since the season started.

But Reka knew from experience that going a block in Ballard with Heath could take hours, and she was so eager to be alone with Jake that she told Heath to catch up with them at the Government Locks. Heath would not look at her and she hurried off so that she would not have to look at him. She wondered where to start, for she'd thought for so long of being alone with Jake and had so much to say, but as soon as they were out of earshot, he settled that question for her.

"He doesn't seem real glad to see me." They stopped to watch the boats passing through the locks, chambers clanking shut, yachts rising like rubber ducks from the floor of a tub.

"*I* am," she said. "And don't worry about Heath. He can't come right out and say what he really thinks, and you ought not to expect him to. It's been a long time, Jake. He's not a boy anymore. But yes, he's glad. He was up at dawn to go down to the market and buy lunch."

"You've changed him."

She looked up from the water. "I haven't done a thing to him. He was like that when I met him and I assume he was like that always. He's a special person and why shouldn't he be?"

"I can think of a few reasons why he could be having a rough time."

"Who doesn't have a few reasons for that? Okay, some are better than others, but finally it's your choice and not your choice—finally it has to do with how you were raised. He was raised to keep going. I can't imagine Maggie taught him that."

He fell distant at the mention of her name.

"You don't want to talk about her."

"It doesn't exist anymore. I don't exist, she doesn't exist, the house we live in has disappeared. It's just me now. Nothing else. I kept thinking it would get better or that I would find a way to exist, but since you left, the only thing that kept me going was work, the forest. And now not even the trees. Not even food. You know how food can be like a reward for the boredom of living? How you can wait all day for a meal and fix your favorite things and sit down to it and all the awful stuff that's making you suffer goes away for a while? Now I eat to keep from dying. I'll put anything in my mouth, I can't taste any of it, it just slides down my throat to my stomach and fuels me for another eight hours. That lunch you fixed was the first real food I've had since that night we made stew and ate in front of the fire."

At the mention of that night, she saw his face flicker in shadow and firelight. She moved closer to him, only an inch, close enough for his sleeve to touch her hand, which was not enough.

"Why are you here with him?"

She sighed. She knew it was coming, had lain awake half the night trying to concoct a response that might please him and satisfy her own questions, but now that he'd asked, she did not know what to say.

"I don't want you to think I'm some kind of creep."

"Why would I think that?"

"Coming here to find Heath, getting to know him? God, even moving in with him? I don't know, I guess you could think I'm trying to find a way to keep you with me even though I know I can't have you and that you don't want me."

"I don't think you're a creep," he said. He spoke so softly she had to lean forward to hear him over the noise of the locks clanging shut and filling with water, and they fell silent to watch again. As the chamber filled, Reka decided this process was unnatural, cheating—a tampering with parts of this earth that were made to exist on different levels. But as the last lock was filled and the boats chugged away into the higher canal, it seemed a miracle, this merging of fresh water and the sea, a miraculous overcoming of odds.

She took his hand in hers and brought him closer to her. After he kissed her he said, "No, I don't think you're a creep. And who said I didn't want you? I've loved you more every day you've been gone."

She collapsed against him, pressing her face against the wet slicker so he would not be able to distinguish between her tears and the rain collected on his coat. She was about to tell him that she felt the same way when Heath's words knifed her face away from the slick vinyl.

"Pretty amazing system, isn't it?" Heath stood behind them, his arms on the railing, his head turned away from the sight of their embrace.

"Quite a feat," said Jake. His embarrassment only made Reka tighten her grip on his hands. She released him reluctantly when Heath suggested they walk down to the terminal, where he launched into a stiffly guided tour, pointing out boats similar to his own, talking to neither one of them about all kinds of mechanical things. Jake appeared to be interested in his monologue, but she didn't even bother to fake it. She felt he was talking only to get to the end of his father's visit, and even though this had been her idea, she didn't want to think about how badly it was going. She had enough to think about, enough to wish for. So much hope that she needn't entertain a thought of the present for months. It worked like that for her: She'd be overtaken with wishfulness and the world would move for her, allowing her to stay still and lose herself in desire.

On the way home they stopped off at Hattie's for an ale. This time she crowded in the booth next to Jake before Heath could choose the seating arrangements. He sprawled across from them, his feet on the seat, and drank two beers before his father had managed half a glass.

"Thank you so much for showing me around the marina, Heath. I really appreciate it, son."

Maybe it was the formality of the thanks that got to Heath; maybe it was his father's tone, decorous and needy at once, as if good manners were all he had left to hide behind but might also allow an entry into the kind of familiarity he desired. Why don't you just say something real, Reka wanted to say to him. Don't talk to him like he's a tour guide at the World of Tomorrow.

Heath studied the taxidermy mounted above the bar, then drained his beer and signaled the barkeep for another. When it arrived he cocked his head to them and said, "I'll say this in front of Reka. I know all about you two, she told me everything, and she obviously can handle anything I've got to say to you."

She looked away herself, at a blue-green steelhead, scared to look at Jake, though obviously he knew her well enough to know how incapable she was of keeping such a secret. She *would* be a creep if she'd led Heath on all this time without telling him the truth. Still, she wished she'd had the chance to tell Jake herself.

She waited for Heath to speak, though she was close enough to Jake to feel his mood. She told herself that he would be relieved rather than angry. She told herself this twice, and then again, and finally she believed it.

"I don't think you did right by me," said Heath. "You knew what was going on and you did nothing to stop it and if you'd just stepped in and demanded she leave me alone and get on with her own life . . . Oh, hell, why'm I even bothering? You know all this."

"I do. But that doesn't mean I don't need to hear it from you. I never have before and I deserve it."

"You were up there with your fucking trees. Hiding out in the woods."

"I'm sorry, Heath."

"You should have just left her a long time ago. You think sneaking around's going to solve problems?"

"Hey, now." He'd pulled his hand out of the pocket of his suit-coat but it just hung there by his side, as if he'd forgotten what he needed it for. "You can say anything you want about how I failed you, but don't think it's your call to tell me how I should be living my life now that you're gone. And gone for good it seems to me."

"I just think leaving her would have made everything easier. You didn't love her, that was plain. What was she to you when you married her?"

"Just a girl," said Jake. He looked surprised by his answer, then resigned to its honesty. "A high school girl."

"I'm going," said Reka, too quickly and with a catch in her throat that made them both stare.

"Stay," said Jake, reaching for her hand as she scooted out of the booth. "Heath wants you to stay," he said, nodding toward his son.

"He does, too," said Heath, nodding toward his father.

"No," she said, shrugging off both of them. "I'm going back."

Outside she did not even bother to wear her hood, and by the time she got back to the house she was soaked. She stripped off her clothes, drew a warm bath. There was wine in the refrigerator Heath had bought for their dinner, and though she was not a drinker, she poured herself a glass and took the bottle along and sat sipping wine in the bath. *Just a high school girl.* She thought of

Maggie at seventeen, a naive beauty in love with a college boy come home from the war. She thought of herself at seventeen, naive in a different way, and desperate enough to fall in love with a boy whose war was of his own making, and one he did not come back from. Had Edwin lived, and had they left town and headed west like they'd planned, they'd have ended up just like Jake and Maggie. How could she ever have thought it might work? She remembered lying awake in prison, dreaming of a life with him even while serving time for killing him. She poured more wine and wondered if people who prove themselves failures at love aren't just deluding themselves when they give it a second try, or a third. She wondered if there were not some people who should not even bother.

But she did kill a man, there's no denying that, she imagined Heath saying to his father across the tabletop crowded with their empties at this very moment. She lowered herself into the tub so that only her breasts and kneecaps and mouth and face were unprotected, her ears safely submerged. It was true: in the records of the district court of the State of North Carolina and in the minds of hundreds who followed her case in papers as far away as Greensboro and Norfolk she had killed a man; there was no denying it and Heath had every right to point this out to his father whom he had not seen for years. He had every right to suspect her, doubt her, question her motives. An ex-convict who pops up out of nowhere, ingratiates herself into their household by listening patiently to his needy, desperate mother. A woman with a secret who placates his mother by sleeping in his old room and allowing her to fix meals and put flowers by her bed, then—the moment his mother is out the door—seduces his father and turns him from a kindly, stoic lover of trees into a sneak, a sinner, an adulterer. Who was she? Cracker stock from down South. Tobacco Road trash.

It sounded like a B movie, played out this way in her head: mysterious seductress who slides into town to disrupt an otherwise settled domestic tableau. That it was not otherwise settled did not seem terribly pertinent to the plot.

When the bottle was empty she drained the tub. She got out and dried off and retired to her bedroom, where she told herself she would stay all night, for it seemed a dangerous idea to see him again. Better to let them both leave. Heath would call when he got to Ketchikan and they would talk and as for Jake, he would probably not even knock in the morning to say goodbye. Good manners would save him. He'd hide behind decorum and his decorum was a wide, safe screen. It would get him back to Red Fork, where he would kiss nonexistent Maggie on the cheek and pull her chair out for her as they dined and take care of the dishes while Maggie watched the after-dinner game shows and knitted a sweater for her nephew. And why shouldn't he be nice to her? She was a high school girl when he married her and she was still that girl to him, innocent and curious about an older man home from the war, and he would stay with her because he had already lost too much and would rather live miserably in confinement than endure the consequences of freedom.

She picked up a novel and tried to read, but someone else's story, some other life with its complications and loose ends and unexpected triumphs and artful conversations, seemed incomprehensible to her. What were these people doing? What did they want from each other? She put it down and waited in the dark for sleep she knew would only come when she had worn herself out with worry.

After an hour or so she heard the back door squeak open. She listened for voices, but heard only the sound of Heath clanging around in the kitchen, opening a beer, peering into the icebox, slamming shut its squeaky door. The same noises she often heard when he came home late and a little tight from Hattie's, noises she'd long ago memorized.

She held her breath, or thought she did. She breathed, but

barely, as she waited for the door to open, a knock to sound in the hallway, Jake to return. Just out taking a walk. Wanted to see the city at night, its hills terraced with lights. He would not see Rainier on this rainy night, but there would be enough to impress him without it. Enough of what they called the Emerald City to keep him interested for a while.

Ten minutes passed. She did not need a clock to keep time. She had her breathing, such as it was. Noiseless, modest, as if taking up too much oxygen might keep him away longer, outside in the fresh night air. There was room to breathe here, in this house shared by his son and his lover. He needed to know that. Heath needed to tell him that. Oh, why did I leave, why did I run? She could have listened all night long to him talking about Maggie and she could have heard worse if it meant that he would, at the end of it, return.

Heath's footsteps in the hallway. He had taken his boots off but she knew his walk, knew the way his weight creaked the floorboard in front of the heat register. It had been so long since she had lived with anyone, since prison, and before that Edwin, and she had been nervous enough in her first nights with Heath to hear everything, catalog it so she would be used to it, know it without having to hear it.

He coughed in the hallway. She could tell where he was, knew that he'd passed the bathroom that separated their bedrooms, knew he was standing outside her door. Thirty seconds later the knock came, and fifteen seconds after that, when she did not answer, he asked to come in. She let his words settle long enough to discourage him, but when he knocked again she acquiesced.

He stood in the doorway, his hand on the knob; she made no effort to get out of bed or turn on the light, which seemed to make him nervous.

"Don't you want dinner? There's salmon left over, I can whip up some cakes. Make 'em all the time on the boat. My specialty."

"I'm fine," she said. She could see him, but what could he see of her? Only the kitchen light shone, and he stood blocking what little light there was.

"You don't sound fine."

When she ignored this he said, "You didn't have to leave. I told you, anything I was going to say, I'd say it in front of you. I know you better than I know him. Hell, you've been more like family to me than he ever has."

Was this what she wanted? For him to feel like she was family? Not if it meant replacing his blood kin. She'd rather be a stranger to him, some woman he met years later when, through guilt or maturity or simply exhaustion, too tired to be angry anymore, he reconciled with his parents only to find them long parted, and his father with a new wife, children maybe. He would be thrilled to find out he had siblings. Thereafter he would remain in touch, they would see him for holidays and visit him here in Seattle and he and his father would find, after so long a pause, that they loved each other and were capable of all kinds of forgiveness.

Wouldn't this be a better way to claim him as family?

He was waiting for her to respond, but she could not tell him of her dream. She thought of how she'd lived her life in Trent after she got out of prison, working, saving money, seeing no one but Rose, with whom she ate lunch every day under the pecan trees behind the laundry, and Randall. Reading novels at night and going to the movies by herself and sleeping occasionally with men who meant nothing to her. She never would have predicted that she would prefer that fierce and empty detachment again, but she felt, watching Heath watch her in the near-darkness, that maybe this was what was left for her.

"Listen, Heath," she said. "That's not true, what you said. He's your father. I really didn't think it was right for me to stand by while you berated him about not leaving your mother. It's none of my business and it made me uncomfortable."

"Well, then, I guess you did right by leaving. Went straight downhill from there."

She waited for him to say more. The refrigerator kicked on, its sudden humming a sound known to her on a normal night, but this was no normal night and she shuddered along with its sputtering.

"Are you going to tell me what happened?"

She watched his silhouette for some sign that he was weakening, that he wanted to talk and needed her to listen, for who else could he talk to about his father but her? But his body was a rigid, black cutout in a dim yellow haze, and she remembered the silhouette some teacher had made of Randall once when he went with a friend to Bible school. His profile from the shoulders up scissored from black construction paper, glued lumpily onto a smudged sheet of white. She remembered where it had hung in the kitchen on Devone Street, beside the auto parts calendar that remained on July 1949 for so long that the edges curled and the paper yellowed and the dates in the squares seemed to dim with age and neglect. No one looked at that calendar, and no one else but her ever saw Randall's silhouette, but she remembered everything about it now, how the artist had done a passable job with everything but her little brother's nose, and how sometimes she had come home from school and looked up at it and wondered if it would weather and rot there like the calendar while Randall in the flesh worked his magic someplace far from Trent.

"I told him to leave."

"Why?"

"I thought all this made you uncomfortable."

He was right. She wanted to know everything, but did she deserve to know what had been said? Wasn't it between them? Even if it had been about her, it wasn't her business really. She knew what she was allowed to know: that Jake was gone, and that chances were slim she would ever see him again. This was enough. Too much to fathom with Heath standing in the doorway, letting in unwanted light.

"I hope the fishing picks up, Heath," she said. "Thanks for coming back for the fair. It meant a lot to me to have some company in Tomorrowland."

He hesitated for a moment, as if pondering a response, then told her he would radio her from the boat. But his statement lacked conviction, and could have just as well been a question: Will I radio her from the boat? Why should I bother? Why not just lock this night away in that drawer where I keep the rest of Red Fork? Why not forget all about the future and what wild plans people come up with to keep themselves from becoming bored in the intolerable present?

After he was gone, she stretched as far as she could beneath the sheets, seeking the curve of the bed with her toes as if it was the end of an earth she longed to prove was not flat after all.

———

WITH A BLACK MAN NAMED Will Boykin, Randall spent the summer of '62 cutting timber and selling it to the rich Trentonians whose wide antebellum houses lined River Road. Once he had gone out with Will to deliver a load to Edwin Keane's father's place.

"I can't go up there," he told Will as they idled in the road, waiting for traffic to thin to turn into the drive.

"How come?"

"Just can't."

"What, you owe that man money?"

"Carry me back to town. I'll be in front of the courthouse, you can pick me up when you're through."

"Your lazy ass can walk to town if you ain't gone help me unload," said Will.

"Fine," said Randall, as he climbed out of the truck. Though he'd never laid eyes on Edwin's parents as far as he knew, he felt it would be a betrayal to Reka to set foot on their property. He knew the mother had visited her in jail, brought her food and books, even lent her money when she came back here to Trent to begin her next prison sentence. But the father had seen to it that she was prosecuted; he had blamed her for his son's death from the start, and had not rested until she was led away by the fat female bailiff, the last time Randall had seen her until she was set free five years later. He would not stoop to stack firewood for those people. Walking up the shoulder of the road toward town he smiled, thinking of how much his sister was still with him.

When no one was buying firewood anymore, Randall did odd jobs for Speed—mopped the store, washed his truck, stocked the shelves—and took his pay in food. He worked when he got hungry, spent the rest of the time searching. He hitchhiked down to White Lake and sat for hours in the August sun on the pier at Goldston Beach, hoping to find his mother. She would bring her grandkids down maybe, and Randall would see them playing in the sandy shallows, and their features would shine in the tea-colored water, and he would watch them closely until one of them got hungry or tired and ran back to find her grandmother, who would be sitting high up the beach beneath the cypress trees, wearing a man's hat to shade her eyes and working a crossword puzzle. He did not care what she wore, did not care if she could even read. He had imagined her tying tobacco behind a tractor under a blaze of August sun, he had seen her working the counter of one of the sticky-floored motels down at Carolina Beach. And he had pictured her up in Raleigh, a tennis-playing beauty with skin to show for it, a prosperous woman with lawyer sons and doctor sons-in-law.

That fall they hired themselves out to a pulpwood crew, spent much of the season logging the cypress out of Serenitowinity Swamp. Will quit after a few weeks, tired of the water in his boots, the mosquitoes thick as fog and the cottonmouths who dozed on cypress knees and fallen logs and were too fat and spiteful to be scared off by the sound of a chainsaw. Randall wore leggings over his waders to ward off snakebite and kept at it, more for the swamp than the money or the work, which was hard and hot and exhausting. But he quickly grew to like the swamp. He remembered his father telling him about how his own father had gotten work logging up north on the Virginia border, the Great Dismal. He, too, had logged cypress for a living. Randall had never been big on carrying on family traditions—in his case it would be wise to forget those who went before him—but working the same trade as his grandfather made him feel as if he knew the old man, as if he were working a crew just the other side of the swamp. And there were the cypress trees to love, gnarled and hideous, their trunks bloated like the thighs of a woman who worked behind the butcher counter at the Piggly Wiggly in town. He hated to cut them down, but just like with the carts he'd welded to ferry hogs to their grisly end, he could not summon the moral outrage required to turn down cash money. It needled his conscience, though—he kept this job because of the swamp, and if he kept at this job long enough, what he loved about the swamp—the lazy old fairy-tale trees—would disappear.

There was something else to love about the swamp, though. It took him a while to figure it out, for at first it was just a vagueness, an inkling of a presence, some spirit that made him feel watched over and protected him from the blade of the saw he wielded which his first week on the job had sliced a tendon in a boy's thigh and the snakes that men with their buildings and highways and cars drove from all over the coastal plain into this muddy and godforsaken tangle. It wasn't until the crew had worked themselves deep into the swamp, past the last rudimentary roads, to places trashless and free from other ugly signs of man, that he recognized the presence of his mother. She was here, had been all along. She hid out here in the daytime and made sure he was safe, and rather than bother picking through the scrub to return to wherever it was she was staying now, she found some high ground to camp on and waited for his return.

He stopped work one day in October. Put down his chainsaw and walked away from the rest of the crew, into the purple shadows of the swamp. She was everywhere present and nowhere visible, God in her universe, and he did not mind that he could not see her because he felt her so completely. His very body altered in her presence, a calm came over his bones and the ache of the hard labor left his muscles. He endured the bugs and the heat because it was worth any sacrifice to be so close to her, whom he had searched for all this time. Years, really, for he was searching for her before he knew it. Those walks he took Reka on when they were younger, long afternoon explorations of backalley Trent, the times they hid out from thunderstorms in abandoned warehouses, the mornings he spent at the river when he was supposed to be delivering packages for the drugstore, even that fateful day when he took Reka to the courtyard of the Episcopal church and Edwin Keane happened to pass by and see him high in the trees calling out hello down there to his beautiful sister—all these hours spent searching for something vague but vital, and here he had found out finally what, and why, and here he had finally found her.

The next day he loaded a burlap bag with matches, his father's duller-than-hell axe, a couple of knives, some fishhooks, a pot and a tin collapsible cup, clothes, two sheets of plastic, candles, the least frayed portrait of his mother folded neatly into eighths and two books he'd borrowed from the public library: the *U.S. Army Survival Manual*, revised reprint of the Department of the Army Field Manual, a severe-looking tome of tan cover and cheap paper, and Mark Twain's *Innocents Abroad*, which was a month overdue already but he was loving every word of it and had several countries to go yet. He stopped off at Speed's store and bought what he could carry of canned goods and other nonperishables, then hiked the five miles down to the edge of Serenitowinity Swamp. He waved over his shoulder to a farmer hauling his hogs to market in a cart he might have welded, improvised a bluesy elegy for the poor, dumb, soon-to-be-dead hogs, hopped the ditch and disappeared into the swamp to join his mother.

―――――――

THE DAY AFTER HEATH LEFT, Reka stayed in bed. She kept the shades drawn and did not bother with coffee or breakfast or books or a bath or scouring the kitchen counters or any of the things she knew might help her mood. She was glad she'd asked Thanassis for time off and sorry, too, for she knew that she would never *not* show up for work even given the way she felt, which was the worst she remembered feeling since she'd left prison. Work was what she knew. It was what you did when you got out of bed in the morning. You do not take time off to make love to someone's husband in a borrowed cabin any more than you cower in bed all day long after losing a lover and making certain in this loss that his son never wants to speak to him again.

But why did he want to speak to *her?* This question kept her occupied while lying abed trying not to feel any worse. Whatever passed between them the night before must have had little to do with her. She was vain to assume so in the first place.

Outside, rain pelted the windowpanes. She remembered how he used to compare her to rain. She tried to think of places where rain was a miracle. Somewhere parched, landlocked, riverless. She would bake there, know rain only in memories of this sodden city and from movies where it rained entirely too much in her opinion. It was hard to find a movie where the streets were not rain-slick. A western maybe. Tom Mix or Gene Autry, the movies she used to take Randall to when he was loping through grade school, a sullen twangy cowpoke with a twig in his mouth.

Sometime during the morning she drifted into a thin, doleful sleep. When she woke sweat-soaked from a bad dream she remembered hearing that you don't dream when drunk. She considered for a while a trip to the kitchen for a bottle of Heath's rye. But even this day was not enough to turn her into a daytime drinker. Not with the father she'd had.

She did not bother with clocks. What need had she of time? She knew that one minute would not be any more or less tolerable than the next, that there would be no gradual healing as the day dimmed its already weak light. Outside a light drizzle alternated with a more wintry Seattle downpour. A day made up only of slightly distinguishable shades of gray.

At some point the rain let up. In the place of rain drumming wood, a knocking on the door. Some fisherman stopping by to see if Heath was still in town, game for a trip to Hattie's. Go away, nobody home. Whoever it was proved persistent, if gentle. A respectful rap instead of a hammering.

She put a pillow over her head. Squeezed out the room, the house, the world, the choices, so many and treacherous, her world was made of.

In her self-inflicted darkness she imagined it was Randall at the door. Soaked and startlingly alive, carrying nothing but his love for her, a need to find her so great that it directed him to this bungalow among rows of so similar ones. But this vision was dim and grainy and flickering like the worn films she'd been shown in high school on matters of personal hygiene. She could not hold on to this image even in her cave and it made her feel guilty anyway, for she knew she did not deserve to find her brother after all the havoc she'd caused.

It was not soundproof, her hideaway. From the hallway came the sound of footsteps. Floorboards creaking by the heat register.

Not Heath come back to tell her everything was fine, not to worry, he'd just sent his father home to fetch his toothbrush. Not Randall.

Who is it? Who's there?

Pillow-muffled cries. The pillowcase was sopping from tears and a kiss of saliva left by her terrified questions.

She slid the pillow off slowly, struggled with its feather weight. Jake stood in the doorway, slivered by the same light as his son when she'd last laid eyes on him.

"The back door was unlocked," he said, apologizing before he was even real to her.

"Don't you talk," she said, throwing back the bedclothes, making room for him beside her. "Not another word."

Sometime near dusk he lifted his body from hers and said, "Can I talk now?"

"Yes," she said, even though she wasn't ready. She needed him in other ways, needed to have him inside her and on top of her and beneath her and alongside her entwined in a dizzy, wordless half-sleep, before she could listen. She needed to know that he was there, that he had not come back to tell her goodbye, that he was, at least for the rest of the afternoon, hers.

"I know I should have told you this earlier. But there really wasn't a chance. Your brother came to Red Fork looking for you."

She felt bones melt in her body, felt herself go as limp as those protestors she'd seen on television disobeying with slack limbs the world's atrocities. But there was a difference—she was not protesting so much as giving in, overwhelmed by the notion that the choices her world demanded would never be fair, that one would eliminate another and there was no sense in pretending that she could ever find security without sacrifices so dear that her joys would always be suspect. People talk about knowing their minds, their hearts, she thought as she struggled to find the frame in her body, so indistinguishable now from the soft mattress, the damp Seattle sheets; people speak as if knowledge, for them, is fact, like the year they were born, the color of their eyes. People talk craziness to help them sleep, but I would rather toss about in the gray unknown dawn than make hard fact from open question.

"Where is he?" Her voice was solid and harsh, as if strengthened by the iron returning to her skeleton.

"I'm sorry. I know I should have said something earlier."

"When, Jake? How long ago?"

"God, a while ago. March of '60, I believe. Two years now. He got himself arrested. He was going house to house, knocking on doors, flashing these drawings of a nude man and asking people if they'd seen his sister. Maggie came to the door and took one look at the pictures and then at him and she slammed the door in his face and called the cops. She wasn't going to tell me. I didn't even know she'd done it, I had to hear about it from Mrs. Bowers, the widow lady who lives next door. She told me how the cops had come and taken the pervert away and after I got it out of Maggie, who he was, I went down to the jail to see him but they wouldn't let me in there. I guess because they thought I was going to try to hurt him since it was my wife who called them on him. I paid his bail and tried to explain to the magistrate that I didn't mean any harm. I had to tell them he was not right, Reka, which they had no trouble swallowing, considering what he'd done. I thought I'd convinced them that he was somebody I was trying to take care of and I arranged with the police to pick him up in the morning but before I got down there, some jailer'd let him go already. Maybe they said something to him about me and he said he didn't know me from Adam, which is true. I guess he was as suspicious of me as the police were. Anyway, I tried like hell to find him. I rode around the county two days looking for him but he disappeared."

She turned away from him, crumpled her body around a pillow.

"I'm sorry," he said. "I was too late."

"It's not your fault," she said when she could. "He was the one who was too late."

"You'll find him," he said.

"No," she said. "I lost my father and now I've lost him."

"I know this isn't much," he said, "but you found me. And for good."

It was what she'd wanted to hear from the start, but it only reminded her of other unfinished things.

"What happened last night?" she said. "Why are you here? I thought you'd left."

"What did Heath tell you?"

"Nothing. He knocked on my door when he got home and he came in for a minute but he didn't tell me anything, really, except that he asked you to leave."

"That's how it ended," said Jake. "But a whole lot more got said than that."

"And are you going to tell me about it?"

Jake sighed and pulled her close, but as soon as he'd settled against her he sat straight up in the bed. She knew there was nothing she could do to calm him, that he just had to fidget through it.

"He thinks I set this whole thing up."

"What?"

"The fair. Thinks I sent you out here to befriend him so that later, after he succumbed to the charms of your friendship, I would get you to bring him to the fair and I would magically show up and we would run into each other and have a reconciliation and I would be able to appease my guilt about losing him, which he maintained I needed to find a way to resolve since there were obviously more crucial things for me to feel bad about now."

"Why didn't he tell me any of this?"

"He meant for you to hear it, I guess. But you left. He didn't try to go after you because he assumed you left because you knew what was coming. Or, as he put it, you knew he was 'on to us.' "

"God," she said. "How could he think I'm capable of such a thing?" As soon as she asked the question, she felt ridiculous. After all, she'd only killed a man and served time for it. How could she be not capable of such manipulation and worse in his eyes?

"Don't tell me," she said. "I'd rather not know."

"Thing is, he doesn't seem to be mad at you. He blames me. He says I used you, that I'm using you still, that I'm not all that serious about you and I'll end up ignoring you just like I did his mother. He feels like it's his job to protect you. You're a sister to him who needs to be saved from an old lech like me."

She thought it would be so much easier if Heath had told her to leave, too. If he had thrown her out of the house last night when he returned, told her he never wanted to see her again. Now she had to live with knowing how much she'd disappointed him, but like a loving parent he was giving her another chance to prove herself to him.

"What now?" she asked.

"I'll go home in a day or two and get some things. We'll stay here while Heath's gone, and then we'll find a place of our own. I'll get a job. As soon as I start making some money, you can go back to college."

"You've got it figured out, haven't you?"

"Not as if it took a lot of time or energy. I want to stay here with you, Reka."

"But what about Heath?"

"I've lost him already, a long time ago. I don't see that the present situation changes anything."

He waited for her to speak, but she stared at the blinds slatted tightly across the window and remembered all those nights staring at another window from her narrow prison cot, when her every desire appeared cross-hatched by bars.

———————

THERE WERE NO TRAILS in the swamp save the rutted logging roads used by pulpwooders, wide muddy tire tracks following the highest ground and dipping in places to fill with tawny water where the dump trucks and backhoes had bogged. Randall didn't mind getting wet. He wore the high waders he'd bought for his pulpwood job, the army/navy surplus leggings he'd found at a rummage sale, stiff olive-drab canvas numbers with hooks and eyes that rose to his shins. He wasn't scared of snakes. Mosquitoes liked him and he did not like mosquitoes but he was philosophical about their presence, as it seemed to him that if he was to trespass in their domain he had no right to deny them his blood.

The survival guide proved indispensable the first night, when Randall realized he had brought only enough water for two or three days. In his guide he learned to tie tufts of grass around his ankles and parade through dew-covered foliage just before dawn. He wrung the water into his one small pot. With the plastic he fashioned a camp on rare high ground safe from the rising swamp water but soft enough to make a fine bed. Sunlight was sparse even in the heat of the day, and often his retreat was shadowed in dark greens and the purple of bruise by high noon.

He kept busy. He killed a squirrel by batting it out of a low limb with a club he fashioned from a poplar branch and a piece of brickbat that had obviously dropped from the bed of someone's logging truck. With the tiny amount of fat from the squirrel he made soap, frying the fat until it rendered, straining the grease into his cup to harden, fashioning potash by pouring water over ashes and collecting the runoff, then boiling the grease and potash together until it thickened and hardened enough for him to collect a small bar of his very own soap. No matter that he did not need to bathe; every morning he rubbed his arms and face with the soap. It smelled only a bit more gamey than his own odor, which he feared would frighten off quarry.

He saw a small bear cub, a coral snake, countless deer. He had not known the swamp was so alive. The only people who came here were hunters and pulpwooders. The swamp covered half the county, and he knew he could lose himself here for months, for even though the swamp backed up on the country club not three miles away, no one would think to look for him here. He was safe in the swamp. He remembered Reka telling him once that it was here, on some road bordering the swamp, that Edwin had the wreck that killed his girlfriend and left him with a back injury so unrelenting that he became a morphine addict. She told him once that Edwin thought the swamp evil, that he had claimed it had sucked his car off the road, down the embankment.

He liked its name: Serenitowinity. He decided it was a mix of Indian and white people, as the *winity* sounded native, the *serenity* something a preacher tagged to it. Serenitowinity soap, he called his new product. Straight from the swamp. He spent a couple of hours drawing a logo for it, in the dirt with a stick.

On one of the trees to which he'd strung his plastic lean-to he hung the portrait of his mother. He talked to her nights. Tried to smooth the blemishes from her face with his bar of soap. No-see-ums and mosquitoes lit on the paper, so thick sometimes it seemed she was sprouting facial hair. He took great care to sweep them off, as maybe she was not as philosphical about insects as he was.

She seemed so at home that he adjusted easily to the terrain. He read to her from *The Innocents Abroad*. Her favorite excerpt was a snippet of a journal Mark Twain admitted keeping when he was a boy:

Monday: Got up, washed, went to bed.

Tuesday: Got up, washed, went to bed.

Wednesday: Got up, washed, went to bed.

Thursday: Got up, washed, went to bed.

Friday: Got up, washed, went to bed.

Next Friday: Got up, washed, went to bed.

Friday fortnight: Got up, washed, went to bed.

Following month: Got up, washed, went to bed.

He decided she liked it so much because it was familiar to her, to them, as the days in the thick of Serenitowinity were not without surprises, but they began and ended in routine and solitude. Here they had only each other. The years they had lost were slowly making themselves up in this new and blissful isolation, in this new and oddly untedious routine: got up, swiped ourselves with soap, went to bed.

He filched bird eggs from nests in trees. Hiked every other day in a different direction in search of a better campsite, for even though he thrived on routine, he couldn't see the point of not looking. Left, right. Not straight but forward, a couple of miles made more by the circuitous what-passed-for-paths, he discovered the Tar slicing arrogantly through the lowlands. He did not know it ran this way, had never taken note of where it forked from the highway. Grand and low and muddy-watered, no banks to speak of, mud sloping into current, the river thrilled and terrified him. He was happy to have the access in or out, and wary of the traffic it might bring. After all, he was in hiding. Lost on purpose.

In a high clearing a quarter mile from the river, far enough so that smoke from his fire would not be visible to boaters and what fool fishermen braved the hike to cast their lines, Randall resettled. Daily he crept down to the water to fish for his one meal of the day. Even though he had brought line, he fashioned his own fish hook from a maple shank and a nail he wrestled from a piece of driftwood. This took time, but what was time? Once he had wasted time, hesitating in Chicago trying to see what he could see. As a result, he had lost his sister forever. Now he vowed never to get caught in a situation that required some schedule more than get up, swipe myself with soap, go to bed. He would emerge from the woods when he could no longer subsist, and with the river so close, and his *Army Survival Manual* teaching him things he doubted he'd have ever learned in the Army, with his mother along for company and his head filled with images from his year of travel and the highly ironic European excursions of Twain, he felt he could stay there forever.

———————

FOR ALL HER DOUBT and guilt and regret, something simple kept her going: Jake was there in the mornings when she woke and there in the evenings when she returned from the diner, and even though she knew he was not hers, the life they improvised during those few weeks seemed as if it could last forever.

But she made herself remember that it was not real. It was paper, a plan, drawings of castles done by dreamy kids. She did not mind dreaminess or cobbled lives, as she wanted always to believe that there was no real difference between the life you imagined and the one you ate and slept and bathed in. Yet he was not hers. He was married to someone else.

She had never been a list maker—lists were for shopping, for tests, Christmas. Yet she found herself thinking in pluses and minuses for the first time ever, and it shocked her and made her think of Edwin, of how foreign it would have been when she was with him to write down words on a page and assign them some fixed value. With Edwin she had made no attempt to define what was good or bad, helpful or detrimental; he had taken her away with him, picked her up like a high wind, and despite the recklessness and fury of the breeze she had never once thought to tether herself to some false wall of fact.

And now Jake, for whom lists seemed similarly inappropriate. But she found herself making them against her will, more from fear that she was making a mistake than desire to claim him. She had made her choice and would stick by him, yet this did not alleviate the need to tally, which scared her. Maybe it was the age difference. But age was the first item on her list, for she was twenty-eight and he was forty-six. She was an old twenty-eight; despite his suffering, he was a young forty-six. She could give a damn about numbers, though the thought of losing him to old age made her wonder if numbers did not add up for a reason. Still, to base one's feelings on arithmetic seemed absurd to her. She thought of Randall, seven years younger, the person she'd been closest to her whole life. Would she ever feel that the numbers separating them made any kind of difference in the way they saw each other or the world? A vision even slightly compatible with yours was so hard to come by, so rare and infrequent, so like a miraculous merging of sun and moon. She felt ashamed, sitting around fiddling with the probability of total or partial eclipse, the distance between heavenly bodies, and yet she could not help herself.

He was married. At seventeen she had moved in with a man, lived in his house with him in a town too small to hide a buried secret, much less a public one. She had slept with married men before Jake and never once for love, and afterward she had never felt for the wife even when she wanted to; even when she wanted to take the side of the betrayed, she sided instead with herself, for whatever reasons she had for sleeping with a married man—commerce, boredom, lust, curiosity—seemed more complicated and more interesting than the particulars of an unsuccessful union. She remembered what she'd said to Bob Smart—Mrs. Bob Smart has her own troubles, I'll let her take care of them—and she remembered the look of shock on his face, as if her lack of concern was a supreme moral failing. Yet she saw no virtue in guilt, no rectitude in recognizing victims. There were too many victims, it had always seemed to her; we're all of us victims of our own schemes and conflicting wants, and to pretend feelings for the people you wrong is to wrong yourself.

A married man, twenty years older. A son befriended with guile, by design. She could write these things down and she could fold the paper up and sneak looks at it and try to feel, but she could not compute, she could not arrive at a figure. There were lines between the words, and in the empty space a missing body hovered, buried between these words and the truth she sought from listing them. A spirit, an inspiration, her brother: he was eraser dust, pencil smudge, a indelible mark whose stain would linger always on any list she made, for every added word meant one deleted, or so it felt like to her. What was the use of listing names and ages and statistics when the spaces held so much more meaning, when omission was more powerful than inclusion?

In her conversations with Jake, much was omitted. They did not speak of Heath. They did not talk of Maggie, of what Jake would say to her and how he would say it, because Reka did not think it was her place to help him plot his defection. Hadn't he already left? Wasn't it a matter of folding clothes, packing bags, signing documents? Paperwork, she told herself even as she recognized that there was nothing remotely simple or detached about paperwork, for your name is sacred, more password or even prayer than noise and syllable, and you cannot sign it, even in the dust of a car windshield, without claiming something for yourself.

The autumn rains arrived. Sifted dampness from the Pacific, from Asia and Canada and other far-off places whose mysteries she felt in the curtained cloud cover, the rolling fog.

"You should go now," she said to him on the second day of a

downpour. They had talked around his leaving for a week. "I mean, if you're going."

"Of course I'm going," he said. "But the thing about it is, I can't say when I'll be back. There's stuff to take care of and I don't know how long . . ."

"I don't care how long. I care to hear your boots on the porch one night when I'm trying to wash the hamburger smell out of my hair. And I care to hear if you change your mind, and I care to be notified about that change of mind at the earliest possible moment."

"What do you mean?"

"I mean I'll be damned if I'll be stood up. Call me and tell me when you're coming back. If you're not coming back, you call me and tell me. Don't write me a letter."

She did not want the evidence lying around for her to reread. She'd rather think of the stories he'd told her about the war, or be reminded of him by a barge of huge, barkless soaking logs chugging through the Sound on the way to be processed into paper. She'd rather his leaving not be processed into paper, rather remember him by the images of blooming and vibrant wood than clear cuts that left behind earth as barren and festering as burned flesh.

"You sound like you have your doubts."

"I don't think it's healthy to not have them." This might have been a lie, or it might have been instinctive protection. She wasn't sure she cared to distinguish between the two, or if she even could. She only knew to steel herself against another defection.

Jake took his leave quietly. He seemed to understand what she needed: for him to go away and come back when he could, without endless discussion, without the wrong kind of baggage for the trip. She hated the sight of him walking out the door, but found promise in the sight of his son's borrowed clothes tight across his body, the yellow fisherman's slicker exposing his knuckles. A uniform of now, of them: She wasn't one to pray, but if she prayed it would be for him to show up in the same getup, for him to hide those clothes in the woods behind his house and change into them for the return journey.

He was gone for three weeks. She kept busy at work for the first few days, then gave in to her loneliness and let the house go to hell and was late for work. Nights she sat in a chair by the window, listening for his boots on the warped porch boards, and though she had spent five years in prison, this confinement seemed to her even more unbearable, for in prison she had so little to hope for except for release. Everything about the work camp—the strict regimen, the abysmal food she ate only enough of to subsist, the insolence and anger and violence of the other prisoners, the cold cinderblock walls and the ribbed metal roof of the quonset hut where Memory Wright kindly but pedantically passed along what she could remember of her rigid Seven Sisters education—conspired to quell any shred of optimism, even dreams. For that reason prison was easier time to do than those weeks when Jake was away from her.

She found thoughts to hold on to during this dark time. She decided that had she never come here to Seattle and tracked Heath down and befriended him, Jake would never have allowed himself that uncharacteristic vacation from his beloved forest. Had she kept on moving, Jake would have stayed with Maggie forever. It was a small but notable consolation to think that her coming here had, on some level, allowed him the courage to leave.

But the more she coddled this thought, the more it seemed the world she had courted since Edwin's death did not work like that. Randall would disagree—he would argue for some mystical governance in which the actions of someone hundreds of miles away could indeed affect you, change you, force you out of a rut—but she could not let herself think this way for the simple reason that Randall could. She had lost him, and it seemed fair punishment as well as rational healing for her to discipline herself not to think like he did. She had given up dreaming. She wanted only reality now, for she had found a place so socked in with fog and surrounded by water, so drastically different from the landscape she was used to, that there seemed no reason to invent. She had found a man to love and she would love him with honesty and without illusion.

There were days to get through, raw short sunless Seattle days. After two weeks passed and she still had not heard from him, she prepped herself for disappointment. Her commitment to reality seemed suddenly foolish to her, as how could she have ever imagined that she would have him in her life forever? She memorized the trajectory of their story and repeated this sequence of improbable events so much that in time they ran nonstop in her head, like the chants Randall used to whisper to himself when he was small and she would take him for walks. He had to set a cadence everywhere he went, as he had seen a war movie and been seduced by the half-sung call and response the troops performed while marching, and ever after he mumbled phrases over and over again in time to the slap of his sneakers against blacktop, and even though it used to annoy her, she found herself still, after all these years, humming these chants silently to herself on long walks. I don't know but I've been told, in the heat of the sun a man died of cold.

Her chants were shorter and darker. Hell is other people, the mistake one makes is to speak to people. She had read these both in a magazine article about some French existentialist and this was the only thing she really bothered to subsume in the article because the whole existentialist deal reminded her too much of Edwin, who was certainly a fan of this Frenchman as every other quote in the article sounded suspiciously familiar and she knew no one else who might go around paraphrasing French existentialists.

She went later and later to work. Thanassis had all but given her the diner now. He came in every day still, but mostly to sit and talk to the other vendors and merchants of the Market and stroke his mustache and scowl at the kids who came in after school for hamburgers and Cokes. But as Jake's absence dragged on, Thanassis began to show up early, though he did not say anything to Reka until the second week.

"Who is he?"

"Who is who?"

"This new one you worry over."

"What do you mean, new one? How do you know there's a new one."

"It's not Heath. He's only away fishing and besides I have not forgotten the look on your face when you used to come in here and sit staring out into the Market all day drinking my awful coffee for free. Now you don't seem like you're looking for someone, you seem like you've given up looking for someone."

She smiled at his accuracy even as she told herself she hadn't given up yet.

"I'm giving you a raise," said Thanassis.

"Oh, come on, Thanny, that's not it and you know it. You already pay me more than you can afford."

"Don't you dare tell me what I can afford. You might run this place but you don't touch the books." He was mock gruff, his glasses sliding down his nose and his big belly straining against the counter. He'd been scraping the griddle and had the spatula raised above his head as if he was about to clobber her. She held her hands up in surrender and he grunted and said, "You let me decide what to do with my money. I might be an old man but that doesn't mean I don't have sense enough to put my money somewhere where it will grow fat and happy."

"I don't need more money."

"How are you going to pay for college?"

She'd not thought about it at all since Jake had turned up, though before he arrived it was all she thought about, and she had managed to put away enough money since she'd been in Seattle to get her through at least a year of school. As soon as he mentioned it, she was glad for the reminder. Her own needs, independent of others, would come first now.

"Okay," said Reka. "You're right, Thanny, I'm due a raise. You can contribute toward my college fund, that's a splendid idea."

She thought of money, college, herself constantly until one Tuesday three weeks after he'd left for Red Fork, she came home from work to find Jake making stew in the kitchen.

He pretended not to hear her key in the lock. As she entered the kitchen he stood facing the stove, stirring his beef stew. She remembered his name for this stew, the same stew he'd fixed for her the day of the freak storm. *Stayabed stew.* She waited for him to turn around and he did not and she understood what game this was and went to him chanting *stayabed, stayabed, stayabed stew.*

"Not even a hello?" she said, hooking her arms around his chest. She felt his ribs, single and hard beneath the skin. His pants dropped from his bony hips, and he looked to have lost at least ten pounds off his already lean frame.

"Just this," he said, turning to her with a spoonful of stew, but she pushed it away and told him that wasn't what she wanted and she brought his head down to hers and pressed so hard against him—breast, groin, lips, forehead—that she heard him gasp.

Then she turned away from him. She wasn't sure why, but she hurt.

"What is it?" he asked.

"My teeth are all gunky," she said. "I had garlic bread for lunch and I didn't know you were coming."

"Hey," he said, pulling her back, holding her close. "Hey, now. I'm here. This is me. I'm back."

For good? she wondered, but she did not want to say such a desperate thing. Still, she worried; she pulled away from him and sat down at the kitchen table and crossed her arms beneath her breasts and held her breath and stared at a square of linoleum. She was suddenly terrified, and she could only think that she had not believed him, did not trust him.

He was back and she was terrified. She didn't know if she'd done the right thing; she knew that there would be no going back. She told herself she didn't really know Jake and she had told herself after Edwin Keane that she would never again fall for someone so quickly.

"I thought you'd be happier to see me," he said.

She put her hands over her eyes and rubbed, hiding her tears, trying to pretend she was only tired. But he was kneeling in front of her and pulling her hands away and she fell into him and let go her lungs and he held her for five minutes of sobs.

"I am," she said when she could breathe again. "I wanted you back here the day you left. But I didn't know if you'd come back and while you were gone, I don't know, Jake, I started thinking . . ."

He waited for her to finish, but she lapsed into tears again. Finally she pulled away and dried her eyes on his shirt and said, "Does she know it's me?"

"Do you care?"

"Enough to ask the question."

"No," he said. "She doesn't know. She knew it was coming, though she will not admit it. She's not big on admitting things. She thinks Heath left because I did not spend enough time with him. She says if I hadn't spent so much time up in the woods he'd have a job in Red Fork and would live at home with us. She seems to think that if I had done my job differently, Heath would choose to live his entire life upstairs, never marrying, never leaving home. Giving her something to do in her old age. She seems to have forgotten that she would not let me spend time with him, which is why I spent so much time in the woods in the first place."

Reka sighed and allowed him to take her hand. "I want to feel sorry for her," she said, "but I can't. I can't imagine doing what she did. I have a brother I love as much as she loved Heath and it looks like I've lost him, too."

"Too?"

"Heath. Your son?"

"I know who he is. And I'm the one who let him go. I could have stayed away like he asked, but I didn't. I had to choose and I chose you because I've already lost him, I lost him a long time ago."

Though she knew this already, she hated to hear it voiced. Somehow it was easier to take when left unsaid.

"We've got to figure out how to tell him."

"Can we eat first?" he said. "My stew's done, and I'm hungry."

"You look like you haven't eaten since you left."

"The misery diet," he said. He pulled her up to him and hugged her close and said, "Which is hereby officially over."

And it was. A new diet took over, clams and fresh asparagus, artichokes and crab legs and Domino's discount salmon, fresh victuals brought home from the market every day for meals that more often than not went unfinished as they succumbed, in kitchen or dining room or hallway and elsewhere, to a heat from which she sought so many things: to nail Jake on the bed, against the broom closet, on the couch, so that he would never leave again. And deliverance from what to do about Heath, who had radioed home several times since Jake returned, and she had not yet found the courage to tell him his father was there, sleeping in his house, his bathrobe hanging in the bathroom. She worried about Randall still, though she kept that worry to herself. She never mentioned her brother now to Jake, and when he brought him up she curtly changed the subject. Her guilt over losing him surely fueled other worries, especially what to do about Heath.

When the lust leveled off after a few weeks' time, she applied for the fall term at the state university and worked longer hours to pay for it. Jake found a job at Boeing installing bathrooms in jetliners. He had a long commute each day, an hour each way on the bus, and she worried that it would be hard on him to be cooped up in a claustrophobic cabin after twenty-some years of having the run of the wilderness, but when she quizzed him he seemed happy with the pay and the co-workers and he did not complain.

It lasted, this peace, until Heath floated home. He radioed on a Saturday afternoon that he was just south of Vancouver Island and would be there the next afternoon. They were wasting the day away in bed, three o'clock in the afternoon, the covers astray and strewn with newspapers and Basic English textbooks. Jake was quizzing her on verb tenses. He knew more than he allowed, and she both respected and disparaged his self-effacing way with her. She found solace in the rigid complexity of grammar, and had a strong grasp already from her work with Memory Wright, to whom a split infinitive was as offensive as a woman walking down the street smoking a cigarette.

"We should have told him weeks ago," said Reka. "And we should have found our own place by now. It's bad enough he has to come home to find us together, but to find us together in his house . . ."

"You're assuming he's against us."

"Seeing as how last time you saw him he asked you to leave, I'd say that's a pretty safe assumption."

"He's young. He'll change his mind when he sees how good we are together."

Reka looked down at her verbs, tried to lose herself in the technicalities of past and future perfect, but suddenly these terms were offensive to her. What past was perfect? How could anyone, even Jake with his open and innocent love for her, believe in a future free from trauma?

"He's not that young," she said. "You think of him as young because he's your son, and you lost him when he was a lot younger. But he's a man now, Jake. He might seem like the angry teenager who ran away from your house, but he's also older and wiser. There are sides to him you haven't seen yet, or at least you haven't seen enough of these sides to understand who he is now."

"What about your little brother?" said Jake. "You think because he's lost to you, because you haven't seen him in several years, he'll have changed that much?"

She resented the comparison even as she acknowledged his point. He wouldn't look at her, and he was obviously hurt; she realized that this was the harshest thing he'd ever said to her. She found herself wishing he'd lose his temper over this, for skirmishes and disagreements made love real. She thought briefly about provoking a confrontation—that way she could act out of indignation and her own hurt, and she would have more options to do whatever it was she was going to do next. But any fight would have to be about Randall, and she did not want to talk about Randall at all to him, and particularly did not want to think about how her brother might have changed.

"We're not talking about my brother, we're talking about your son. I've got to think about what I'm going to tell Heath."

"I'll tell him. I'm his father."

"You are, that's true. But I'm the one sharing this house with him, and when he left I was living here alone and he'd asked you to leave, and now he's coming back to find you still here and it seems my responsibility to explain how that came to be."

She didn't want to tell him what Heath had said the night he came in from Hattie's, that she was more like family to him than his own mother and father. But if it came to it, she would. Surely it would hurt him, but it might be the only way to get him to understand that blood ties, in this case, were not everything. In fact—and she hated to admit this, as it made her fear that someone else might have taken her place in Randall's life—the simple fact of kinship might not mean anything at all.

"We'll both tell him. I'll wait for you to get off work down at Hattie's, and we'll walk in together."

"No," she said. "I have to do this on my own, Jake. I don't want to lose him, too, and I'm afraid he'll hate me if I put it off on you."

"Who says you'll lose him? You keep assuming the worst here."

"It's my best quality," she said. She was trying to lighten the tone, but she wondered if there wasn't more truth in this comment than she intended.

"If you do lose him, you've still got me. And I've got you. Like I said, Reka, I've already lost him. I might have laid eyes on him again, and I might be all the more eager to have my son back, but I made my choice. I chose you, and if he can't understand that, if he continues to have a problem with it and decides he doesn't want me in his life, what will I have lost?"

Reka looked out the window at the dry-docked boat in the neighbor's yard. Heath was on his way right now, his boat slicing through the Sound toward home, and she was just as confused as she was when he left her that morning and a few hours later Jake climbed in her bed.

"I'll tell him," she said. " I was the one who showed up out of the blue and befriended him. It needs to come from me. You wait at Hattie's like you planned, call me from the pay phone out front around seven."

Jake acquiesced without argument, but he was distant for the rest of the evening, and that night both of them tossed across the bed so wildly that she imagined they were aboard the *Red Fork* with Heath, stowed in the hold as Heath guided his boat through the treacherous currents of home.

Jake got up early in the morning and left before she managed to get out of bed. When she heard him leave, she called Thanassis and asked for the day off.

All morning she kept busy cleaning house. When there was nothing left to scrub or scour, no part of the floor not swept or mopped, she brewed a pot of coffee and sat at the kitchen table going over her lines. She'd had them memorized ten times over as she cleaned, but now every syllable seemed wrong. She stared at the fat round clock hanging on the wall, as vibrantly white in the shadowed room

as a harvest moon. Endlessly it ticked against the ghastly early afternoon silence. Edwin had loved this time of day, and hated it, too. He
told her once that everything bad happens between the hours of
noon and three, and that great thoughts came to him always in
these hours, that in this time his desire and his love was at its peak,
yet everything good was overshadowed by the lengthening shadows
of early afternoon, everything joyous was drowned out by unnerving stillness. He spoke of unspeakable violence behind the quietude.
She did not understand what he was talking about until now.

Heath would be standing before her in this room in mere minutes. She needed more time to think. It seemed that all the world,
the rest of her days, depended on this decision.

Reka poured more coffee and sat down at the table again, determined to see this thing through. She tried to convince herself that
Jake's choice was the right one. He was devoted to her no matter the
cost, and didn't she deserve that kind of devotion after Edwin, who
found ways to push her away even as he promised his love for her?
She'd only ever loved a man who was incapable of loving himself,
and now she had someone who loved her enough to sacrifice his
only son to keep them together.

But did she want to be responsible for such a thing? Could she
live happily with Jake knowing that her love had led him to make
such a choice? If Heath was not chosen, he might as well be dead.
They would not see him and he would have children whom Jake
would never meet. She felt suddenly furious at Jake for bringing up
Randall the day before, comparing him to Heath, for now she found
it impossible to keep them straight in her mind. She imagined Jake
asking her to choose between him and Randall. Once she had sacrificed Randall for herself, so that she could escape from the scene
of the crime and not be reminded of how that crime had scarred
her, but she would not give him up for anyone else on this earth, not
even herself if she had it to do over again, not even Jake.

Once she had sat in another kitchen trying to make up her mind.

A dark and humid afternoon; she sat beside a cot where her lover lay slumped in an intermittently coherent trance, trying to get him to say those words that she needed to hear from him, the promise that he would take her far away from the place she felt she hated, the place she blamed for all unhappiness and misfortune. She'd told herself then that it all boils down to a few minutes, people's lives together, comes down finally to a frank and naked quarter hour of words that most people manage happily to avoid. When her lover asked for more medicine, when he claimed he needed it in order to tell her what she wanted to hear, she took refuge in a dream of someplace far away and free from the weight of her present, some crisp blue plain where she would see her breath always, where her words would leave trails.

"Good God," she said aloud. Her words bounced from the walls of the tiny kitchen, but they did nothing to disturb this malevolent quiet and so she said them again and followed them with tears and then sobs. She stood up from the table so quickly that she overturned the chair and the noise it made as it hit the floor was not loud enough to pierce the silence that had settled over all of Seattle, it seemed, the whole country, even Trent.

She thought of Randall leading her through the streets of Trent, on his way to another of his special places, alleyways and abandoned warehouses and church courtyards, which were all he needed of the world, for each site was transformed by his imagination into something exotic and daring and foreign.

Thinking of Randall only worried her more. She searched for some other image to get her through this moment, some appealing landscape like the frigid plain that she might fixate on while she told Heath that she loved his father and would do anything to stay with Jake, even if it meant Heath's hating her for it, even if he was never able to speak to them again.

That frank and naked quarter hour of words that most people manage happily to avoid. To think that she had let herself believe that a life could boil down to words, that a quarter hour of talk could make everything right. The worst part was not that she had convinced herself of this simple idea, but what it had allowed her to do.

She remembered thinking earlier that, had she not come here to find Heath, Jake would have stayed with Maggie forever. Even though she realized that the world did not revolve around the choices she made, it seemed in these last desperate moments before Heath arrived that her actions might travel across the country like a wave of atmospheric pressure, transported thousands of miles to change someone without their ever knowing it. Maybe he's guiding me, too, she thought. Maybe Randall right this minute is making some choice that will help me make up my mind.

Oh Randall, I'm coming. Wait for me, I'm on my way.

Outside she heard a car door slam and held both breath and body until no footsteps echoed in the hallway. She hurried to the living room, surveyed the street from behind the blinds. Someone visiting her next-door neighbor. Safe, anxious to escape, she ran to the basement for her suitcase.

After she'd stuffed all she could carry into her bag, she sat down to write Jake a letter in the notebook he'd bought for her to practice her verb tenses. She'd made columns at the head of a sheet that was otherwise empty, and under headings that read, "Present, Past, Past Perfect, Future Perfect," she scrawled her goodbye.

> Dear Jake,
> I couldn't tell him. I stayed home from work to tell him but I couldn't. I love you, I want to stay, but when it came time to tell him I got scared. I should have let you tell him like you offered, but I was the one who found him and it wasn't your job to tell him, for in a strange way (and you know this so I know even if it hurts you'll understand) I know him better than you do. I do not want to give up knowing him that way. I've lost too

many people. Some of them are dead. They don't bother me as much as the ones who are still alive.

I'm going to find my brother. He's out there somewhere, he's not dead. I'd know it if he was dead, and he's not. I will find him, I've not tried hard enough. I need him right now, need to be with him. Maybe when I find him, get him back, I will not be so scared about losing Heath. But I don't think it works that way, Jake, I don't think I get to trade off people like that, I don't think you'd want me to do that even if I could bring myself to do it. I want to say this: I'll be back soon. But there's only this instead: I love you today, even more than yesterday, and I would do anything to spend my life with you. Anything but come between the two of you. Anything but make him hate me, and worse, hate you, too.

If you go back to her I'll understand.

Don't try to find me. Whether you stay here with Heath or return to Red Fork, find something to do outside. Go back to your trees. Miss me when they bloom, miss me just as much when they shed.

Love, Reka

WATER BECAME A PROBLEM. There was food everywhere—nuts and plants and roots his survival guide taught him to find and identify and prepare, small game he caught with ingeniously rustic traps diagrammed in his yellowing, mud-stained bible, or miraculously chased down and caught by hand. He snared birds in a contraption attributed to the Ojibwa Indians, caught more fish than he could eat, though even as he tired of eating them he kept catching and cleaning them, for their bones were useful to him. He found a thousand ways to put them to work; his life seemed dependent on fish bones, as essential to him as matches, which he ran out of soon enough, but no matter, for there were other ways to make fire.

But not water. He had the Tar, slow and frothy, leech-filled, too toxic from the runoff of textile mills to drink. He had the swamp, which even if boiled tasted sulfuric and gave him diarrhea he learned to cure by brewing a tea from the bark of hardwoods, rich in tannic acid but so vile-tasting that he usually threw it right back up.

Water everywhere. His days began to lose themselves to the pursuit of it, he dreamed of it and spoke its name, rain was grace to him, he ad-libbed the methods of procurement taught him in his manual and multiplied his various rough cisterns and catching devices and still he did not have enough to drink.

He knew he would have to sneak back into the world. He spent a week trying arbitrary trails in search of the golf course he knew bordered the swamp. On the seventh day he heard through the woods the mechanized snarl of lawn mower and chainsaw. Sound carried in the swamp, insulated by dense scrub, amplified by water. He heard children splashing in a pool. Ladies playing bridge at the clubhouse dining room, their voices slushy with mimosas, slender cigarettes and hushed gossip. Next door in the dark, private bar, the clink and rattle of ice cubes, the bray of bankers. Someone on the tennis court double-faulted and blamed Jesus, God and that lesser deity Dag Gum. He heard clubs swishing air in practice swings. Crack of wood on golf ball.

At the edge of the wood bordering a long fairway he found and pocketed a half-dozen muddy balls. He would bring them back to the swamp where they would be transmuted, no longer orbs batted around lawns, but some other magical object, the purpose of which he and his mother would determine. A long fairway stretched out of sight, brilliantly coiffed and green, too orderly and groomed for the taste of a man used to the tangled anarchy of Serenitowinity. It hurt his eyes to look at it. Yet he could not turn away, squatted at wood's edge for the highest heat of the afternoon, sweating in his long sleeves and watching men move down the overly manicured grass on foot and in carts.

Suddenly he remembered: He'd been here before. Years ago, when he was seven or eight years old. It had snowed, a rarity in Trent, and the snow had stuck, even rarer, and there was enough of it to sled, rarest of all. His brother, Hal, had asked his father if he could take him sledding, and despite Reka's protests—for she barely let Randall out of her sight then, and she did not trust Hal at all because he had chosen her out of all his other sisters to torment and ridicule, and was only interested in playing with Randall or even acknowledging him when he was certain it would provoke Reka's jealousy—their father had ruled, for once, in Hal's favor.

"He won't get no more chances in this lifetime," he'd told Reka. "Not unless the world gets ready to give up the ghost and the goddamn weather goes crazy like the Bible thumpers claim."

"Who said anything about Bible thumpers?" said Reka, tearing up now. "You're always talking about Bible thumpers." It was true; with each drink their father talked louder, crazier trash about preachers and their gullible followers.

"I'll take him sledding at the graveyard," his sister said. "There's a hill over there."

"If you're an ant," said Hal. They all knew that the fairway of number nine out at the country club was the only passable hill until the Piedmont started its pitch and roll just past Raleigh. It was man-made and grand, and there were narrow concrete cart paths that wound through the woods alongside the fairway, perfect for sledding.

"You let him out of your sight and I'll have your ass, Hal."

"Come on, buddy," Hal said, pulling Randall away from the fireplace in the kitchen. On the back porch Randall pulled one of Hal's stringy sweaters down over his hips, layered himself in crusty mittens and galoshes donated by the clothes closet run by the Bible thumpers from whom his father was not too proud to accept donations. He stuck his head back in the kitchen to say goodbye to Reka, but she turned away at the sight of him, as if she blamed him for this betrayal.

"It'll do you good to have some time off from taking care of that boy," he heard his father say to her as Hal pulled him out of the door and into a car loaded with loud smelly boys. He sat on his big brother's lap and was quiet. He remembered now the beery smell, the way the boys shouted at each other, the words he'd heard out of his father's mouth coming awkwardly and brashly from their own: shit, fuck, goddamn, fuck.

"Let's git him primed so he won't cry if he falls off the sled and busts his head open," said the boy squeezed next to him. He lifted a beer bottle to Randall's lips and Hal knocked it out of the boy's hand and told him to go fuck a duck, which made Randall laugh until the bottle landed in his lap and soaked through to his underwear and then his legs and he thought the other boys would think he wet his pants and he tried hard not to cry. Hal lit a cigarette and the smoke went straight to Randall's nostrils and made his eyes tear up and finally he closed his eyes and tuned out the bragging and the empty shouts and imagined he was already on the sled with his brother, flying on land, down a hill as big as he'd seen, threading trees and other sledders, Trent transformed by falling freezing water into not Trent.

Hal and his buddies had only one sled between them, which Hal, who Randall realized with a pride that embarrassed him was the leader, took for himself. The others made do with sheets of cardboard and battered metal trash can lids which they carried like shields as they left the car by the side of the road and ran out onto the slope. Sledders were everywhere. The top of the hill was thick with them, lined there like trees, a bulwark of overly bundled boys and girls who all turned to watch Hal and his friends struggle up the slippery bank. Randall could feel the hate coming from the crowd;

he knew without knowing why that he was not welcome, that Hal and his kind were not wanted here, and he knew also without knowing that this was why Hal was here. Not to take him sledding. Not to wrest him away from the overprotective clutch of Reka. Not to mess with her mind, as he used to say to her. No, he was here because he wasn't supposed to be, because it was off limits to him. And Randall understood also that this was why he was along for the ride.

Hal pushed right through the crowd waiting their turn to sled, pulling Randall along by the mitten.

"Hey, Johnsontown, there's a line," a shaky voice called from the crowd, but Hal had taken over the front of the sled already and told Randall to hook his arms around his waist and as soon as Randall touched him Hal pushed off the bank. The breeze was icy and biting and Hal made no effort to steer; Randall was terrified and as elated as he'd ever been in his life. They came to rest three quarters of the way to the next green, and Hal toppled off and pulled Randall into the snowbank and said, "What about that, little brother?"

"Again," said Randall. He had not thought of this night in forever; he had thought of Hal hardly at all since he had seen him at his father's funeral. Maybe he was dead, too. Wouldn't doubt it, the way he was living when last seen. Randall thought of this night with the sled as the best time he'd ever had with his only brother. One of the very few good times.

But later that night there had been trouble. The country club kids and the sons and daughters of Trent's finest grew tired of Hal and his friends hogging the slope and the Johnsontown taunts grew louder and bolder. Less terrified than eager for a good seat to witness the battle, Randall ran into the woods, the very woods he hid in now. From behind a tree he watched his brother break a boy's sled into pieces and beat the hell out of anyone within swinging distance with a piece of the metal runner and he watched Hal's buddies whoop bloody war and attack with their trash can lids and the night ended as it would so often come to an end with Hal, sirens and handcuffs, blood and oaths, beer poured out onto the side of the road, foamy yellow in the snow.

A policeman drove Randall home. His daddy was passed out on the porch. When the policeman woke him to tell him what happened, he slapped Randall's toboggan off his head and told him to get to bed. Crying, he tiptoed into the room Reka shared with her sisters and tried to shake her gently awake as he so often did when he was scared nights but she only whispered, *You made your bed*, and turned away from him in the dark.

Now Randall watched the fairway turn from black and white sparkling snowscape to ostentatiously verdant carpet again. Was this where and when he had lost her? Was this where he'd made his bed? Or was it later, when he'd taken money from Edwin Keane one fall day while delivering him medicine, payment rendered for leading Reka into his snare? Or later still, when he'd slept with his brother's girlfriend, and accepted her curse as if it was his due?

As he crouched in the shade, contemplating his question, a golf cart filled with boys he recognized from his days at Trent High rattled down the path, then stopped not twenty feet from where he hid. Braxton Jarrell, whose father ran the jewelry store, and Bobby Wright, who had tried to have his way with his sister Ellen at a dance down at Williams Lake one night. Why weren't these boys off fighting that war? Why were they standing free, within spitting distance almost, drinking their sweaty bottles of Miller High Life in the golden hours of summer, singing the hits on the radio to themselves, patting their Sansabelt bellies, thinking no doubt of which Johnsontown girl they'd backseat down at Williams Lake tonight, still up to the same cheap kicks, while he was holding his breath and searching, like some hairy hunter-gatherer from the ape ages, for life-or-death water to subsist for another day?

What was this world? And where was he in it? He felt defeated, comparing his own fate to that of the fools in front of him, who had always been there, and whom he had never let bother him before.

And what difference did it make when and where he'd lost his sister? Like his mother she was with him everywhere now, he could not look at a golf course without remembering her, and this world seemed to have always been carried like mist between the two of them, in their minds and words and crazy dreams. Golf courses, church courtyards, prisons, high lonesome towns in Montana—perhaps she had forsaken him for those places, perhaps she had to make a choice and in his absence had vowed to live on this earth, but that did not mean he had lost her. He could stay in his woods forever and feel her presence no less. He longed to lay eyes on her, but he knew that, should he not see her again, she would be with him always in that dim, busy strip behind his eyelids. Wherever his sister was, whatever sacrifices she had made to allow herself to live on solid ground, he could find her, could enter her thoughts like a drop of rain replenishing this very earth.

He stayed around the river the next day, and that night returned to the golf course. There was a moon, and no streetlights, and the dew had coated the shorn grass of the fairways and he cussed himself for not bringing his watercatchers. But he needed more, he needed gallons, and he sneaked across the course, keeping to the greens, avoiding the streets where the country clubbers slept in assumed safety. He avoided houses with dogs. From the back of a huge split-level made up mainly of panels of glass—it was built in a pine thicket and there were no curtains and Randall watched a light switch on and a sleepy woman in a robe walk a baby, her words mouthing some lackluster lullaby—he stole a plastic bucket, which he lugged up on the back nine and abandoned when he came to the shed where the maintenance crew kept their gear. A windowpane was missing; he did not even have to break to enter. A dark garage filled with mowers and tools, a small kitchen where the groundskeepers took their breaks. He ransacked the refrigerator, bagged a half-dozen Tupperware containers; whatever it was he'd eat it, mold and all. He took crackers and a jar of peanuts and a white, grease-dappled bag filled with day-old donut holes. Out back he found a couple of gas cans and took them into the bathroom and rinsed them with soap for close to an hour until the gas fumes were gone, and he filled them with water and balanced them over his shoulders with a hoe handle and entered his woods just as the sun came up. Back at camp he broke his fast on donut holes, an absurd culinary invention he told his mother, hard proof of man's inability to surrender himself to the mystery of that hole that so often appears in the center of things.

THE DAY SHE LEFT she took a bus downtown to the station, then switched to another that would take her to Tacoma, where she checked into a ragged motor court near the airport on the SeaTac strip. Here she stayed for three days, struggling with an emptiness stronger than any she'd ever known. She did not sleep, eat, read, or watch television. Did not bathe or brush her teeth or listen to the radio. She went out for crackers and ginger ale, which she nibbled and sipped. Took to the bed, which she sprawled sideways across to prohibit memories of the bed she'd shared with Jake. She did not want to acknowledge his side of the bed. She did not want to think about his side of this situation at all, though it plagued her, kept her up nights, made her mumble crazy incantations that sounded not a little like prayer. Please, please understand I beg you please don't hate me please. These words she wheezed, her heart skipped and thumped wildly, she kept herself clothed and even sweatered to avoid seeing the skin that only hours ago had been sealed against his own.

What was this? She had known pain before, more than her share. She had spent time in prison, and she told herself over and over that this was not prison, she was free to move, free to leave. No one was telling her when to eat and when to walk, no one was making her decisions for her. Yet why did this come so close to prison? Why in some ways did it feel worse? She could go anywhere, but there was nowhere to go to get away from the thought of him, the memories and the grief and the guilt. She could not move about in the world of people and commerce, of taxis and restaurants, hills and flowers and trees, for what she was doing was not living. Nights the emptiness turned intolerable; it was as if someone had died, someone she could not name, but she knew this death anyway, from gut and spleen, in teeth and marrow. Randall? Good God, she thought when she came to her senses enough to see where she was, there is nothing wrong with Randall.

But there were more crazed and delusional fears, more unanswerable questions to ponder. Was it easier to be left or to leave? She knew she had no right to the grief she felt, for it was owed him, she was the one who had left. And she had been left before. She had had a lover die; she had served time for killing him, even though it wasn't her fault. She had allowed herself to be punished for leaving him even though he left her, alone on this earth. To have Jake die, she thought now, was easier. She shivered at the thought of it, let the tears run; she dried herself off with the pillowcase and said, No, it's not easier, if Jake died now I would not feel any better, I would feel worse. And then, God, it would be so much better if he died, if he was gone and I could not make it up to him and I would not have to worry every minute if I should return to him.

She worried every minute whether she should return to him. Who cares what Heath thinks? He is a grown man, as old as Randall, and she would not think of consulting Randall about her romantic life. She did not understand her decision fully, though she knew it had to do with both Randall and her fear that she had failed so much in the past, had proven herself so wretchedly unequipped to love, that she must sabotage a love so real it made what she'd had with Edwin fade, tatter. But not forget—she would never forget Jake. She would believe in the purity of her love for Jake even as she threw it away. She would tell herself the biggest love lie of all time: I left you, baby, because I loved you too much.

After three days she took a shower. Fetched fresh clothes from her unopened suitcase, put herself together. Went out for breakfast, managed an egg and two strips of bacon. The people she saw in the pancake house were not people at all, for they seemed to be behaving in ways she neither recognized nor understood. They knew what they wanted to eat and they checked their wrists for the time, for they had places to go; once they arrived at these places they busied themselves with things to do, and these things occupied their minds completely, they were able to add, subtract, talk on the phone, write memorandums to their subordinates, fill out an order form, make change, prepare an omelet, hammer a nail. It was miraculous and meaningless at once. She felt as if she were viewing them through glass, and the layer separating them was her overwhelming desire transmuted into a transparency that both allowed her to observe and kept her from participating in such industry.

Walking back to the motel, she saw lovers in a car, idling at a stoplight. The man leaned over for a kiss and as the light turned green a truck driver ground his gears and leaned on his horn and Reka smiled her approval at the braying of the truck horn. My sentiments exactly. She took delight in assuming the clichéd role of a woman who had lost in love and hated all lovers now, all love. She delighted in this even as it disgusted her, for she did not want to put herself in any category at all, much less the embittered lovelorn misanthrope.

The next morning at the airport she handed over money she'd saved for tuition without regret, for it seemed dangerous for her to indulge in pity. Who was she to think that she could have everything she wanted, and at the same time? She bought a newspaper and hid behind it while waiting for her flight to be called, resolved and anxious to leave this place so sodden and filled with mist.

But once they left the earth, her resolve weakened and she shook with sobs. The man sitting beside her tried and failed to console her and the stewardess brought her blankets and a Coke and beneath her the earth passed by unnoticed, as if she had ascended so far above her old life that she could never again be satisfied with the ground beneath her feet.

WHEN THE WATER RAN OUT he went back for more. Soon it became habit, these midnight excursions. Nightly roam of the country club. He stalked the sleepy fairways, napped in sand traps sunken in fog. Followed the swish of sprinklers left on to water the greens. Occasionally he filched dinner from the maintenance workers' shed, but he left his woods not for food or water now but for other reasons, unknown to him yet crucial.

During daylight he swore never to leave the swamp. He had his life there, his bible to tell him how to survive, his mother to keep him company. He could close his eyes and know she was everywhere, in the whisperings of the pines above his head, the slow muddy sliding away of the Tar. In the thin smoke from his campfire, birds singing so close they seemed to beat their wings inside of him. In wind and what scarce sun reached him beneath his canopy.

But night would come and he would hesitate, deliberate, drift finally toward the clipped lawns alongside which citizens slept in their showy white-brick boxes. He told himself he returned to remind himself of what he was not yet ready to return to.

What was this world he was not ready for? He was well into his twenties and had never loved a woman. He'd had women, a half dozen; he'd even had one man. But he'd had nothing at all like the love people spoke of as if it were a conversion, a baptism in some hallowed-watered river. Liquid redemption that left one cleansed, free afterward to love and be loved. Such a cleansing did not seem deigned for the Speights, nor did the love it promised, unless one of them had proved him wrong while he was gone. He hoped it might be Reka, but he could never really see her tied down. If he was not going to have her in his life, he wished her a gypsy. Besides, who could she find who would love her like she needed? She lived so much more in this world than he ever had, and what she needed was a wordly love, the kind he never even expected. He was content to stay in the woods and know that his mother was there with him, his real mother, not the woman his father had married who had died just weeks before he was born, but the woman his father had kept secret and therefore treasured all the more. He and Reka were the product of a mystery. This seemed the way it should be, the way he liked it.

Something good was wrong with him. He was by himself in this world, as Delores had predicted, but never alone. He had his girls: his mother, Reka in thought and memory and even on some distant party line, crackling with the quotidian commerce of a thousand distant tiny towns like Trent. Their exchanges floated over the country, tracing the sky like the ephemeral trails of jetliners.

He did not need people. What had family ever done for him anyway? He thought of his father, as hard to talk to as a tree. Hal, who had taught him little save how to get yourself locked up every week. His other sisters, who passed right by him on the streets of Trent without a word during those days before he left.

He had no need of a job, or money. The only jobs he had held seemed absurd to him now. Weld ships for a war he did not understand. Let himself be kept by a rich artiste who treated him as a case study for the great unwashed. Sit naked for months in front of a roomful of strangers, losing himself to the pursuit of a mother who appeared finally, magically, in every rasp of charcoal against paper, every tentatively drawn collarbone. Ferry drunks to the closest package store through the ravaged history of beleagured Poland.

None of these jobs was real. He could do anything so long as it was not real. Sleep with his brother's girlfriend. Wake each morning of his life to the hoot of an off-key owl whose song was so plaintive, so redolent of foghorn and Dobro and all the other saddest sounds on earth, that he had named him Hank Williams.

Returning to his camp in the thin dawn light, he felt ashamed for leaving his mother alone all this time. As if he were her protector, there to guard her against the elements. But he knew, once he lay his head down and let his body go invertebate, let his spirit rise, that she was as powerful a force here as any other. He knew she was here long before him, that he had not brought her here in a ragged sheath of newsprint, that she had existed here as long as the cypresses so regal and fat-trunked and ancient, as long as the river they rose from.

"THIS IS AS FAR as I can go," said the cabdriver as the Checker heaved its way down the rough two-track leading to her father's shack. She pulled out her pocketbook and counted out a handful of the bills, too distracted to even care how much it had cost to take a cab from the Raleigh-Durham airport sixty miles east to Trent.

"Want me to carry your bag down there for you?" the driver asked. He seemed worried about her, an obviously exhausted, red-eyed woman disappearing into a hole in the woods with nothing but an overnight bag.

"I can manage," she said. She stood in the high grass watching the yellow cab back up the rutted road. Listened to its motor chug until it was replaced by the eery quiet of early afternoon.

Once she'd hit town she had the cabby drive her around for a while. There were things she wanted to see: the house on Devone; Edwin's bungalow, which it seemed Thomas Keane had finally sold. It lay far back in the lot, spruced and brightly painted, and she was glad to feel nothing at all at the sight of it.

As the cab rattled across the bridge spanning the sluggish Tar she'd pushed herself up in the seat to stare at the indolent current and wondered if she was too late, if he'd gone already and for good this time.

But she'd come to her father's house, because she knew nowhere else to go. No use bothering her sisters; they would be the last to know Randall's whereabouts.

She entered the clearing and stopped at the sight of the shack settled in the curve of the pasture. Behind it loomed the dark-mouthed swamp. As she crossed the yard a squirrel-loosed branch fell on the tin roof, disturbing the early-afternoon silence with a crack as loud as a gunshot.

She set her bag on the porch and sat for a while, catching her breath, in the splintery old rocker her father had brought from Devone Street. She pretended she'd find her brother inside, that her search would be over, she could tell him to pack a bag and they'd leave on the next bus. If Randall was inside he would hear her and come out to greet her. She did not feel quite strong enough to go in there, not yet. She was scared of what she'd find in this shack, which from a distance resembled the face of her father, its peeling paint flaking like her father's weathered face, the sun-touched tin of the roof shiny-silver as his hair. Whatever made her think she could make it out of here alive?

Early afternoon ticking away. She got up slowly and peered through the brown and saggy screen. Through the filter of the screen the drawings appeared to be abstracts, and she was shocked to find when she made her slow way inside that they were realistic. Lifelike studies of a nude Randall in the same pose, a dozen times over Randall. She looked at his drooping penis and quickly away. The drawings were done by different hands but shared a seething power, as if something in the subject's immodesty pushed each artist to an honesty they'd never before known.

Only after studying the drawings for a few minutes did she wonder how they got there. No one else could have put them there. He had been here, he'd come back; maybe he was here still, gone to the store for milk.

She was so happy she held her breath. With the first inhalation came the tears: He was back here, in this place they schemed to leave together. Living in this shack where their father had wasted away his last years. For all her yearning to see him again, she was devastated. It seemed her fault, his presence here; she blamed herself for leaving him, blamed herself for leaving Red Fork before he could find her there.

Restlessly she paced the two tiny rooms of the house, growing more and more distressed at each sign of him. Someone had wired the place, which surprised her. A record player sat on a bureau in the corner, stacks of albums beside it. She flipped through the selections: Charlie Parker, Thelonius Monk, Don Cherry, Coleman Hawkins. She knew the names from Edwin, but had never been able to care much for the music. To her it seemed an affectation of Edwin's, something he wanted to like because he had read in a book that this was the type of music for people who could think for themselves. She did not think her little brother capable of such an affectation, but then what did she know of his capabilities? She never imagined him back here, isolated in this dreary cabin with nothing but his jazz and his drawings and his crazy talk offered to squirrels and bees, the field mice who made their home in the walls of the shack and the black snakes who wrapped themselves around the pipes beneath the kitchen sink or stretched out flat as belts in the sun striping the porch. Living alone like Edwin with his records and his thoughts. Oh God, Randall, I'm sorry. I promise never to leave you again.

_____

FOR WEEKS HE RESISTED the call of the country club, stayed close to camp. He collected tap roots and foraged for the mushrooms he'd learned to trust. He swam in the river and afterward pulled a leech from his crotch and sang to it a song halfway his own and the other half stolen from his days with Cyrus and Benny.

Bleed me with leeches, bloodsuck tango
Wash me with dirt, suck my blood,
Come back to me sister
It's fixin' to flood.
Mama's frying chicken in some bacon grease
Down the road down the road down the road apiece.

But the pull grew intolerable. One night he stole through the woods, once again entered the shed where the maintenance men stored their tools. He opened the door to the freezer and stuck his head into it, singing softly to himself as the cloudy blue cold washed over him. Loaded a grocery bag with Tupperware containers. He spread his feast out on the green of the eighth hole, which wound around a figure-eight-shaped lagoon. During the daylight he'd heard golf carts rattle across the bridges spanning it. Cattails fenced it from the green, and ducks poked around its algaed banks. He picnicked on turkey hash. Some sort of casserole with potatoes, hamburger and cheese. Barbeque, the first bite of which tasted for all the world like it came from that greasery out on 403, run by some

Flemings who his father claimed were kin. The next bite tasted strange, chemical, and left an aftertaste so acrid that Randall vowed its makers were no kin to him.

There were canned peaches for dessert. Randall poked the lid open with a knife he'd borrowed from the maintenance workers and sipped the syrup, which was so sweet it made his belly ache. He lay back on the green and thought he saw, in a flickering of leaves at the edge of the woods, his mother. Calling him back to camp. The woods began to quiver, his vision blurring. He turned on his side and threw up his peaches, turned back to look at the dark line of trees. The whole forest was wavy, patterned, moving. It was only his mother, he told himself, for she was everywhere in the swamp, beneath the surface of the brackish water, in the tree whistling when a storm blew up, beneath the bark he pulled from trees to boil for his medicinal tea.

He could use a belt of that foul tea now, for he threw up again. Emptied his stomach of food and then water and then nothing at all but noise, a fearsome intestinal groaning. He twisted on the green, his stomach cramping, his body wracked. He grew cold; shivers became tremors. To steady himself he chanted: I don't know but I been told, three-legged woman ain't got no hole. Bleed me with leeches, bloodsuck tango. An hour passed, two: in a thin window of clarity he went over everything he'd eaten lately, all the leaves and roots, the fish he'd caught in the Tar. Could have been the latter, easily. Could have been anything. His stomach bubbled, his bowels churned and jellied. Could have been anything at all. What made him think he could survive on the advice of their army? He decided they'd planted something in the guide to edible plants, something poisonous, lethal. Until he remembered the barbeque.

Sometime in the night a dog came along and sniffed the flood of vomit he lay in. His mother came, too, creeping out of the woods to crouch beside him. She put her hands inside his shirt and wept over his skin, swore over the clamminess of it. She peeled away the drenched clothes and tied them around him and dragged him toward the treeline. Come on baby before they find you out here dying over something you ought not to have had your hands on in the first place. His father hated a thief. I hate a goddamn thief, Randall had heard him say. Out of nowhere did he make this claim. Once he and Reka stole a pack of Teaberry's from the drugstore where his father worked and she had felt so guilty that she stopped him before he slipped stick one in his mouth and made him put it back in the pack, which was murder, so tightly packed it was, and ordered him to take it back and put it right up on the rack. But it's open, he said to the dog, who looked up from his sniffing and studied him and knew better. I know better than to pay attention to any old thief. Said this dog: In the morning the maintenance men are going to drag your smelly ass right up to the pro shop and call the cops. What good would it do to return it, who's going to buy an opened pack of Teaberry's? Something bad wrong with him now. Maybe it was time. High time. Give in to whatever the world had in store for him. Past time: to fight, to keep on searching for things he could only dream about. Better it be their barbeque than one of the trusty mushrooms he'd learned to live off of. All right, goddammit, he'd said, snatching the gum from her hand and marching into the drugstore to stick it back up on the rack, although this is not how it had happened in real life. In real life she'd always let him win.

He lost thought. Trucks geargrinding on some highway detoured right over the putting green. His every organ burst as they pummeled him into the earth, the thick-treaded tires pushing him down to the water line. Three fourths of the world is water, four fifths of the body. He closed his eyes and floated, and inside this watery darkness he wept, for it seemed time, high time, past time, and it was spiked barbeque and soon they would come for him.

After another hour of retching, he heard voices, opened his eyes to see two men climb out of a golf cart. He lay in his shallow grave and listened to the voices of the living.

"God Almighty. What's he weigh, eighty?"

"Shit, Lou, I feel bad."

"How come?"

"Look at him. Raggedy as a broomstraw. I'd a known, I'd a let him have his free lunch."

"How were we supposed to know?"

"What we going to do with him?"

"Hey buddy. Fellow. Can you sit up?"

"Get him some water, Mark, he's sprung leaks on both ends."

"You stay with him in case old Hayes comes through on his six o'clock front nine."

"Hayes wouldn't pay him no more mind than if it was a crushed turtle. He's got to get in his eighteen before the bank opens."

After a silence, plastic nudged his lips and he drank. He blinked and the men came close to him, too close. He turned his head aside to throw up the liquid.

"In and out."

"Look fellow, we're sorry. We . . . "

"Hell, Louie, don't apologize. He's the one been stealing our goddamn lunch."

"Well, what we going to do with him?"

A pause. The switching on of sprinklers and the nervous silence of men deciding his fate. Finally the apologetic one said, "We got to take him home."

"Look at him. He ain't got no home."

They debated over whether they would get caught if they snuck off for a while.

"Depends on where we got to take him."

"Where you want to go, bud? We'll take you anywhere."

"Goddamn, Louie. Now he'll be wanting a ride down to Myrtle Beach."

"Speed's store," said Randall. The words tasted foul in his mouth, as if they too carried poision. He screwed up his face and spit them out onto the grass.

SHE LIVED ON RICE, potatoes and sadness at the edge of the swamp. The emptiness she had felt back in the motel room did not leave or even lessen, was compounded by the ghosts of the men in the two slanted rooms of the shack. The cot she dozed on most of the day and night smelled of sweat, and she could have sworn it was her father's smell, though she knew it was impossible for any part of him to have lingered this long. There were other signs of his presence here: a pair of his overalls flung in the corner in a puddle, a pocketknife she recognized lying open on the mantel. The place was as unkempt as it had been the last time she'd visited it, that day she'd come to tell her father she was leaving, goodbye, be sure to pass this note along to Randall so he'll know where to find me always. The disorder seemed even sadder since it contained not only remnants of her father, but also of her brother. Piles of books, a recorder made of beautiful red wood, a Marine Band harmonica case, those records. He had no call to be living here like this. Nor did she.

Three weeks after she arrived she grew sick. Weak and nauseated, too fatigued to do much but lie about on the cot all day. Rice and potatoes no longer nourished her. She spent hours dreaming of the seafood dishes Thanassis would cook for his family on weekends, she craved all kinds of food not native to the sandy flats around her. A tenderness in her breasts confirmed what she would not let herself believe. Finally she called a cab from Speed's store to take her to the doctor and found that she was more than two months gone.

For a week she lay abed talking herself into and out of calling

Jake. What good would it do to tell him if she would not see him again? As devastating as it was to have lost him, she was thrilled to have carried away some part of him, some part of them. But he had lost a child already, had spent years deprived of his offspring. It seemed cruel to her to keep him from his own blood again.

But she could not see him. She made a choice. Now that she was alone in the woods, isolated and sick and wasting away all the money she'd saved for college, her choice seemed inordinately selfish, even cowardly. Yet she stuck with it, for every time she thought of returning to him she was reminded of Edwin Keane, how she had let herself do terrible things to keep him with her. Even inject him with the poison that killed him.

And what if it did not work out? Would she not be even more devastated than she was now? Though she had survived half her life cocooned within the bounteous rooms of her imagination, more emptiness and desolation was impossible for her to fathom. The thought of losing him to anything less than death, and of suffering any more than she already had, was inconceivable. Having lost so much, it seemed the only thing worse for her was to lose her baby, whom she took to calling Randall regardless of sex.

She went to the doctor for checkups, came home to the shack by the side of the swamp. She bought herself a television she could not afford and grew so disgusted with its meager and offensively melodramatic offerings that she sold it to Speed for half of what she paid for it. She began to live for her weekly rendezvous with the bookmobile, which traveled the county and stopped each Thursday at Speed's store. She was usually the only browser, and the kindly librarian let her linger inside the van while she made her choice.

One day her sister Martha showed up at the door. It was cold out, and Reka sat by the stove in nightgown and quilt, reading *Madame Bovary* for the third time since she'd returned. She hugged her sister with genuine affection, for it seemed ludicrous of her to hold on to her old indifference. Like as not, her sisters were all she had in the world now, though that did not make her seek them out.

"Girl I work with at the telephone company said she seen you at Doc Simmons. I told her she was crazy as hell, won't no way. But she was in your class at Trent High and swore up and down and damned if she won't telling the truth. How long you been here? What are you doing here? Why didn't you call nobody, Reka?"

Embarrassed, Reka made coffee. She kept herself wrapped tight in the quilt to hide her burgeoning pregnancy, though a half hour into Martha's visit she let the wrap fall and Martha saw immediately and did not take her eyes away from Reka's stomach until Reka said, "Going on four months now."

"Is the daddy in the picture?"

She lied and said she never wanted to see him again. That this was why she had come back to Trent, she had nowhere else to go, it seemed to her as good a place to raise a child as any. Martha looked at her suspiciously; she had chosen to stay here, would not ever leave or even think of leaving herself, but she knew there were better places for Speights to raise their children.

Reka changed the subject. To Randall.

"Hell, he could be anywhere," Martha said. "I hope for his sake he ain't in jail. He wouldn't last a month in prison. He's not right, Reka."

"What do you mean, he's not right?"

Martha pointed to the drawings that still hung ragged and yellowed on the walls of the shack. She told her how he'd shown up one day, how he too had hidden out in this shack (just like she was doing now, though Martha stopped short of saying this) and got crazier and crazier. Let his hair grow out and worked for a year or two welding out at McCullen's ironworks but got fired because he looked a damn sight, hair all down his back, thin as a hoe handle. Other welders refused to work with him is how she'd heard it. All but the Negroes and hanging out with Negroes didn't make it any easier for him. After that he set himself up running booze, made money off of drunks and kids who couldn't get across the county line to buy their own. The police got on to him after a while and how he'd been living since she had no earthly idea.

Reka began to cry. Tears dripped off her cheeks onto her swollen belly but she made no noise at all. Her sister rose and came to her side, kneeled beside her and took her in her arms and told her there was nothing she could do, she ought to have learned long ago that she couldn't live that boy's life for him, he had to find out for himself what he was made of, thank God he wasn't made of the same stuff as their daddy or Hal. She went off on Hal then, told Reka about him getting arrested with a girl he had the nerve to bring to their father's funeral, how it made the papers up in Norfolk, Hal and this girl running a prostitution ring right out of their house in Virginia Beach, servicing sailors and anybody else with the change. There was a trial and this girl, Delores was her name, she refused to testify against old sorryass Hal and it was all in the papers about how she slept with damn sailors because he asked her to and they needed the money and she got her friends in on it and all Hal did was sit back and drink up the profit and this girl Delores was quoted as saying she would do it all again if Hal asked her to because she was in love with him and it wasn't his fault and if they were going to send anybody to jail it ought to be her because nobody forced her to sell herself, she did it of her own mind. Said they ought to let Hal go free.

"And did they?"

"Hell no," said Martha. "He got sixteen years, but not just out of that. He was wanted for a whole slew of other things, too. That girl-friend of his, they let her loose with a suspended and run her out of town."

Reka stopped crying.

"What are you going to do?" her sister asked.

She couldn't tell her the truth. That she was going to wait right here for her brother to return, that she would wait as long as it took, that she would die here if it came to that. That she knew this was not what she should do, what she needed to do, but that she would not return to the man she loved until she knew for sure her brother was not lost to her again, forever.

"I'll stay here until the baby's born."

"You come stay with Ronnie and me. We got two girls in high school, good babysitters both of them. They can look after the child while you get some kind of work. What you living off of, anyway?"

Reka told her about the money she saved for college. She declined her invitation and told her she was fine here, which made Martha angry.

"I hate this damn place. I ought to of got Ronnie to bring his backhoe down here and tear the damn place down. You seen yourself what it done to Pa. And then Randall. Come back here to give up, both of them. This might as well be one of them intensive care rooms up to the hospital. Chances are slim you'll make it out of here in one piece. You might not think it will happen to you but I swear, Reka, you ought not to be living out here by yourself regardless of what all happened to them. Nowhere ain't safe these days."

"I'll stop by and see you when I'm in town," said Reka.

Martha turned sullen. She said she was glad to see her, but that she hadn't changed one iota. Still as stubborn as always. Well, you know where I'm at. Call me if you need anything. I'm still your sister. And was gone.

Randall gone, too. She didn't trust her sister's assessment of his mental health, for she knew how her sister saw the world, knew she would judge all men by the bigoted obstinance of her husband. Still, making money buying booze for underage kids? She couldn't have made that up.

She grew tired and large and cranky. She stayed home and read, went to town to see the doctor, stayed for dinner at her sister's ranch house out in an ugly new subdivision called Sir Trent Acres, came

home to her retreat. It turned hot. For weeks Reka dozed in the stifling room. After years away the heaviness of the air seemed like a
language she could not speak. She could not comprehend how she'd
survived it. She told herself she'd been spoiled by Seattle, where
humidity and heat were mutually exclusive, at least to her notion.
But it was hard to breathe here, harder still if you were six months
pregnant. She thought only of Jake and of Randall. When she was
in town and saw a phone, she fixed her gaze on the black box, willing it to vibrate with bells and news. Come get me Jake, I love you.
Take me back home with you. Come get me Reka, it's your little
brother, I'm down at the bus station, I'm home.

One June morning she got up early, swept the house, fixed herself some cheese toast, returned to bed with a book. But she could
not concentrate, could not free her mind to follow the black blocks
of words running across the page, could not see them as anything
other than smudges violating the white crisp paper. She let the book
fall to the floor with a thud and drifted. Outside, the breeze picked
up. Wind swayed the flimsy pines, their needles sweeping the sides
of the house. Crazed bird cries and the baritone hum of the breeze.
She looked out the window to watch the coming bank of black
clouds. She'd forgotten these late-afternoon storms that blew up
from the coast and often spawned tornadoes and slightly less violent
spells of high wind and hail.

When the rain arrived, its pelt on the tin was deafening. Beneath
the noise she thought she heard someone calling to her. Someone
singing. A song she did not know, a song without melody or even
structure, the kind a child sings when alone or in a crowd, sings to
herself while entranced with the assemblage of found objects, leaves
or rocks or the pieces of a jigsaw puzzle.

But it went away, or was drowned out by the coming of heavier
rain.

The roof leaked. She got up to fetch a pail but realized she did
not care, it wasn't her house, it wasn't even Randall's.

Whose was it then? A dead man's. It belonged to the past. A time when she was marooned in this town by fear and inertia and guilt. What had changed in the years since? She looked to the heavens for a lightning strike to send her out into the rains while the shack burned down to charred bricks and a sheet of flame-rusted tin.

Instead the rain lightened, then quit. She rose from the cot and moved to the door to watch the world come to life. Slowly the clouds passed and the sun appeared, lighting a last pocket of daytime like another room, some secret place known only to a lucky few. Mist rose from the drenched foliage. Out of this mist her little brother appeared, soaked to the skin, his feet bare and muddy.

She would not cry. Why should she cry? He was alive and she had him in her sights after all these years and that was nothing to cry over. Never again would she forsake him, not until one or the other of them left this world for good would she not know where he was, how he was. Who.

She stood trembling behind the screen. He did not see her until his feet stained the porch with mud.

"Good God," he said.

She flung the door open and his arms were around her and then they were laughing at the awkwardness of the embrace, her hard belly in the way and Randall not knowing how to hold her, what to do with her girth. Her laughter turned wet and his eyes misted over and she closed her eyes finally, unable to look at the way this world had altered him.

But it was there behind her eyelids, sihouetted against the darkness. His gauntness, the lines around his eyes. She'd never thought of him aging, changing. He looked exactly, oh too exactly, like his father.

"Good God yourself," she said to the vision fading behind her shut-tight eyes.

"Eureka," he mumbled and they held each other for days and he broke into a song, wordless and chaotic, the song she thought she'd heard beneath the rain. He seemed not at all conscious of his humming and she had to remind herself that he was not a child, he was a man now.

"I came to find you but you were gone." He spoke into her hair, his head on her neck.

"I know."

"How do I hug you?" he said, and they both laughed again and broke their embrace to look each other over.

"Boy or girl?" he asked.

"How should I know?"

"Girl," he said. "You ought to call her Virginia."

"Boy," she said. "I'll call it Randall."

"And does this boy have a father?"

"Of course he has a father."

"In the picture, I mean."

She stepped back from him. "Come on, Randall. That sounds like something Martha and Ellen and them might say to me."

"You're right," he said. "I'm sorry." He grinned, held his grin and widened it until she said, "What?"

"Well, does he have a daddy in the picture?"

"You almost met him in Red Fork, Montana."

"You mean the guy who bailed me out?"

She nodded. He said he feared for his life and got the hell out of there and she said no wonder after that crazy stunt you pulled and he asked again about the father of her child and she said she'd tell him the whole story and he said he wanted to hear everything but first there was stuff he had to tell her. Let's go inside, I need a cup of coffee.

He heated water at the stove while she sat on the cot, trembly from the shock of seeing him again. She caught him smiling at her from the kitchen every few seconds and there seemed so much to say that they did not know how to be around each other. So much had passed. So many things to say. She wanted to save him first and tell him the story of all the years later but how do you go about picking right up again with a ghost?

He brought her coffee and lifted her feet up off the cot so that he could slide under them.

"You don't know how long I looked for you," he said. "As soon as they buried Pa I took off. But I'll tell you all about that later, first there's something else. Something big."

"Good or bad?"

"More along the lines of incredible," he said. "But if you put a gun to my head and made me choose one I'd say way more good."

"Okay," she said. "Ready."

He lifted her feet up, scooted off the cot, walked to the walls where the pictures hung.

"You know who this is?"

"Of course," she said. "It's you. A younger you. Whole lot more of you than I really need to see."

"Yeah, me, okay, me, who else?" He scampered through his sentence like a giddy child anxious to show off what he knew to a teacher. She imagined his hand stretched as high above his desk as it would go, I know I know please Miss Peterson pick me pick me I know.

"Okay, I give up." She wasn't much interested in playing games they might have played when she was last close to him, before Edwin, but she wanted to hear him out and knew she must play by his rules.

"Who else, Randall? I don't know who. Pa?"

"Not Pa," he said. She could see the disappointment clouding over him, as quick and filled with fury as the storm that had just passed. She'd never thought of him as fragile, but maybe it was there all along and she did not want to see it, for had she acknowledged such a thing she would also have had to acknowledge her part in making him that way.

"It's our mother," he said.

"Really?" She did not have to feign surprise, for her mother looked nothing at all like either one of them. "I'm sorry, I see Pa, I've always seen more of him in us than her. I guess the rest of them take after the Taylors but for some reason we didn't get any of that . . ."

"Not her," he said. "Our real mother."

She waited. Watched his lips, his eyes; a hard smile took over his face, the kind of smile that comes from self-righteousness or delusion. She'd seen that smile before: Bob Smart, Edith Keane, Maggie Whitener. She felt suddenly nauseous, quelled the queasiness with curiosity.

"Who do you mean?"

"We have a different mother. He had a lover, see, no one knew about her. Her name's Virginia. I've been staying with her this whole time. She lives alone out in Serenitowinity near where the Tar cuts through and she taught me how to survive, and I wouldn't put it past her if she brung you back to me."

"Stop, Randall. Wait. Slow down. How do you know he had this lover? He tell you that before he died?"

"You know good and well he wouldn't of ever told me such a thing. He didn't need to. It came to me when I saw those pictures, and it was there anyway, beforehand. Remember how we used to always wonder how it was that we were different from the rest of them?

"Sure," she said, but she wanted to say: That was a game, just talk. We weren't like them—we aren't—but that's no reason to go inventing some phantom lover and following her around the forest going slowly mad.

"That's why. We're only half-kin. Same father. But our mother is what makes us who we are. You always used to claim it was some secret part of Pa he never got to use, we inherited it and that was why he was easy on us and why he beat the hell out of us too when all he'd do to the others is switch them every once in a while. Remember how he used to talk nasty in front of Martha and Ellen and them but around you he kept his mouth clean, acted all prudish or something? He would not even acknowledge sex around you; if two old muddy dogs got stuck screwing in the front yard he wouldn't have let on he knew what the hell was going on if you were there. Why do you think he acted that way? Don't you know he couldn't look at us, either of us, without seeing the only woman he ever loved?"

She tried to breathe in the heaviness that had returned with the passing of the storm. If he wants to believe this, why not let him? How could it hurt? I've got him back, he's alive and maybe I could even take him back west with me and Heath will give him a job on the boat and hard work and family will heal him in weeks.

"I came back to find her and I found her," he said.

"You found your mother in the swamp," she said. It wasn't a question.

"Our mother. Ours. Yours and mine. I knew she was alive still, I'd of known it if she was dead. Just like I knew you were alive and that we'd find each other and I'd get to tell you this to your face and I'd get to give you all the letters I wrote you over the years a whole slew of them . . ."

"Randall," she said. "Our mother's dead She died just after you were born. I remember her. She smelled like soap and she liked to work in her flower garden and used to sing hymns to me at bedtime and just because you can't remember anything about her doesn't mean you have to go making her up as someone else. I'll tell you what I know," she said, "I can help you know her," but he was not listening to her. "No," he was saying, "no, no, no," and he was shaking his head wildly like he'd done when he was a child and she was trying to tell him something he could not believe was true.

"Nope. Alive."

"Listen to me, Randall," she said. She pushed herself up from the cot and crossed the floor to him, tried to hold him but he sensed what she was going to say and would not let her touch him. Please listen to me she said and he said nope, alive, still here and she reached behind him and ripped the drawing from the wall. What are you doing Reka, who are you now to do this to me, those drawings I've saved them for years, they're what kept me going the whole time you were gone. He was yelling and she was crying and moving around the room snatching the ancient crinkly newsprint from the walls and balling up the drawings and tossing them on the floor where his clothes and books and papers lay in piles. No no no, she was yelling, that's not the answer Randall, don't you do this to me I came all the way back here I don't want this I don't want to ever fight with you, and he was following her around the room gathering the drawings in his arms, spilling half of them onto the floor and bending to scoop them up again, crushing them to his chest and repeating through coughing sobs "She's here, I found her, my mother, yours, ours."

He ran out into the yard. He had the drawings in his hands and he fell into the grass and rolled there. She watched through the screen. Like an acrobat he rolled himself upright and kneeled again to the wet ground and began to unravel the crumpled drawings and stretch them out in pieces, which with a terrifying smile on his face he set to work reassembling.

She sat down on the cot. Inside she felt the baby kicking, upset no doubt by the sudden tilt of this world she felt suddenly terrified about bringing him into. She said his name over and over and thought of his father and wished him here, for she knew he was the only one who could help her now. With a shallow breath she spoke to her brother outside and not his namesake inside of her. I cannot help you Randall. I can not save you. How could she take away the things he dreamed, the thoughts he'd conjured up to survive her leaving him? She let her head fall against the wall, linked the ache in her body to the men in her life: Edwin Keane in her head and Randall in both of her trembly arms, Jake all over, Heath and her father in her heart. How could she live this life without them, and how could she carry them all with her?

Randall's name replaced with Jake's. With each repetition, each soft monosyllabic bite, she understood that even he could not help her out of this, that he would be loving her still, was waiting for her, but that he would not appear suddenly out of a passing storm like Randall. And she did not want him to, for then he too would be lost to her, stumbling through some other world where mysterious lovers lurked in swamps and a family's troubles lay between the sidewalks and littered vacant lots of a small, ruined town and the far more dangerous folds of the imagination.

I am coming back to you, Jake. As soon as I can. Now.

She thanked him and God blessed him and she thanked their son she carried inside her and she asked Jake to secure a place for Randall on Heath's crew. But this was all she could do for him. The baby kicked and just as suddenly resettled and she raised her dress and rubbed that part of her that had arrived to save her, save them all.

She found the box of matches on the mantel. Lit one and dropped it, watched it go out before it hit the pile of clothes and papers she'd kicked up in the middle of the floor. Without the energy it usually took her to kneel she lowered herself to the floor and struck another, rose again when the flame caught and spread. Calmly she moved about the room adding things: her father's things, Randall's recorder, his books, the record albums Edwin Keane had taught him to love. A packet of letters addressed to her that she found in a box beneath his bed. The box beneath his bed. The sheets off his bed.

Mice ran squealing from the walls. Outside, jays chased each other out of the swamp, squawking, losing blue feathers in the wind.

She stood in the glow of the fire with her dress hiked up to her rib cage again, watching the flames turn her belly golden before moving slow as smoke outside to join her little brother squatting in the mud, clawing at fragments.